KNOWLEDGE ITSELF

KNOWLEDGE ITSELF

SHELLY CAMPBELL

MEGAN KING

To Liam, Ella, Lily, Finn, Sam and Gabby. You can take on the world and do big things. Never doubt it. We love you to bits.

CHAPTER
ONE

When I was nine years old, I broke my brother's back.

Vinton smashed something of mine, a gift from our Uncle Nate—my favorite grown-up in the whole world. So, naturally, I fried a circuit and ran away down the train tracks that clung to the steep incline separating our city from the lake. Uncle Nate always came through the train tunnel when he visited, all booming voice, scraggly beard, and smile-lined eyes. He wasn't afraid of the wastelands, and I wanted to be just like him—maybe without the beard.

Vinton followed me, because he was two years my elder and high on responsibility. We weren't allowed outside the shelter of our city after sunrise, a rule born just after I was. That's when the sun had expanded and dark spots marbled its surface like bruises. Constant solar flares overloaded electrical grids and wiped out power worldwide. Bird migrations messed up. Food crops died. The solar storms never stopped. And they changed everything.

We weren't even a *real* city. Our settlement looked nothing like the pictures from years ago: crowded with sleek glass skyscrapers, cars clogging massive boulevards, and people streaming down sidewalks like ants. Those places fell to ruin after the collapse.

Containing nearly two hundred people, we were the biggest settlement for hundreds of kilometers. Our founder, CEO Kahn insisted on titling us as a city, but we were more of a commune. Vinton said that some rich guy had paid meg cash to have this place built, surrounded by bare, eroded bluffs painted in green patinas and clay reds. He died before his fancy end-of-the-world hide-out was ever finished, so the contractors he hired took it over when the power grid collapses began. Our parents were among them. Their world shrank down to three top-of-the-line industrial generators, some commercial greenhouses, and rows and rows of Seacan shipping containers converted into homes. The metal walls worked like Faraday cages, shielding us from the sun.

We all knew the cautionary tales: outside was poison. Get caught unprotected and your skin would blister. You'd go blind. You'd get cancer. Your hair would fall out of your head—or grow in places where it shouldn't—I couldn't remember which one it was. Vinton believed all of them, I'm sure.

On the day I ran away, neither of us knew the last torrential rainstorm had washed out the train tracks, leaving a gaping hole just beyond the exit of the tunnel. My brother, as always, wore his stupid favorite dress shoes with no grips. I caught myself before I fell. He didn't.

I still remember the awful thud he made as he hit the shale bottom of the ravine, arms and legs rag-dolling as he rolled toward the lake, head cocked at an inhuman angle. Vinton shattered his legs and fractured his spine. He would never have gone Outside if he wasn't chasing me. It was my fault.

Two nights later, I was between the Med building and home —Mom had sent me to get more pillows to prop up Vinton's ruined legs—when Uncle Nate stepped into the streetlight where the boardwalk intersected the path to the lake. His hiking pack made his silhouette look monstrous, like a sasquatch lumbering out of the dark, but his voice warmed me to my toes.

"Hey, Beetle!" That was his nickname for me.

I stumbled toward him and smashed into his legs, sobbing. He smelled like pine needles and warm summer nights.

"Hey. Hey now. What's wrong?"

"I-I was coming to see you in the train tunnel and—"

"Honey, your face!" He squatted to my level, his fingers hovering over the blisters marring my cheeks. "What happened? Are those burns?"

"Vinton fell." I gulped. "We were stuck Outside for a really long time, and I tried to use mud for sunscreen, like you do, but it didn't work."

"Vinton fell?"

I nodded, blubbering, "And it's all my fault. He's hurt bad. He can't walk."

Nate shifted, the contents of his pack rattling. He dabbed tears from the corner of my eyes with his sleeve while his warm, blue eyes examined mine. "Where's your mom, Beetle?"

"Stay away from her!" Mom's sharp voice made me jump.

Nate and I both spun to the Med building where she stood rigidly holding the door.

"Anne? What happened?" Nate straightened, still holding my little hand in his big, rough one. When she didn't answer, he gestured to my cheeks. "These need bandaging."

"Stay *away* from her!" Mom barked again, tears glittering in her eyes. She stabbed a finger toward her brother. "You. It's *your* damned fault they went down to the tracks in the first place. All those crazy thoughts you put in her head! Encouraging her to go Outside. Get out of my damned sight before I call the Firewalls! Iris, go inside right now."

"But Mom ..." I sniffled.

"I said now!" she bellowed.

I flinched and slipped my fingers out of Uncle Nate's warm grip, even as he squeezed my hand.

He smiled down at me uncertainly and spoke under his breath. "It's okay, Beetle. Go to your mom. Everything's gonna be fine."

But that was a lie. I wouldn't see Uncle Nate again for six years.

AT FIFTEEN YEARS OLD, I'd long since re-routed my dream of being like Nate. I'd converted from hiking boots to stiletto pumps. My face bore the scars of the sunburn from that tragic day with Vinton, but I was properly pale now and had perpetual headaches from wearing my dark hair in a severe French twist instead of the loose braids of my childhood. I kept my nails manicured short enough to type without clicking. I only spent time outside on quick stints between the Work Commons and Cache buildings, clacking down the wooden boardwalk in a pencil skirt, bathed in the pale glow of LED streetlights and faint stars with the steady hum of generators in my ears. I never ventured to the train tracks or the lake.

My world had contracted to a desk that only had room for cracked flat screens and overflowing mounds of dog-eared files. It seemed like sparse repayment for trapping Vinton in an uncomfortable chair for the rest of his life.

On the bright side, all of my excruciating effort at curtailing my random thoughts and cramming into the confines of what my family considered normal had paid off. The Shareholders reviewed my school files earlier this semester and—despite my corporate aptitude tests showing anomalies—they'd announced that I was a prime candidate for a Search Engine position.

Mom overloaded a circuit when she read the email. I hadn't

seen her beam like that since Vinton earned a Browser position two years ago—a job he only qualified for because Dad's friend was a Browser too, and our family paid through the teeth to modify one of the motorcycles the Browser's used to accommodate a paraplegic. I just had to ace my year nine placement assignment and I'd be set.

The project was a collaborative one, meant to test not only aptitude, but determine whether we could function as team players. We were legally considered adults upon successful completion. My fingers froze over my keyboard when I read my assigned partner's name: Robert Lycos.

Well, shit. I'd had a crush on him since year five when Vannevar Baran spammed a picture of my best friend, Olivia Teoma, across the school network with the biting quote "Dirty Girl" and a circle highlighting her soil-blackened fingernails.

Robert had come to her defense. *You're full of malware, Vannevar. Don't forget, Olivia's family feeds us all.*

I'd never seen anyone stand up for a gardening family like that and hadn't realized that sort of nobility existed in a boy. Robert instantly seemed smarter, more mature, and cuter than anyone else my age.

Heat rose to my cheeks, and I pressed my palms against them as Robert's name stood out in bold type on the screen. *Normal. Just act normal, Iris. How hard can it be?* Having already grilled Vinton for details of his year nine experience, there wasn't much else on the scrolling page to surprise me. I skimmed through the assignment outline.

Subject: Nickel Iron Batteries

Oh thank Sol. I can work with that. Batteries were something that intrigued me. If I'd been saddled with a subject that didn't interest me, there would have been no way I could have forced my brain to focus. The subject was followed by instructions on when and where to pick up our reference material drives, task lists, and formatting for the final presentation, all capped with the trite warning that any unauthorized access of Cache information would result in immediate disqualification and irreversible cutback of food creds.

Honestly, creds were the furthest thing from my mind. *Robert Lycos.* How was I going to spend the next three weeks with him and not blurt out something absolutely idiotic?

Robert Lycos with eyes as moody as the lake before a storm and that quiet but authoritative voice.

"Shit," I repeated. As if I needed any help in the distraction department. What would he think when he read my name? How in the wide world was I supposed to concentrate on anything when I couldn't stop looking at his lips? Was that normal, staring at lips? I bit the inside of my cheek and shook out my hands until they stopped tingling. *Reboot, Iris. Get a grip.* My messenger pinged, and Robert's name popped up in an impatiently blinking tab. Smoothing my clammy palms over my stiff skirt, I clicked open the tab.

> Robert: Ready to spend the next three weeks researching
> batteries? Eye roll. I'm going into sleep mode just
> thinking about it. Generator maintenance. Coding. Hell,
> even paper preservation would be more interesting than
> batteries.

My throat tightened. *See, you haven't even said a word, and he's bored with you already.* I clamped my teeth to cut off the thought. Splaying my fingers to stretch them, I inhaled slowly. He wasn't bored with me, just the subject.

> Me: Shareholders want to see if we can find something
> new. Something the first Search Engines missed when
> they read their files, right? We do that with batteries,

they'll flip a breaker. We'll be dock ins for Search Engines
for sure.

That sounded confident, right? Mature? I jabbed the send key before I could delete my message and stared hard at the blinking dots ticking away the seconds between my reply and his answer.

Robert: Optimism. I like it. I never thought you were the
Search Engine type, Iris. Full of surprises.

Heat rose up in my throat and pooled in my cheeks. "What's that supposed to mean?" I blurted. *Why wasn't I the Search Engine type? Not smart enough, not focused?*

"He likes you."

I jumped and whirled at the unexpected voice over my shoulder. "Mom!" I hissed, reaching to snap my laptop monitor closed, even as she coolly scanned the messages on the screen and glared at the sloppy mess of files piled like fall leaves on my desk.

"Hello? Privacy?" I said.

She patted my shoulder and smoothed back a wisp of hair that had escaped from my updo. "You'll do fine. There's plenty of reference material on batteries. Just *finish* what you start. Watch your writing, Iris. That left hand of yours. We need to work on underwriting. You're such an overwriter, always smudging, and the Shareholders will dock you creds for that, you know. They demand neatness."

Trust my mother to be more concerned about my penmanship than anything else at the moment. "Yes," I mumbled. Agreeing was the only way to make her go away.

"I don't know why they allow left handwriting in school anymore. Such important documents to be scribed. It'd be far easier if they'd just taught you properly when you were young."

"Being left-handed isn't corrupted, Mom."

"It may as well be." She huffed as she clacked away from my desk to frown at the weather station above our sink. "How they ever expect to produce any decent Search Engines from your generation, I'll never know." Mom was a Search Engine. It was a revered job with a hefty food cred salary, and she never let any of us forget it.

I stared after her, nostrils flaring, barely controlling my breathing. This wasn't about being left-handed or a Search Engine. No matter how much I pretended at normalcy, Mom knew just what subtle jabs to pin into our conversations to remind me that she saw the real me. No matter how hard I worked, I needed improvement; I needed to be better than my messes, my trailing sentences, and unfinished projects.

"Lay off, Mom." Vinton's wheels creaked as he pressed his chair back from the desk opposite mine. He was home for a few days between survey runs. Even though he'd been an adult for two years, he'd continue to live with us until someone in the city died or was expelled from their Seacan. Only metal buildings shielded from flares, and metal was scarce. Our city didn't grow. That meant we lived with our parents *forever*. Sol help us. "The Shareholders aren't going to care if she's left-handed as long as she can ferret information out of a hard drive."

I wanted to thank my brother for coming to my defense, but a picture of a ferret squirming through circuit boards and cables overwhelmed my mind. *Focus, Iris. Damn it. Just focus. Not on ferrets and not on Robert Lycos's lips. You need this project.*

CHAPTER
TWO

stood on the boardwalk at dusk while people scurried around me like ants. The setting sun painted a swath of clouds in reds and oranges so thick I half expected the sky to drip color. No one else stopped to take it in. Polished shoes clacked past me, along with a current of smart blazers, fitted skirts, and trousers with crisp creases. Search Engines, Shareholders, and Browsers headed for work. Coveted jobs like these were what Robert, I, and every other year nine junior executive, were competing for.

As color bled from the sky and mosquitoes settled over the dirt streets, the Basic workforce made their commute next. Cache was my dad's department, curators of the largest hardcopy library this side of the mountains, maybe even the largest in the country. I waved at him as he passed. Power Supply Unit, Firewall, Food Bank, and Med, they all filed to their respective buildings to start their shifts. The Gardeners would come last, once the streets cleared, walking the opposite direction of everyone else, heading home from their dayshifts. Gardening was where Corporate put people who couldn't find placement anywhere else.

In the lull, I grappled with an old internal battle, deliberating whether being late for school was worth staying to wave at Olivia on her way home from work. We'd been effortlessly close as kids, giggling in school, racing between the benches of the greenhouses, and cradling hatchling birds in her oupa's pigeon loft, but it had all unravelled once Olivia started working as a gardener full-time. She attended all her courses online. Then her computer crashed and her oupa couldn't afford a replacement. I couldn't message her anymore. We weren't even awake at the same times. In no time at all, my closest friend felt further away than I ever thought possible, and I started every evening like this, toeing the border of our separate worlds. Most nights I didn't stay because most nights Olivia didn't wave back at me anymore. Besides, this was year nine, my last chance to prove myself to Corporate.

"Hey, Iris. You coming?"

I jolted at the sound of my name shouted from far down the boardwalk.

Robert waved at me as he held open the door of Work Commons. "Okay, partner?"

"Yeah." I gulped and waved back, feeling suddenly warm. "I'll be right there." And I turned my back on the greenhouses as the Gardeners started filing out.

"YOU EVER TAKE A BREAK?" Deep into subfiles of an NREL Watt hour capacity study, I strained to reel my attention away from my computer screen. Robert's lips were talking to me.

"W-what?" I stammered.

"A break. You know. Stretch. Eat. Increase your productivity and all that shit?"

I didn't, actually. Not early on in a project like this when there was so much to absorb, and all these connections were clicking in my brain. This was when I could focus. Later on, when it wasn't new and exciting anymore, I'd fizzle out, I knew it. But now, alone, I could get lost for hours hunched over my laptop, highlighting notes and references until my stomach cramped with hunger and my legs tingled from sitting for too long. Leaving the file on my screen half-read felt like forcing a speeding train to jump the tracks and expecting it to finish its journey unscathed.

"Um, I've just got to dig into this one a little more." *That sounds so much better than I'm afraid I'll lose momentum and crash this project.*

Rows of divided workstations stretched beyond the cramped cubicle Robert and I shared, crammed with other students poring over files and squinting at screens. Cables slithered over cheap, threadbare carpet. Bare LED light bars flooded the entire double Seacan with harsh white light, and despite the rattling of the old air conditioner wafting out trickles of cool relief overhead, the air smelled like sweaty feet and canned tuna. Work Commons held none of the elegance of the high-end corporate offices.

Robert's lips pursed as he twirled a thick fountain pen between his fingers. "Team project, Iris. Come on. I feel like you're still researching when I go to sleep at dawn. You're gonna burn out. Or make me look like a slacker. Just a short break?" He flashed me a grin that made my insides jelly.

Of course, I blushed and mumbled, "Yes."

We shuffled out of our cubicle and past Jean and Charles, then Vannevar and Claude who snickered. When we exited the Work Commons Seacan, warm night air rushed in and clashed with the air-conditioned environment. The balls of my feet ached as we meandered down the boardwalk between Work Commons and Cache. I was simultaneously overwhelmed by the urge to take off my shoes and mortified by the idea of doing it in front of Robert.

Besides, my legs looked good when I was in heels. I wondered if he was a leg man. My hand found my cheek and scrubbed at the scars there, like I could wipe away my blush before Robert noticed it.

He did notice. *Shit.* He was staring at me.

"Does it still hurt?"

"What?"

"Your scars. You're rubbing them. They still hurt?"

"Ah, no." I ducked my chin to my chest. "Bad habit, I guess."

"You know, all of us think you're a badass."

"What?" I snorted and looked up wide-eyed. Robert's smile was genuine, not mocking. "All of who?"

"Us guys. Actually, pretty much everyone except Vannevar, but she's a flamer. I mean, you were a kid, and you just went 'frag it' and took off out there." He beckoned toward the gully leading to the lake and the train tracks. "Outside. On this big adventure. You didn't give a shit about what anyone else thought."

And look what I did to Vinton. I gulped, pressed my palms against my cheeks and turned away from Robert to wallow in familiar, sour guilt.

"Hey." He grabbed my hand. "I didn't mean—shit." His thumb stroked my knuckles as he shook his head and exhaled before pinning me with a nervous, hungry gaze. "I'm totally fragged right now. Like, you're different, but that's what makes you shine. I think your scars are hot."

And then Robert Lycos pulled me toward him and kissed me. I knew that a normal person would concentrate and burn this moment into their memory forever, but I got lost in his smell and whether or not he minded that I was taller than him and did my breath smell like the egg sandwich I ate for lunch. Then it was done. We went back inside, and I couldn't even remember how Robert Lycos's lips felt on mine.

TWO DAYS LATER, I stumbled upon the motherboard of all discoveries. It seemed innocuous at first, just a duplicate pdf file forgotten in a download folder pulled from a hard drive the Browsers had labelled *Ballard Emerald Residence*.

Emerald was code for Seattle. I'd seen it on a map once, a coastal city far to the southwest. I wondered how much our Shareholders bartered to get the drive. My city's Browsers had already mined every computer within easy reach when I was still a toddler. Houses, garages, shops, all of those had been long since stripped. We took paper books too, but those were exceedingly rare. The first winter after the power outages, people burned anything they could to stay alive. Books went first. Thank Sol, circuit boards made terrible firewood.

Browsers like Vinton had to travel further and further from home to find unstripped computers. Residential stacks were our bread and butter. While the closest data center to us held invaluable masses of data in its arrays, it was all encrypted, and even if we found the encryption keys, we didn't have the gear to interface with their media.

Residential hard drives held onto the internet in easily accessible fragments. Bits and pieces lodged in browser caches like broken glass. Downloaded files waited for us to puzzle them all together into a bigger picture. That's what Vinton did, rode out with his partner on his modified Sommer 462 (a small fleet of the German diesel motorcycles had been sourced and shipped to our city long before the collapse) and brought us back pieces of the past in the form of dusty hard drives. Once recovered, Search Engines like Mom mined for the most current cached info and anything new to add to our database. We were rebuilding the Internet, pouring it all back out onto paper and regaining knowledge lost to circuitry for years, but it was a tedious process of sifting through corrupt files and duplicate caches for nuggets of new information.

And I'd found one, something new, something *big*. I was sure of it. *Shit,* I straightened in my seat as I compared both copies of a maintenance guide for an Iron Edison Nickel Battery bank. One was labeled with a newer date. Both contained the same number of pages, table of contents, first and last paragraphs, but as I scrolled through the older document, I noticed a subtle difference in some of the diagrams and a small added paragraph cautioning about battery life reduction in elevated temperatures. It was a different version of the same guide.

"Robert?" My voice came out as a croak.

"Yeah?" He leaned back from his screen beside me and stretched his back until it popped.

"Come look at this. Tell me I'm not crazy."

"What is it?" His chair creaked as he shifted.

"Duplicate content, but check this." I tapped a manicured nail against my screen where the extra paragraph was slotted between a graph and a footnote. Robert smelled like sleep-warmed bedsheets, cloves and sweat, a wholesome sweat though, nothing like Vinton's foul socks. *Focus, Iris.* "I-I couldn't find this anywhere else."

Robert scanned the screen, lips moving as he read.

Would it be wrong to kiss him right now? He had really nice hands.

"What's eighty degrees Fahrenheit in Celsius?"

"Uh." I blinked. "Twenty-five? Twenty-six, maybe?"

"Shit. It gets hotter than that in battery storage for sure, doesn't it? I mean, like half the summer it's got to be warmer than that in there."

Our battery storage Seacan looked like a bunker, soil

mounded over it for insulation and air vents punctuating its length. They weren't for cooling though. Nickel iron batteries vented hydrogen gas. "It's warm, all right, for most of the year," I murmured.

"Are you seeing this?" Robert grabbed my shoulder and his voice shifted up an octave, loud enough that the rest of Work Commons dropped into silence. Heads craned over cubicles. "A ten-degree temperature rise can double the wear on the cells. *Double.* Shit. This is big, Iris. This is gigabyte."

I bobbed my head, swallowing at the implications. "There's no air conditioner for the batteries, right? If we moved one over there. The gen set can't handle more load, but if we cut power somewhere else—"

"We could potentially double the life of the batteries." A radiant grin spilled over Robert's face. His cheek dimpled, and his voice dropped to a whisper as he tucked his face close to mine. "This is huge. *Huge.*"

His eyes were pale up close, like a winter sky. I wondered what would—

Robert kissed me before I could finish the thought, with every student in Work Commons staring. I savored the warmth of his lips on mine, and by the time I opened my eyes, Vannevar looked like she'd dry-swallowed a handful of pills and they were still stuck in her throat.

"You did it, Iris." Robert's cheeks looked as flushed as mine felt. "We did it. The Shareholders are gonna overload when they see this. We're in."

CHAPTER
THREE

Within a week of our initial report, the Shareholders arranged the transfer of the Work Commons air conditioner to Battery Storage. A blanket memo stated that they had re-prioritized climate control, and citizens were welcome to share workspaces in homes equipped with evaporative coolers. They distributed cooling vests that nobody wore because they looked ridiculous over our dress shirts.

Vannevar and Claude greeted me with open, angry snarls every time I set foot in the oven-like atmosphere of Work Commons. They called me Basic Bitch and made every effort to trip me when I rushed by their cubicle.

"Ignore them. They're just jealous." Robert pressed a hand against my damp back as I folded stiffly into my chair.

"They all hate me," I hissed around the pen clamped in my teeth and scratched at the hair stuck to my neck.

"That's my pen."

"Sorry." I wiped it on my shirt before holding it out to him.

"Keep it. You've already started that page in black ink. May as well keep going, and you know what? Frag Vannevar. She's just trolling you. Corporate thinks you're worth your weight in copper, now. We'll be swimming in food creds while Vannevar eats shit off her own shoes."

I smiled outwardly at Robert's jab, but inside my thoughts wrinkled and clung like my sweaty shirt. The high of our discovery had worn off days ago, and there was nothing left to our assignment now but routine write-ups and filing. The Shareholders had happily accepted our preliminary findings but hadn't congratulated us, offered us coveted Search Engine, or even thanked us. My gut churned with an emptiness I couldn't place, and my mind refused to stick to task.

Who gave a damn anyways if the handwritten instructions posted on the wall across from the battery banks were fading? Dad or someone else from Cache could scribe a new set in neater printing than mine, and the Shareholders knew it. But Robert said it'd show initiative, and he was right. *Just reboot, Iris. Can't you finish anything without slacking?* Breath leaked out of me in a stale puff as I smoothed the paper before me and remembered Mom's words. *Finish what you start. Underwriting, Iris. Hand below your work. Don't smudge.*

Early that morning, as I slipped into my bunk above Vinton's, my messenger pinged. *Robert,* it had to be. No one else chatted this late. In fact, aside from Vannevar's trolling, no one messaged at all. Pulling my laptop out of its charging dock, I climbed back into bed and opened it on my lap, smiling.

Robert: Hey, have you seen my pen?

"Hello to you too." I frowned and typed my response.

Me: I gave it back to you.
Robert: You tucked it in your hair after lunch and that's the last time I saw it. Could you look for it?

I snorted.

Me: Now?
Robert: Look, I hate to be a glitch, but that pen is kind of important. It belonged to my Grandfather.

"Shit," I whispered.

Me: I'll check

I couldn't find it. I swept through my whole house and Work Commons. The next night, Robert and I searched everywhere in between, but I'd lost it: Robert's medium nib, soft grip pen, the only possession, he confessed, he'd had left of his dead Grandpa. Robert told me not to worry, but he didn't kiss me after that.

My inferior pen splotched ink on the pages as we wrote, and my hands shook whenever our arms brushed. I rewrote so many pages of our report that eventually Robert mumbled something about wasting paper and said he'd scribe the final pages himself. I felt relieved when he said it, *relieved*. Part of me was crushed, but my whirring mind leaped at the opportunity to drop the last loose ends of our project into someone else's lap. I wanted to be done. I needed the Shareholders to assign us our cred rating and our future job assignments and be finished with it.

Three weeks after handing in our final report, on a weekend, I received an email from the Shareholders. This was it. The rest of my life in one job posting memo. I held my breath, my finger hovering over the title. I couldn't believe they'd ranked us so soon. It usually took months.

Re: Nickel Iron Battery Collaborative Analysis Report 9AECLY

Upon review of page 46 'Battery Bank Electrolyte

Replenish Schedule' under 'Detailed Watering Instructions' an error was noted on paragraph 4 a) line 2, as written: 'Depending on usage most batteries should be watered every 1-4 years.' Please note that the proper scheduled interval is every 1-4 months with best work practices dictating checking battery levels monthly.

As this document falls within Critical Equipment Compulsory Procedures, an adequate peer review should have been conducted prior to report handover. If unaddressed, this inaccuracy in the reproduction of a posted Critical Equipment Maintenance Document would have directly led to a breach in a Mandatory Maintenance Schedule, and the degradation or destruction of Critical Support Equipment. For an oversight of this magnitude, the Behavior Modification Matrix indicates a repetition of year nine junior executive training for Iris Ecosia and Robert Lycos (hereafter referred to as the Offenders). In addition, dates have been reserved on the Offenders personal calendars to attend mandatory training on Document Archiving, Shareholder Fundamental Rules, and The Critical Role of Penmanship in the Modern Corporate World. If the Offenders wish to register a formal objection, a query session can be scheduled with Shareholder Public Relations Liaison Mr. Paul Lycos with five business days prior notice.

Knowledge is Power,

Douglas Baidu

Executive Assistant to CEO David Kahn

Cold tingling crept up my arms and legs. Saliva flooded my mouth. My breath fluttered, shallow and frantic, like bird wings. *A course on penmanship. It was me. It had to be. Robert's printing is neat. Tidy. He triple checks his work, and he doesn't smudge.* I scoured the email again, flinching at words that seemed to leap off the screen. Fundamental rule. Critical Equipment. *Oh Sol*, Robert's dad was the public relations liaison. He'd know it was me too. My fault. I'd ruined everything. Corporate was making us retake year nine. I'd set Robert and I back an entire year from our peers and lost us our place in line for the coveted Search Engine positions.

"Oh Sol." The words fell out of me as coarse as gravel, followed by a rapid, expanding heat. I shot out of my chair, caught my shin on its leg and plunged into our kitchenette. Gripping the counter, I swatted the faucet to one side and vomited into the sink.

"Iris, you okay?" Vinton called from his bed.

Bile burned my mouth and nose and another heave rocked me. Thoughts clogged, grinding in my skull like a computer hang up. *An entire year behind my peers. How could I possibly catch up?* I could live on dried beans. The Universal Resource Locators had topped off our bulk storage during their last trade. Mom and Dad wouldn't let me starve, but career base salaries were calculated using our year nine cred balances. The more creds you could save per month, the higher your future base salary. It was supposed to encourage frugality—I'd already cut down my consumption this year in preparation and so had every other year nine student. And for what? Now I was back at square one, a year behind everyone else and bumped to the back of the line on the career path list. And this didn't just affect me. *First you crippled Vinton and now Robert.* Sol, I'd put his whole future at risk.

"Iris?" My brother's voice rang sharp in my ears, like an echo. Was it an echo? How many times had he called and I hadn't heard him? His bed shifted and wheels squeaked as Vinton maneuvered into his wheelchair.

I wiped my mouth, sucked a trembling inhale between my teeth and ran.

"Iris! What's wrong?"

Slapping open our door, I stumbled into the gray of late dusk. Diesel fumes, dust, and the clicking of grasshoppers assaulted my senses. I held my breath against the nausea boiling in my stomach and trotted to Robert's house as fast as my heels and fitted skirt would allow me.

CHAPTER
FOUR

Raising my hand to the door, I paused with my palm hanging inches away from the metal panel. I wiped my mouth, smoothed my hair, and pressed both hands against my cheeks for several, shaking exhalations. Then I knocked.

Robert's dad answered. His expression was as unruffled as his impeccable pressed shirt when he recognized me.

"Um, hi, Mr. Lycos. Is Robert home?"

"He is," he answered and then pressed his lips into a tight line.

I swallowed in the awkward pause, cringed at the lingering sourness in my mouth, and pressed on. "Could I speak with him please, sir?"

Something shifted in Paul Lycos's eyes. I couldn't place the change in emotion. Was it pity? I couldn't tell. I sucked at reading people.

Robert's dad gripped the edge of the door, sighed, and nodded slowly. "Yes, Iris. I'm sure that could be arranged. One moment, please." He closed the door on me like he was afraid I'd bolt past him, some sort of wild animal trying to raid his kitchen. I stared at the metal panel before me. The cracks in the paint looked like tiny dead trees in a pale blue desert.

When Robert opened the door, I didn't have to ask if he'd read the email, his red-rimmed eyes, tight jaw, and the way he looked over my head instead of into my eyes told all.

"Robert, I'm sorry," I blurted before the swelling ache in my throat dammed up my words.

He sniffed, glanced at the space between our feet and shook his head in a small, tight motion. "I don't think it's a good idea to talk right now."

Prickling heat crawled up my scarred cheeks and spilled out in shameful tears, but I kept my voice steady when I spoke. "I—I can tell them it was my fault. *My* error. Your dad could talk to the Shareholders, and they won't hold you back."

"It was a *team* project. They won't grade us or dock us individually, and you know it."

I blinked, trying to clear my washed-out vision. "It's not fair to—"

"Who said anything about fair, huh, Iris!" He looked at me now, eyes colder than clouded winter ice. "You wanna talk about fair? How fair is it riding the discovery that made you the Shareholder's sweetheart, and letting your partner do all the legwork after that? Huh?"

"I didn't mean—"

"How fair is it just dropping the ball, Iris? I worked my ass off. I wrote out procedures until my fingers bled, and you just sat there like a fried circuit. You picked the low hanging fruit and left all the small stuff for me. People that *care* don't do that, Iris. Normal people don't do that."

Normal people. There it was. A deep sob gripped me, and I smothered it. I wasn't normal, and even Robert saw it now.

Someone moved behind him, pressing the door further open even as he gripped it to obstruct my view. She ducked under his shoulder, all gobs of blonde hair, caked makeup, and whitened teeth. "Hey, Basic B," she snarled.

"Vannevar." Robert's tone was soft and full of warning. He shook his head, but didn't defend me like he had with Olivia, all those years ago. He just let the silence build between us like choking smoke.

Vannevar ducked her head, faking chastisement but glaring at me under her lashes. Her hand reached for Robert's, and he didn't draw away.

He'd never invited me into his house. Not once.

I turned and fled, blinded by stupid tears and wobbly on my heels. A part of me wished that Robert would call my name, so I could turn back and face him. But he didn't.

Normal. No matter how hard I tried, I couldn't even fake it. There was something wrong with my brain, and I couldn't fix it. An anomaly. A virus in my circuitry, and I couldn't wipe it clean.

I WENT TO THE GREENHOUSES. Crashing to my knees in an aisle flanked by fronds of kale and spears of chives, I gulped down air fragrant with peat moss. There was no light in here save for the pale halo of the streetlight outside filtering through the plexiglass. A fan rattled overhead as I scrubbed my palms over the runs in my nylons. No fixing that. Nylons were expensive. No fixing any of this mess I'd made. *Oh Sol,* I bent over wheezing, I wanted to go back. Back to being a kid when Vinton still ran like the wind, Olivia saved iridescent pigeon feathers for me, and it was okay to have messy braids and a wandering mind.

"Iris?" A voice skewered me.

Shit. I sagged and swiped the tears from my cheeks. "Hey, Olivia." My voice wobbled.

"What are you doing here?" She stood with her arms crossed in the gloom.

"I-I just wanted to be alone. I thought your shift was over."

"I *live* here." My face must have screwed up in confusion because she sighed and shook her head, clouds of copper hair haloing her round face. "Oupa gave up his lease on our house years ago and converted part of the loft." She pointed to the metal staircase outside that led to the aviary where we'd once trained pigeons together. "You didn't know?"

I frowned. "I wave at you on your way home."

"I walk Elise's family home at shift change. Vannevar's been hassling them, and they don't feel safe walking after dark. If you ever waited long enough, you'd see me coming back." Those last words held more bitterness than the kale and chives around us.

"I'm sorry," I mumbled. *Zuse, how could I not know she'd moved?*

The greenhouse door lock beeped and clicked as someone swiped their wristband. Olivia turned, and I scrambled to my feet as two men strode in. I squinted but couldn't recognize their silhouettes.

"Ah, an early customer. We're not quite open for the evening shift yet, I'm afraid," the first man called.

"It's just Iris, Oupa." My childhood friend spoke my name like it tasted sour.

The second man stepped around Olivia's grandfather. His height and the unwieldy pigeon cages strapped to his back made him look inhuman.

My heart seized, and my fingers tingled.

"Beetle, that you?" he asked.

Nate. The uncle who I called Sasquatch because he looked too savage to be human when he popped out of the train tunnel, long arms swinging and mud caking his skin. It was really him. My eyes stung with fresh tears. He hadn't changed. Same smile lines, same full beard and easy grin. *Oh Sol.*

"Jesus, look how tall you got! And all dolled up like one of them. How do you even walk in those shoes?" He stopped himself as he closed on me. "You okay, Honey?"

My chin quivered, and I shook my head.

"Liv, let's give them a moment," Olivia's oupa murmured.

She let out a soft snort and turned her back on me. The greenhouse door closed quietly behind the pair, and Nate held his arms out from his sides like it was taking everything he had to hold back from scooping me into a bear hug. "I'm, uh, sorry it's been so long."

A fierce ache swelled in my throat. "You've been coming here the whole time? Six years?" Of course, he had. My uncle was a Universal Resource Locator. His group orchestrated the barter of goods our city couldn't produce like diesel and plant fertilizer in exchange for knowledge from our Cache. But I'd stupidly assumed that when my mother forbade Nate from seeing us he'd sent another URL to replace him.

"Mostly during the day when you're all sleeping."

"That makes it better?" I barked. *Frag, what else have I missed? Olivia living with the birds. Sasquatch under my nose this whole time.* My fists balled up, and my uncle lowered his arms.

"Beetle, believe me, I miss you and Vinton something fierce. Anne just thinks you're better off without me around. And she's your mom. I've gotta respect that. Look at you, all grown up, though. She must be so damned proud." The honest warmth in his voice stung me more than anything else so far tonight.

"She's not," I croaked.

"Hey, now." He shrugged the pigeon cages off his back and crouched down to my level. "Course she is."

I kept shaking my head because I couldn't speak. Nobody was proud of me, not Mom, not Dad, and certainly not Robert. Several agonizing moments passed punctuated only by my sniffling and the warbling pigeons behind Nate.

"You wanna talk about it?"

I clamped my jaw.

He sighed and nodded. "That's okay. How about I talk then?" I loved this about Sasquatch. He didn't push. He told me once that he'd nicknamed me Beetle because bugs never travelled in straight lines and neither did my thoughts. He was patient enough to walk that crooked line with me. Nate had never cared how long it took or where we ended up. "You remember that time I gave you the envelope?" he asked.

Of course, I did. It was my last happy memory of him before Vinton fell and everything changed. Nate had tugged on my braid and given me a present, for no reason at all, because that's how he was. It was an envelope of snap pea seeds with the name Beetle printed in smudged blue ink across the back. Inside were instructions on how to grow them Outside. It had been a challenge.

"Wind that big brain up, Iris," he'd said. He was the only adult who thought I was smart.

School had told us the sun killed edible plants unless they were shielded from UV rays within a greenhouse, but I had planted the snap peas Outside and they'd grown. They'd flowered. Plump pods had ripened along their length right up until the day Vinton discovered them and smashed them because I was breaking the rules. And then he'd fallen.

"Did the seeds grow?" Nate's question brought me back to the present.

"Yeah."

"You know why? 'Cause they're stronger than anyone gives them credit for."

"I'm not strong, Nate." My voice cracked. "I made a mistake. I messed up big time. There's something wrong with me."

He didn't wait then, just leaned forward and pulled me into a hug firm enough to make my ribs creak, like he could press all my broken bits back together if he held on tight enough. "Beetle, you listen to me now." His words were muffled in my hair. "You're the strongest person I know. There is *nothing* wrong with you. It's this place. You ever want out of it, you just let me know."

Out of it. He's offering to take you Outside. The thought terrified me after what had happened to Vinton. "No," I choked. "I don't want to go Outside anymore, Nate."

He flinched but didn't let go. "Well, okay then. Go kick some ass. You've got more brains than half the carpet-walkers in this place. Screw them all. You'll figure this out, whatever it is." Nate leaned back and held me at arm's length. "Shit, I wrinkled your fancy shirt."

A tired laugh burst out of me. "It's okay."

The greenhouse door beeped again, and Olivia leaned in. "Your mother is looking for you. She's calling your name up and down the whole boardwalk."

"Frag." Anger and anxiety flared in my belly.

"I better lay low 'til the coast is clear." Nate backed away and winked. "Go get 'em, Beetle."

I marched out of the greenhouse with heat blooming in the dark pit of my stomach looping outward like a plasma flare and vaporizing my fear. *Nate's right. Screw them all. Robert picked Vannevar over you. You let him see the real you, and he dropped you. Olivia thinks you're a fake. And your own mother still treats you like a nine-year-old.* I breathed in cold night air and exhaled heat. *Show them all. The Shareholders value hard work and frugality. You'll just have to work harder than everyone else. Save every cred.*

Surplus creds rolled over annually and increased your base salary average. I could earn more than Robert next year and increase my chances at Search Engine if I cut my creds hard enough now. Food was my biggest expense. I could starve for a year if it meant salvaging my salary and my future career.

Besides, Robert was a boy. He put away twice the calories I did. He ate like every meal was his last. I could outrank him. Vannevar and he could go frag themselves. I'd show them all what Beetle could do when backed into a corner.

CHAPTER
FIVE

irewalls were one of the two factions of our society who were allowed to carry arms. Browsers were the other. While Vinton and his partner were allowed to sign out small handguns to protect against marauders while out on a data run, Firewalls were armed with semi-automatic rifles with sizable ammunition magazines. They dressed in bright blue combat helmets and stark camouflage fatigues. Just their stern presence was usually enough to ward off any sort of petty crime in our city, but when it wasn't, the Firewalls had been authorized by CEO Kahn to use force.

Three years ago, they'd shot a woman, Nora Yates, because she wouldn't leave after Kahn announced her expulsion from the city. She was an alcoholic who'd used up all her food creds on moonshine and then had been caught stealing on the job from Food Bank.

I remembered rushing out of Work Commons with all the other students when we heard the screaming. The Firewalls had pulled her outside during her work shift. They'd deactivated her wristband, locking her out of Food Bank, the greenhouses, and Cache. Then they'd marched her to the edge of the city, the path down to the railway. She lost her shoe on the way, and when the blue-helmeted guards escorting her shoved her away, she kept trying to bolt back toward home. Until they shot her in the leg. She crawled away after that. And her shoe stayed on that path like a solemn marker for weeks afterward.

That wasn't going to be me. I was going to show all the Shareholders that I was more than my failures. I could still do big things. I could bounce back and start my career stronger than ever. I could be an asset instead of an anomaly.

Squinting through streaks of rain, I recognized Vannevar and Claude's dad posted in front of Food Bank in their blue combat helmets, holding their assault rifles under their raincoats like cradled babies. Cache and Food Bank were guarded twenty-four seven. I splashed past them and held my wristband up to the scanner beside the door. Vannevar sneered and Claude's dad stared, but I'd grown used to staring by now. It barely made me blush anymore.

The door beeped, locks clicked, and I stepped inside, wiped my boots on the mat, and nodded to the gateway clerk. Nora Yate's replacement. Eva, Evelyn? Something that started with E. I couldn't remember. *Just get it over with and get out.*

I peeled off my soggy rain slicker and the jacket beneath, held my arms and my bag out to the sides and shivered as I stepped onto the scale in front of the gateway. The clerk raised her eyebrows at the readout. Weight was measured down to the gram here. Food Bank prided itself on precision. The whole system was set up so that I couldn't walk out of here with any unaccounted weight.

"All right, Iris." The clerk nodded as I stepped off the platform. She stood, shuffled around her desk and patted me down quickly—sometimes people filled their pockets with rocks so they could replace them with stolen food once inside. "Come back with a nice full bag, okay?"

I pursed my lips and pressed through the cage gate without

answering. Saliva flooded my mouth as I passed shelves of dehydrated soups, smoked meats, and canned fish, beef stew with sliced potatoes, tuna casserole. Sol, I would kill for tuna casserole. Swallowing, I pulled my gaze from the shelves to my shuffling feet and walked past. Twelve more steps and then a left to the beans, past the plank with the big knot at the end. My survival had distilled into small things like this, walking through Food Bank without looking up at the well-stocked shelves of food beyond my budget. The smell of dried basil overwhelmed me, and I breathed in its deep, ripe tones, lost in a dream of basil goat cheese on crackers. *Move it.* I swallowed again, pressed my elbows against my ribs and made my selections quickly, returning to the clerk with three scoops of dried beans and a can of oranges. The oranges were expensive, but I couldn't afford to neglect my vitamin C right now.

"We're overstocked on canned corn right now." The woman —Elaine, her name was Elaine—recorded my purchases on the manifest, frowning at my deflated bag. "Big shipment came in from out East, and it's on at half cred. Do me a favor and take some off my hands? I don't know where they expect me to store it all."

I collected my bag and my can and stepped on the scale. "Maybe next time, Elaine." I smiled tiredly.

"Willpower. Give me some of that, would ya?"

I clamped my teeth together. "Balance?" I asked.

Elaine clicked her keyboard and scanned her screen. "You've got three-hundred to spare for this month, honey. You wanna live to see whatever you're saving for, yeah?"

Bite me, Elaine. We all know what I'm saving for. My whole damned career. The scale beeped, and the front door unlocked. I let my arms flop to my sides and winced when the can of oranges thudded into my thigh. Shrugging into my jacket, I wrapped my raincoat around me and got the hell out of Food Bank.

Vinton was home again, and he'd promised to bring me kale.

I needed it for iron, but I couldn't bring myself to set foot in the greenhouses, not since the last time I went in and the smell of chives overwhelmed me to the point that I cried. Nate hadn't made another appearance since that night, and Olivia seemed farther away than ever. My brother would buy the biggest bunch of greens he could find, and he'd pay for it out of his own food creds. I couldn't stop him, but I told him if he bought anything other than kale for me, I wouldn't eat it.

Despite their cushy jobs, my family didn't have any creds to spare. Sol knew how much my parents had spent on Vinton's paraplegic modified motorcycle so he could qualify for his esteemed Browser job. I wouldn't have them suffering for another one of my mistakes. They'd tried to force food on me this past year, but you can't bargain with someone with nothing to lose and everything to gain by starving. My base salary and my future were on the line here, and I could literally define my long-term success by not eating up creds now.

It was the only thing I could control, and with the end of my second round of year nine approaching, I'd only have to gag down boiled beans for ten more days. At first, I hadn't minded it. I hated eating, all the steps of cooking a meal, the undivided attention it required, the texture of certain meats, it all threw me off. At first, beans were my best friends. I knew what to expect. They were full of protein, fast and easy to prepare, and I could be done eating and back to working sooner. But it had been almost a year now.

Ten more days and all the starving would finally pay off. I'd saved a record number of surplus creds. When they rolled over, if I got my coveted Search Engine assignment, I'd be making more than Robert, I was sure of it, and a selfish part of me couldn't wait to rub that in his and Vannevar's faces. If I never saw another bean after that, it would be too damned soon.

I dawdled as I closed in on our Seacan, despite the cold ribbons of rain creeping down my neck. Overhead an LED streetlight blinked to life and washed me with harsh white light, highlighting every drop of rain. *It's still early.* I had wanted to get to Food Bank before the evening rush, but that meant returning home with my paltry haul while Mom, Dad, and Vinton were still home. I stood in front of my own door for a long moment, flapping my soggy hands and gathering precious energy to face my family. Flicking a wet strand of hair out of my eyes, I grabbed the door latch and hauled it open.

"You're up early." Dad hunched over the table cradling a chamomile tea in one hand and frowning over his glasses at his tablet. "Shopping?" He straightened and glanced at the bag clutched in my hand. "Something other than beans, I hope?"

"I bought oranges," I deflected.

He studied me with tired eyes, and I knew what he saw. A daughter wasting away. A wet wisp of the round-faced girl he once hugged. I hadn't let my parents hug me in a long time. They both looked at me like I was breakable, but Dad saw deeper. Beneath my frailty, obstinance ran bone deep. Sometimes, I thought Dad knew it was all I stood on. He didn't try to topple it like Mom did, because he didn't see it as a challenge; he recognized it as a part of my whole.

"Oranges." He sighed. "That's a start, I suppose."

"Vinton's getting me some kale later too." I stared at Dad's fingers, stained black with the ink he worked with all day in Cache. I couldn't remember a time when his fingers weren't ink stained.

"Kale's not food." Dad slurped his tea. "Anyone who tells you otherwise is lying. I'm making cabbage rolls later if you'd rather."

"Sounds good. Maybe I will." I nodded.

We both knew I wouldn't. This wasn't just about creds. I was punishing myself for the mistake that had lost me Robert and trying to live up to the admiration I'd seen in Nate's eyes that night in the greenhouse. Cabbage rolls wouldn't help any of that.

"Hey, Iris?" Dad looked up.

"Yeah?"

"You okay?"

"Yeah," I repeated.

We both knew I wasn't.

With Mom showering in our tiny cubicle bathroom and Vinton still asleep, I retreated to my bunk with my laptop and headphones and pulled the divider curtain closed on the only private space I'd ever known. I needed to wrap up my second year nine assignment. The Shareholders partnered me with Elise, the gardener Olivia walked home every night. She was a year younger than me. Her parents could still afford to put her in school part-time, but she was happy to let me do all the work on our project. She didn't care if we passed or failed.

"I'm a Gardener," she'd snapped when I called her on slacking. "Corporate wasting my time with paperwork isn't going to change that."

So I completed our group project on preserving paper on my own. All of it. It was remarkably easy, really. Getting the air conditioning torn out of Work Commons and then screwing over your crush's career cleared one's social schedule nicely. Besides, when I cordoned myself into my bunk space, I didn't even have to dress in business casual, wrestle my coarse hair into an updo, or deal with people. I could wrap my brain in music and work uninterrupted.

But it wasn't without distinct disadvantages. I could only pick at threads on my bedspread for so long before my whole body ached for movement. Swatting the curtain aside, I'd dive out of my bed, but our Seacan was too cramped and narrow to pace properly, even when it was empty. Most days, I felt like a wool sweater, crackling with static, every fibre quivering on end with nowhere to discharge. I used to jog when I energy-bundled like this but running burned calories I couldn't afford right now.

Soon I'd be big time. I'd be making more than Vannevar and Robert both. I'd wipe that smug grin off her face, and he'd stop looking at me like I was some sort of starved stray he wanted to save. And I'd eat tuna casserole. All the tuna casserole.

I waited until my family left for work to pace, and I proofread the final copy of my assignment for the hundredth time. When Vinton got back home, I already stood gagging over a boiling pot of beans, headphones still blaring in my ears. The vibration of our Seacan door closing alerted me to his presence, and when I turned, his lips were moving.

I peeled my headphones back from my ears. "What?" I asked.

"Beans again?" He snorted. "You just love torturing yourself, yeah?"

"I love a big salary. Ten more days and I'll have another chance at Search Engine." I held my face away from the pot as I stirred.

"Here's your kale." He reached back and unhooked a bag stuffed with crinkled greens from his chair.

"Thanks. What do I owe you?"

"Iris, don't." Vinton snapped.

I set the spoon down and stared at the steaming water pooling beneath it in the shape of a duck's head. My pulse pounded at my temples in perfect time to the tinny music still leaking from my headphones. Another headache. I wouldn't miss the headaches. "Don't what?"

"Don't plow through life without taking help from anyone. You're not meant to do it alone. That's what family is for."

"It's just kale." I watched the duck-head water stain warp and absorb into our wooden counter.

"Exactly. It's just kale. You don't bloody owe me for kale, okay?"

I owe you for breaking your back, I thought, but I swallowed and said, "Okay." Picking up the spoon, I wiped my sleeve over the water smudge and went back to stirring beans.

At supper, I pressed the mashed, bland mush to the back of my mouth and swallowed several gulps of water to get it down. Mom cut into a fat, steaming cabbage roll swimming in tomato sauce. I looked away when she noticed me staring.

"Have you been getting your period, Iris?" she asked.

I hacked, speckling our tablecloth with half-chewed food. "What?" I rasped.

"You heard me." She jabbed her fork into a chunk of crumbling meat.

"Uh, I'd really rather not talk about this at the table." Judging from the stunned look on Dad and Vinton's faces, I was pretty sure they'd back me on this one. My fingers jerked toward my headphones still hanging around my neck.

"I think it's the perfect time to talk about it, and don't you dare put on those headphones," Mom continued, unruffled. "When a woman doesn't *eat* enough and her fat stores drop below a certain point, she stops menstruating. It's called athletic amenorrhea, and it's a serious indicator of osteoporosis and malnutrition. It's a simple enough question, Iris. Yes or no."

Frag, she couldn't do it. A whole damned year and she just couldn't stop pushing. Nothing was good enough or big enough for her. "Thanks for the biology lesson, Mom." I pushed my half-finished bowl away from me despite the hollow ache deep in my stomach, and I stood. "You know what? I think I've lost my appetite."

I hadn't had a period, not for months.

"Iris," Mom hissed, but I put on my headphones and walked away from the table without answering her.

Ten days and this would all have been worth it. Junior Executive School would be done. I'd get my big job assignment and a padded salary to go with it. I'd show them all that they couldn't knock me down.

CHAPTER
SIX

urns out, I didn't have to wait ten days to find out my fate. Five days before Junior Executive School ended, CEO Kahn invited us to his monthly Town Hall meeting. The city didn't actually have a hall, so ceremonial speeches from our founder were delivered from a podium in front of Kahn's lavish house when the weather allowed it. They were live streamed when it didn't. The CEO and all the other Shareholders—including Robert's family—lived in their sprawling, stitched-together Seacan houses in the downtown core. I logged out of school early and trailed behind my classmates until we reached the core. The wide dirt street was already clogged with people in formal business wear.

I scanned the crowd for my family but didn't find them. It wasn't uncommon for people to attend from their desks if they were busy. CEO Kahn valued production, and so long as you saw his face on a regular schedule, he didn't care if you worshiped him digitally or in person.

I tucked into an alley where I wouldn't get overwhelmed by the crowd and wrapped my arms around myself. The wind was cold and the clouds blotting out the stars to the west flickered with strobes of lightning. I hoped Kahn would get this over with quickly.

Our CEO approached the podium on time, as always. He wasn't a tall man, but his impeccably tailored suit, hawkish eyes behind thin-rimmed steel glasses, and the way he held himself as if he was comfortable with every awed gaze in a crowd made him seem larger than life. He didn't fidget with his notes before puffing up his chest and speaking clearly into the microphone. "Knowledge is Power."

"Knowledge is Power," we all repeated back.

"Not a lengthy agenda today. I won't keep you all from being productive." He smiled as if that were some inside joke, and every Shareholder in the crowd made sure to paste a knowing smile on their faces too.

Someone in the crowd shouldered toward me, and my stomach dropped when I recognized Robert. I tucked further into the alley, but he'd already spotted me. Soldamnit, I'd done my best to avoid him all year, completing my schooling online and avoiding Work Commons. I'd deleted his emails without reading them. Trust him to corner me now at a town hall meeting when I couldn't escape without the Firewalls noticing. I held my breath as I scanned the blue helmets and recognized Vannevar's pale blonde hair. If she saw me go, she'd make sure the Shareholders knew about my absence.

"Iris." Robert stood beside me, his eyes pinned to CEO Khan as the man droned on about power-saving measures and team-building opportunities. "You've been a ghost in the wiring lately."

"I recommend it. You don't have to deal with people," I murmured without looking over. Frag, why did he have to smell so good?

"Look, I know you've been avoiding me, but we need to clear the air about what happened last year."

"No, we don't," I answered sharply.

He shook his head and tried again. "It's not my fault you messed up, but I should have proofread the report."

"We're good." I ducked around him to press into the crowd ahead of us and flinched when he grabbed my hand.

"Iris, wait," he whispered. "It was a typo. Nobody asked you to kill yourself over it. Don't be so damned sensitive."

Sick heat flushed my face. He didn't even know, did he? Robert, in his cushy, spacious house didn't even know that those of us who weren't swimming in creds had to *starve* in year nine to earn a living wage later. And I had to starve most of all to make up for a year lost. Had he even made an effort this year, or was he a dock-in for Search Engine, regardless? I twisted my hand out of his grip and clenched my jaw hard enough to make my teeth ache.

"I'm just trying to understand you," he blurted.

"Yeah?" I snorted. "How about not leading with the 'Don't be so sensitive' line next time. Hell of an opener, Robert." I turned to leave, but right then CEO Kahn said my name from the podium.

I froze.

"—For her admirable work ethic and excellent budgeting skills, which have made her a leader amongst her peers this year, the Shareholders would like to present her with the Model Citizen of the Month award, as well as accept her application for one of our Search Engine openings."

You misheard. I raked a bony hand down my face and sucked in my sunken cheeks. CEO Kahn had said someone else's name, and my fried brain misheard it.

"Congratulations, Iris Ecosia. And next on the agenda"— Kahn peered over his glasses at his notes—"I am overjoyed to announce that the Licklider family's application to add a child to their family has been approved. Charles Herzfeld has accepted a promotion to Senior Power Supply Unit ..."

The rest of our founder's words were drowned by the

buzzing in my head. I turned from Robert and ducked down the alley as the clouds covered the moon overhead.

As I trotted home in a daze, Vannevar's older brother Peter called out to me from his post in front of Cache. Her whole damned family was Firewalls. "You check the west, and I'll get the east?"

"Yeah," I answered absently, even though I didn't really register what he was saying. *I'll figure it out later. Focus, Iris.*

Our Seacan was empty when I got there. Mom and Dad were likely watching Kahn's speech from their offices, and Sol knew where Vinton was. I opened my laptop and clicked on the confirmation email titled *Search Engine Application Acceptance*. My throat dried out as I scanned it. *Model citizen. I'm a model citizen.* I balled my hands into fists as they started shaking. At the bottom of the email, the Shareholders posted my starting salary—everyone's wages were posted 'to promote transparency,' CEO Kahn said. It sat there like a victory flag. *3500 creds per month. Oh Sol.* My knees jellied. *That's huge. That's Meg.* It was nearly as much as my parents made, and five-hundred creds more per month than the average starting salary for a Search Engine.

It had paid off. All the bellyaches and mashed beans. All the staring and starving, it had all paid off. Tears pricked my eyes, and breath blew out of me. This was big. Model citizen, Iris Ecosia, and all I had to do to earn the Shareholders' highest praise and a big salary was starve and become a workaholic. I poured out of my bunk on wobbly legs, abandoning my laptop. I needed to get out of here before Vinton and Mom and Dad swamped me with hugs. I needed to eat.

The weather station above the sink pinged an alarm, but I ignored it and dove out into the night without my jacket. I didn't need it. Thick, humid air hung over our city now, stirred by an anxious wind. Gravid, restless clouds hemmed the valley in from the west, but I had a bit of time before it rained. I hurried toward Food Bank with my arms crossed over my chest.

Something wriggled in the back of my mind as I scanned the building storm, but I couldn't fish the thought out of the spinning current filling my head.

You're forgetting something. I felt dizzy, and I wasn't sure if it was the email or the thought of eating real food that was causing it. Whatever it was, it could wait until I filled my belly. I didn't need to save surplus creds anymore. I was salaried. Corporate. I deserved this.

Elaine looked up from her console where CEO Khan's speech was still playing on mute. "Couldn't resist my corn offer, could you?" She smiled.

Good, she didn't know yet. I didn't have time for empty congratulations.

"I'm, ah, actually craving something else, thanks." I fought not to shift my feet on the scale and waited for the click of the gate lock.

BY THE TIME VINTON, Mom, and Dad streamed through our door, the whole Seacan smelled like cheese and cream sauce and baked tuna.

"Iris! Oh my Sol." Vinton wheeled toward me, a bright grin pasted across his normally stern face. Without setting his brakes, he pulled me down and flung both arms around me, crushing me into a hug while his footrests dug into my shins. "You did it. They announced it to the whole damned city! Big time. You're making more than me. I can't believe it!"

Browser was one of the highest paid positions. It paid more than most Search Engines. They got danger pay because of the risk of running into marauders.

My brother slapped between my shoulder blades, and I

winced. Sometimes I forgot how strong he was, despite his paralysis.

"Careful, Vinton," Mom scolded, but her bright eyes met mine and she nodded, blinking away tears.

"This calls for anything but beans!" Dad leaned over Vinton and squeezed us both.

"I made a casserole," I answered breathlessly, extracting myself from their embrace to crack open the oven door. The waft of heat, the bubbling cheese, and plump, fresh green peas nestled between pasta shells nearly undid me.

"Only you would celebrate with tuna casserole, Iris." Mom shook her head and smiled.

"Remember that one birthday when that's all you asked for. tuna casserole?" Vinton snorted. "We actually gift-wrapped canned tuna."

"It was good. It was a great birthday." I blushed and closed the oven door. "Don't make fun of it or you don't get to eat any."

A crescendo of thunder cut off any comeback Vinton may have had.

"Whole world's celebrating with you." Dad pointed upward with one ink-stained finger. "Fireworks and everything, Iris. We're so proud of you."

I grinned and spooned out cheesy slabs of piping hot, perfectly creamy casserole for everyone. As we sat at the table passing small talk and dinner rolls, rain leaned into the Seacan in dark vicious waves and thunder resonated through the support ribs of our walls, making us wince, but the generators chugged steadily away outside.

I'd done it. I'd course-corrected my life, and I didn't have to worry now.

I had already cleared the table and was doing dishes with Vinton when the hail hit. It thudded off the metal roof and rebounded against the walls. At first, we all grinned at each other at the enormity of the noise. It wasn't the first hailstorm we'd ever endured, but it never ceased to amaze us how overwhelming the sound of it was cooped up in our metal box. It was too loud to speak over. As the storm flexed and our Seacan shuddered, our smiles dropped from our faces. Dishes jittered in the sink between my soapy fingers. Vinton yelled something in my ear, but I couldn't hear him, even when I bent close to his face. If we had windows, they'd have shattered by now, the thought pressed through the cacophony around me.

In ten minutes, it was over. The wall of hail receded into fitful rain, and Vinton pulled at my wrist.

"You got your storm checks done, right? You were on panels with Peter this week?"

Peter. Panels. Solar panels. My legs sagged and my brother gripped my wrist as I slid down the cupboards and sat hard on the floor.

"Iris!" he barked surprised.

"Did she faint?" Dad's chair squealed as he shoved back from the table.

Oh Sol. Peter told me to check panels on my way back from the town hall meeting, didn't he? *You check the west, and I'll get the east.*

"Iris, you okay? Look at me." Vinton leaned toward me.

Peter had *reminded* me. The weather alarm had pinged, and I ignored it. I'd gone to Food Bank. I walked right by the west panels without checking them, and Vinton had been trying to ask me for the last ten minutes. A horrible heat tingled through my chest and soured in my stomach.

My brother grabbed my face, and I reached up and clutched at his warm hands with cold, wet fingers. "Iris, what's wrong? Tell me what's wrong."

My gaze fluttered to his. I couldn't stop blinking and swallowing. "I, uh, I don't think I closed the louvers." Years ago, the city had installed protective metal louvers over all our solar panel banks. If you were on panel duty, you cleaned snow, dust, and debris from the panels, made sure they were oriented at the proper angle for the season, and closed the overhead louvers when storms came.

"Oh Sol." The words flew out of me, and I bent at the waist, slipping out of Vinton's grip to hold my head in my hands. "I didn't do it. I didn't close the louvers."

"That's why there's two of you on duty. Redundancy," Vinton said. "Peter would have checked them too."

I shook my head "We divided rounds. He said he'd check the east panels if I checked the west."

Dad stood over me and cleared his throat. "They're built tough, solar panels. They're made to withstand hail."

"When they're new!" I squealed and rocked back until my head hit the cupboard "They're old and brittle now. That's why the city installed the louvers, right? Shit. I forgot. Peter reminded me, and I totally forgot."

"I'm sure they're fine, Iris." Mom patted my hair down, but she didn't sound convinced. We sat in wretched, resigned silence until the rain stopped.

It was too soggy out for Vinton's wheelchair to manage, but the rest of us pulled on over-boots and raincoats and went outside to check the panels.

The sky was still dark and the ground greasy with slick clay as we rounded the generators and slogged toward the solar fields.

Rows upon rows of tilted black panels huddled under opened louver tops.

They weren't fine.

CHAPTER
SEVEN

h Sol. I stumbled through the last few steps to stand before the west panels. One in the larger bank was smashed completely, and big cracks snaked across the faded plexiglass of another. I had no idea how much a solar panel cost, but it was more than I could ever repay the Shareholders. Even if the city could find replacements for the parts I broke, they'd cost more than I could make in a lifetime. Cities fought wars over solar panels. People killed for them. I was finished. Done.

Zuse, I'd gone through hell for a whole damned year. I'd only just made it, and I was ruined. It was all for nothing.

My flashlight trembled in my hands as I ran my fingers over a crack I could reach. Something cold slipped down my spine, ice rain snaking down between the hollows of my vertebrae.

"We'll sort it out." Mom came to stand behind me. Her voice was so damned steady. Too steady.

The crack snagging my nail looked like a roadmap or a river or blood veins. "Don't, Mom. I won't let you all suffer for this."

This was a huge offense. Generators, batteries, and solar panels were Critical Support Equipment. Last year my printing error had endangered the batteries. My neglect just now had damaged a major component. I would lose my esteemed job—there was no way the Shareholders would let someone so irresponsible into the role of Search Engine—and my cred balance would be zeroed immediately. My family would have to pool their creds to feed me with food meant for their own mouths.

No. I clamped my jaw and shook my head. "This is my fault. My penalty."

"I said we'll sort it out, Iris. You're not the only one on the hook here. Your partner should have checked these too." Mom's voice never changed, but it was as hard as steel.

My stubbornness came from her. I could fight her, but I wouldn't win because I was already weak, and she knew it. *Peter will hate me for this. One more person I've pulled down into my mess.*

We trudged back to the house through the mud in silence. Vinton nearly ran us over when we opened the door.

"Well?" he gulped, scanning our faces.

Dad shook his head slowly.

"Two panels cracked," Mom croaked, peeling off her overboots.

"Shit." My brother slumped, brown eyes shifting and unfocused. "Shit!" He slammed a fist into the padded arm of his chair. "You both broke protocol. This isn't all on you. Was anyone else out there yet?"

"I don't think so," Dad said. "Just us for now."

Vinton clenched his jaw and nodded before leaning toward Mom and fixing her with an earnest gaze. "I'll take her to Nate's. We can take the bike right now. I've seen the maps, and I'm pretty sure I know where his place is. It wouldn't take more than two days, and when I get back, I could say I was on a data run."

Nate had offered to take me away from the city last year in the greenhouse. I'd turned him down and he'd disappeared again, for a whole Soldamned year.

"No. Absolutely not." Mom leaned away from my brother, her face tight with horror. "You aren't scheduled for a run for what, two more days? Besides, Browsers always travel in pairs. You never go out alone. You *can't*. They'd think you stole the motorcycle, and that's all we need on top of this."

"I'll take her then," Dad said quietly. "We'll go on foot. You can tell the Shareholders that Iris ran when she saw what she did, and I went after her to try and bring her back."

"Stop talking about me like I'm not here," I snapped.

"John, don't be ridiculous!" Mom yelled. "You haven't walked more than two miles a day in your life. You don't even have proper shoes. Neither of you do."

"Send a pigeon," Dad fired back unfazed. "If Nate knows we're coming, he can meet us halfway."

"John, I'm NOT sending my daughter away with him!" Mom's voice cracked, shrill and uncontrolled and utterly unlike her.

My head spun as my strait-laced, corporate family talked about escape and mutiny. None of this seemed real.

"Anne," Dad spoke her name quietly. "We don't have much time. The Shareholders will launch an investigation to see where to place the most blame, but that won't take more than a week. What if they detain her?"

Detain. As in jail? We didn't have a jail, did we?

"You know if we don't send her, Kahn will make her work for the rest of her life without pay. That's slavery. Do you want that for our daughter?" Dad said.

"Of course not!" Mom snapped. And she sent a pigeon to Uncle Nate, the brother she hadn't spoken to for seven years.

THAT MORNING we couldn't sleep. My cred account froze a few hours after the sun came up. Someone from Power Supply Unit must have noticed the drop in panel output and gone to investigate.

At noon, when most people would be sound asleep, a harsh knock on the door made all of us jump.

"Don't open it," Vinton hissed.

I goggled at the latch.

"We're here for Citizen Iris Ecosia," a loud voice from outside announced.

Claude's Dad. *Oh shit.* The Firewalls were here—during the day. They'd come take me away like they did with Nora Yates, the alcoholic. I tried to swallow, but my throat stuck together and I gagged instead.

"We just need to question her, but if you don't send her out, we'll shoot the door latch. It would be a shame if a round ricocheted and hit somebody."

Shit. Shit. Shit.

"Iris, you don't have to go with them. You're not even dressed. There hasn't been an investigation." Mom clutched my arm, but I wrenched out of her grasp.

What else could I do? Let them shoot at my family? I straightened my pajamas, yanked on a set of tinted goggles, and opened the door to the blue helmets and the blinding sun.

THE FIREWALLS MARCHED me past the generator building. I felt utterly exposed. The sun was so bright it made me squint through my goggles. We turned toward a set of small Seacans beneath the generator exhaust stacks. I'd always assumed the containers were tool sheds. Turned out they were prison cells. Claude's Dad shoved me into a space barely large enough for a cot and a bucket on the floor. Neither him nor the other blue helmets spoke as they locked the Seacan door behind me. Even if I could have slept, the hum of the generators reverberated through my organs. My mind felt like glue gumming up in my skull. I knew I should be scared, but all of my emotions were stuck.

The cot pinched the back of my knees until my legs tingled, so I stood and paced, my slippered feet scuffing against the cold floor. I twisted my wristband on my arm. And then I heard the yelling, barely audible over the roar of the generators.

"Let me out of here! Soldamnit, I didn't do anything wrong. She said she checked the west bank! She said she'd check! I did my rounds. This isn't my fault." It was Peter, howling at the top of his lungs, but I was the only one close enough to hear him.

I winced with every thud of his fists pounding against the metal wall beside mine and imagined what he might do to me if there were no barriers between us.

An hour later, he stopped yelling. The door to his cell squealed as it opened, and the blue helmets took him away. Two hours later, they came for me. We marched through the blazing daylight to Work Commons. Inside was stifling as always, but entirely cleared out save for one table, four Shareholders, and across from them, an empty chair for me.

They questioned me for hours about the events leading up to the solar panel 'catastrophe'—their words not mine. After awhile I couldn't even remember the order of the events. My mind spun out, and I studied the pattern on the worn industrial carpet between my feet and offered one-word answers. It was dusk by the time the Firewalls escorted me home with firm instructions to my parents that I was not to leave our Seacan.

The next day, the Shareholders grilled me again. Always alone. always the same questions, and always for hours. For two days after that, Vinton said they called half a dozen peers my age as character witnesses: Robert, Olivia, Elise. Vannevar. I cringed when I thought of the slanderous picture she would paint of me. She'd always hated me, but now I'd hurt her big brother. Peter was being investigated alongside me, his career hanging by a thread. blue helmets stuck together, and I'd inadvertently dealt Vannevar's family a blow they wouldn't soon forget.

A week after I smashed the solar panels, I was escorted home from a cross-examination to find Mom sitting on her bed in her pajamas, bawling and spitting vitriolic curses at a long ribbon of paper twisted in her fist.

Pigeon mail. I frowned. *Zuse, Mom never swears.*

She must have just read the p-mail before I came in because Dad was hovering around her gaping in confusion just like I was. She wouldn't answer us when we asked her what was wrong.

Nate said no. The thought sent ice down my back. *I turned him down in the greenhouse and he changed his mind about me.*

Dad peeled the ink-stained letter out of Mom's hand to read it.

"This is from Nate's URL group. They got our message." He frowned, scanning the tiny printing across the ribbon.

The end of it curled toward me, and I picked out the subject line. To: Anne re: Iris Visit, but before I could read any further, Dad gagged and flopped onto the bed beside Mom. "Oh my Sol," he exhaled. "He was shot. He died."

My legs sagged, and my insides loosened. "Nate?"

Dad nodded.

No.

Not my Uncle Nate. Not Sasquatch.

Now I'd never see him again. He'd died in a raid on some unknown road a month ago. Shot in the chest, the letter said.

I think I know what that feels like. I pressed my hand over my sternum. *Struggling to breathe with all my organs leaking into each other and my life slipping away. I think I'm there too, Sasquatch. If I was ever your beetle, I'm squashed now.*

CHAPTER
EIGHT

On the day of the verdict, the blue helmets told me to get dressed and took me to the Seacans behind the generator again. This time, we arrived at the same time as Peter and his escort. Undiluted malice twisted Vannevar's brother's face when he saw me, and I froze until Claude's Dad steered me into the dark safety of my cell. Until that moment, I'd never once considered that the Shareholders might be putting me here for my own protection. My relief passed quickly though.

Sol, I couldn't stand this, crammed into this tin can with no room to move and nothing to do. Hours passed. Light blazed through the cracked seal in the door. I kicked the plastic bucket to pieces, peeled off my blazer and scratched my arms raw trying to ease the anxious itch deep under my skin. Pathetic relief washed over me when the blue helmets opened the door at dusk.

You shouldn't be happy to see them. The path they're leading you down now is a dead end.

They led me to the downtown core. It was well past sunset, and a crowd had gathered when most people should already be at work. David Kahn perched behind the raised podium in front of his house, and my family stood separate from everyone else with tears in their eyes.

Peter's family stood surrounded by supportive blue helmets. He stood as far away from me as his escort would allow him.

CEO Kahn was going to use us as an example. Our punishment would be public.

Paralysis soaked my limbs, and I sagged in the grip of the blue helmets on either side of me. Claude's dad's rifle slipped from his shoulder, and he shrugged it back into place and gripped me tighter. "On your feet, kid. Don't embarrass yourself."

If I could have breathed, I would have snorted. *Embarrass myself? He thinks I'm worried about embarrassment?*

Dad stared down at his feet, and Vinton was too short in his chair. He was blocked by the crowd between us, so I caught Mom's eyes and she nodded at me with pursed lips and smoothed her updo. *It's my hair she wants to fix.*

A thud sounded from the podium microphone followed by a resonant squeal. David Kahn tapped a finger on it once more, cleared his throat, and said, "Knowledge is Power."

"Knowledge is Power," we all repeated back reflexively.

"Let's call this meeting to order, shall we? I'll not mince words." David turned and pinned me with a predatory gaze as honed and polished as the rest of him. "Citizen Iris Ecosia."

I flinched at the sound of my name on those thin, stern lips.

"You were on panel duty last week, correct?" He stared over his glasses. "With Peter Baran as your partner?"

"Y-yes, sir."

"The louvers were left open during last week's storm. Was there some sort of malfunction?"

I clamped my teeth so hard they ached and shook my head slowly while David studied me like I was a maggot on his dinner plate.

"Then I'm not sure I understand the problem that led to the destruction of two pieces of critical equipment, Citizen Iris. Won't you enlighten us?"

"I uh …" Thoughts sprayed across my mind like short-circuiting sparks. I tipped my head up and squinted at a moonless sky with gobs of stars half-swallowed by clouds towering in the west. "I forgot."

"Zuse," someone snarled from the audience.

"No, she didn't!" Peter shouted. "She told me she would do first checks on *all* the panels before the storm. I started my redundancy checks after her but only got the east bank done before the hail got so bad, I had to go inside."

No. It wasn't like that. Peter had said he'd check the east if I checked the west, hadn't he? I hadn't lied.

Heat choked me. I focused on Kahn, the keen intensity of his eyes, the sharp gray highlights of his flawlessly styled hair, his twitching cheek muscle, because if I looked at my family now, I'd cry. It wouldn't embarrass me, but it felt like the kind of hysteria that would irreversibly unravel me. "I didn't lie. I just forgot," I said.

"You forgot?" Our founder repeated.

I nodded, heart hammering between my ears and adrenaline convulsing my fingers.

"How unfortunate. Do you have any idea what the replacement cost of the equipment you *forgot* to protect is?"

I knew it was as far out of my reach as the stars above us.

Kahn gripped both sides of the podium like it would fly away if he didn't. Peering over his glasses to pluck the correct figure from his notes, he said, "One-hundred-and-forty-three-thousand credits *each* for two replacement panels. How do you intend to repay the cost of your forgetfulness, Citizen Iris?"

"You know she can't," Vinton's hard voice barked before I could open my mouth. I turned to see Mom slapping him, gaping with horror.

"That's right, Citizen *Vinton*, is it?" Kahn's hungry gaze parted the crowds around my brother who suddenly looked frail in his wheelchair, despite his teenaged bravado.

Shit. Don't let him look at Vinton. My throat worked. *He's already paid too much for your mistakes. Your whole family has. Kahn can't take this out on them. It has to be me.*

Squaring my scarred shoulders between the two blue helmets holding me, I spoke in the loudest, brashest voice I could muster. "I don't know. Doubling the life of all of your batteries should be worth something, shouldn't it?"

There was nothing subdued about the gasp that sucked the sustenance out of the air around me now. Peter smirked, and Claude's dad gripped my arm tight enough to pinch nerves.

Thank Sol Almighty, David Kahn's dissecting gaze swung away from Vinton and back to me. "Pardon me?" He enunciated each syllable like a dart.

I resisted licking my lips and instead thrust out my chin. "I said, I saved your batteries. I found the original maintenance file with the operating temperatures in it and saved every single one of your batteries from getting the life cooked out of them. How much is that worth, because I don't remember getting paid any creds for that."

"Iris!" My mother yelped.

The entire crowd inched away from my family as if our waywardness was something visible and contagious.

The guard beside me sucked air between his teeth and flexed his fingers on the grip of his gun, but David Kahn didn't look at anyone except me. Watery relief mixed with icy fear in my chest, and I struggled to breathe past the slurry. *Good. I pissed him off. It'll just be me now. Whatever happens next will just be me.*

Without removing his heated gaze from me, Kahn covered the microphone with one hand and leaned to one side, beckoning his executive assistant, Douglas Baidu, from the crowd.

He whispered something to his assistant, nodded, and then cleared his throat.

"We have a verdict. Citizen Peter Baran, for not fully completing the redundancy checks specified in Critical Equipment Procedure Rule 4.1 A, the Shareholders of this city have elected to fine you twenty-thousand credits payable immediately."

Twenty thousand. I sucked air through my teeth. That was nearly a year's salary for a Firewall.

"Citizen Iris Ecosia, you have violated Critical Equipment Procedure Rule 4.1 B and are hereby banned from ever holding a salaried position in this city. If you find menial employment, any credits you earn will go toward replacing the critical equipment you damaged. If you are unable to find an employer to take you on, your citizenship will be revoked, and you will leave city grounds? Do you understand?"

The words rushed over my head like cold water. I remembered Nora Yates screaming, blood gushing from her thigh, her lonely, slender shoe left on the path to the railway. Sweat prickled my armpits and saliva dried on my tongue. No one would hire me, not after this public fiasco. *I* wouldn't hire me.

"Do you understand?"

"Yes," I croaked.

Kahn dropped his attention from me immediately, like I was so far below him, I'd already ceased to exist. "Move to adjourn?" he asked.

"Seconded," Claude's dad growled from my right.

"I'll hire her, David," a voice I recognized spoke quietly but firmly, and I turned toward it gaping, as did everyone else. Olivia's oupa. Had he just addressed our CEO by his *first* name?

"I'm sorry?" Kahn raised his eyebrows.

"I'll hire her. You owe me a Gardener. It's been pushed from the budget for three years running now, and I'm getting old. Her creds go toward funding for new panels. And I get to train another replacement before I die. Everybody wins," Olivia's oupa said.

"You have workers and your granddaughter. Train her," Kahn answered dismissively.

"You've cut my staff in half the last decade. The greenhouses as well as animal husbandry and pigeon training called for a staff of at least twelve in the original plans, did it not? We're worked to the bone, David, and you know it. If one of us falls ill or injured, you risk crippling the lion's share of the city's food supply and your communication system. This seems an ideal solution for both of us."

Kahn sighed loudly enough that the microphone caught the noise.

"Motion to accept Iris Ecosia as a permanently unpaid Gardener?" Olivia's grandfather ventured.

"Seconded," Dad barked.

We all waited for our founder's response. Only he could call the vote, and it wasn't really democratic, because he could veto if he wanted. He was the CEO. That's how it worked.

Sweat trickled down my back, and I choked on the smell of Claude's dad's tobacco breath as David Kahn measured me like he was calculating my weight in creds. "All in favor say aye," he said.

My family responded immediately. Around them, their peers started to nod and say, "Aye" as well until well over half the crowd had responded.

"Fine." David pressed his glasses up his nose, and my legs jellied. The rest of his words swirled above my head like a swarm of gnats, buzzing and barely discernible. "Motion passed. Move to adjourn."

"Seconded."

"All in favor."

"Aye."

"Aye."

"Aye."

"Meeting adjourned. Knowledge is Power."

"Knowledge is Power."

Bile rose in my throat, sick, sticky relief. *Oh Sol. I'm employed. I'm a Gardener. What the hell just happened?*

THE NEXT DAY, my family traded their occupancy in our Seacan for one half the size because they couldn't afford to feed me and pay the lease on our house too. Vinton grazed his knuckles because his chair barely cleared the narrow walkway to his bunk, and there wasn't any room to turn it around once he got there. All of the food creds I had starved for over the last year were replaced with a zero balance. I hadn't thought I was capable of crying over a number, but I sobbed when I saw that zero underlined in red on my screen.

It would be red-lined for the rest of my life.

Every cred I ever made would funnel toward the bill I'd accrued when the solar panels broke. Even the creds I earned selling my laptop and my business clothes went toward my debt. And my family would use their creds to keep a shelter over my head and food in my belly. I'd never be a contributing member in my household.

Every mistake I made, someone else suffered for it.

CHAPTER
NINE

The next morning, as my family settled into their beds, I woke and inventoried the only clothes I now owned: three long-sleeved, cotton shirts, two pairs of loose slacks, five pairs of underwear and socks, one wide-brimmed hat, and a pair of matte black flats.

Breathe, Iris. It's a fresh start. It wasn't a big dream, but I had always wanted to grow things when I was little, get out from behind a desk. Just water some plants. How hard could it be?

I dressed, braided my hair into two loose plaits like I'd done as a child, and strode toward the greenhouses under the naked light of dawn. We worked during the day because the greenhouse grow-lights had burned out long ago, and Kahn said it wasn't in the budget to replace them. That's what Olivia's oupa told me last night when I asked. He and Olivia stood silhouetted outside Greenhouse One, waiting. I wiped my clammy palms on my thighs. I hadn't spoken to her since that night with Nate. I'd whittled my life down to nothing in the last year. *Olivia was like a sister to you once and you unfriended her to chase after your big Search Engine position.*

I scuffed to a stop in front of them and waved my hand like

an idiot. "Hi, Olivia." My throat tightened as I realized I still didn't know her grandfather's name. We'd both called him Oupa as kids. *He saved your life. Literally saved it, and you don't know his name.* "S-sir," I stammered.

He returned my awkwardness with a gentle smile. "Johan is fine, Iris."

Johan. Johan. Memorize that. Mnemonics. Joyful Olivia Has A Nice … Grandpa?

"*Those* are the shoes you're wearing?" Olivia jutted her chin toward my feet and scratched one of her eyebrows with short-clipped nails.

"Yeah." I grinned uncertainly. "They're the ones on my feet, so yeah."

"You'll roll an ankle, for sure. Did you bring goggles?" Her dark eyes appraised me with all the intensity of a coder searching for malware.

She hated me. *And why wouldn't she?* This past year, I'd poured myself into the corporate mold and stayed there, walled off by screens and deadlines. I had never thanked her and Johan for letting me be a part of their family growing up. I'd never even said goodbye. *Because you're selfish, and you don't think of anyone else.* I ruined every life I touched. Olivia was smart to keep me at arm's length now.

Swallowing against my self-sabotaging thoughts, I rolled back my shoulders and reset the tightness pinching my face with a forced smile. "I didn't bring goggles." *Tell her you couldn't find them this morning. You lose everything.* "I thought a hat would be enough. Do we need them in the greenhouses?"

"*You* do. Look at how pale you are!" Olivia waved a dismissive hand, and suddenly, I was ashamed. Her skin was so dark it made her eyes and teeth stand out. Johan's was the same. When we were young, Olivia had nicknamed me *the Ghost*. I wished I were something insubstantial now, because my presence seemed to be insulting her more every second.

"When was the last time you were out in the sun all day?" she demanded. "Your skin and your eyes won't be used to it, even with a hat on."

"I, ah, thought the glazing filtered the UV."

"Not all of it, and we're outside between the houses a fair bit to tend to the chickens and goats."

I broke our gaze, blinking down at my already dusty slip-on shoes. When we were little, Olivia had always been the fun one, the accepting one. *Way to frag this up too, Iris.*

"Liv," Johan spoke in a quiet, firm voice, "why don't you go see if we have some spare boots and goggles at home, hmm? What size are you, Iris?"

Size? Goggles came in different sizes? "Uh …" I swallowed. *He means feet, you idiot.* "Oh, eight and a half."

"We don't have half sizes," Olivia mumbled before striding away from us, red hair floating like a billowing storm in her wake.

"Come on. I'll show you the ropes before the sun gets much higher." Johan waved a gnarled hand, and when I glitched, he took my elbow and guided me inside. "Olivia doesn't like big changes. She'll come around."

I doubted it. I wouldn't come around if my childhood friend abandoned me because she wanted a coveted job instead. I'd be cold as the coming winter too.

Johan toured me through all five greenhouses, stoked the fires in their woodstoves, and cleared the air intake screens on the circulation systems as we went.

We hadn't lit our woodstove yet. It was late fall and the first snow had already fallen, but the new Seacan was so stiflingly small that our body heat kept us warm. Johan explained that the greenhouses weren't nearly as well insulated as the retrofitted shipping containers were. "And our plants don't have blankets," he added with a wide grin, like it was the funniest joke in the world.

I tried to smile, but my insides were still twisting up over the hardness in Olivia's eyes. Johan had assigned her to train me. It would mostly be her and I all day, every day, from here on out. *Get used to it, Iris.*

As soon as Olivia rejoined us, and I'd donned my goggles and boots, we got to work. I'd naively assumed that working at the greenhouses would be somewhat similar to visiting them. Meandering down restorative rows of green, inhaling the smell of dirt, moss, and fresh flowers, misting water over glossy leaves while occasionally pinching off a wilted stem, that's what I thought it would be like. After all, I'd grown Uncle Nate's peas with only the barest of care. I supposed plants sheltered by the greenhouses required even less dedication. Stupid girl. I hadn't a fragging clue.

That first day, we mostly lifted. Bags of sand, bags of soil, shoveling compost into wheelbarrows, transferring sopping wet trays of plants from one bench top to another. Olivia directed while the resident tabby cat, Luan, weaved underfoot, tripping me every other step. When my back screamed from lifting and I started panting and swaying in the humid heat, Olivia had me switch to repotting plants.

She watched over my shoulder the entire time, like I was four years old and incapable of working unsupervised. Luan yowled in rejoinder, tail twitching and eyes as cold and intense as his master's.

"Break up the root ball or it'll get bound. I already showed you how," Olivia snapped.

She was right. I had no idea what I was doing. This was nothing like planting Uncle Nate's seeds, and I was clueless.

"I told you. Watch for pests, they'll ruin an entire tray. You missed one over here again." Olivia pinched her lips and held up a gyrating, maggot-like grub so close to my nose, I wondered for a horrified second if she meant to stuff it up my nostril. "That's three trays now. Pay attention."

My head swam and the humidity made it hard to breathe so I nodded instead of answering. The other Gardeners in the greenhouse moved as far away from us as they discreetly could.

Olivia crushed the fat grub underfoot and then kicked it to Luan who batted at it for several minutes before turning up his nose in regal disinterest.

"Don't leave any air pockets behind, and—frag, don't tamp down the soil so hard!"

I froze with my filthy hands buried deep into a large pot with a gangly vine. Dirt had crammed so far under my nails that my fingers throbbed. "Which one is it, Olivia? Don't leave air pockets, or don't tamp down the soil?"

She snagged the edge of the pot, yanking it toward her hard enough to spill soil all over the bench top.

The plant jiggled between us like it was shivering.

I stood with my hands outstretched like a bird about to take off. Soil caked between my fingers. The other workers straightened and stared. *Do not shake your hands. Just don't.* "I'm just trying to understand," I offered quietly.

"It's both. No air pockets *and* don't tamp down the soil. Even an idiot could understand that."

We didn't talk anymore after that.

I ate my lunch of cold mashed beans alone at the potting table, and when I limped home that night, my feet had blisters from swimming in oversized boots, my back felt like a crimped cable, and my hands were cracked and dry. My family had already left for work, so I showered, rolled into bed, and clamped my headphones over my ears. Along with an old MP3 player, they were the only personal luxury I'd kept. If I tried to sleep without sound filling my ears, my scrambling thoughts grew too loud, like mice in my head. But even with the music, I couldn't sleep that night. My eyes throbbed. They felt gritty whenever I closed them even though I'd worn the goggles and hat all day.

The next day Olivia had me refill the sandbags I'd emptied yesterday for potting mix from the pile by the henhouse. My eyes burned, and my head pounded. Everything outside seemed too bright, colors too close. My shoulders screamed when I threw my weight into the shovel to break up the compacted sand, and Olivia critiqued my every move, just as she had yesterday.

"You jump on the shovel like that and you'll wreck your feet."

We repotted, swept, moved tender plants away from the chillier outside wall zones, chopped wood, stoked fires, and released a new batch of ladybugs into Greenhouse Three. By the end of day two, I realized working here meant constantly soaked clothes from sweating or watering, and hands that cracked until they bled. And, my Sol, the back pain. We never stopped lifting or bending or tripping over damned Luan.

How could anyone disrespect the Gardeners? How could anyone do this for their whole lives? I was breaking, literally breaking. I returned home every night that week utterly drained, unable to do more than mumble at my parents as we crossed paths. I was too tired to eat. While I lay in my bunk with my back screaming and my feet swollen, my family navigated around each other like finely programmed droids in our abysmally tiny Seacan. Vinton took double data run shifts just to get out of the house. He literally couldn't get ready at the same time as Mom and Dad. There wasn't enough room to squeeze around his wheelchair in the mornings, so my family woke and went to work in shifts. And I pretended to sleep through chaos in a tin can.

Even though my limbs were heavier than sandbags, I couldn't sleep. I couldn't ever shut my mind off when it was tired, and this past week had stretched my starved body to the limit. I wasn't used to manual labor, and the swing from night shift to days was more jarring than I'd anticipated. It was eerily, horribly quiet during the day. I almost welcomed Olivia's berating when it came because, at least, it broke the silence. I could listen to something other than the short circuiting in my head. At night, every sound of the city outside, awake and moving on as if I never existed, needled me.

A week, and they've all forgotten you. That's all it took. I missed the idle chatter of Work Commons, the clack of my keyboard, Soldamnit, I missed Robert and walking under the stars at lunch break. The sky at midday burned into my eyes and stayed there like a permanent afterimage. Even through the filtered Plexiglas of the greenhouse, there was nothing gentle about the bright blue. It was harsh, and so was everything else about my days.

CHAPTER
TEN

"Come on," Olivia muttered. "Put your back into it. I'm not filling this whole thing myself."

I didn't answer, partly because answering didn't help, but mostly because I could barely breathe. My hands, soaked inside their gloves, slipped on the handle of the water hand pump, and my back cramped with every downward stroke. We were manually filling the five hundred-gallon reservoir tank because the electric pump had broken yesterday, and Power Supply Unit hadn't sent anyone to fix it, yet. The other Gardeners were busy elsewhere, so Olivia and I were pumping in shifts. We'd been doing this for two hours already, and the reservoir was only three quarters full.

She watched me pump for five more minutes before ordering. "Switch."

I sagged, expecting to rest while Olivia took over, but she handed me a paper face mask and ordered. "Put that on and pour in three of those bags." I blinked at faded plastic bags she'd indicated, stacked at the opposite end of the greenhouse, each marked twenty-five pounds.

"Okay," I sighed. My face mask clung to my mouth and

pinched my nose. Wisps of hair escaped from my braids and plastered against my face. I heaved the first bag onto my shoulder, carried it back across the length of the greenhouse, slit open the top, and dumped its blue powdered contents into the massive vat in front of me.

Olivia masked up and stirred.

Flecks of grainy residue caked my arms and clung to my braids. "What is this stuff?" The mask muffled my voice, and Olivia didn't answer. "Should I be worried?"

"Not if you wash off once we're done," Olivia puffed as she returned to pumping. "It's fertilizer. Don't breathe in any of it and you'll be fine."

Luan sat bunched on the stack of fertilizer bags, glaring at me judgmentally as I grabbed another bag. Frag. I couldn't do this for much longer, and Olivia knew it. Even the damned cat knew it. *Don't seem weak. Keep talking.* "Fertilizer?" I gasped. "Isn't that what the compost is for?" Blue crystals dissolved into milky, swirling clouds like young galaxies forming in the water.

Olivia sighed loudly and enunciated each of her words like she was speaking to someone who didn't understand English. "Compost was enough before the sun storms. Now, every plant in here will die without supplementation. The sun does something to them, and compost isn't enough to keep them healthy."

"Plants outside." I spoke between exhales. "They don't die."

Olivia froze and gaped at me for a moment before snorting. "Yeah. Trees and scrub grass. You eat trees? Cactuses? Anything we grow for food needs this fertilizer or it dies. You gonna get that last bag, or what?"

Uncle Nate's snap peas didn't die, not until Vinton stomped on them. The rogue thought burned through my mind and made me flinch. Why now? Oh, Sol, Nate. Swallowing against the swelling ache in my throat, I strode toward the fertilizer bags and heaved the third bag over my shoulder, but my brain wouldn't let the question go. It kept circling back like an open loop programming fault. "How do you know plants die without it?"

"Because three years ago the URLs upped their barter price for it, and the city wouldn't pay. When we ran out, we lost every crop in here, just like they said we would. It all wilted within days." She sniffed and pinched her mask tighter over her nose. "The city pays whatever the URLs ask for it now."

I digested Olivia's words slowly through the growing fog in my head. Dizziness swamped my brain, swirling like the cloudy water in the vat. It must have been an URL group from further west. Nate wouldn't gouge his own family, would he? Zuse, stop thinking about him. Tears pricked my eyes, and I focused on the stamped lettering on the bag before me. It was faded and the plastic was brittle and yellowed. "Where's it from?" I croaked.

Olivia shrugged. "Somewhere overseas. URLs ship it inland from Vancouver, and it's worth its weight in copper so don't spill any."

Another URL group then. They could have upped the price and Uncle Nate was just the middleman. Had to be. I pictured the smile lines creasing his mud-crusted face, those vivid blue eyes, and the way he threw his head back when he laughed. *Hey, Beetle!* Saliva filled my mouth. The vat in front of me tilted along with the rest of the greenhouse. I stumbled and grabbed the lip of the container. The bag I was pouring slithered out of my grip and hit the ground with a smack, before sagging and spilling out a stream of blue powder into the dirt.

"Hey!" Olivia snapped.

She just said don't spill any, idiot. I bent to scoop the precious fertilizer back into the bag, but my gloves were stiff and my fingers clumsy. I leaned hard against the vat, swallowing nausea.

"Sit down." Olivia's fingers clamped my upper arm, pulling me down.

I spilled it. I fragged this all up, big time, gigabyte. They'd fire me and I'd get expelled, and I couldn't go to Nate because someone shot him. Someone fragging shot him, and I never got to see him. He said he'd take me away. I should have gone, and now it's too late. I gagged and sat down hard, clawing my mask off my face.

Olivia plopped down beside me, stripped off her gloves, and pressed my head between my knees. "Head down. Breathe."

"I can't," I wheezed.

"Yes, you can. Deep breaths."

"I fragged up," I gulped. "I frag up everything I touch."

"When was the last time you had some water?"

"I'm wired wrong. There's something wrong with me. Anomalies."

"Where's your water bottle, Iris?"

"And everything I touch I break. The peas, Vinton, you, Robert. My whole family. Oh Sol. Nate. Nate died. They shot him."

Something about Olivia's voice sounded urgent, but I had to blink at her for several seconds before her words shot through the mess in my skull. "Iris! Your water bottle."

Water bottle? I sat up to gape at her. Heat flushed my scarred cheeks and words bubbled past my lips like scalding water. I couldn't stop them. "My uncle died, and you're asking me about a damned water bottle? I don't *have* one, Olivia. I don't have *anything,* and I never will except damned mashed beans, and my family is suffering to make sure I have even that. I can't *afford* a water bottle, okay? And you haven't let me take a break for the last two damned hours. Am I suffering enough, yet? Or do we just keep doing this until I'm dead, huh?"

Olivia pinched her lips.

My eyes felt hot and itchy, but tears wouldn't come. I sniffed loudly. "I give, all right? Whatever this game you're playing is, *you* win. I'm done. I'm sorry. I'm sorry you've been shoveling chicken shit for years while I was stuck behind a desk. I'm sorry I was an asshole friend. I'm sorry about it all."

Her boots scuffed beside me. We sat in silence for several hard breaths before Olivia sighed and said, "I was just waiting for the asshole friend apology."

Laughter barked out of me, genuine and unguarded. "Am I supposed to kneel and beg?"

Olivia's teeth flashed in a lopsided grin. She slapped my knee. "Nah, on your ass in the dirt is close enough. I'm sorry too, okay? Stay here, and I'll get you something to drink."

I leaned back against the fertilizer vat, swallowed by its shadow, taking deep breaths until my nausea faded and sweat cooled on my back. Luan alighted from his stacked bag throne and bumped his head against my shins until I scratched behind his ear. By the time Olivia returned, I felt nearly well enough to stand.

She balanced a jug of water, a thermos, and two wax fabric parcels in her arms.

My mouth watered even as my mind cringed at the sight of a wrapped lunch that was almost certainly not mashed beans. Oh Sol, if she ate her lunch in front of me, I'd start crying again.

"Quit looking at me like some sort of martyr. It's to share." Olivia shooed Luan away, spread a square of cloth away from the cistern, and threw a damp rag at me. "Wipe off. I don't want fertilizer on my food."

I shook out my braid and wiped down my arms and neck while she unscrewed the cap on the thermos, flipped it over and filled it with water from the jug. "Water first." She held it out. "Drink slow or you'll puke. You look greener than anything else in here."

"Thank you." I sipped my water while Olivia refilled her own bottle.

"Nate died?" she asked quietly.

"Yeah." My throat closed after I said it, and I squeezed the cup in my hand until my fingers ached.

"How? When? Sol, I'm sorry, Iris."

"Couple months ago." I swallowed and rubbed my chest. "Shot on the road. Probably marauders."

"Zuse." She shook her head. "That's fragged up."

We didn't speak again until I'd drained another cup of water and handed the thermos cap back to Olivia. Luan curled against my hip and batted at my braid a few times before settling into a warm, purring pile, oblivious to everything around him.

"Here." Olivia poured a generous amount of steaming red liquid into the cap. "You look like shit. The caffeine will do you good."

"Is that …" My words dried in my mouth.

"Black tea? Yeah, it is."

"Olivia, I can't afford that. Zuse, *nobody* can afford that. Where did you get it?" I squirmed and eyed the surveillance camera mounted high above us. "I can't take it."

Green tea was our city's caffeinated drink of choice since coffee went extinct. Only the elite among us could afford black tea. Johan had shown me this week that both leaves actually came from the same cultivar of *Camillia sinensis*, but processing black tea involved a precise drying, rolling, and fermentation process that made it three times more caffeinated—and three times more expensive—than green tea. Only the most elite among the Shareholders drank black tea. My parents bought a packet *once*, for their twenty-fifth wedding anniversary.

"I can't take that," I repeated blinking up at the camera.

Olivia snorted and deftly maneuvered herself so that her back faced the camera and shielded me. She pushed the cup into my hands. "Zuse, Iris. I didn't steal it. Who do you think processes the entire supply for the city? They don't just keep Oupa around for his pigeon-training skills and his green thumb. He's the fragging Tea Master, and he sets aside his own private stash before the Shareholders come for their harvest. It's kind of like a salary. Drink up."

I savored a long inhale of flowers and spice before taking a tentative sip. It was bolder than green tea, with earthy, caramel undertones. It tasted like summer giving way to fall, and its warmth eased my raw throat. "Thank you," I sighed and passed the cup back, but Olivia waved me off.

"You need the whole cup. You look like shit. Been sleeping at all?"

"Not really." I swallowed a bigger gulp of tea.

"Shift change will do that to you. It'll come. I'll just have to work you harder, I guess." She grinned again. "Lunch first." Olivia unwrapped two sandwiches: thick slices of tomato, creamy hummus, and crisp sprouts on corn bread. "Johan always packs too much." She shrugged and passed one to me, ignoring the tears filling my eyes.

"Thank you." I sniffed.

We ate in silence, sitting side-by-side amidst the quiet hum of the greenhouse fans while snowflakes clotted on the opaque Plexiglas panes above us and Luan slept at my side. I got lost in the texture of the bread and the mix of salt and tomato juice stinging my cracked lips, how the sprouts squeaked between my teeth as I chewed.

When we were done, I stood, stiff but steadier on my feet than before. Luan stretched and stared at me balefully for interrupting his nap. Olivia and I filled the rest of the cistern and checked all the drip lines running from the vat for leaks or clogs. Caffeine buzzed through my veins and lifted me into a level of sharpness that felt like breaking the surface of murky water. For a few hours, I wasn't a frayed wire. Everything connected and fired, and I lifted out of the fog. Zuse, no wonder the Shareholders paid so much for black tea. This was meg.

When we were done for the day, Olivia closed and locked the greenhouses. "Come on, I want to show you something before you go."

She nodded toward the stairwell that led up to Johan's house and the adjoining pigeon loft. I hadn't been up there since we were kids. It felt like too much, the tea, the sandwiches, and now this invitation. It was too big of a shift for me to grasp, so I stood there gaping like a cornered animal.

Olivia frowned, smoothed back her cloud of red hair and shook her head.

This was it. She was nice to me, and I just fragged it all up again.

"You know what?" She smiled tiredly. "Stay here then, and I'll be right back."

She trotted up the metal stairs with an energy I envied. Johan's thick wood door slammed behind her. I'd pinched my fingers in that door so hard once that my finger bled, and Olivia cried when she saw it. Oupa had put aloe juice on it and a bandage made out of my own hair ribbon. I swam in the faded memory, until the door slammed again and Olivia descended.

"Here." She held out a book. An actual Soldamned book, just like the ones that lined Cache which the Firewalls guarded twenty-four seven. I gaped at its yellowed pages and tattered edges while Olivia still spoke. "When I can't sleep, books always help."

"This isn't from Cache," I mumbled.

"Nope. It's Oupa's personal stash. He collected them before the collapse. Did you know he said that people just gave them away, back then? Sometimes they threw them in the trash, there were so many. That's how cheap it was to print them back then."

"He didn't have to surrender them to Cache? The Shareholders say—"

"You might have noticed that Kahn and Oupa don't exactly see eye-to-eye on most things. Kahn wants his tea, Oupa keeps his books. Here. Take it."

"What's it for?" I squinted at the title and the faded picture on the cover.

"What?"

"What section of study?" My laptop was gone, but Vinton could update my continuing education file for me on his, and I needed every cred I could put toward my crippling debt.

"It's fiction, Iris." Olivia wrinkled her nose. "It's just a story. No cred attached." She tapped the cover. "This one has pirates on solar sail ships. It's good."

I frowned down at the faded painting of a black sea with an aggressive, sleek bow cutting through frothing waves. "Good for what?" I mumbled and winced at the words I'd only meant for my head.

Olivia snorted. "For fun. Zuse, Corporate really got in your head, didn't they? People used to read for *fun*, Iris. Try it." She flicked the book against my chest and turned back toward the stair. "Come tomorrow actually ready to work, yeah?"

"Yeah," I murmured.

I read about solar pirates that night cradled in the sea of sound my headphones poured out. The book had an old map of Africa with trade winds and currents that no longer existed. It was a ridiculous, exquisite waste of time, and I fell asleep with it open on my chest for the next two days. That's when it struck me, one morning as the words swam on the timeworn pages, and my mind came down from a glorious caffeine swell courtesy of Olivia's tea. There weren't any tomatoes in the greenhouses. They were all harvested before I started working there. We'd had tomato sandwiches with sprouts and hummus. I'd never forget them, that undeserved peace offering from days ago. Where had Olivia gotten fresh tomatoes if there weren't any in the greenhouses?

CHAPTER
ELEVEN

meant to ask Olivia about the tomatoes the next morning, but she was chopping wood and I was on chicken duty. Despite the faint smell of ammonia, I didn't mind the coops. There was an odd warmth to the mustiness within, the way the hens, still fat with sleep, clucked to each other like gossipers sharing the latest rumor. They clotted around my feet while I filled their troughs. I raked their run and marveled at the efficiency of the roll-away nest boxes that funneled laid eggs down an inclined chute and into a central collection bin where the chickens couldn't peck at them. After I inspected each egg for cracks, I sorted them into cartons to take to Food Bank.

Smiling at the guards, I tapped my wristband against the door panel until it beeped and let me in. "Forty-three this morning." I stacked the cartons on the gate clerk's desk.

Elaine squinted at her computer screen for several moments before popping open each carton to confirm my count. Thank Sol, it was Elaine. The other girl couldn't count, and she glared at me like I was some sort of Trojan horse.

There was a camera mounted in each coop above the nest box's roll-away trays. Food Bank's gate clerks kept a running tally of egg count in the bins, and if my delivery didn't balance, the shortfall came off my cred balance. I couldn't earn money, but the Shareholders had made certain there were numerous ways for me to accrue more debt.

"Why a dozen a crate still?" Elaine frowned as she counted. "Would it be such a sin to keep a simple ten to a box? Who's the CEO who decided twelve was the proper amount of eggs?"

"English in the first century, I think," I offered. "One egg sold for a penny and twelve for a shilling which equaled twelve pennies."

Elaine snorted. "First century! They teaching you nonsense from the first century in business school?"

"History of Economics. Important stuff. See, I knew I'd need it someday."

"Forty-two."

"What?" My smile dropped from my face. There was forty-three. I'd counted twice. I hadn't fragged this up.

"My count is forty-two," Elaine repeated, her face unreadable as she held out an egg.

I stared at it dumbly. It was some sort of trap. Sol, why couldn't I read people better?

"Go on. There's no cameras in here. It's all done by count or scale. You know that." Elaine pushed the egg toward me. "You need to get some meat on your bones, girl, or you'll drop my next shipment and crack them all, and then where will we both be, hmm? Forty-two. That's my count." She smiled warmly.

"Uh—thanks." I bobbed my head, cheeks warming as I pocketed the egg. "I, uh, I was planning to do a bit of shopping. Vinton said I could put it on his creds."

"Good. On the scale with you then." She nodded.

I stood on the scale, arms spread and egg heavy in my pocket. The gate clicked, and I rushed through, jumping as it clanged behind me. How would I explain this to Mom? We couldn't afford eggs, and she was going to ask how I got it. I wasn't some damned charity case! Only I was. Of course, I was. I'd never earn a single cred for my family again, and they'd be the ones who suffered from that. I blinked at the floor and navigated the familiar path to the only shelf I could afford. *Soldamn beans.*

The gate clanged again, and I hunched my shoulders and sucked in a long inhale that burned my nostrils. Whoever was shopping this late wasn't coming to the dried bean section anyways. *Relax, idiot.*

Dress shoes clacked smartly against the warped plank floor, closing on my aisle. I stared down at my own feet, toes curling in the rubber boots Johan had given me, now dusty and crusted with chicken shit. *Please, just keep on walking.* But like one of those nightmares where you show up in Work Commons and your computer is wiped or you've just utterly forgotten how to power it up, the dress shoes closed in on me, stride unfaltering until they entered the periphery of my vision and scuffed to an unsteady stop.

I recognized them. Square-toed loafers freshly polished. Navy pants with a sharp crease, and a black belt with a classic, understated matte silver buckle. My eyes refused to look further up, even as the back of my neck tingled and my stomach snarled into a knot. *Let him talk first. Don't say a thing.* Zuse, why now, when I was in boots and mucking overalls?

"Hey, Iris."

"Robert."

"So," he whistled through his teeth, "you come here often?"

I did look up then because I couldn't gauge by his voice if he was joking or making fun of me. Joking. I decided as I studied the softness of his pale eyes. What the hell? Had he not been at the meeting where my whole life changed? How could he joke?

"You look good," he said.

I snorted. "You're full of malware."

"No, I mean it. Dayshift suits you." He waved his hand over

his face. "Your coloring looks good."

"My coloring?" I squinted and scanned Robert's face until his cheeks flushed.

"And I like your hair in braids. Suits you," he said.

"Zuse, I'm sorry," I said. "Is this supposed to be the part where we both reach for the same bag of beans and our hands inadvertently touch and it's *electric*?"

Despite the hardness in my voice, Robert grinned. His teeth were so straight. "Like in old romance movies," he said.

I cocked a hip and slipped my hand into my pocket like I was confident, but my fingers wrapped around the egg that wasn't mine, concealing it. Its weight grounded me, like a sun-warmed stone. "You watch old romance movies, Robert?"

His blue eyes crinkled, Soldamn him, and he leaned closer. "You won't tell anyone will you? I'm just meg into happy endings. Can't help it. What about you?"

I *was* reading a romance, in fact. It was the third book I'd borrowed from Johan's eclectic library. "No." I shook my head. "No romance. I'm more into tragedy, you know, a realist."

"A realist," he repeated.

"What's your handle, Robert? What are you doing here?" *Shit. Shit. Shit.* Why couldn't I just play along with the meaningless small talk? Everyone else could. I'd watched them my whole life, just pinging, back and forth, but I couldn't stand the indirectness of it all. I always grabbed a conversation by the throat and choked the meaning out of it.

Robert's shoulders sagged. I hadn't noticed before that his shirt was wrinkled and his tie hung slack around his neck. "I, uh, I've been thinking about you since the meeting."

So he had been there. "Yeah?" I gulped.

"I messaged you twice this week," he pressed.

"I don't own a laptop anymore. We sold everything."

"Oh." He stared intently at the dried beans flexing his fingers and holding his breath before blurting out his next words in a heated pile. "It's shitty what they did to you, Iris. To your family. You're not the first soldamned person to ever forget to close the panel louvers. I checked."

"Well," I raised my eyebrows, "I'm the first one who forgot when it counted."

He licked his lips. "I've been researching—"

"Congrats on the new Search Engine job by the way."

"Would you shut up for a second and let me talk?"

The rebuke was so soft and tired that I did shut up.

"One of the panels didn't even have any cracked cells. Just the Plexiglas was damaged. I went and checked. That one's still putting out at the same capacity as it was before. It just needs a new Plexi cover sealed over top, and that's what the Shareholders should have done with all of them anyways, instead of the damned louvers. I'm trying to source a supplier for Plexiglas now." He screwed up his nose and shook his head. "Anyways, the other panel. It only smashed one corner, looks like we lost twenty-one of the seventy-two cells and that means it only lost a proportional amount of output. It's still running at seventy percent of what it was before."

"So?"

He pinned me with a pleading gaze, and I shivered. What was he asking for? What did he want?

"Iris, I know this isn't any of my business, but what exactly did the Shareholders charge you with? Kahn was just posturing when he spit out that number at the meeting, wasn't he?"

I swallowed the heat lapping up my throat. "No, he wasn't. Two three-hundred-watt solar panels. Total replacement cost. 286,000 creds."

Robert exhaled slowly and ran his hands through his hair. "Shit. They don't cost that much. I checked."

I already knew. I'd had Vinton check for me after the meeting, but the numbers didn't really matter when you were already an indentured servant for life. Debt was debt.

Robert turned back to the shelf, cocked his fist, and punched the nearest sack. The shelf rattled in protest. "Shit," he hissed.

I jumped.

"They scapegoated you, Iris! You're their head on a pike. Peter got a fine that the Firewalls pooled together to pay, but you, you're their grand example of what happens when you don't keep your nose to the line like a good little corporate slave, Zuse! They told the whole city that two panels were *entirely* destroyed, because of you, and only the crew in Power Supply and I know otherwise, and they'll all keep their mouths shut if they want to keep their jobs." He paused but his eyes darted, and I knew he wasn't waiting for me to answer. Robert was working it all out, like I had with my brother, weeks ago. Peter had the Firewalls. My parents had hardly any connections at all, and they'd used up all their favors getting Vinton his job and his bike. I wasn't a scapegoat. I just wasn't *connected*.

"Do you know they have air conditioning in the board room?" he blurted.

"What?" I frowned.

"Yeah. It's fragging on even when no one is using it for a meeting, and so is the heat in the winter. While we sit frying in Work Commons all summer, sacrificing for the batteries, the Shareholders are wasting electricity keeping an empty mahogany-paneled board room climate controlled. Bastards."

"Search Engines don't have to worry about Work Commons." I tried for a half smile. "Have your own office now, I bet. You can use that board room any time you like. Won't be a waste then."

Robert stared at me like I was speaking in binary. "That's not the point." He moved to grab my shoulders but stopped when I stepped back. I didn't want him to get his suit dirty.

"Is that tailored?" I asked. "Your mom sews?"

"Why do you do that?" Robert snapped.

"What?"

"Change the subject. Refuse to look me in the eye. Look, I tried to apologize about our project, and you wouldn't let me. Every time I talk to you, you just phase out to some place I can't reach."

"Sorry."

"I don't want *sorry*, Iris." His voice cracked, and then he whispered, "I want to know what's going on inside your head."

Everything. All at once. I cleared my throat. "Tangled up thoughts. It doesn't matter now. I don't need to think much in the greenhouses."

"Iris, you were a dock-in. You *literally* starved for Search Engine. Why would the Shareholders do this to you?"

"Nothing personal," I choked, stroking the egg in my pocket. "Just business."

Robert shook his head. "No, that doesn't make sense. Why you? Why now?"

Was this what he came here for? My throat burned. Some pep talk on the fair and noble leadership of our city? Zuse. He was seeing it now for himself, wasn't he? And he wanted me to confirm or deny it. Shelter his little egg or break it. "Robert," I sighed. "My dad isn't the public relations liaison for David Kahn."

His lips pinched into a thin line. "I'm good at this. I got in because I'm good at this job."

"You are." I nodded. "You will be."

"No." Robert pulled on his tie like it was choking him. "That doesn't explain what they did to you. Those solar panels are operable, Iris, but they still let you burn."

I shrugged, even though my shoulders felt too tight. "They don't like how I'm wired." It's what my mother had always feared. She'd been right. "I'm different. The scores in all my early testing show anomalies, and I showed them that I keep making the same stupid mistakes. Now, they don't trust me. They needed someone in Gardening. Olivia's grandpa is getting old, and so are most of the other Gardeners. When they're gone, the crew will be halved. They needed another trainee, just like he said at the meeting. Nothing personal, Robert. Just business."

He looked so downtrodden in his rumpled shirt that I reached and patted his arm.

"Sol," he blurted, hands shaking.

"It's okay," I lied.

"Don't say that. I can file a report about the panels. I could apply for a reassignment. They might listen if—"

"Please don't." My gut clenched. I couldn't handle anymore big things right now. I grabbed Robert's upper arms, heedless of the proximity of his pressed cotton shirt to my chicken shit coveralls. "Robert, look at me."

He did. Pale eyes like the lake under a winter sky.

"You were there. No one else would have hired me if Johan hadn't spoken up. My family is already suffering for this, and I don't need you to stir things up any more, got it?"

"It's not fair," he said, like I'd said it a year ago, sobbing at his doorway.

"Not all endings are happy ones," I replied gently.

"I miss you."

I froze. That, I did not expect.

"Don't freak out, not in a creeper way." Robert wiped his nose, a whisper of a grin returning to his face. "I miss our conversations, our walks. Everyone else is so full of bullshit. You always get to the point."

"Your *point* being?" I needed to get out of here. My brain was thunking into a lower gear, unable to process Robert missing me, frayed wire, rubber-booted, egg-stealing me.

"I'd like to walk again with you sometime."

"What about Vannevar?"

He wrinkled his nose. "Frag Vannevar. She's such a bot."

"I'm sure she'd like to hear that."

"Walk with me sometime, Iris. Under the stars?"

"Gardeners work dayshift, Robert. I'm sleeping then."

"Dusk then. This Friday? There's supposed to be a meteorite shower. I promise I won't keep you up late."

I shook my head. "You can't afford to show up to work late. You just got the position."

"Yeah? Well, word has it that my dad is the public relations liaison to David Kahn. I do what I want." He couldn't say it without cracking a self-deprecating smile. "Come on, Iris. I just came from work now. They know I put in my hours. One walk. Friday."

"All right." I gulped. "I'll walk. I have to get to work now."

Robert grinned. "Good seeing you, Iris. I mean it."

"Go to bed, Robert."

I WALKED HOME. Easing our door shut behind me, I set the egg from my pocket in a mug on the top shelf, relieved to hear snores coming from Vinton's and my parents' bunks. I didn't want to have to explain myself right now, not with my gears still spinning from Robert.

"Iris, is that you?" Mom's muffled voice called through the bathroom cubicle door, and I jumped. Zuse! I hadn't heard her in there.

"Yeah, it's me," I whispered.

"What are you doing here?"

"Just grabbing an extra layer of clothes. It's cold out today," I lied. "What are you doing still up?"

"I'm fine. Keep covered up out there," she said, and then I heard her vomiting. Loud, wretched heaves that should have woken everyone in the Seacan if we weren't all so exhausted.

"You okay?" I asked uncertainly.

"I'm fine," she said, and we both knew she wasn't.

Naked fear gripped me and punctured my lungs at the sounds of her gagging. *You can't get sick, Mom. None of us can.* With my creds gone, my family couldn't afford to miss any days of work. They were barely covering the lease on this shed, and we didn't have money to buy more beans until next month. *Please, Sol. We can't get sick.*

AT LUNCH, Olivia shared her meal with me again. *I should have brought the damn egg to trade,* I thought as I relished the taste of cucumbers with fresh dill and salt. "This is amazing," I said around a mouthful. "Fresh dill?" We'd just reseeded our entire crop of dill. Olivia and Johan had harvested the mature rotation before I came. I knew it because the desiccated fronds still lay on the drying racks in the lean-to near Greenhouse Four.

Olivia met my curious gaze with a steady one of her own. She swallowed and shook her head. "No, it's dried." And I knew she was lying. I could taste the difference between fresh and dried dill.

"It's good." I smiled lopsidedly, and when Olivia returned it with a sly one of her own, I realized it then. She knew that I knew. Sol, first the tomatoes and now the dill. Had she been intentionally sharing her lunches just to let me know? That the Gardeners had a side-operation growing right under the Shareholders' noses? Was Elaine in on this? The greenhouses might not be so bad with these kinds of perks.

"Where?" I asked, but Olivia's smile dropped off her face, and she clammed up. She wouldn't speak to me again until I changed the subject, and I was so scared of toppling our tenuously re-built friendship that I didn't mention it again.

MOM WAS STILL sick when I got home that night, too sick to go to work. Dad and then Vinton got ready in awkward silence while she curled in her bed clutching her pillow, sweat plastering her hair to her face.

When Dad leaned down to touch her forehead, she hissed, "Don't be stupid, John! What if it's something catching?"

He absorbed the acid of her words unflinchingly, like he always did. Turning to the sink, he soaked a clean cloth, wrung it out, and folded it before laying it across Mom's forehead. "If it's catching, we live in a metal box the size of a phone booth, Anne. We'll all get it anyways. You sleep beside me for Zuse's sake."

"You should sleep at my office, or I should," she mumbled.

"Now you're delusional." He shook his head and poured her a glass of water. "You don't have a comfortable piece of furniture in that office. Just relax. Drink lots of fluid. All that jazz. Iris, don't let her go to her office."

I nodded past the music buzzing in my headphones, pretending at casualness, like even acknowledging the seriousness of this would give it traction but ignoring it would make it go away. Mom was like an avalanche, but so was whatever hit her. If Dad and Vinton got sick, we'd eat up every last cred to our name within a week. The security deposit on this shed, paired with the penalty for exiting our lease early on the last one had eaten a hole in my parent's savings.

Don't think about it, Iris. Don't get all tangled up in what you can't control. Dad used to say that when I was little and hyperventilating over some snag I couldn't free myself from.

That was the problem. I thought, struggling to breathe past the tension in my chest. What on Earth did I control now? It was all out of my control.

CHAPTER
TWELVE

boiled my absconded egg for breakfast while Mom still slept. Olivia's black tea coated all my ragged nerves in smooth warmth and clicked my brain into that elusive sweet spot of focus that was becoming more and more common for me since my introduction to caffeine, physical labor, and reading for pleasure. They weren't big things, but together these small things were saving me. I returned the tattered romance novel and borrowed an old survival guide from Johan's library.

He cracked a small smile when he saw my choice. "Not so romantic, that one," he said.

"Oh, I don't know, Oupa." I grinned. "I find the idea of surviving positively dreamy."

He pointed with a thick-knuckled finger. "Half of the plants identified in there don't grow here anymore."

"That means half of them do, right? Good bedtime reading for a pioneering greenhouse intern."

Johan nodded approvingly and, blessedly, didn't crush the hope he must have seen in my eyes. I was scrambling for control, for some way to bring in food for my family. If the worst happened, and we got sick and faced starvation, maybe there were still edibles out there if I knew where to look. Me—a girl who hadn't ventured into the real Outside since Vinton fell— Ha! Vannevar would probably make a better gatherer than me. But I absorbed every page of that survival guide like it was the last thing I'd ever read.

Dad got sick the next night. My parent's begged Vinton to go stay at a friend's house, but he shook his head.

"None of the other houses have ramps. The Shannon's tore out the one at our old place as soon as they moved in. I'm fine here. Besides, snow isn't supposed to stick to the ground for another week or so. I'm going on a run day after tomorrow. Be out of your hair soon."

"Iris." Mom sighed like saying my name was some sort of obligation. "You could ask to stay with Olivia?"

"I think I'm already imposing on them enough, Mom. We'll get through this, all right?" I tried to sound confident, but I winced every time my parents coughed or hobbled to the bathroom that night.

The next night wasn't any better. When I came home from a bone-wearying day of re-potting lavender and aloe, the tang of stale bile and sour sleep thickened the air in our Seacan.

"Your shift," Vinton croaked, already in his chair, shrugging into a grease-stained work shirt. "I've got to change the oil on the bike with Mark before we go."

Mark was my brother's Browser partner. Probably more than just a Browser partner, but I didn't ask. Mom thought Vinton hadn't ever brought home a girlfriend because of his wheelchair. I was pretty sure the chair had nothing to do with it.

"How are Mom and Dad?" I asked.

Five total days lost wages between them. I swallowed, surveying everything in the room except my parents' bunk. My gaze snagged on a level gauge outside the bathroom stall wall. Looked like the water was getting low in our rain reservoir too, and we couldn't pay for more. I should check Oupa's barometer tomorrow to see when it was supposed to rain. I wondered if we could haul water from the lake somehow?

"Are you even listening, Iris? Don't ask me a question and just zone out." Vinton yanked his comb through his hair.

"Sorry," I mumbled. "Hey, are we allowed to haul water from the lake for personal use?"

"What?" he snapped. "Zuse, focus, would you? You asked how Mom and Dad are doing, and I'm telling you. Like I said, they had a rough patch around noon, but I think they're through the worst of it." He started shaving.

"How are you?" I asked, placating.

"Bulletproof as usual." He nicked his chin and swiped at the bead of blood, swearing.

"Yeah, bulletproof." I smiled despite the fear coiling in my guts. Sol, he reminded me of Nate sometimes. I wondered if Vinton saw the resemblance.

"You think you could check the price of dried ginger? It'd settle their stomachs."

"Yeah," I nodded. "No problem." Big problem. Ginger was bloody expensive, and both of us knew it.

"Tell Food Bank to put it on my cred again. I'll send them an email today." Vinton pointed toward his shoes.

"Got it." I grabbed the pair of old loafers and slipped them onto his feet.

"Oh!" he said as I straightened. "I almost forgot. That Lycos kid came by just before you got in." He smiled indulgently.

Shit. Robert. What day is today?

"He said he'd meet you at Work Commons for your stroll tonight. Is that what the kids are calling it now, *strolling*?"

"We're literally just walking."

"Yeah, sure," Vinton called over his shoulder as he wheeled out the door. "Be sure to practice safe strolling."

"You too. Make sure Mark checks your dipstick after that oil change, yeah?"

A rare blush colored Vinton's cheeks.

I snorted and closed the door behind him. There certainly wasn't enough water to indulge in a shower, so I sponge-bathed and changed into my second set of work clothes while I waited for dusk. My parents slept through it all.

Frag it. I couldn't lay in here all night thinking about starving. Vinton was distracting himself with Mark. I deserved to see Robert too.

WORK COMMONS WOULD ALREADY BE busy by dusk, and I didn't want to wait for Robert outside while my former colleagues paraded past, so I lay in my bunk and counted the lines in the ceiling panel above me until I was certain I'd be late. Robert was pacing the wooden walkway when I arrived, and I admired the broadness of his shoulders in his fitted suit jacket until he turned, saw me and straightened, flashing a quick smile.

"You made it."

"I haven't forgotten where Work Commons is." My face flushed and Robert's smile fumbled.

"That's not what I meant."

He smelled like aftershave, and for a moment, I lost myself in that, the fact that he could afford the stuff, that he needed to shave at all at our age. I wanted to see him unshaven. I hadn't seen a beard on a man since Nate. It wasn't the style in our city. *Stop thinking about Nate, Soldamnit.*

"Shall we?" Robert offered his arm awkwardly, and I hesitated before slipping my hand into the crook of his elbow. The fabric felt firm and tightly woven under my chapped skin. "Perfect night for it." Robert pointed up, and I gawked at a deep, dark sky rich with stars.

"For what?" I mumbled. *Sol,* I suddenly felt lost. Out of sync, like when audio and video tracks didn't quite line up.

Robert glanced down at me. "The meteorite shower. You okay?"

"Oh yeah. The week just got away from me. Mom and Dad are sick so no one's sleeping much at our place. You know how it is."

I expected him to draw away then, at the mention of illness. People stared at us as we passed them on the walkway because we were two cable ports that didn't mesh, Search Engine and Gardener. I regretted taking his arm, and I couldn't get my thoughts sorted with the distraction of his closeness, but Robert didn't let go. He slowed his pace and faced me, frowning.

"I hadn't heard. Are they okay?"

No. "They will be, I'm sure. Just some sort of stomach bug. No big deal." The biggest deal actually. We'd run out of creds soon if they didn't get better, and then what? We'd all be Nora Yates: expelled, desperate, and deleted like corrupted files.

"Are you okay? Do you need anything?" Robert pressed.

"We'll be fine." I pasted on a false smile as we walked past the throbbing hum of the generators running. Glancing at the tiny shed beside it, I shuddered before turning away. A cold wind rushed up the hillside, carrying the smell of ice up from the lake and the forlorn call of geese. They should have been gone by now. It was late for geese.

"Oh wow." Robert pulled me to a stop past the end of the walkway and the streetlamps where darkness swallowed up the edge of the residences. His head tipped up, and I followed his gaze to see a flare of green and pale pink roiling through the sky like a rippling flag. Northern lights, harbingers of another solar storm.

"You'll be busy tonight prepping for this." Procedure dictated that every piece of electronics be secured in Faraday cages or EMP bags before a solar storm, every electrical cable disconnected and rolled up, and all removable circuitry panels stowed. "You sure you have time for a walk?"

"I'm sure." His face looked pale and drawn in the phosphorescent light.

"Because I can go." I pulled my hand away from his arm, coldness prickling in my stomach. *This was a stupid idea, Iris. Why did you say yes?* My family was sick, and I was just ignoring it to go walking with a pretty boy. And what had I thought it would feel like, walking beside him in blue-collar clothes, toeing the border of the world I lost?

"Don't, please." He caught my hand in his and there was something so quietly desperate in his voice that I didn't pull away. "I've been looking forward to this all week, Iris. Seeing you. Just give me a chance, okay?"

"A chance to what?" I asked carefully. "We're moving in different circles now, Robert. You've got Vannevar." She's wasn't going to starve to death soon.

He frowned down at our clasped hands and snorted. "Vannevar and I were never a thing, okay? She wants us to be, she tells everyone we are, but we haven't ..." He exhaled slowly. "She's not my type. What I want is the chance with you, Iris. I want to start over. I was a jerk when you came to my door. And I'm a jerk for not trying harder until now."

I shook my head. "You were right, Robert. Everything you said was right. I'm not *normal*. I can't handle big projects, and even the Shareholders can see it." *This was a mistake.*

"Hey." He placed his hand on my scarred cheek softly, and I let him, Soldamnit, I just let him. "Normal is overrated, Iris. Frag normal."

His thumb drifted over the edge of my scars, and he shifted closer, pale eyes reflecting the Northern lights above us as he searched my face for something. *Permission? Frag it, Iris. Let him.* When was I ever going to get the chance to kiss him again? He was as out of my reach as the stars.

I closed the rest of the distance between us, and this time, when Robert Lycos kissed me, I swam in every second of it, the faint taste of spearmint on his tongue, the smoothness of his clean-shaven jaw, how he held my face like I was something precious. I pressed it all into my short-circuiting mind, because this was the last time it would ever happen. I wouldn't walk with Robert again. I didn't deserve to distract myself from the mess I'd made of my life, and I wouldn't risk dirtying his reputation with the Shareholders. I ruined everyone I touched, but oh Sol, I'd enjoy this moment while it lasted.

We didn't see any falling stars, but it didn't matter. When the Northern lights faded, Robert murmured that he should get to work, and I floated back down the walkway home, my throat aching with equal parts elation and agony. Robert liked me. He didn't care that I wasn't normal. He wanted to start over.

But there was no starting over for me, no earning my way up the corporate ladder, and I wasn't about to hold him down at the bottom with me. If I just let him go, Robert would get too busy to see me, like he had for the past year. Search Engine was a position that demanded a lot of time. Robert would forget me, and I'd have to be okay with that. Zuse, that had been some kiss though.

That night I bought dried ginger on Vinton's cred, and when I got home, the Seacan smelled like lemon disinfectant and Mom was sitting up in bed, the hollows of her face exaggerated by the blue light of her laptop screen.

"Feeling better?" I asked quietly, careful not to wake Dad.

She nodded and pushed her glasses up her nose. "Just catching up on work, you?"

"I'm good, Mom." I set down the packet of ginger. "Ginger tea?"

Her gaze snapped to mine, peering at me over her frames. "Where did you get ginger?"

"Olivia's oupa," I lied easily. "He says that's how he pays

overtime. It's just a small packet." Impulsively, I added, "Sometimes he pays in eggs too, the one's the chickens crack before we get to them." If Elaine from Food Bank decided to be generous again, I didn't want to have to explain myself.

"You're working hard then. Good." Mom nodded sharply before softening, "Yes, some tea would be lovely. Make a pot, and your father can have some when he wakes up. We're both planning on getting back to the normal schedule tomorrow." She smiled, but her lips were too tight and her face too sallow for it to look convincing.

"Sounds good, Mom," I spoke offhandedly with all the casualness of an apathetic teenager, because it felt like if I hoped too much for her health, the world would flip me a big Frag you and Mom would relapse. I put on my headphones and slept until Vinton came home halfway through the night to catch a few hours of sleep before he'd leave on his data run.

After he got up and packed, we sat on the front stoop of the Seacan together in the predawn light while my parents still slept inside. I perched on the edge of the wooden ramp while Vinton crouched in his chair, fiddling with something deep in the undercarriage of his modified motorcycle as it sat propped on its sturdy retractable landing gear.

"You ever see anything out there?" I asked.

He jiggled a glow plug cap. "I see lots of shit out there, Iris. Marauders. Bears. Honest to Sol prostitutes. Sometimes they're just standing out on a road in the middle of nowhere. It's surreal. You're going to have to specify."

"Food-wise?"

"Like, in the houses? Canned goods? Hell no. That stuff got cleared out years ago, and if it hadn't, it'd be bursting with botulism."

"No, not that." I tugged on my braid. "Like Outside. Old Gardens. That sort of thing?" If Olivia was growing food outside the greenhouses, it *had* to be possible. If I'd grown snap peas as a child, Outside couldn't be poison. Or maybe it had been at the start of the collapse, but it was healing now.

"Rhubarb," Vinton said.

"What?" I wrinkled my nose.

"Every damned house has a massive patch of rhubarb where their garden used to be. Sometimes the house isn't even there anymore, but the rhubarb is. I didn't even know what the stuff was until Mark pointed it out. He said his grandma used to make pie out of it."

"So you've found gardens then?"

"Zuse, Iris." Vinton straightened, frowning and wiping his fingers down his shirt. "We're not doing this again, are we? I've told you before, it's a fragging desert out there. There's nothing edible. About four runs ago, Mark tried a few of those rhubarb leaves, and he got the shits for days. It's poison. It's *all* poison. Get it through your head."

So where was Olivia's food coming from then? Another greenhouse? One they built hidden away from here?

I passed Vinton a coiled SATA cable, and he stuffed it into the bike's saddlebag beside his rented handgun. He still needed to tie his foldable chair onto the rear rack, but I knew better than to offer to help before he asked. My brother despised that sort of thing, people assuming he couldn't do it himself. He rode Outside and fended off marauders and prostitutes for Sol's sake, and I'd already pissed him off asking about gardens again. So, I watched as he heaved his travel chair up onto his lap, wheeled it over to the motorcycle's rack and started lashing it down.

He didn't call me over until he'd wheeled parallel to the bike, set his brakes, heaved a leg over the motorcycle seat, and pulled himself up using the centre grip on the handlebars. "Move the chair back, would you?" he asked.

I did. "You good?" I asked.

"Always." He frowned. "We travel in pairs, Iris. We have

guns. And we're too fast on the bikes for anyone to bother with us."

That's not what I was worried about. I mean, of course I worried about marauders, but that's not what I was worried about right now. Licking my lips, I said, "Not sick?"

Please be okay. Vinton hid sickness. He wouldn't tell us if he felt bad until it was too obvious to mask. His paralysis had done something to his immune system, so he got sick often. I'd read up on it back when I had computer access to Cache, but I couldn't figure out if spinal injuries caused immune system paralysis or if it was just the constant urinary tract infections that wore his immunity down. Either way, Vinton's stubbornness was stronger than any immune system out there, stronger even than Mom's obstinacy. He'd hate me for asking if he was ill.

"You know what I *am* sick of?" He glared down at his knobby knees. "These Soldamned Velcro straps." He sniffed, propping his leg up onto the broad foot pad of the motorcycle. "They're too low to do up with both hands, and I can never get them snug enough one-handed."

I let myself grin at his crotchety deflection and secured the thick Velcro straps below both his knees that held his legs pressed against either side of the gas tank. "Your shoelace is untied. Why the hell do you have a pair with laces anyways?"

"They're Dad's. One of my loafers fell off on the road, somewhere between here and Sorrento. I didn't even know until we got home, and I can't afford new shoes." He inhaled deeply and pinned me with an examining gaze. "Besides, I never know when I might need a nice long pair of shoelaces to strangle the odd kludge bag for accosting my sister down by the generators."

My fingers froze over the shoe I was tying. "Y-you were watching us?" I squinted, heat prickling across my cheeks as I absorbed his words. "What are you doing spying on us, you stalker?"

Vinton tapped his thumb on the electronic shifter. "I don't know. What are you doing kissing a guy who's ignored your existence for like a year, Iris? Learn to stand a little further from the street cams if you don't want anyone to see you. I was just watching out for you. The guy crawls back out of the woodwork and you just trust him?"

I'd forgotten about the streetlamp cameras, a whole row of them down Generator Ave so that every angle of Cache and Food Bank could be viewed remotely. Robert would have known we'd be seen. He didn't forget things like I did. *What the hell?*

"It was just a damned kiss. And I'm not a kid, Vinton. I'm *sixteen.*"

"He thinks you're a honeypot. He just wants to dock you and be done with it."

"You're an asshole, you know that?" I bolted up to go inside but Vinton grabbed my wrist. I bit down on the urge to yank my arm free because doing so might pull him right off the bike and he wasn't wearing his helmet yet.

"I'm a brother," Vinton said. "I'm *supposed* to be an asshole. So I know other assholes when I see them. Have you looked up his starting salary, Iris? Cause I did. Corporate listed his wage as 3500 on the public salary sheet, but if you look up the entire Search Engine budget and take away what the others are making, he's raking in *4500* cred a month. How do you think he pulled that off, huh? How's pretty little Robert making more than anyone else? He got the Shareholders to fudge the *transparency* numbers for him. You starved for a year to boost your salary. Sure doesn't look like that's what he did."

"Robert's good at his job," I mumbled, digesting that figure. *4500 creds. What the hell?*

Vinton snorted. "He better be. His Shareholder daddy bailed him out and that wasn't enough for your boy, so he took that job right out from under you, Iris. And he doesn't feel like he took quite enough, so he wants to bang you too. I'm just saying, you don't have the creds or the permission to have a kid, so I hope you've got your Soldamned head on straight."

It was never on straight. "You know what?" I barked, jamming a finger toward the shoe on Vinton's foot. "Tie your own damned shoe. I'm not your caretaker, and you're sure as shit not mine."

Lunging around the motorcycle, I headed for the greenhouse and went straight to the goat pens to muck out stalls because that's what was on the schedule today. *This is your life now, Iris.* I huffed as I stabbed at sodden straw peppered with goat pellets. Robert was making 4500 creds a month, and I was just shovelling shit.

At lunch, Olivia didn't even ask if I'd brought anything to eat, she just waited until the other Gardeners had gone back to work and wordlessly handed over a thick roll of sourdough bread stuffed with sprouts, goat cheese and purple basil. *Purple basil.* We didn't have purple basil seeds in the greenhouses. We only grew green in here. I chewed in silence while Luan rubbed against my leg and meowed piteously for scraps. Olivia watched me. She was waiting for me to say something this time. This was it.

She was down to her final bites before I glanced up at the overhead camera and held my half-devoured roll close enough to my lips to cover them.

"None of this is from our greenhouses, is it?" I spoke without looking at her.

"Some of it is," Olivia answered without looking back, popping the remainder of her sandwich in her mouth before brushing the crumbs off her thighs. "Ready to chop some wood?" She stood and left.

Sol Almighty, what the hell was she waiting for? Was this some sort of big test? Because it felt like it was. Zuse, I was starting to hate secrets.

I BROKE my promise to myself not to see Robert again. Turns out it was considerably harder to ignore him when he knocked at my door than it was to delete his emails unread last year. And on evenings when Vinton was home, it was particularly delicious to see the sour look on my brother's face when Robert and I left together for our nightly walks.

I relished those evenings, bitter and snowy as they were. I could spend them with Robert instead of Mom who picked at me for information about our "budding relationship" as she called it, or Dad who said nothing except, "I trust you, Iris," even though his eyes said otherwise. My parents had recovered enough from their illness to pull in some creds, keep us off the edge of starvation, and judge my life choices.

Robert just talked about his day. He drew me into the nostalgia of my old life, asking my opinion on search strategies and bouncing ideas for cataloging systems. He spoke to me like I hadn't changed when everything else around me had, and I ate up every bite. We kept our short trysts away from the street-lamp cameras, and while Robert's kisses were hungrier over the next nights, they weren't demanding. He was a gentleman, everything the corporate world said he should be, and I thought I could control the dizziness of it all, which was incredibly stupid, considering my track record.

It's a fifteen-minute walk, a little thing, I reasoned. How much trouble could I possibly get into in fifteen minutes? A small part of my frayed mind reminded me that it had taken less than that to lead Vinton through the railway tunnel to the fall that nearly killed him. The typo that prompted my year of starvation took only seconds. Forgetting to close the solar panel louvers took even less time. Given fifteen minutes, I could get into worlds of trouble. The thought burned through me, and I pushed it down and ignored it, because every stolen moment with Robert felt like it might be the last connection to my old life I'd ever have.

On the night of our fifth walk, it was snowing. Bloated, wet flakes churned down around us, clotting the streetlamps like so many white moths. We didn't walk for long, because the wind was picking up, and I didn't own a winter jacket. I don't even remember what we talked about, but I remembered the kiss and how Robert, despite my fussing, draped his coat over my shoulders before we parted.

"Take it. I have another," he insisted even as he shivered.

"I can't, Robert. The Shareholders started auditing me once a week." The inspections had only started recently, and I had no idea what had prompted the increased interest.

"Yeah, and?"

I clamped my jaw. This wasn't how I wanted our walk to end. "They'll take the coat. They take anything they don't think is essential and put it against my cred deficit." The only reason I still had my headphones and Johan's books was because Vinton hid them in his bunk for me.

"Zuse, are you serious?" Robert spat, and when I nodded, he snorted and shook his head. "And a winter coat isn't *essential?*"

"Not one like this." I shrugged nervously beneath the heavy, felted wool trench with its silk lining.

Robert chewed on his lip and his anger for a moment before snapping his fingers and nodding. "*Borrow* it then. They can't take it if it's mine. I'll sick my father on them."

A whisper of a grin pressed through the dark expression on his face. It was a joke, I was sure of it, but it still froze the smile on my face. *Your father. The one who bailed you out and fudged the public wage sheet numbers while I starved.*

"I expect you'll keep it safe for me in the meantime, yeah? Hey, what's wrong?"

"Nothing." I smiled and blinked up at the snow. It was

falling so thickly now, it swallowed the sounds of everything around us.

"Borrow the coat, please."

Robert hadn't screwed me over. It wasn't his fault he was rich. He was my friend. He was starting to be more than that.

"Okay." I nodded. "You should go. You've got no coat now, and you'll be late. I don't think Corporate likes their Search Engines showing up looking like wet rats."

He grinned, pulled the collar of his coat up over my neck and kissed me one last time. "Sleep tight, Iris," he said before trotting toward his office.

I was walking home, lost in the smell of Robert's coat, and mindlessly weaving between the early dusk commuters on their way to work when someone side-stepped into my path and shouldered me hard.

My feet scrambled on the snow-slicked planks. They swept out from under me. I landed on my back, breath barking out of me as my head smacked against the boardwalk hard enough to bounce. I couldn't see the snow anymore, and I couldn't breathe. When I tried to roll to my side, dark nausea clutched at me. Blinking against it, I opened my mouth wide and pulled in a trickling wheeze of air.

Shadows coalesced above me, but I couldn't bring them into focus.

"Oh, look who I've run into," a forced bright voice chimed above me. "It's Basic Bitch."

Vannevar squatted over me.

Saliva pooled in my mouth and pain rang through my head like a bell as I strained to sit up, but I couldn't. The street yawed and tilted around me.

Three other forms materialized behind Vannevar, and I wondered if they'd come to help me until she leaned in close enough that her gobs of blonde hair brushed against my cheek.

"Had a nasty fall?" she purred. "That's what happens when a dirty girl wanders too far from her pen."

My throat soured with bile. Dark spots swam across my vision like ink spills. *Reboot, Iris. Breathe.* She couldn't do anything with the street cameras recording, could she? I searched for the closest one, on the lamp post over Vannevar's shoulder, but she followed my gaze before turning back to me with a small pout.

"Cameras are out, Basic B. I'm not sure it's safe out here in the dark."

Oh Sol. Oh shit. "No," I wheezed, and one of the bodies standing behind Vannevar swept forward and kicked me.

CHAPTER
THIRTEEN

My body folded around the foot as it dug into my side, and I couldn't remember what happened after that. I think they kicked me more than once, but pain was already roaring through me so brightly it burned everything in its path. I curled into an egg, but they kept breaking me open, laying into my back, peeling Robert's jacket off me in rough jerks like wild dogs fighting over scraps.

Someone grabbed my braid and yanked me toward their face, washing me in hot breath. They were speaking, but I couldn't make sense of the sounds. Everything slipped past me like snowflakes. I grabbed at my hair with feeble hands, nausea curling up my throat. The fist that held me shook me hard.

"Did you hear me?" Vitriolic words poured into my jumbled head. "You listening?"

Vannevar, it was Vannevar. She was shaking me. My thoughts formed slow as sap.

"Stop rattling her so hard. She hit her damned head," a male voice berated. *Claude?* I couldn't tell.

"You're the one who fragging kicked her," she barked over

her shoulder, but then pressed her face back toward mine. "Look at me, Basic Bitch."

I'm trying. Frag, I can't …

"This is from my brother. He's too chicken shit to get payback, but I'm not, you hear? And keep your filthy hands off what's mine. Stay away from him, yeah?" Vannevar snarled. She didn't need to say who she meant. I knew. Everyone knew. I tried to nod but couldn't because she was still holding my hair. Wet breaths sawed out of me as I stared back at Vannevar and tried to convey it with my eyes.

Yes. I'll stay away. Oh Sol, my head.

"Hey!" A voice across the street barked.

Vannevar jerked and let go of me.

"What the hell? Hey!"

She and her lackeys scattered. Their feet clacked up the boardwalk, slipping as they went. Robert's coat flew behind them like some sort of victory flag.

"Sol! Are you okay?" Someone skidded to her knees beside me, heedless of her practical skirt and nylons.

I flailed in the snow like a turtle on its back and blinked up at the face before me. Elaine. It was Elaine from Food Bank. Forty-three eggs.

"Are you okay? What'd they—Zuse, you hit your head. You're bleeding."

I told Robert I'd look after his coat.

"Can you stand?"

They took it.

"Hey, can you stand?" Elaine leaned over me. "Let's get you out of this snow, yeah?"

I'd forgotten about the snow—I forgot everything—but now, past the pain, my back felt cold and my hands were shaking. I sat up, blinking at the fat flakes like I'd just woke up here. My fingers felt like ice as I pressed them to the back of my head. They came away smeared with red. *Snow's not red.*

"Let's get you up, okay?" Elaine grabbed me under my armpits, and I got my wobbling legs under me. I was tangled and dull and chewed up, like a dog toy.

"All right." Elaine steadied me, wrapping her arm over my shoulders. "Where do you live now, honey? I can't remember."

I formed the words slowly in my head and pushed them out sluggishly, "By ... by the chicken coops."

We started walking. As I stumbled beside Elaine, a shadow passed us on the boardwalk. and I flinched hard.

"It's okay, honey." She held me steady. "We'll get you home."

Two more people passed us. That's when it hit me. People going to work. They strode by us pointedly avoiding our presence. People had been walking by the whole time. The whole time while Vannevar and her nulls were beating on me. And no one had stopped except for Elaine.

I was still processing that bitter thought when Elaine guided me right past our house.

"Stop." I tried to turn my head, but the whole world spun with it and my hand swung wildly when I pointed.

"Here?" Elaine raised her eyebrows and, when I nodded, she steered me toward our Seacan. "This one? I thought it was a storage shed."

It probably had been.

I leaned against her hard as she slapped her palm against the door until the latch squealed and Mom's face poked out.

"Iris? Oh Zuse." She gaped, opening the door wide to usher us in. "What the hell?"

"Bunch of kids swarmed her. Had her on the ground when I got there." Elaine pursed her lips. "Joseph's daughter. That tall kid she hangs with, Claude? I don't know who else. Viruses, the lot of them."

"John!" Mom barked over her shoulder as Elaine pressed me into her arms. We stumbled a few steps toward my bunk, and Mom sat me on the edge.

"I think she hit her head pretty hard," Elaine called from the entry. "They were right under a street cam if you want to download the footage later."

"Thank you. Thank you so much," Mom gushed, an uncomfortable smile swimming on her face.

I wanted to tell them that Vannevar had shut off the cameras, but my head felt heavier than the bags of soil we hauled at the greenhouses.

"Iris?" Dad's voice sounded frightened. He grabbed my shoulder. "What happened?"

"She hit her head." Mom pressed a cold cloth against the back of my head, and I flinched at the pain.

"They were beating on her. A bunch of kids," Elaine elaborated from the doorway.

"Who was beating on her?" Dad bristled.

"Vannevar and Claude, apparently." Mom shook her head and inspected the cloth.

"And two others. I couldn't see their faces," Elaine said. "Email me later for a witness report? I'd be happy to file one."

"Of course. Thank you, Elaine. We appreciate that." I could tell that Dad wanted to offer something more, but there wasn't even room in the Seacan for all of us to sit at once.

"Do you need anything? Bandages? I'm working Med tonight," Elaine said.

We couldn't afford bandages. We could barely afford beans.

"We'll be sure to stop by and grab some later," Mom answered, tipping my head up to the light so she could look in my eyes. "I think we'll just have her sit for a bit. Thank you. We don't want to keep you from work."

Even Elaine recognized Anne's subtle tone of dismissal. "It'd be no problem at all."

"We'll come by in a bit." Dad's smile looked broken. "Thanks again, Elaine."

My parents were embarrassed, my aching mind realized. Of

what? Me? Our house that used to be a shed? The fact that they were not dressed in appropriate business casual? I couldn't pin down which one it was, and I wanted to lay down, and my ribs hurt.

Elaine left, and Mom braced herself in front of me and started asking all the right questions, the one's that needed more than a 'yes' or 'no' answer, but her words kept running together like dripping paint. Dad boiled water for tea, but all I could focus on was the strange sounds coming from our tiny bathroom. My gaze rolled sluggishly toward the door and settled on the shape of Vinton's wheelchair folded nearby. My brother had been home since the snow started. Couldn't motorcycle out to steal pieces of the internet when it was snowing. In between Mom's repeated requests, the muffled gag of vomiting filled the room. Oh Sol, I realized. Vinton was sick.

The weight of it all tumbled down on me, and I cried until my stomach ached.

MY PARENTS TOOK two more days off work to care for Vinton and I. Robert knocked on our door both days even though my mother curtly told him that I wasn't well enough for visitors. By the third day, we ran out of beans. My head stopped spinning enough that I could look after my brother on my own. My parents went to work. They had to if we were going to eat this week.

Vinton's stubbornness didn't ease with illness. Several times, he refused my help when I caught him trying to transfer from his bunk to the bathroom. He swore when he fell and fumed silently when I gripped him under the armpits and hauled him like a sack of potatoes across our cold, cramped floor.

"Don't plow through life without help, isn't that what you

told me?" I puffed. "We're family, Vinton. We all need help sometimes."

"No one needs help to take a piss," he spoke through clenched teeth, forehead slick with sweat.

"I'm sure my day will come." I adjusted my grip. "I'm holding you to it. You owe me one assisted piss."

My brother snorted and twisted out of my grip to grab the reinforced rails bolted into the wall. "I've got it from here." When he was healthy, Vinton was strong enough to pull himself onto the toilet or the shower bench on his own. I wasn't so sure about now, but I decided to give his battered dignity the benefit of the doubt and closed the door between us.

"Let me know when you're done."

"Frag off, Iris." His voice cracked.

A knock reverberated through the front door. Ah Sol, I sagged. *Robert.* Maybe he hadn't heard us.

"Iris?" he called tentatively. "Look, I know you're in there. Please, I just want to see if you're okay."

Pressing away from the bathroom door, I shuffled past the bunks and the kitchenette, and opened the front door. Snow gusted in, and I winced.

Robert stood on the wooden landing without a coat. Dark circles ringed his eyes, and his tie was crooked.

"I'm sorry I lost your coat," I said.

"What? Zuse, I don't care about the damned coat, Iris. I care about you." He ran a shaking hand through his hair. "Can I come in?"

Our house reeked of sour sickness. "No." I hugged the door tighter to myself. "Vinton's sick, and there's no room in here."

"Right." He swallowed and nodded. "Of course. Look, I just want to know what happened. I saw Elaine's witness report. I scanned the video feeds, and they cut out for a whole hour that morning. What did she do to you, Iris?"

Bile rose in my throat, and my sore head pounded. I didn't

have time for this. For Robert. As much as I wanted to feel the steadiness of his arms around me right now, if Vannevar found out, if she hurt me again, my family would lose more creds missing work to tend to me. And she was a Firewall. I couldn't afford to cross the Firewalls again. "She bumped into me on the boardwalk." I shrugged. "I fell and hit my head."

"Bullshit," Robert spat. "She threatened you. She hit you, didn't she? For Sol's sake, I swear she's got a circuit missing. She cut the camera feed?"

I nodded.

"You're going to testify, right?"

"I'm not."

Robert froze, his mouth hanging open. "What'd you mean you're not? She assaulted you, Iris! Over a damned coat!"

Over you. And you know it, Robert.

"I can't afford this right now." I shook my head and gripped the door hard as the movement made my head throb. "I can't afford to piss off someone like Vannevar. I can't afford a proceeding. I can't afford the time off work, and I sure as hell can't afford to get hurt again. Let's just leave it, okay?"

"Leave it?" He hissed. "What's your bandwidth? What did she say to you? She threatened you, didn't she?"

"Robert, it's not a big dea—"

"No," he barked. "Let me help you, Iris. I want to—"

"You want to help me?" I raised my voice to match his.

"Please." He held his hands out. Snow settled on his rumpled dress shirt. "I want to fix this, Iris. What Vannevar did was *wrong*. What Corporate's doing, turning a blind eye to an assault report, *that's* wrong."

How did he know Corporate turned a blind eye? I squinted. They *had* closed out my testimony report on the same day I entered it, but no one else would know that, unless … Had he been looking through my personal files?

"You want to fix this, Robert?" Heat pooled at the back of

my throat. "You turn around and go to work and don't come back here again."

"W-what?" His blue eyes searched my face, shock slackening his features.

"I don't want to see you anymore. I don't want you knocking on my door, understand? If you want to help me and my family, leave us alone and keep your nose out of my personal files." And I slammed the door so that I wouldn't have to look at his broken face.

"You good out there?" Vinton called weakly from the bathroom.

"Yeah. Golden," I said, but I couldn't stop my hands from shaking. "You?"

"Way to let Lover Boy down easy."

"Frag off, Vinton."

A WEEK after my incident with Vannevar, I went back to work a partial shift at the greenhouses. Vinton was still sick and getting worse. We were taking turns staying home with him. Yesterday, Mom and Dad had pooled creds to buy him a prohibitively expensive anti-nausea medicine because he hadn't kept water down for two days. We were out of beans again, so we'd been living on two eggs a day, courtesy of Elaine. Two eggs between the four of us.

"I can't wait anymore," I blurted to Olivia while we were alone pinching back seedlings. "I need to know where you're growing your extra food."

She stared at me, unreadable, her green-stained fingers still poised over the flat of seedlings before her. I couldn't stand the yawning silence between us, the chance that I might be wrong about her. "Vinton's really sick, and we red-lined yesterday,

Olivia." My voice wobbled.

"Shit," she exhaled, sagging over the plants. "*All* of you?"

I snorted and shook my head, immediately regretting both as pain lanced through my still-bruised skull. "All of us whose creds weren't already screwed."

Last night, Mom cried when she checked her cred balance. Dad and her had passed maximum allowable debt percentage— red-lined. Vinton would red-line today. He'd told me as much, in utterly defeated tones, before I left this morning. Now, my family's wristbands simply wouldn't allow them access to Food Bank and Med, not until they reduced their debt. The only reason *my* band still opened either of those doors was because Gardeners supplied Food Bank and Med with produce and medi- cinal herbs, but I couldn't buy anything once I got inside.

My family had three options now. We could leave, if Vinton wasn't sick, and we could afford transportation out of here for him—he couldn't motorcycle in the winter. Even if he could, we couldn't afford to buy the vehicle my dad had paid so much to modify, anyways. We could stay and starve until we lapsed on our Seacan lease, and then we'd be homeless. That was the more likely outcome. Or Olivia and Johan could stick their necks out and save us.

Why would Olivia have given me all those hints if she hadn't wanted to let me in on their secret? They must need help main- taining it. Their little operation had grown too big to handle alone. I'd counted on that when I'd asked her my question moments ago, but I didn't feel so certain now with her staring me down, and I'd break if she shut me down again.

I licked my lips and tried a different angle. "Do the other Gardeners know?"

She held my gaze and moved her head almost imperceptibly side to side.

"Look, if it's a hidden greenhouse somewhere out there, you know I-I can maintain it for you," I floundered. "You've trained me well enough, and Sol, I won't tell anyone, Olivia. You know the other Gardeners can't stand me. I don't *have* anyone else to tell." Not since I brushed off Robert.

Olivia ducked her head away from the overhead camera behind me, masking the motion by petting Luan at her feet. She spoke in a low, flat voice. "There's no greenhouse. That'd be too big to conceal. We have a field, a garden with row covers, but we've already pulled the last of the produce off of it. It's a hard job, Iris. Johan and I were waiting to see if you were strong enough."

Her last words sounded like an apology. Heaviness settled between my ribs, sharp and stiff. And I hadn't been strong enough? Zuse, I did everything she asked! It was early winter now. Unheated row covers could only extend a season so long. Olivia and Johan weren't growing anything right now. I'd sampled the last of their harvest in Olivia's shared lunches. Tears pooled in my eyes and my words swelled in my throat until I could barely breathe. It was too late. I finally found out it was possible to grow food Outside, and it was too damned late.

"Besides, I don't need you to look after plants. I've been doing it on my own for years," Olivia muttered, straightening.

"I understand," I croaked, blinking away tears and flapping my hands like an idiot. *Shit.*

"I didn't mean it like that, nullskull. Zuse, I won't let you starve!" Olivia reached across the potting bench and grabbed my hand to soften her words. "I meant, I don't need you to look after plants *because* I need you to hunt."

"W-what?" I blubbered.

"We hunt in the winter. Oupa and I."

"Hunt what?" Winter had always seemed dead and barren here.

"Rabbits, geese, turkeys, gophers. Big horn sheep when we're lucky, but the greenhouses are eating up all of my time, and Oupa is getting old. He wants to teach someone else to hunt. You're tough, and occasionally you know when to shut up, but Johan wanted to wait and make sure you were dedicated first. He didn't want to let you in on this if you were just going to fold." She smiled and shrugged. "He was impressed when you came into work even though you were all beat up. Plus, he says you've read that whole survival guide front to back twice now. That's where he learned to set snares himself."

"I don't think I'm hunter material, Olivia."

"You're survival material, Iris. Always have been. Especially lately."

I didn't have the strength to tell her she was wrong. I'd survived so far by pulling those closest to me down with me. A hunter? I'd never killed anything bigger than a spider in my entire life, and I was pretty sure that gutting an animal wasn't as detached and scientific as it looked on the pages of Oupa's survival guide. I wasn't cut out for this. This was big. I'd been Corporate for most of my life.

And you hated it. Admit it, Iris. I'd hated nearly every second of it, uncomfortable suits, sitting still for hours, ridiculous, mundane filing. I had never fit in, no matter how hard I tried, and I'd loved being Outside once. Before Vinton fell, I'd dreamed about being like Nate, as a girl. I'd dreamed about doing big things. This was it.

Olivia was offering to help my family. We would starve without her.

I cleared my throat. "When do I start?"

CHAPTER
FOURTEEN

Um, what are those, exactly?" I blurted.

Olivia's oupa eased down the steps from his loft in the gray, pre-dawn light, cradling two weapons that looked like medieval versions of the semi-automatic rifles the Firewalls carried.

"What are they *exactly*?" Johan raised his eyebrows as he alighted the last few steps. "Well, I believe yours is a Vixen two recurve with one-hundred-and-fifty-pound draw weight. And mine is a ..." He held the weapon up and squinted at the lettering on the side. "Mine's a Vortex. Higher draw. Two-hundred-pound."

I gaped at him, swallowing as I took in quivers lined with short arrows. "English please, Oupa."

He grinned. "They're crossbows. You'll be using this one." But when he held out the bow, I backed away from it like it was a coiled snake. It looked like one, all tension and wicked curves, rippling with camouflage patterns. I didn't want to touch it.

"Olivia said we'd be setting snares. L-like in your guide-book." I shook my head. "She didn't say anything about zombie apocalypse weapons. I can't shoot that." This was a mistake, Sol. Who had I thought I was when I said, yes?

"Come now." Johan tucked the weapon back under his arm and offered me an easy smile. "I'll take you to our target range. They are simple tools, I promise. You only need to remember a few details in order to stay safe." He started walking up the hill without waiting to see if I'd follow.

I stood frozen for several breaths before trotting after him. "Oupa, I'm not the best at remembering details." I gulped.

"I've noticed." He nodded, climbing with an ease that belied his age. "But if you forget these ones, you'll amputate a thumb, or shatter an arrow and get shrapnel in your face."

Zuse. Blood drained from my cheeks and Johan turned and chuckled at my horrified expression. "That should make it easier to remember the details, yes?"

"Sol, I hope so." I swallowed.

We walked for several kilometers, stopping only to put on our goggles, cinch down our hats, and smear our cheeks with sunscreen as the sun crept over the eastern horizon, painting the undulating, snow-crusted hills in golden tones. I'd forgotten how it felt, dry grass crackling underfoot, black-capped chickadees calling in cheerful tones from clumps of sage brush gleaming with hoarfrost. Boulders the color of old copper jutted up from the white-like oxidized islands. The sharp smell of woodstove smoke stung my nostrils, and the sun warmed my scarred cheeks and shoulders. It was all overwhelming and more than a little terrifying for someone who'd spent the majority of her life scuttling down the city boardwalk from Seacan to Seacan at night. Of course, I'd spent more daylight hours outside since my demotion to Gardener, but this was no trip to the chicken coops or the goat run. This was *Outside.* Outside of the safety of the city, the awnings over the boardwalk, the UV shielding of the greenhouses, alone in nature with the bald-faced red sun creeping over us. I tried to blame my shortness of breath on the inclined terrain, but even when we crested the hill and Johan slowed, I kept gulping for air.

"Here." He pulled a canteen from around his neck and passed it to me. "Sit. It's normal for young people like you to feel anxious when you get out into the open. Olivia was the same when we started. I promise it'll pass. Real freedom lies in wildness, not civilization."

I gulped several stale sips of water, wiped my mouth, and passed the canteen back. "You used your quote voice for that last part."

"I have a quote voice?" Johan's brown eyes always gleamed like he knew an inside joke. It was infectious.

"Who said it?"

"Charles Lindbergh. Ancient history." Johan sighed.

"Father of commercial aviation, wasn't he?" My voice wobbled, and I crammed the brim of my hat further down my face. *Just ignore the sun and breathe, Iris.*

"Yes, but he loved nature. He said if he had to choose, he'd pick birds over airplanes."

"He'd have loved the post-collapse world then." I snorted.

"Yes." Johan craned his neck, blinking at the pale pink sky. "I like to think he would have." He held out his hand, and I took it and let him help me to my feet.

My knees still felt loose as we walked. Anxiety banded my chest. Johan looked so incongruent, striding ahead of me under the harsh light, with a crossbow slung over each shoulder. I'd always known him as Olivia's oupa, the introverted pigeon keeper who dabbled in tea-making, but right now, he looked like Nate. And that was throwing me, the memory of my uncle aching in my chest, the sky yawning above me like I'd always hoped for as a girl, but it was too damned much.

I didn't really know Johan at all, and I was following him further from the city than I'd ever been in my life. "How much longer?"

"To the target range? We're nearly there," Johan replied assuredly, but his words didn't soothe me.

The sky was about to swallow me up. Zuse, it was *too big* out here. Too bright and stark. I couldn't get my mind to unlatch from that morning at the bottom of the ravine sitting beside Vinton with his legs twisted the wrong way, paying for all my stubborn wishes. That's what happened when I tried to do big things. I hurt people. I tried to control my breathing, but it loped beyond my control, faster and faster. *Distract yourself. Keep talking. Say something. Anything.* "Where did you get crossbows, Johan?" I puffed between inhales.

"I ordered them from a catalog before you were born. Did you know that before the collapse, you could just order online, and a truck would deliver boxes right to your doorstep?"

Sometimes I forgot that the old world had been so recent. It had crumbled just after I was born. It may as well have been a million years ago, but Johan and my own parents had touched it and lived it, that fragmented past our city clung to with unbreakable resolve. "The world was ending, and you bought crossbows? So you *were* expecting a zombie apocalypse then. Bad luck no one saw the solar flares coming."

"Oh, we saw them." He shifted the crossbows on his shoulders, scanning the horizon. "The sun always had occasional vigorous cycles before the collapse. We had satellites specifically to track solar activity. Mapped out the whole coronal surface. We even stockpiled spare parts, high voltage transformers locked away in caverns below mountains. We had twelve hours to prepare the national power grids for coronal mass ejections. We saw them coming, Iris."

I knew all this. We'd learned it in school, but I'd never heard Johan talk about technology, and this felt so much more immediate than skim-reading history from a dusty hard drive. I didn't want him to stop because he was distracting me from my ratcheting heart and the odd, overwhelming sense of guilt about being Outside. "What went wrong? If you could see the solar storms coming, why did everything fall apart?"

"Have you ever been down to the lake when it's *really* windy?"

I had, as a child. Those mornings waiting for Nate. Pain still prodded my heart whenever I thought of him. I nodded.

"Then you've seen those big waves coming. You can't stop them. Sure, you can try to dampen the effect or fortify your shoreline so that the onslaught doesn't erode it, but if those waves keep coming, and they're big enough, you can't stop all of them. Eventually, they overpower everything in their path." He shrugged.

Like anxiety.

"And that is what happened to us. The first few solar mass ejections, we saw them coming and took the proper measures, the next ones wiped out the satellites, and then we were blind. After that, well." He shrugged ruefully. "Didn't matter how many spare transformers a nation had. The solar flares kept coming and we couldn't rebuild fast enough. The power grids collapsed. And here we are."

He made that last announcement as we scrambled over the lip of a scree-filled valley. A wide, snowy grassland stretched before us, edged on the far side by a copse of stunted coniferous trees. On the near side, a small, open-sided shed scrabbled together from mismatched sheets of corrugated steel provided welcome shade from the looming sun. Large stuffed canvas bags with circles painted on them dotted the meadow in increments to the tree line. As we closed on the shed, with its generously overhanging roof, I noticed that the open-front side had a wide shelf set between the posts at about chest height. It was otherwise unadorned and empty, save for drifting snow.

Johan set both crossbows on the shelf. "You rest here in the shade, and I'll go clear the snow off the targets. Then we can get started."

I didn't want to get started. Zuse, I knew I needed this. My family needed me to be able to feed them so we didn't all starve. If we got expelled, I needed to know how to do this so we wouldn't die, but Sol, I'd never been so out of my element in my life. And it must have showed because Johan clucked his tongue when he returned. "Iris, you're looking at me like I'm your executioner. We are just shooting bolts into targets. That's it. Perfectly safe."

"What about the part where I amputate my thumb or an arrow explodes in my face?" I countered.

"Easily avoided." He chuckled, picking up one of the crossbows. "Come on, they don't bite unless they're loaded. Let's show you the basic parts first. I'm assuming you've never shot a weapon?"

"Up until today, I'd assumed you'd never shot one either."

"Do you doubt your mentor's experience?" Johan asked playfully. "I'll have you know, I hunted before the collapse. Bow hunting mostly, but I haven't been strong enough to draw a compound bow in years. That's why I ordered the crossbows. They're easy, Iris. Just point and shoot. With practice, you'll be proficient enough to hunt with one in a few weeks. Perfect for beginners."

Or girls on the edge of starvation.

I tried to pay attention as Johan pointed out and named every component: the stirrup and riser, the limbs and the deck, the arrow retention spring and the safety latch, explaining each part's function along the way. Then, he showed me how you could screw different arrowheads into aluminum-shafted bolts, field tips for targets and broadheads for hunting.

After that, Johan demonstrated cocking the bow, latching the safety and loading the bolt before he leaned on the shelf. Squinting down the sights, he disengaged the safety and squeezed the trigger. The crossbow snapped, and an arrow answered with an immediate *thwap*, buried deep into the circle of the target marked twenty yards.

"Make sense?" Johan asked.

I nodded dumbly. He still hadn't told me how to avoid chopping off my own digits. Zuse, targets wouldn't feed me. I needed food now.

"All right, now walk me through yours." He held out the smaller crossbow and waggled it until I gingerly grabbed it by the stock. It was lighter than it looked. "Show me how to load it," Johan ordered.

Oh, Sol help me. "Okay," I exhaled. "Foot goes in the stirrup. Safety in the fire position."

"Good. Foot all the way in. Do you want to cock it with the rope puller or by hand? It's easier with the puller—more mechanical advantage—and it will shoot straighter. By hand is faster, but if you set the string unevenly, you'll shoot crooked every time."

"I-I don't know," I stammered, overwhelmed by all the information.

"Here," He pulled out a rope with handles and pulleys and hooks. "Like this. Hook on either side of the rail and pull back until it clicks. Very important that you hear that click."

"Okay." Sweat prickled my armpits.

"Keep talking."

"I-I don't remember what's next." *Zuse,* I felt like a child.

"That's okay. Safety on. Always safety on next. Press it down."

I thumbed the safety down, loaded a bolt with its odd colored fletching notched into the rail.

"Arrow all the way back against the string. All the way back," Johan urged. "Never fire the crossbow without an arrow in it, and never without it pressed all the way back. That's when limbs crack or arrows shatter."

"And when do I cut off my thumb?" I rasped.

"Oh, Iris." Johan put his hand on my shoulder. "Just breathe. Take your time. Now, keep your finger away from the trigger, but hold up the crossbow as if you're going to fire. Only ever point it at something you want to shoot."

"Seems like common sense."

"You have no idea." He chuckled. "There!" he exclaimed and tapped my hand, the one clutching the foregrip. "You see how you're holding it? With your thumb over the rail like that? What do you think would happen if you fired right now?"

I tucked my thumb down. "The string would hit it."

"At three-hundred-feet-per-second with one-hundred-and-fifty-pounds of force. That, my dear, is when you cut off your thumb." Johan held up three fingers, and for a moment, I was horrified that he was going to show me he was an amputee and I'd never even noticed, but his digits were all intact.

"Rule one." He tucked a finger. "Only point at what you want to shoot. Rule two: Never dry fire the crossbow, and rule three: keep your thumb and fingers below the rail. Simple as that. Ready to fire?"

Not even a little. "Okay." I nodded, sweat and sunscreen stinging my eyes.

"Keep that stock snug against your shoulder. That's right, and don't be afraid to use the shelf to stabilize. That's what it's there for."

"How do I aim?"

"See the notch on the back sight and the front one too? You want to line those up. Your target circle should be in the middle of the front notch."

"Got it." I clenched my teeth.

"Disengage the safety."

I thumbed the latch up.

"Fire when ready, my dear."

I held my breath and squeezed the trigger. The crossbow bucked in my hands, but I didn't hear the arrow hit.

"You closed your eyes." Johan smiled softly.

"I missed?" I felt like crying. *Zuse,* I needed to be good at this now. If I was a slow learner, we'd be homeless: Vinton, Mom, Dad, all of us.

"Don't look so down." Johan pointed to where a bolt had snagged the top corner of the target. Then he slapped my shoulder and laughed. "See? Even with your eyes closed, it's easy to shoot. You can do this, Iris."

Bolstered, I cocked and fired the crossbow a dozen more times after that, sometimes using the rope pulley, sometimes hand-cocking, but always with Johan's steady, calm voice guiding me. "Were you a teacher before?" I asked as I lined up another shot.

"We're all teachers in our own way. We've all got something to share that the world needs. That was the whole original point of our city, wasn't it?"

Wasn't that still the point? But we didn't *share* the information that Vinton and the other Browsers gleaned from pirated hard drives and rare books. We sold it to the highest bidder. I fired, oddly satisfied at the *thunk* of the bolt near the circle of the target and the bite of the stock against the hollow of my shoulder. "You weren't a teacher, then?"

"No."

"A gardener? Tea Master?" I grinned as I braced the crossbow, slipped my foot through the stirrup and pulled back on the string. "Pigeon keeper extraordinaire?"

His eyes crinkled as he smiled back at me. "Those were hobbies. I was a bit, uh, eccentric, let's say."

"What then?" I lined up my shot.

"I was a partner in a construction company. Toward the end, we specialized in off-grid builds and survival pods. Disengage your safety and check your hand placement. Every. Single. Time."

"Survival pods. Kind of like David Kahn's company?" I

murmured as I thumbed up the safety and peered down my sights. Before Kahn was our CEO, he was the head contractor who'd designed and built our city for some rich client before the collapse started. When the guy died before his project was completed, David Kahn took over, founded Corporate, and started scavenging information lost when the internet crashed.

"It *was* David Kahn's company, in fact," Johan answered my question quietly. "And mine. We're partners. We built this place together."

My finger twitched on the trigger. I missed my shot, sending a bolt whizzing through the long grass. "Holy shit, Oupa," I blurted. "You were *Kahn's* business partner?"

He stared after my arrow, raised his eyebrows and murmured, "I still am, a silent partner for the most part."

"What happened?" I asked, gobsmacked. What on Earth had the *co-founder* of our city done to get demoted to the lowest ranking job in our society?

Johan fixed me with a stern gaze. "Nothing happened, Iris. I happen to like gardening. Do you hate it so much?"

You insulted him. *Shit.* "No—I mean—it's great, Oupa." *Shit. Shit. Quit calling the co-founder of the city "Oupa."* I wiped my sweating palms down the front of my shirt. "It's saving my life. I can sleep at night. I've never been able to sleep."

"See?" Johan nodded. "Not all of us were built to be stuck behind desks. David loves it though. He loves civilization, the order of it, the technology, pushing people toward a common goal. And production. He's always believed that a person is only worth what they can produce. 'Knowledge is Power' and all that."

"And you?" I asked.

"I'm Charles Lindbergh." Johan smiled wistfully. "I like technology well enough, but I'd trade it all for wilderness. Wilderness is what's keeping me alive. It's not poison out here, Iris. It's paradise. Wilderness grows and adapts. It self-balances. It provides without fail. And I'm proud to provide for those in our city who need it. There's a whole side to our home that you've been kept blind to, Iris. And I'd like to show it to you. If you'd let me."

It's not poison; it's paradise. Outside. My dream since I was a little girl, to learn about Outside, Oupa was handing it to me, ready to teach me all about it. And it wouldn't hurt anyone. If I did it right, it would save my whole family. There was nothing bigger than that.

"I'd love that, Johan," I rasped.

CHAPTER
FIFTEEN

I was initiated into Johan's underworld with a bag of potatoes. When we returned from that first day of crossbow training, Olivia met us behind the chicken coops holding out a full-to-bursting burlap sack. "Payment for your first day, oh mighty hunter." Her teeth flashed in the dark.

"Olivia. I-I can't," I spluttered, wide eyes taking in the red-skinned tubers peeking out the top of the bag, each one bigger than my fist. From the gardens, I presumed. If I'd kept my designation as Search Engine, buying this many potatoes at Food Bank would have cost me two weeks of salary. Potato plants took up a lot of real estate, even if grown in stacks, and we didn't have a lot of room for large crops in the greenhouses, so limited harvests like potatoes were expensive. I couldn't remember the last time I'd eaten one.

"Oh, not to worry. They're not all for you." Olivia snorted as she hoisted the bag into my arms. "Here's your list." She held up a strip of paper, and I skimmed over a few family names and their Seacan numbers before she stuffed the paper into my front shirt pocket.

"I don't understand." I shifted the burlap bag and looked to

Johan for guidance. Olivia followed my glance and rolled her eyes.

"Didn't you teach her *anything* out there today?"

Johan laughed and waved Olivia off. "That's part of my route, Iris. I'd like you to divide that bag amongst the four families on that list and your own. You'll be making weekly deliveries of vegetables and, Sol-willing, fresh meat to those addresses. Now, this will involve some very early mornings hunting and checking trap lines with me, and some late-night deliveries to avoid the evening work crowds. I hope that a modest supply of meat and vegetables for your own family will be adequate recompense for the extra work?"

Tears sprung to my eyes, and I couldn't wipe them and hold onto the unwieldy sack at the same time. Blinking rapidly, I gulped several times before nodding. I could provide—actually provide—for my family who'd sacrificed everything for me. I didn't have words enough to thank Johan for that.

"Come now." He gripped my shoulder and continued warmly. "You've worked hard in the greenhouses. You were patient with us, and you proved yourself. It's the least Olivia and I can do."

Olivia tapped at the list in my pocket. "Two knocks on their doors, then pause, and two more knocks. If they don't answer, go around the back of their Seacans, and there'll be a bin buried there marked with a large stone. Avoid the street cams if you can. Should be easy enough. Most of these houses are far from the core. Got it?"

"Is-is this ..." I faltered and licked my lips. "Are we doing something illegal?"

Olivia snorted again, brushed her mass of red hair from her eyes and shrugged. "Last time I checked, delivering potatoes wasn't against the law."

"It is if someone thinks I took them from greenhouse stock!" I hissed. "What am I supposed to say if someone asks where I got all this stuff?" Vannevar had beaten me on the street for accidentally getting her brother fined, for kissing Robert, what would she do if she caught me with food that wasn't mine? My chest ached with sudden tightness. "Potatoes are *meg* creds, Olivia. People are going to ask."

Johan cleared his throat. "We only deliver on nights that coincide with the schedules of Firewalls who know what I'm doing. I'm feeding their families. They won't ask you any questions, Iris."

"What about the people on this list, huh? What's stopping them from ratting you out to Corporate?"

Johan smiled, and it maddened me. "Would you tell if it meant cutting off your only food supply? Anyone desperate enough to need our services will keep quiet. We're their last option ahead of expulsion."

"Tell me why I am avoiding the cameras again?" I swallowed.

"Because David Kahn doesn't appreciate my 'Experiment in Charity' as he calls it." Johan sniffed. "He knows we're feeding people, but he doesn't believe in hand-outs. Besides, there's no need to flaunt what we're doing, Iris. The families we're helping, they don't need their reliance on us broadcast citywide. Our best work is quiet work, understand?"

"No." My scarred cheeks flushed. "I don't understand. Kahn knows what you're doing? He knows about the gardens? Zuse, Johan, you nearly break me before telling me, but Kahn knows?"

"He doesn't know about the gardens, and Iris, it's imperative he doesn't find out. He thinks I'm feeding people spoiled vegetables from the greenhouses and that the potatoes are pulled from my seed stock for next year's crops. He doesn't know about Elaine's eggs. He thinks I'm a failure as a hunter, and he has no idea about my outside gardens. He isn't stopping us, because he thinks we're bound to fail. There's no way I can keep the greenhouses producing expected outputs while feeding so many people with seedstock."

"Why is he letting you do it though? If he hates it so much, this charity of yours, why let you go when he could just as easily stop it?"

Johan sighed. "Long story, Iris. Let's save it for another night. For now, I just need to know if you can deliver this food to the people on that list."

I clamped my mouth shut and nodded. I tried not to feel shut down. And I made the deliveries that night. Some of the families, after getting over the initial shock of seeing my face instead of Johan's or Olivia's sobbed openly when I handed them their food. They shook my hand and thanked me so profusely that guilt swamped me, because I hadn't planted the potatoes or tended them. None of this had been my doing.

But it could be. I could still be a part of something big. I could be a contributor to this city in a foundational way, like Nate was when he was alive. This could be more meaningful than anything I could have done as Search Engine. Saving lives, literally. I was beginning to understand what Johan loved so much about gardening.

Over the next weeks, Vinton recovered from his illness. Having missed so much desk work, he'd have to extend his hours for the next month and double his data runs in the Spring to pull his cred out of red-line. My parents couldn't ease his debt, having just reconciled their own. They did their best to feed our family of four on their scanty salaries, but it was my weekly contributions of potatoes, carrots, and rabbit meat that saved us. At first Mom and Dad were terrified when I revealed that Johan was teaching me to hunt and paying me out of his personal food stock, but they weren't strait-laced Corporate sweethearts anymore, not since Kahn made me an unpaid worker.

"We can't take this, Iris. They'll confiscate it all!" Mom yelped.

"I don't think they can." Dad rubbed his upper lip thoughtfully. "Even if they proved the food belonged to Iris, and not the rest of us, I've never seen Firewalls take food before, have you?"

"Well"—I raised my eyebrows—"they can't take it if we eat it all first, and they only come audit once a week, right?" Most of the families on Johan's delivery list were red-lined, I was sure of it. No way he'd keep dropping food to them on a weekly basis if he knew the Firewalls would confiscate it.

"Amen. Eat it all!" Vinton brightened, slapping his thighs. "Finally, Iris suggests something I can get behind."

Turns out, we didn't have to worry about the Firewall's audit. We left a single carrot for them to find as they rifled through my possessions later that week, and they saw it, but didn't take it or list it on the tally. Food was a loophole then. We could eat as much as I could catch, grow, or gather outside of the greenhouses and Food Bank with no worries of it being taken from us. Kahn would let it ride, just like he let Johan's experiment in state welfare ride.

"But you said before he didn't like what we're doing. Why let us try when he could just as easily crush our efforts?" I asked Johan the question he'd put off that first night and he got very still before answering me.

"David and I got drunk one night, way back at the start of the collapse. We were arguing politics—we often did—and I was pressing the need to care for those who were unable to contribute to society in a tangible manner." He chuckled bleakly. "I *am* getting old, after all, and so is David. Soon neither of us will be able to contribute much to society. But I'll never forget what he told me that night, Iris. He was so crass when he said it. He told me, 'There's always going to be a portion of society that's a rock in your shoe, Johan. They make the whole rest of the body stagger with the pain of them. Now, do you extract the pebble from your shoe and cast it away, or do you endure it until it infects your foot and sickens the whole body?'"

Zuse. I shuddered.

Johan smiled, but the brightness in his brown eyes wasn't joviality. It was fire. "You see, Iris? David doesn't see us as a threat. He doesn't know about the gardens, and he sees what I'm doing as a joke. He believes pure capitalism is the only road to success, and that we'll crumble under the weight of trying to support those who can't pay us. So long as we keep limping along quietly, so long as we don't shirk our day jobs, and so long as *we* don't become the pebble in David's shoe, he won't stop us. He would dearly love to see me fail so he can rub my face in it. He's so sure of himself, he allowed me to take on extra staff." Johan prodded a finger toward me. "*Guaranteed*, he knows I'm not just teaching you to take over the greenhouses, but he doesn't care because he's sure we'll fail and his capitalism will prevail. He's trying to make a point."

My face warmed. "Some of those red-line families he's trying to starve out *are* contributing to his society right now! Working their asses off to pull themselves out of debt while he keeps getting richer off their efforts. Charging them rent on bloody tool sheds he has the nerve to call homes."

"That's the other reason he's not stopping us. We're feeding some of his poorest and most productive workers for him. He doesn't have to."

"Sol Almighty," I exhaled. "Why are you partners with this guy again?"

Johan shrugged tiredly. "Maybe I'm trying to make a point too. What David has built. All this." He waved his hand toward the city. "It can't last forever. It's too top heavy. Eventually, it'll all come crashing down. Before that happens, I'd like to show him how to adapt and live in the world now, not in some echo of what it once was. We were close once, but maybe I'm no better than David is. I'm waiting to see him fail too. We're two old men, both sure that we're in the right, waiting for the other one to fall. Some partners we are." He sighed.

I rolled that information in my head. Adapting and living in the world now. That's what Uncle Nate had done too. That's what he'd been trying to teach me before he died, way back when he'd gifted me the snap pea seeds, how to evolve past what Kahn's Junior Executive School had taught me, to be unafraid to ask questions, and to live in harmony with Outside instead of in opposition to it.

Soldamnit, I blinked rapidly as the enormity of it all settled on me. *I've ended up right where I was supposed to be after all, Sasquatch.*

"THIS PART of the operation is not exactly legal." Olivia pinned me with a hard glance as we trekked together northwest of the city. Insects buzzed drunkenly around us, only recently thawed by the warming spring air. Trumpeter swans flew overhead, their brusque calls echoing down the valley and their wings whistling with every downstroke. While Olivia kept talking, I wondered what the best position for a hunting blind on the shoreline might be. If I could bag three or four of the big birds on their morning sojourns to the lake, we'd be set for the week.

"Are you even listening?" Olivia slapped my arm.

"Ow," I huffed. "The swans ..."

"You can hunt later. You're mine right now, so don't go flying off with them. This is more important than any damned bird. The whole year's harvest depends on this."

I chewed on my lip. "Run me through it then, if you don't mind, our not exactly legal operation?"

Olivia jammed a loose wisp of hair back under her sun hat. "It's simple. Everything needs supplemental fertilizer to grow. Everything in the greenhouses *and* everything in our fields. Sol knows we tried, but we could never get a garden to take without it. The sun doesn't sterilize the plants, it leeches the soil somehow." She shook her head. "Remember when I told you we ran out of fertilizer a few years back, and lost everything in the greenhouses?"

"You lost the fields too?"

She nodded, lips pursed. "We walked out one day, and they'd just wilted. Rows and rows of food we were counting on. That winter was brutal. We nearly didn't make it."

Any condolences I could offer would sound trite, so I changed the subject instead. "Kahn still believes that everything out here is poisonous? He's not just preaching that to funnel everyone into buying from Food Bank? That's why Johan doesn't want him to find out about the gardens right? I mean, if he did, if he knew that it was possible to grow food Outside, he'd want to cash in on that right?"

"Finding the place would involve wandering far outside of the city, in daylight. Not exactly Kahn's style. No, he thinks the sun poisons outdoor crops just like everyone else does." Olivia smirked as we pressed through the grasslands, and then down an eroding, green-tinged gully into a wooded area.

"So he honestly believes that Johan's 'Charity Project' runs on nothing but spoiled greenhouse produce and seed stock for next year's greenhouse crops?"

Olivia shrugged. "It's all so far beneath him, he doesn't really care. He thinks we're hunting and trapping and skimming off our own seed stock—which would be totally unsustainable because Oupa and I are the ones who'll have to pay if the greenhouses underproduce next season. That's why David thinks we'll fail."

My head spun. "Won't he get suspicious eventually when you don't? When people with no cred keep on eating but the greenhouse seed stock isn't suffering at all? He's going to find out about the gardens at some point, isn't he?"

"Yeah, that's the plan, eventually." Olivia shrugged again. "Oupa's hoping that we've fed enough mouths by then, that they'll be on our side. Enough of them have been burned by Kahn that they're ready to leave the city if they know they won't starve by doing so. Our CEO will be left with a half-empty city, no idea how to run the greenhouses, no pigeons, and no black tea if he kicks us out."

The air filled with the chatter of squirrels and tentative birdsong, but it wasn't enough to ease my anxiousness. "So, until then, you steal supplemental fertilizer. Is that what this is about? You said it was worth its fragging weight in copper. For Zuse's sake, Olivia! Kahn would probably legalize public executions if he caught you and Johan stealing something so valuable."

In the midst of the collapse, executions had actually become fairly commonplace. We'd read about them in history class. None had taken place in our community, of course—although Nora Yates had been close. Kahn was too *cultured* for that, but elsewhere, amongst the riots and raids, URL groups reported several communities who hadn't hesitated to hang their criminals at their boundaries as warning signs to potential thieves. Some continued the practice to this day.

David relied on his Firewalls instead. They hadn't killed or hung anybody ... yet.

"We're not *exactly* stealing." Olivia held a branch aside. "We have a side deal with the URLs."

"A side deal?" I gulped. So that was the illegal part. No one was supposed to deal directly with the URLs. It was all Corporate-controlled trade. "Who has a side deal?"

"Oupa and I. We needed extra fertilizer for the gardens, and the URLs needed a reliable communication network."

I stopped in my tracks, gaping at her back until she turned. "Pigeons?"

She nodded.

"Are you shitting me? You're trading *pigeons* for the most expensive good we purchase? Are these people idiots?"

Olivia pushed up her hat brim to glare at me. "It's your *uncle's* group. Nate always struck me as a bright man, no?"

I winced at the mention of his name and stumbled to catch up as Olivia tromped through the brush away from me. I hadn't really thought about it, but of course Nate's group would be carrying on without him. Where else would all our traded goods be coming from? *The outside world didn't stop just because your uncle died, stupid.* Had he been a part of this then? Running the underworld with Olivia and Johan? "You traded pigeons with my uncle, while he was still alive?"

"Not *just* pigeons," she spat over her shoulder. "The best of Johan's breeding stock. The fastest, most reliable carriers we have. Nate's group still gets first pick every season. They have the finest network of birds this side of the mountains. No one can relay information faster, I'm told."

Holy shit. Then why had it taken a week for them to p-mail Mom and tell her Nate had been dead for a month? My chest ached. I scrubbed at it as we walked. "What's the deal then?" I croaked.

"The URLs set aside a portion of the fertilizer shipment at a safe drop before it ever reaches the city. They fudge their accounting so that it only shows the inventory that actually *arrives* at the greenhouses, like Elaine does with the eggs. We pick up the surplus at the drop and take it directly to our gardens." Olivia stopped in front of an eroded hillside laced with exposed tree roots. She toed the loose soil a few times until the hollow rattle of tin crackled beneath her feet. Bending down, she brushed away a layer of twigs and leaves exposing the corner of a corrugated sheet of metal. Then she peeled it away from the hill's face, revealing a hewn cave nearly as tall and wide as I was. Stacked within were rows and rows of fertilizer bags.

"Mother of Sol," I whispered.

"It's not technically stealing if it never reaches the city, and we paid for it fair and square."

"It's trading outside Kahn's Corporate umbrella. Not exactly legal."

"I believe those are the exact words I used," Olivia snapped.

I waited for fear to creep in. This wasn't delivering potatoes; it was bigger, moving goods outside of Corporate trade agreements. I'd been mouthy at the public meeting where David Kahn stripped me of my job, I'd been a pebble in his shoe, and Johan said he didn't forget that sort of thing. Did I really want to side trade with his URLs? Break his laws?

Beetle would do it. The bright thought crept into my head so unexpectedly I smiled.

Beetle always wanted to do big things. She would cut off her braid to be a part of something Nate had had his hands in. Moving goods. Just like an URL. Right where I was supposed to be.

BY LATE SPRING, I was a Gardener, a somewhat proficient crossbow hunter, a trapper-in-training, a delivery woman, and a mule for not-exactly-legal goods. The fertilizer bags at the hillside safe drop were about three kilometers from our hidden northern gardens. Olivia and Johan had taken turns hauling a bag at a time in hiking backpacks to the crops. Every two weeks, they mixed two bags of fertilizer with rainwater from an underground cistern Johan had dug when he'd tilled the first hidden garden plot. It was a painstaking process, but it only happened bi-monthly, and I quickly worked my way up to hauling two bags at once, a fifty-pound load. I'd never been in better shape in my life.

Johan was right. Outside life suited me. I craved the movement and the sweat and the ever-changing scenery. My mind was free to wander unfettered while I hunkered in tree stands on game trails or checked trap lines or weeded. My soul felt healed when I saw sunrises now, not scarred. When I needed to focus, Johan's exquisite black tea gave me the caffeine boost I needed to pull my frayed wires into order. Every day was different than the last, and at nights, I fell into my bunk and slept like the dead.

I thrived in a way I'd never thought possible. I learned to love the Outside I'd feared for so long.

Mom stopped questioning my every move. Dad spoke to me like I was his equal, and Vinton eyed me with something akin to admiration. Olivia kept me in check, and Johan was the grandpa I never had. Nothing was missing. I had everything I'd ever wanted. Well, I *thought* I did.

But everything changed on the day Olivia added another name to my weekly delivery list.

Robert Lycos.

CHAPTER
SIXTEEN

Robert Lycos?" I wrinkled my nose. "This is some sort of joke, yeah? Robert's the furthest thing from redline there is." 4500 creds a month away to be exact.

Olivia coughed and studied the ground between her feet, uncharacteristically silent.

"What?" I demanded.

"You haven't heard?" She exhaled, dark eyes studying me through frizzy locks of hair.

"Heard what?"

"Ah, Zuse." Her shoulders dropped. "I keep forgetting you don't have a laptop anymore." Olivia owned one now. She'd confided it had taken her seven months of saved wages to purchase it. "Don't you ever read the news on Vinton's?"

"Yeah," I snapped. "I have loads of time between hunting at four in the morning, hiking six clicks round trip to fertilize and weed, keeping up my day job, *and then* delivering at midnight. Sometimes, I do crossword puzzles, you know, with all the spare time I have."

I waited for her to toss something snide back at me. Olivia

always did, but instead, she broke eye contact and focused intently on picking dirt from beneath her nails.

"Frag it, Olivia. Spill!" I barked.

She flinched, puffed out her cheeks and exhaled. "Robert's mom killed herself."

My stomach dropped. "What?"

"I guess she had some mental health issues. Elaine says she's been unwell for a few years now. She stayed at home. She didn't work. Did you know that?"

"She *had* to work." CEO Kahn expelled adults who didn't. He'd threatened to do it to me before Johan stepped up and hired me.

"Guess not if your family is rich."

I shook my head. Zuse, I didn't even know the woman's name. Robert had never mentioned her. Had I ever even seen her?

"Robert says she hung herself in Paul's office. She hated that he worked such long hours, and she didn't want Robert finding her at home."

"Oh Sol," I murmured, lips numb. *Oh, Robert.* "When?"

"Three weeks ago. They had the funeral last week."

"*Three* fragging weeks, Olivia?" My voice cracked. "And you never thought to tell me?"

"Zuse, sorry Iris. I-I thought you already knew. Everybody was talking about it. I figured your family would have told you."

They might have, if I ever saw them, but I left before they woke up and didn't get home until they all slept. I doubted I would have woken even if they'd tried to rouse me. Heat pooled at the back of my throat. "Okay," I choked. "Okay. That doesn't explain why Robert is red-lined. He *is* red-lined, right?" Most of our clients were.

"He's, uh, in and out."

"He lost his job?"

Olivia shook her head slowly. "No, he's still a Search Engine."

Thank Sol. Maybe he hadn't earned it. Maybe his Dad bailed him out, but Robert worked hard for that job. "What then?"

"His Dad just lost it, I guess. Total nervous breakdown. Paul hasn't worked since he found her in his office. He told Kahn he won't go back, and that house they're in? Have you seen how lux it is?"

I hadn't. I knew it was big from the outside, but the one time I'd showed up at the door, Paul had guarded it like there was something he didn't want me to see inside. I'd assumed it had been Vannevar visiting his son. I'd never dreamed he was protecting a mentally ill wife. Vannevar had known about her, and I hadn't. Robert had only ever shared conversations about work with me, never home.

"That place is nearly the size of one of the greenhouses," Olivia whispered. "I can't imagine how much it costs a month to lease or heat in the winter. Robert can't afford it on his Search Engine salary, not without his dad working, and the lease is locked in. He can't afford the penalty payment for bailing, so he came to us for help. He's sure it's temporary, that Paul will come around and start working again, but until then ..." She shrugged.

"They can't afford food."

"Pretty much." Olivia sniffed.

"How the hell does Robert know about our *charity* program? Kahn knows, but none of the other Shareholders do."

"Elaine got worried when they stopped coming to Food Bank. She told me, and I told Robert."

"Shit, Olivia." I ran my hands through my hair. "His dad could leak our whole operation. We'd be done!"

"His dad is *sick* right now. He doesn't even leave the house. Robert says he won't tell, and we need someone in Corporate on our side."

Heat crept into my cheeks and burned my throat. "This is ridiculous. They should just eat the penalty and downsize. Other people need our food more than those two do!" I sputtered.

"Housing is short right now. I don't think there's anywhere else for them to go, and Robert is trying to maintain an image with Corporate."

Corporate could frag themselves. I shook my head. "Why me, Olivia? Put this one on Johan's run." I hadn't seen Robert since the week after Vannevar jumped me, when I'd sent him away for trying to help me.

"After Douglas Baidu, Paul is practically David's right-hand man." Olivia fidgeted. "He and Johan don't exactly see eye to eye. They've argued a few times, and it got heated. I don't really think it's the best thing right now to send Oupa sneaking around his property, not with Paul unhinged."

But it was safe for me? I didn't have time for this, catering to Robert Lycos or explaining to Olivia why it was a bad idea. I'd never told her about the beating. She'd swallowed the story that I'd slipped and hit my head and that's why I'd missed work.

Vannevar had warned me to stay away. She was a Firewall. She carried a semi-automatic rifle for Zuse's sake.

"There's bad blood between Robert and I too, all right?" I rasped. "I'm not the person for this job."

"There's no one else. Johan is overworked as it is. You *know* he is, and I'm absolutely bogged at the greenhouse. Besides, it's only a couple of streets over from your last delivery." Olivia gripped my arm, dark eyes pleading. "Look, we'll make it a back-door drop. Just leave his deliveries in the bin. Don't even knock. No contact, all right?" She held out the list.

My stomach churned. "It's temporary?"

Olivia nodded. "We need Robert's support with the Shareholders, Iris. They keep cutting maintenance funds for the greenhouses. We need this almost as much as he does."

"All right," I croaked, but I wasn't.

COLD MIST CONDENSED on my hair and cooled my cheeks as I slogged through the backsides of the core tenement lots. The air was sharp with the smell of rain and the diesel exhaust from the generators. Red, chalky rivulets ran down from the banded hillsides above the city toward the lake. Slimy clay caked my boots and spattered my pants, and I slipped several times trying to identify which hulking fortress of Seacans was Robert's house from the back. Even though the street was nearly deserted at one in the morning—the lunch crowd had already returned to work—I kept far from the reach of the pale boardwalk street-lights. I hoped to finish my last delivery unseen. Then, home to a hot shower, music in my ears, and bed. In three hours, I had to be up to check the southern trapline. *So let's get this over with.*

A pale green rock nearly the size of my head had been set in the shadows of an alcove in Robert's barren back plot. I bee-lined for it, unslinging the burlap bag from over my shoulder with soggy, wrinkled fingers. Between the rock and the wall, there'd be a buried container with a watertight lid. I'd asked most of our clients to drape an old rug over their bins before burying them—it kept them cleaner and easier to expose—but as I toed the soggy mess behind the marker stone, my foot hit bare metal and my heart sank. "Zuse," I swore under my breath. *No rug.* I'd have to scrape back an inch of mud to access the bin. *Fantastic. Just fantastic.*

I left the food in the bin with a recipe for stew and went home that night with mud up to my elbows.

ROBERT LEFT a note in the bin the next week on the back of the recipe.

> Stew was wonderful. Dad ate seconds. I haven't
> seen him sit down to a meal for weeks.
> p.s. Are you supposed to eat bay leaves? Asking for
> a friend.
> R.

I grinned, deposited the food in the bin, and jotted my reply on the back of my recipe for Crispy Duck.

> R.
> If you have to ask if you should be eating some-
> thing, the answer is usually no. Tell your friend
> not to eat the bay leaves. The packet of dried
> flower heads aren't for eating either! They're
> for chamomile tea. I thought if you or your dad
> are having trouble sleeping?
> I.

We wrote back and forth like that for days.

> My mom used to make me chamomile tea when I
> had nightmares as a kid. I still love the smell.
> No one talks about her. It's like she didn't even
> exist.
> R.

> People can be such monumental dicks—Yours
> Truly included. They aren't doing it on purpose.
> They think they'll hurt you if they mention her.
> My parents do the same thing with my uncle.

What was your mom's name? What was her
favorite color? Did she have any pet peeves?
p.s. The bird this week is a spent laying hen. You'll
need to boil her on low heat for six hours with
an onion. Then debone.
I.

That seems to be the key to interacting with most
fine birds: keep the heat no higher than a
simmer for a long time or else they go all tough
on you, right? ;) Mom's name was Moira. She
didn't change it to some whack-job internet
pioneer name when she got here like most of
the others did. She loved green. She said it
reminded her of spring, but she never went
Outside. Pet peeve? Oh Sol, she hated mouth-
breathers with a passion.
R.

Are you calling me an old bird?
p.s. Ugh, Mouth-breathers. I'm team Moira on
that one.
I.

Have lunch with me one night? I can bring a table
out back. I won't mouth-breathe. Pinky swear.
R.

I don't think that's a good idea. Do you need
more tea?

The next week I walked into Robert's backyard in the middle
of the night without stopping to check my surroundings.

"Hey, Iris," A voice sounded from the dark, and I leaped back, nearly throwing the bag.

"Son of a bitch!" I barked, stiff with shock. "Robert!"

The shadow leaning against the alcove wall shifted. "Sorry."

"Zuse, you scared me! There are eggs in here." I held up the bag accusingly. "*What* in Sol's name are you doing?"

"I hoped to convince you to have lunch with me, Pen pal." He shuffled forward.

I clenched my teeth and shook my head, blinking up at the stars. "No contact delivery. That was the arrangement." *Sol, don't be such a jackass, Iris.*

"I won't keep you then. I can take the bag." He sounded so wretchedly hurt as he held out his hand.

"I-I'm sorry about your mom," I stammered.

"I know," he said, arm still outstretched.

Give him the bag, stupid. "There's, uh, eggs from Elaine, carrots, potatoes, and a goose. I already plucked and washed it. It's oven ready."

"We don't have geese, do we?" Robert wrinkled his nose, accepting the sack like I'd just passed him a severed head.

"No, we don't, Robert." I watched the cogs turn as he took that in. *Yeah, he'd had no idea about the hunting. Nice going, Iris. Way to slip up.*

"Wild? You killed it? Shot it? With what?"

I deflected quickly. "Well, it's generally bad form to try to pluck them while they're still alive, so yeah I killed it."

His teeth flashed in the dark, but I couldn't tell if it was a smile or a sneer. "Iris, the mighty hunter. You always were a badass."

I snorted. "It's not like we had some epic woman-against-goose combat to the death. I just shot it. Let's keep that between you and I, yeah? The less Corporate knows the better."

He nodded slowly. "I've never cooked a goose," he

murmured and when I didn't answer him, he turned back toward the front of his house, shoulders slumped.

"Hey?" I called softly, and he turned like a sluggish sleepwalker. "I put a recipe in there, like always. You can do this."

He sniffed and nodded once before walking away from me.

I couldn't fall asleep that night. Robert's wrung out voice and expressionless eyes wouldn't leave my mind.

"I BURNED THE OUTSIDE, and it was raw in the middle," Robert blurted.

I'd prayed for my whole delivery run that the alcove behind Robert's house would be empty when I got there, but he sat waiting again on a stool, on his deck, limned in moonlight.

I sighed. "The goose?"

He nodded.

"Did you cover it?" I'd handwritten the recipe for roasted goose with vegetables copied from Olivia's computer.

"I didn't have a big enough pan with a lid. I just cut off the cooked meat and kept putting it back in until it was done."

"That's one way of doing it." I raised my eyebrows. "It must have been as dry as a shoe by the time you were done. Aren't you supposed to be working?"

"I am. I-uh-check on Dad at lunch break."

Paul still hadn't left his house then. "It's rabbit this week. How about you try a stew again. Your dad liked that, didn't he?"

Robert smiled faintly. "Yeah, he did."

"Good. Here." I passed him the sack and pulled a square of folded paper from my pocket. "Your recipe, Pen pal."

"Thanks." He took the paper and as I turned to leave, he added. "Your handwriting still sucks, by the way."

"Yup." I waved over my shoulder as I left.

CHAPTER
SEVENTEEN

The sky was clear and needled with cold starlight on my next delivery night. Frog song ricocheted between puddles and the sharp astringent smell of sagebrush stirred around me as I headed to Robert's. He was sitting on a blanket on his back deck, waiting.

"Meteor shower tonight." He gestured toward the horizon. "You've missed some big ones. Come sit for a bit? I promised you falling stars on our first walk, and I never did deliver."

I shook my head, but my feet were so tired, and he looked so doggedly hopeful when he held up his hand, my resistance crumbled. "Ten minutes. No longer," I said.

"Deal." Robert patted the blanket beside him and lay back with his arms crossed over his head.

I eased down beside him and swallowed hard. I'd forgotten the smell of him, the faint aftershave. How, when we were close enough to brush arms, the space between us felt like unsettled air before a storm. This was a mistake.

For several breaths, we shivered and blinked up at the sky.

"Did you know you could see satellites from Earth when they were orbiting, before they were all crippled and fell?"

Robert murmured. "You didn't even need a telescope. You could just spot them cruising through space."

"Really?"

"Yeah, my mom told me about it. She had some program on her phone. There was this massive international station up there too with astronauts on it twenty-four seven, and you could map out which nights it would be flying over your part of the sky. You could just look up and see it flashing past, and maybe they'd be looking down at the same time. All those hundreds of kilometers apart, but still connected."

He shifted, his cold fingers slipping into mine. I knew I should pull away, but his hand was shaking, and I didn't think it was from the cold.

I chose my words carefully. "There are some distances that are too far to connect."

"I keep falling into your orbit, Iris."

A laugh burst out of me. "Frag, that has *got* to be the cheesiest pick-up line I've ever heard." I snorted and covered my mouth.

Robert laughed too. We couldn't stop once we started.

"Shh!" I gasped. "Someone will hear."

"Nah, the frogs are too loud," he whispered, swiping tears from his eyes and stroking my hand.

We fell into silence, suddenly serious again. I couldn't gauge the sudden switch in mood. My heart pounded in my throat.

"No one laughs with me anymore, Iris. It's like they think it'll break me."

Two flashes streaked across the sky, one after the other, leaving twin ribbons of smoke cutting across the black. Gasping, I pointed. "What do you wish for?" Then I turned to him, still smiling. I could do this. I could keep this casual.

"This." Robert pulled me toward him and kissed me, his thumb tracing down my jaw and his body warm against mine.

My breath caught in my throat, and a delicious tingle

smoothed down every thought in my head before cascading down my spine. Robert pressed his hand against the small of my back, and it felt like it had always belonged here. We'd always belonged here.

Only we didn't. Our programming was incompatible. Robert lived in a world so alien to mine, we may as well have been born on different planets. And I had a job now. People would starve if I was caught. Paul Lycos was on the other side of this wall right now. Still, it took every strand of strength I had to peel away from Robert's embrace. He froze when I did.

"I think we should go back to being pen pals," I said, and while I still could, I stood up and walked out of his yard.

THE WEEK AFTER WE KISSED, there was no note from Robert in the bin, and he'd left the lid ajar and exposed. I deposited a sack of potatoes, some basil, and two prairie grouses. Then I sealed the bin properly and buried it.

My backpack went missing the next day. It was just an old hiking pack I'd borrowed from Oupa, but its padded straps and reinforced seams made it perfect for hauling the fertilizer bags to the gardens, and I'd tucked my latest recipe for Robert in the front pocket—Rosemary Chicken.

"Where did you leave it last?" Olivia sighed as I turned Greenhouse One upside down searching for it.

"Here, in the alcove. I always pick it up on my way out."

"Borrow mine 'til you find it, and for Sol's sake, get out from under my feet would you?" she snapped. "You and the cat both."

Yuan yowled in agitation, threaded through my legs, and bit my hand when I tried to pet him.

I STILL HADN'T FOUND my hiking pack by the time I made Robert's next delivery. It was late night, but the back lot was still thick with the kind of humid quiet heat that preceded a storm. Sol, I wished the rain would let up. It had been an unbearably wet spring and, as a result, I'd spent all week slogging through the muddy hidden garden, digging up potato plants whose leaves were blotched brown with blight. Each stricken plant had to be carefully extracted, bagged, sealed and burned. Late blight was a fungus whose spores could ride the wind for miles and survive a winter in the compost heap. If I didn't correctly identify and burn every plant showing signs of infection, we could easily lose the whole potato crop—and the tomatoes too. It affected both.

I tucked into Robert's alcove just past midnight, peeled back the muddy rug, and unlatched the bin lid.

At first, I didn't process it when I saw the full burlap sack from last week. Then the wet stench of rotting meat hit me. I stumbled back gagging. What the hell? He didn't take the food. "Robert?" I gulped.

Shit, what had he eaten all week? Something was wrong. "Robert?" I called louder, heartbeat filling my head as I threw down this week's delivery and stumbled toward the front of the house, heedless of the street cams. "Robert? Hello?" I slapped my palm against his front door several times and called his name loudly enough that the blue helmets in front of Cache, way down the street, turned their heads. No one answered Robert's door.

Nausea clawed up my throat. The thick stench of spoiled food still clung to my nostrils. *Shit. Shit. Shit.* Where was he? He wouldn't have done something stupid, would he? Him and his dad, alone in their grief?

"No," I yelped and hammered on the door again. We'd been talking. We'd kissed. And I had shut him down at his most vulnerable moment. I backed up from the door. The Lycos's were rich enough, they might have a shuttered window or two in this place. Maybe I could bypass the door and climb in. "Come on, Robert!" I hissed but couldn't find any access points. I spun toward the side alley and slammed into someone on the boardwalk.

"Iris?" Strong hands gripped my shoulders: pale blue eyes, warm aftershave, crooked tie.

It took me several seconds to put it together while my pulse hammered at my temples. "Robert?" I blurted and fell into him, gripping him in a strangling embrace. "Oh Sol … I thought—"

"Iris. What's wrong?"

"I opened the bin, an-and everything was rotten, and Zuse, Robert, I thought something happened to you." My last words were muffled as I tucked into the hollow of his shoulder. "You didn't answer your door."

"I was at work." Robert stroked the back of my head. "Look, Dad found the bin, Iris. He was furious when he found out I was taking charity. He screamed every time I went near the backyard this week. I was afraid the Firewalls were going to take him away. Then he dressed this evening—for the first time in Sol knows how long—and he walked to work with me."

Relief loosened my knees and tightened my throat. I choked back a sob. "Have you had enough to eat?" I gulped.

"Let's go inside."

The suggestion hit me like a slap, and I recoiled at the unexpectedness of it. "What?"

He kept his arm wrapped around me, but his gaze was locked over my shoulder as he whispered in my ear. "Easy. I'm not being a creeper, okay. The blue helmets at Cache are watching us. How about we step away from the cameras?" He pasted a smile on his face, waved brightly at the guards and guided me toward his front door.

"Wait." I pulled back. "My delivery. I dropped it in the side yard."

"You go on in." Robert held the door open. "I'll go get it. Be right back."

Zuse, this is not how I planned to visit Robert's house. The door closed, and I turned and blinked at a foyer larger than my old house, tiled in slate, paneled with bright white–washed wood, and with a modern, twisted metal chandelier hanging above me like some sort of sleek, robot spider.

The door opened, and I jumped. "Give me a sec, okay?" Robert patted my shoulder, flapped out of his jacket, and strode toward the back of the house clutching my food delivery.

I took in fat leather couches, thick slab bookshelves full of elegant knick-knacks, sleek granite countertops. *Sol Almighty*, I gulped. What was I doing here? I didn't belong here. A large analog clock, all wood and brass ticked loudly from the sitting room, and I counted the beats in my head until Robert returned empty-handed.

He strode toward me with relief plain on his face. "You wanna sit?"

I backed away from him and shook my head. My muddy arse on those couches? Not a chance. I felt dirty just standing here.

"Sol, I'm sorry." He closed the distance between us and grabbed both my cold hands in his. "Look, I didn't mean to scare you. I've been working so many damned hours, I lost track of what time it was. I thought I could sneak back here and clean things up before you came, but Dad's been ..." Robert deflated. "He's not ready for work. He blabbed to the other Shareholders about the food bin, but he spouted so much other nonsense, he just came across as a madman. I can't handle him and my job at the same time, Iris. They have me at the office nearly twenty-four seven now, an-and he keeps tearing the house apart. He's in his office, taking the drawers of his desk apart right now. It's like looking after a fragging child." Tears pooled in his eyes. "He's supposed to be the parent, right? *He's* supposed to be the one cooking and cleaning and telling me everything's going to be okay. I feel like I'm being pulled a hundred different directions at once, and there's nothing to hold onto. I can't look after all *this*." He waved his hands at the opulence around us.

Zuse, how many mouths would the lease on this house feed? I swallowed and latched onto a similarity between Robert and I, however tiny it was, because *this* was reminding me of the vast divide, the one I couldn't ever cross. "I know that feeling, being pulled a hundred different directions at once. My mind always does that. It never slows down. I always feel unanchored and drifting, and people think that I'm not paying attention or I'm lazy or I don't care, but I do care. I care about you, Robert."

He rubbed his thumbs over my fingers. "I care about you too, Iris. Always have."

"I keep letting you down. I don't mean to. I'm wired all wrong, but I'd never hurt you on purpose."

"Hey." He cupped my chin and tipped it up until I met his gaze. "I love how you're wired, Iris. The whole damned rest of the world is wired wrong. You're a badass. Never change. Now, will you come and sit down?"

But I couldn't. Not with tears running down my face and my chest ready to explode. *Never change.* How on Earth could I fit into Robert's world if I didn't change? I shook my head, and Robert blinked up at the huge spider-like chandelier.

"I can't get close to you if you keep pushing me away, Iris. I'm sorry about *this*. The money, the house, my asshole dad, and his Shareholder cronies; but I'm not sorry about *us*." His voice broke. "I just feel so alone right now, like I'm hanging over this edge and I can't hold on anymore, you know?"

"I'm here," I choked and fell into him. "You can hold onto me, okay? I'm not going anywhere. I promise."

I promise.

What a stupid thing to say. And what a stupid girl I was. As Robert and I clung to each other, I had no idea that this would be the last night I spent in the city as I knew it.

CHAPTER
EIGHTEEN

We held each other in the foyer until an intercom beeped and then crackled.

I jumped.

Paul called for his son and panic leaped into Robert's blue eyes at the hysterical sound of his dad's voice.

"It's all right," I whispered as we broke apart. "I'll go take care of the mess in the bin. Go talk to him."

"Thank you, Iris." He sniffed and stroked my scarred cheek.

"I know you're there. Answer, damn it!" Paul snapped, and Robert flinched.

I kissed his cheek and pressed out the front door before he could stop me.

The Firewalls at Cache were looking the other way when I slipped into the side yard. Pulling my shirt collar over my nose, I entered the back alcove, held my breath and plucked the sodden bag out of the bin, avoiding the vile brown slime oozing from within. Robert liked me just the way I was. My chest burned. He didn't care how I was wired. He wanted there to be an *us*. Setting the sack on the far side of the lot, I sopped up the residue left in the container with several handfuls of grass, sealed the lid and buried it. Without a proper cleaning, the bin would still reek, but Robert wouldn't be using it again, not now that Paul had found it. Sol, I hoped Robert was right and the Shareholders hadn't taken Paul seriously when he babbled about the bin. I didn't want to dwell on that right now. The buoyancy of Robert's words and the way he'd held me like I was the most valuable thing in his lavish house filled my heart with a lightness that wouldn't be tamped down.

I took several cleansing breaths of fresh air before grabbing the putrid burlap bag, holding it straight-armed in front of me, and stumbling out of the alcove like a zombie. As I passed the side yard, movement caught my eye. I jerked toward it, half-expecting Robert had come back out. One last kiss, perhaps?

But it wasn't Robert.

It was a Firewall.

I froze as one of the guards from Cache stared me down.

Shit. I held out my free hand so they could see I held no weapon. My legs tingled with the urge to run.

The blue helmet widened their stance and shrugged their semiautomatic from their shoulder.

Shit. Shit. Shit. Don't run.

"Drop the bag," a shrill, familiar voice ordered. Wisps of blonde hair haloed her face beneath her combat helmet, and my stomach lurched.

Vannevar. She wasn't supposed to be on shift tonight. Johan had said he'd checked the shift schedules. Soldamnit! Of course, it'd be Vannevar.

"Sure thing." I crouched slowly, set the lumpy bag down and edged away from it.

"You," she sneered, raising her weapon and pinning me in its sights, "come here!"

She's going to shoot me. Cold nausea rooted me to the spot. I hunched my shoulders and spread my trembling hands further apart, breathing in hitching gulps.

"I told you to come here, Basic Bitch," she hissed.

"It's j-just garbage, Vannevar," I stuttered, throat closing. "I'm just taking out the trash."

"I told you to stay away from him, and you just went into his fragging house, didn't you?" She slunk toward me, out of the reach of the streetlights and their cameras, rifle aimed steadily at my head. "Robert's dad hates you, you know that? Ever since you started sticking your tongue down his son's throat. Know why we started inspecting your place weekly? Why the Shareholders keep shitting on you? All Paul's doing. And if I tell him you stole something, he'll believe me. He'll thank me for putting you down. No one will even recognize you after." She giggled, and it sounded so out of place, my neck tingled. "If I shoot you in the head from this range, they won't even be able to find all the pieces."

"Please don't." My words came out high and reedy. But she closed on me as if she hadn't heard. *This isn't happening.*

Vannevar flicked the safety off. Her eyes were hard pinpoints of light in the dark and her smile a twisted snarl.

"Please don't!" I wailed, crumbling under her glare, shielding my head with my hands as my knees hit the damp grass. The air thickened to a slurry of panic and soured meat. I gagged and whimpered as Vannevar's boots squelched to a stop near my ear.

She bent down and grabbed a fistful of my hair. Something cold and metallic jammed against my temple. *The gun.* Wet breaths sawed out of me. A buzzing filled my head, angry and raw, like the sound of a wasp's nest crushed underfoot. *You won't even feel it, Iris. Just breathe.*

I did breathe.

For far too long.

An eternity later, Vannevar yanked my hair hard enough that my neck snapped to the side, and I yelped like a kicked dog. The gun against my head withdrew. Adrenaline leached out of my bones like acid, and when I finally gathered the nerve to glance up, she was gone. The side yard was empty.

I scrambled to my feet and trotted home on loose legs, snot still running down my face, and my chest stiff with fear. Curled in my bunk, I willed myself to take deep and even breaths, but I couldn't sleep. I hadn't done anything wrong. She couldn't get rid of me if I hadn't done anything wrong, a small voice in my head insisted, but of course it lied. The Firewalls could do anything they wanted. They shot Nora Yates in the leg just because she didn't leave the city fast enough. I was stealing Vannevar's boyfriend. She'd destroy me.

I peeled myself out of my bunk at four in the morning still dressed in the same mud-smeared clothes from hours ago. Shrugging into my jacket and boots, I padded out of our Seacan before my family got home. The grass was clotted with dew, the sky bloated with low, heavy clouds, and the air smelled marshy from the breeze blowing off the lake. Crickets sang in the gloom. The bare bluffs marbled in green looked like an alien landscape. I picked up my crossbow and Olivia's hiking pack at Johan's while he slept, and I was careful not to slam the heavy wooden door on the way out.

I checked the west trap line, because it was the farthest one away from the city, and after I'd walked its whole span, with two fat rabbits to show for it, I felt calmer. I could handle this. I reset a spring snare and concealed it. I could handle Vannevar. She was all lies and empty threats. If I gave her a wide berth, she'd forget me.

Sol, I was stupid. Vannevar wasn't the kind of person who forgot, and neither was Paul Lycos or David Kahn.

Dawn had bleached into early morning and the cold smell of oncoming rain hung in the air by the time I cut south toward the fertilizer drop point—it was a scheduled fertilizer run week. I was about halfway there when I heard something I'd never heard Outside before: harsh and even footsteps, crashing through the brush toward me with a steady cadence.

Another person. Someone running. I slipped off the path and tucked behind a dense copse of scrub, dropping the rabbit carcasses, and setting my foot in the stirrup of my crossbow. The click when I drew it sounded like thunder in my ears, but the oncoming footsteps didn't falter as I nocked a bolt, aimed back toward the trail, and thumbed off the safety.

You a Firewall now, Iris? You going to shoot a person, are you? I clenched my teeth. Only if they tried to shoot first, I decided.

Whoever was coming wasn't concerned about masking their presence. Branches snapped and boots thudded through the soggy undergrowth loudly enough to scatter every animal for kilometers. *Marauders?* But they travelled in groups, and this was obviously only one person, a very winded one from the sounds of it.

I exhaled, set my shoulders, and peered down my sights as the runner closed on the spot on the trail I'd just vacated. *Please, whoever you are, just run on by. Sol, please.*

They did. I only registered the pale flash of their shirt and a stuffed hiking pack on their back as they trotted by, but it was enough. I recognized that shirt. Pale green, and the hiking pack, that faded orange, that was Olivia's grandpa's pack.

"Shit," I whispered, lowering the crossbow and quickly uncocking it. "Oupa?" I had aimed it at him. I'd just aimed my crossbow at the man who'd told me never to aim at anything I didn't intend to shoot. Scooping up the rabbits, I stumbled onto the path, blinking at his retreating back. "Johan?" I called out to him.

He skidded to a stop, whirled, and pinned me in the sights of his own crossbow.

Zuse. I hadn't even seen it. "It's Iris!" I barked, holding my weapon low, and the rabbits high, like white furry flags of surrender. "Oupa, it's me!"

"Iris!" He exhaled, arms sagging, breath rattling out of him explosively. It wasn't until he lowered his crossbow that I saw it wasn't drawn. Of course, it wasn't. Oupa was too smart to run with a loaded weapon.

"What are you doing out here?" I stumbled toward him.

"Oh, Iris." He folded in half, swaying on his feet.

Zuse, was he … crying? "Hey." I unslung my canteen and strode toward him. "Hey, take some water."

"I found you. Thank Sol," he rasped. I scanned his flushed face and shaking hands while he took several loud swallows of water. He looked ready to drop.

"Let's sit down, yeah?" I took him by the forearm and guided him to the side of the trail. He leaned against a tree, sides heaving like bellows.

"I don't need to sit."

Had he *run* all the way here? "What happened? Is Olivia okay?" I asked, chest prickling with anxiety.

"It's not her," Johan puffed, shaking. "She's fine. Look, I need you to listen carefully." He gripped my arm with strong fingers, dark eyes pained but resolute. "I don't know how, but …" he broke off, shaking his head. "Someone's framed you, Iris."

"What?"

"Framed you."

"Framed me? For what?" I couldn't quite grasp Johan's words. This felt like the start of one of those cheesy fiction novels from his shelves.

"They have video footage of you in Greenhouse Five." He gulped. "This morning, time-stamped 3 a.m. You're stealing fertilizer bags."

"W-what? No," I stammered, shaking my head. "No, I was in bed at three in the morning, and I came straight here. What do you mean they have video footage?"

"It looks like you, dressed in dark clothes, black hair braided just like yours, wearing your backpack."

Shit. "I don't *own* any dark clothes, Oupa. And I lost my backpack. I haven't been able to find it in weeks. You know I only take fertilizer from the drop point. You *know* that."

Johan nodded grimly. "I don't think you lost your pack, Iris. This was planned."

Oh, Sol. My knees jellied. Vannevar's words cut through my mind. *Robert's dad hates you, you know that?*

"*This* is fragged. A video, Johan?" My head swam with heat. "They can't convict me on just a video." I swallowed against a sudden dryness in my throat. "Can they?"

The look he gave me was anxious and injured, like Dad's eyes had been years ago right before he'd told me my dog died, or Mom's when she'd read about Nate getting shot. "They have more than the video. The Firewalls found your backpack stuffed behind the chicken coops. Inside, there were two empty fertilizer bags, and several strands of your hair snagged on one of the clasps."

Oh Sol. Vannevar had pulled my hair, hadn't she? When she'd jammed her rifle against the side of my head.

Johan held up his wrist and tapped his wristband. "The only people with clearance into the greenhouses after midnight are Gardeners and Firewalls." He shook his head, frustration pinching his brow. "But *no one* was in Greenhouse Five last night. That's where Luan sleeps. He gets agitated if someone unfamiliar enters his territory. You've seen him. He yowls all morning, and this morning he was calm, Iris. Utterly calm. I double checked the entry logs and there's no record of entry after hours. Whoever framed you didn't do this last night. They planned it. They made their video ahead of time and inserted it into the camera live feed this morning. They masked the fertilizer inventory so that it didn't show a loss until today."

Vannevar had shut off the cameras when she rushed me on

the boardwalk. The Firewalls kept track of fertilizer inventory because it was a critical asset. *Zuse.* Air leaked out of me, and I doubled over, choking on nausea. How long had she and Paul Lycos planned this for? Weeks? Months?

"What am I gonna do?" I wheezed.

Johan pressed away from the tree he'd been leaning on and slid the orange pack off his shoulders, still breathing heavily. "You need to run."

"W-what? No."

"Listen, David won't expel you for this, he'll *sell* you. And I can't protect you. If they find you and bring you back to the city, I can't protect your family, either."

"Sell me?" I gaped. "What the hell does that mean, Oupa? Sell me?"

He shook his head and pressed his pack toward me. "There's no time. I packed everything I could think of. There're extra bolts for the bow in there, and the survival guide too. Keep the rabbits."

"No," I murmured weakly, my brain freezing into a slush of panic. "I didn't steal anything, Johan."

"I know you didn't, but we don't have time. The whole city has started a grid search for you. They've already de-activated your wristband."

I clutched at the silicone band around my wrist. Deactivation, that was as good as a death sentence.

"I sent a pigeon to your uncle's URL group. My fastest bird. They'll know you're coming. Just follow the train tracks west, and they'll find you. It takes about a week to get to their settlement on foot from here."

"Johan?" Tears pooled in my eyes as the enormity of all of this clutched me by the throat. "My family?"

He pulled me into a fierce hug. "Olivia and I will take care of them. I promise," he whispered into my ear and then pulled back, blinking away tears of his own. "You have to go now, Iris.

Stay off the main roads. Keep within sight of the train tracks. They follow the river. And don't light any fires big enough to draw attention."

"I-I can't," I stammered, losing track of Oupa's words as bile burned up my throat and a cold wind surged up the wooded path.

He gripped my shoulder and gave me a firm shake. "You can. You are stronger than you think, my dear." He held up the orange pack, and I set down my bow and the rabbits, trading Olivia's empty pack for Johan's stuffed one. It was heavy, but not as heavy as two fertilizer bags. "How long?"

"Five days. Less if you walk fast," he answered.

"No, how long until I can come back?" I croaked.

"Iris." Johan pinned me with an achingly firm gaze. "You can't come back. Not ever. I'm sorry." Then he reached out and ran a rough thumb over my scarred cheek before turning and trotting back down the path the way he'd come. "Go. Now. I'll try to throw them off your path," he shouted over his shoulder.

I raised an arm to wave at him, but Johan didn't see it. I don't know how long I stood alone on the path after that, swallowing cold air like a beached fish. A crow squawked above me. I jerked. Then I turned west and started trotting away from the only home I'd ever known. It felt like falling through ice and plunging into dark waters.

Johan's words swelled in my head as it started to rain. *You can't come back. Not ever.*

CHAPTER
NINETEEN

The must of mold and wet plaster hung in my nostrils as I quietly loaded my crossbow and crept through the interior of the abandoned bungalow. Avoiding the broken glass littering the matted carpet, I methodically cleared every room except the basement. The stairs looked steep and warped from previous floods. Several steps had caved in, revealing ribbons of termite damage. An uninterrupted layer of dust coated the rest. No one had accessed this basement in a while.

Satisfied that I was alone, I limped back onto the covered front porch, uncocked my bow, and sucked several breaths of fresh air before sitting heavily on the steps. I shrugged out of Johan's hiking pack and shivered. My back was the only warm spot left on me, and I felt exposed with nothing but my soggy jacket between me and the yawning doorway behind me.

My gaze flicked to the crossbow at my thigh. *Stop it.* I clenched my teeth. *You already checked. There's no one there. Reboot, Iris.*

Flipping open the hiking pack, I pulled out the extra pair of socks Johan had packed. I'd already worn them once, wrung them out and rolled them into a spare shirt, but they were still only marginally less damp than the ones on my feet now. Damned rain.

My work boots leaked, not enough to have inconvenienced me on my regular half-day hunting treks, but I'd been walking for *two* Soldamned days in the rain. Right now, I'd sell my own teeth for a dry pair of boots.

Picking at the laces, I eased off my footwear and blinked down at the faint pink stains blooming through both white socks. *Okay, no big deal.* I sniffed. *Three. Two. One.* I peeled back the wet fabric and hissed as white, waterlogged skin sloughed off with it. Before I could lose my nerve, I stripped the other sock off too. "Shit," I whispered. Thick flaps of pasty skin clung to my heels revealing a layer of raw, tender pink beneath. It looked like my feet were melting. *Trench foot.* That's what the survival guide called it.

That's all it took to break me. Two days walking in the rain. Some badass I was. I couldn't look at the tattered soles of my feet anymore, and I couldn't fix the problem, so I did the next best thing. I ignored it, shifting my gaze to the muted horizon far across the valley.

Misty clouds hung shelved halfway up mountains grooved with erosion and ribboned with bands of colored clay. Sage brush peppered the foothills like mint green flocks of sheep. Below that, the river coiled, churning, brown and bloated. The railway tracked beside it, a rusted line of stitches on a fresh rolling landscape marred by scattered ruins like the house behind me. No smoke from any of the chimneys. Good. If I had any neighbors, they weren't arrogant or stupid enough to announce their presence in broad daylight. I just needed one night out of the rain. If I could air out my feet, if the damned sun would come out, I could dry out and pick up the pace.

Johan had said it would take five days, but what if I was going too slow? What if Nate's URL group got the p-mail and just didn't care to pick up some stray city dweller. What if my family was expelled or David was starving them out? Did Johan and Olivia even have enough time to hunt and provide for all the families they needed to feed without me? I'd seen several huge flocks of geese as I fled. If they were migrating further north already, we'd be leaning heavily on the trap lines until fall when we hunted big horn sheep, and I'd taken half of the city's hunting weapons, leaving Johan and Olivia with a single cross-bow. What if that bow broke? Or David confiscated it? What would he do to Johan if he found out he'd helped me escape?

Stop it! I pressed my knuckles against my temples. Sol, I hated the mess of thoughts that swarmed through my head. I didn't have any music to drown them out, and humming as I walked made my throat sore. Last night was the worst. There were no trees to shelter under. I'd huddled in an open field with rain pelting the crinkling fabric of my emergency sleeping bag. My brain wound up so much that any ideas I'd had of sleeping crumbled. I spent a miserable five hours shivering, sobbing, and failing to rein in my spiralling thoughts. I could never go home. I didn't even get to say goodbye to Vinton or Mom and Dad. Or Robert. Robert who wanted an "us."

Stop. Focus on here and now. I needed to air out my feet, but first I needed to eat. It had been too wet to start a fire, but I needed to cook the rabbits before they spoiled. If I was careful, I could start a small fire in the house. Its old walls would shutter the flames from outside view, and with no moon out, the smoke from the chimney wouldn't be as obvious at night. I wouldn't be the first. The living room already bore scorch marks under a pile of half-burned furniture. *Wait for dark. Roast both rabbits. Dry out your feet. Good to go.*

But exhaustion pulled at me. The idea of wrestling socks back onto my swollen feet, shoving them back into my boots and gathering kindling from around the house, paralyzed me. My mind insisted that I focus instead on Vannevar with a gun to my head, Robert with his arms around me, and Johan telling me I was strong. That was a lie. I'd never felt so broken and weak.

Slumping on the steps, I imagined all the ways I could kill Vannevar until the wind picked up and dusk swallowed the view across the valley. Then I eased on my socks and hobbled back into the moldering house. I built my fire away from the broken windows. Briefly, I considered searching the house for anything useful, but this place had likely been looted hundreds of times since the collapse. Besides, my feet burned. I devoured half of one of the rabbits and bagged the rest of the meat—I still had a roll of plastic bags in my jacket pocket that I'd used to contain blighted potato plants in the gardens.

Belly full and meals packed, I propped my bare feet in front of the smoldering fire and lay back against my hiking pack, surrounded by my own drying clothes. I glared up at the blackened ceiling with its burst bubbles of peeling paint. Someone had wedged a headless plastic doll into the crooked chandelier. I stared at its skewed limbs for a long time before slipping into the exhausting current of my thoughts and letting them carry me away.

THE CLOUDS HAD CLEARED by morning. Steam oozed out of the pores of wet earth wherever the sun touched, and the weather-polished mountains glowed with warmth. I followed the turgid river and the overgrown train tracks south for several hours until the banks of the river widened and the remnants of a town broke into view, all crumbling grid work and rows of faded roofs, crowned with a rusted, white water tower.

I'd never seen a town before, other than in pictures. From this distance, if I squinted, it was easy to imagine it as vibrant and crawling with people. Sol, it was sprawled out so much more than our city. Every house boasted massive overgrown yards, and the trees were huge, dotting the crumbled streets in orderly rows like green soldiers. Overhead power lines and tangles of wire were draped everywhere. Abandoned cars rested against weedy curbs, flattened tires melting into the asphalt. I'd never seen a car in real life, either. The Sommer 462 motorcycles Vinton and the Browsers used didn't count. They weren't *real* cars with the capacity to haul a whole family encapsulated in upholstered luxury.

As tempting as it was to take a closer look, there was no way I was following the river through a town. A single bungalow had been anxiety inducing enough. I couldn't even count the number of dark windows peering out at me now. Too many hiding spots and narrow streets. It looked like the perfect spot for marauders to pick off a slow fledgling traveler like me, and it's not like I could outrun them.

Despite airing out my feet last night, they were still waxy, wrinkled, and raw. Putting on boots this morning had felt like stepping into boiling water. I could still walk—what other choice did I have?—but running was out of the question.

I skirted wide around the town, limped up the steep hillside, and followed the wide plateau southward. There was no cover here. I was exposed, but if I had pursuers, at least I'd see them coming. I'd have plenty of time to load my bow. Midmorning, I stopped to slather sunscreen over any exposed skin and don my wide-brimmed hat and goggles. The tube of zinc cream Johan had included was nearly squeezed out. I had enough for two more applications before resorting to covering myself with mud like Nate used to do. *Sasquatch, I'd give anything to have you travelling by my side, right now.*

My feet jarred with every step, but the pain was manageable, and it gave me something to focus on. I counted my steps in my head as I went. It helped keep thoughts about my family at bay. At 18,305 steps, I encountered my first fellow travellers.

I had just crossed a railway bridge when voices echoed ahead, where the tracks curved around a shallow bend. Gripping my crossbow tighter, I skittered down the loose gravel bank beneath the bridge and tucked under the iron trusses. Pressing back against a rusted beam, I held my breath and cocked my head.

Three voices. Maybe more. One of them sounded high and shrill. A woman or a child? By the time they reached the bridge above me, my legs were cramping from crouching too long. The bridge clicked and creaked as something heavy trundled overhead. I peered up through beams streaked with bird-droppings, but only saw shifting shadows. Heavy feet clomped, and the snort of a horse punctuated the thick air.

A supply train. Not marauders. A supply train. Nate's URL group used them to stock our city. After Vinton's devastating fall from the erosion-damaged tracks west of the tunnel, a supply train group had spent months repairing the rails, paid jointly by Nate's URLs and our city. We needed that track. It was an arterial route for moving goods. Our own diesel supply was shipped from the west via a tanker car hauled by a huge team of horses. Just past the tunnel, the supply train hooked hoses to our receiver pipeline, and the city pumped diesel up to the generator reservoir tanks. It happened once a month, except during the winter when the tracks took longer to clear.

As this supply train cleared the bridge, I saw two sweating bay horses hauling a flatbed car stacked with an assortment of crates and plastic wrapped goods. Someone had tacked razor wire around the entire perimeter of the deck except the rear, where two men sat cradling rifles. Another man wearing a bulky vest flanked the horses, and a woman with a machete paced atop the crates, peering down the tracks through a pair of binoculars.

I squinted. Two more people sat crouched amongst the cargo with their arms behind their backs, like they were tied. Their faces looked drawn and tired, and they were dressed differently than the others. *What the hell?*

Before I could contemplate them further, they were over the bridge and gone. Bless Sol, none of them had looked down.

I kept a healthy distance from the tracks after that, staying just close enough to keep them in view. Three more supply trains passed before nightfall. They were smaller, faster units, manned by a single person on a modified diesel handcar fitted with a supply deck. The operators seemed to have specific territories because I saw two of them swapping cargo at a transfer point designated by a tall red post before zipping back the way they came, motors purring. *Like ferrymen over a river of steel.*

The terrain changed over the next few days as I worked my way southwest. Stern mountains towered, jagged and bristling with pine trees. The river carved through a steep ravine, and the railway clung to shelves of rock above it, occasionally crossing the water on high, stilted trestle bridges. In some spots, I didn't have a choice but to walk the rails and pray that if a supply train saw me, they weren't as lethal as they appeared. Whenever I stopped to rest, my feet pounded intensely enough to bring tears to my eyes. I loosened my laces, but didn't dare take off my boots to survey the damage beneath, because I was afraid I wouldn't be able to get them back on again. With the aid of a stout walking stick, I kept hobbling onward, but I didn't find Nate's group on my fifth day of travel. That night, I holed up under the skirt of a huge pine tree, curled my knees to my chest and bawled.

I'd been too slow. I hadn't reached Nate's group, and they weren't even looking for me. What if Johan's pigeon didn't even make it? Sometimes hawks picked them off en-route. The rabbit meat was gone. I didn't stop to hunt, and I'd eaten everything else Johan had packed me. I had messed up my feet so bad, I could barely walk, and I was alone. *No one is coming, Iris. You're going to starve out here.*

I couldn't stop shivering, and when I pressed my hand to my mud-smeared forehead it felt flushed. My feet were infected. I was sure of it. Sol, I'd messed this up, just like everything else I'd ever tackled. My chest squeezed so hard I couldn't breathe and for several hours, I gasped with my heart battering at my ribs and a deep dread licking at my raw nerves. I was certain I wouldn't make it until morning.

But I did. I woke before dawn, stiff and covered in pine needles. My muscles felt like frayed bow strings as I maneuvered to stand. I whimpered as my feet screamed in pain. Mornings were the worst. It felt impossible to take a single step, but I did, because I knew the pain would settle into a numb heat if I could push through it. And if I didn't start walking, I was dead. *Vinton would walk until his feet wore off if he could.* I reminded myself. *He's got more willpower than you'll ever have, Iris. Just keep counting steps.*

On the afternoon of my seventh day, I was shuffling up an incline on the tracks. An elaborate pulley system with long lengths of chain and massive gears was anchored into a thick steel frame at the crest of the hill. I presumed it was used to tow loaded rail cars up the incline, but thankfully, it looked unmanned. I was studying it when a voice called out behind me.

"You lost, little girl?"

My walking stick fell with a clatter as I spun and raised my crossbow. It was loaded. Stupid, I know, but I also knew I couldn't fumble my ragged foot into the stirrup and load it in time to respond to a threat, so lately, whenever I walked the track, I pre-loaded my bow and relied on the safety to keep from skewering myself.

Three men stood on a hand car. I hadn't heard it coming. Why hadn't I heard it coming?

"Whoa there." One of the men raised his hands, but another one raised his rifle while the third grinned in a very unfriendly way. "Jumpy one, aren't we? I was just being a decent citizen, you know? We could have run you over, but we stopped. Gentleman-like, yeah, Gren?" He nodded to the grinning man with the handlebar moustache at his left.

"Yeah, gentleman-like," Gren said and then sucked something out of his teeth.

"Gentlemen don't point guns at ladies," I said. *But marauders do.*

"Don't look like a lady to me," the man with the rifle guffawed but didn't lower his weapon.

"We could give you passage, if you like," the first man said. "Be happy to take that heavy pack and that crossbow off your hands and whisk you off to wherever you want to go. Quick as you please." He patted the electric motor behind him.

Battery powered, that's why I hadn't heard them coming. "I'm good, thanks." I gulped.

"I think we misunderstand each other, miss," the moustached man growled. "That wasn't an offer. More like an order, yeah? Last time I checked a gun's still faster than a bow."

"We could just shoot you," the first man added brightly, removing his cap to wipe sweat from his brow. "Then we could take your pack and weapon without having to make room for a passenger at all."

Shit. I hunched lower and thumbed the safety into the fire position.

"Don't be stupid now!" the armed man barked, flicking his own safety off. But then his gaze shifted over my shoulder, up the hill, and he faltered.

"She's not the one being stupid, Darrin," a new voice boomed from behind me. I flinched and glanced over my shoulder. A bearded man flanked by a large group of people, all bristling with guns, stood on the crest of the hill. "I believe you three are outside of your territory? Mitch, it'd be a real shame if you lost your stretch of track for breaching etiquette and threatening one of my wards."

"S-sorry, Nate. I didn't know," the man named Mitch stammered, swatting the barrel of his comrade's rifle down.

Nate. My mind absorbed it slowly. I turned, straightening even as my throat closed.

"Shit. Is that—is that a bloody crossbow?" The bearded man smiled, skin crinkling around his eyes, mud caking his hair. "That is *badass*, Beetle."

Beetle. My bow wobbled in my grip. "Nate?" My legs sagged, and I managed to thumb down the safety before I crumpled onto the tracks. It was him. There was no mistaking the concern in those blue eyes as he ran toward me.

Sasquatch was alive.

CHAPTER
TWENTY

y reconciliation with Nate was nothing like the long-lost reunions in Johan's novels. There were no crushing hugs, back slaps, or bright smiles. There was, however, a lot of hysterical crying on my part. I remember several people telling me to breathe and shoving canteens of water and chunks of food at my face. They put me on some kind of cart, like I was cargo, but I only remember slivers of the trip to Nate's compound: a kind lady helping me into a warm shower, dressing in clothes that smelled freshly line-dried, and falling asleep in a massive, lumpy bed.

When I woke, my feet were hot, dry, and throbbing. I peered down to see them bare and elevated by a stack of cushions. A knitted wool quilt draped over the rest of me. I was in a bedroom, like the ones I'd seen in the abandoned bungalow—not a bunk, but a whole damned room dedicated to a bed. This room was wide, spacious, and white-washed. The dry *thud* of someone chopping firewood drifted through a propped open window—a real glass window with all its panes intact. My gaze focused on the wooden door framed between my lobster-red feet.

"Nate?" I'd seen him. That had been real, hadn't it? "Nate!" I called again, pressing up to my elbows.

The door creaked open and a wiry woman with a nose piercing looked me over with a tired smile. I recognized her from last night. She'd helped me shower. "Thought I heard you. Hang on," she said. "I'll go track him down. He's been waiting for you to wake up."

She left the door open. The floorboards in the hallway creaked as she retreated through the house and thumped down a set of stairs. I scanned the rest of the room but couldn't see my pack or crossbow anywhere. There was a chipped glass of water on a bedside table and a pink lamp with a torn shade. In the corner, a wicker rocking chair. That was it.

I was still surveying the room in a numb, half-awake daze when something thundered up the stairs. Claws skittered over the hardwood in the hallway, and I braced myself as a large dog nosed open the door and wriggled toward me, whining and quivering. I froze as its cold nose nudged my hand. Its tail thumped a quick tempo against the side of the bed.

"Maisie!" Boots clomped up the stairs. "Maisie, come." Nate filled the doorway, lanky, tall, and effervescent in that raw, boyish way of his, and suddenly I couldn't breathe.

Nate. Alive. And right in front of me.

The dog bounded back toward him and pressed against his side.

"She didn't scare you, did she?"

Maisie breathed an insulted sigh. Her upright ears folded back, and her brown gaze fixed unblinkingly on me even as her tail kept thumping.

"She's a big baby for a German shepherd." Nate chuckled. "And harmless, I promise." He crossed the room in three long strides and eased into the rocking chair. "How's the bed? You get any sleep?"

"It's bigger than my whole house," I croaked.

Nate threw his head back and laughed. "Yeah, you all like your 'compact living' up in the city, don't you?"

His laugh is what broke me. Zuse, I'd forgotten what it sounded like, how it filled up every corner of a room. Tears welled in my eyes, hot and unstoppable.

"Aw, Beetle, honey. Shit," Nate said. "Don't cry. I'm sorry."

Maisie left his side to lean against my bed, licking my hand. I clutched at her black fur, thick and softer than goose down. "No crying, huh? How'd you like me to react then, Nate? I thought you were dead. All of us thought you were. And you just let us think it! All this time. My mom …" Another sob gripped me.

"Hey now." He leaned forward, palms spread. "I didn't mean to hurt anybody. Let me explain—"

"Mom lost it when she got that p-mail," I hissed. "Shot in the chest. Dead on some road. That's what it said. I mean, Zuse! What the hell, Nate?"

"I *was* shot. Look here." He pulled the collar of his shirt down to reveal a puckering scar just below his collarbone. "This one went right through. The other one, I took it right in the chest. That's why we wear our flak vests concealed. Guy would have gone for a head shot otherwise. Shame it would have been to ruin this perfect mug." He smiled again, gently.

"Marauders?" I swiped at my wet cheeks.

Nate's face sobered. He scrubbed at his beard before raising his eyebrows. "That's what *someone* wanted it to look like, yeah."

"W-what?"

He leaned forward and studied my face for a long moment before nodding like he'd decided to share a secret. "I said someone wanted it to look like marauders, Iris, but it was a set up. We were doing a road run. Not our usual turf, but an avalanche blocked the rails, and we were rerouting a big cargo train. Five horses and carts. My people spread pretty thin and me, like an idiot, right out front. We're pushing aside this car blockade when this guy pops up over one of the hoods, and the horse beside me screams and crashes down."

Nate stared down at his hands and then cleared his throat. "I'm thinking the horse kicked me, because, next thing I know, I'm lying on the road, feeling like my chest is caving in, blinking at this poor animal quivering on the pavement beside me. All around there's these little pops, like popcorn in a greased pan. That's when I realize the guy had shot me—he shot the horse too—and we were shooting back.

"I want to tell my people to stop wasting ammunition, because I can see my shooter's feet under the car, and they're facing away from us now. He's just crouching behind his cover, and he's not dumb enough to stick his head up while we're strafing him. Doesn't take long for my crew to figure that out on their own. And as soon as they stop firing, this guy bolts. On foot, we could have had a shot at him, but he's not on foot. He had a motorcycle leaning up against that car. I'm lying there, starving for air, when he fires that thing up and peels away from us. My people must have been shook, because not one of them hit him. They all turned into Storm Troopers." He smiled half-heartedly.

"Storm troopers?" I asked.

"Bad joke. Before your time. Sorry."

"So a marauder shot you." I wriggled my feet and winced at the pain. "I don't see the set up. I don't see why you lied about dying."

Nate scraped the rocking chair closer to the bed. This close, he smelled like freshly dug soil and citronella. My throat ached. Nate had always smelled like Outside. How had I forgotten that smell?

"The motorcycle the guy rode off on," Nate said, "it was a diesel."

Of course, it was. Every internal combustion engine since the collapse was diesel powered. Gasoline had such a short shelf life. Diesel was the only other viable option. "So what?"

"I'd bet my beard it was a Sommer 462."

Like Vinton's bike? I snorted. "Just because it was a diesel? What the hell are you saying, Nate?"

He leaned forward and reached for my hand, but I jerked away and badly disguised the motion by petting Maisie.

"Shit, No. I'm not saying it was your brother, Iris. Jesus!" Nate exhaled and tipped back in the creaking rocking chair. Gazing out the window, he said, "Look, I'm sorry I brought it up. Maybe we'll talk about this another time, yeah?" He stood, and Maisie did too, slipping away from my hand.

No, don't go. You just got back from the dead. "I'm fine," I squeaked. "Uncle Nate, I'm good. Finish your story."

He didn't look like he believed me, so I squared my shoulders and added, "Besides, you haven't even got to the part where you grovel on your knees and beg for forgiveness for not sending a damned p-mail all this time. And don't think that sending your dog in here first to soften me up is going to get you out of it."

Nate snort-laughed and shook his head. "You haven't changed one bit, Beetle. I'm working up to the apology part. Pinky swear." He sat back down and picked at a loose strand of wicker on the arm of his chair.

"The motorcycle," I prompted.

"Before the collapse, there were only one or two manufacturers of diesel motorcycles in the whole world. And I've put on a hell of a lot of miles since then. From the coast, all the way to Alberta. Sixteen years now. As many years as you've been alive." Nate frowned and pinched his lips into a tight line, digging at the chair. His next words were quiet but firm. "And in all that time, the only time I've ever seen a diesel motorcycle, it was between the knees of someone from your city. The man who shot me, Iris. He was wearing a blue combat helmet. Only one place I've seen those too."

I thought of Vannevar with her gun to my head, blonde hair fanning out beneath her blue helmet. "A Firewall? That's ridiculous. Who the hell would wave a flag like that, Nate? Attempted murder with every signpost pointing back to our city? It'd be stupid."

"Or intentional," Nate said. "Somebody wanted my URL group to know who took me out."

"Kahn? He's Corporate, not some cutthroat." I wanted to bite my tongue as soon as I said it. CEO Kahn had let the Firewalls shoot Nora Yates. Johan said he'd *sell* me if he caught me. I remembered his hawkish eyes behind those thin-rimmed glasses. Kahn was as cutthroat as they came.

"Corporate and cutthroat always go hand in hand." My uncle broke off the sliver of wicker and started jabbing it into the armrest. "I—uh. I don't know if Johan ever told you, but my group, we put a bit of a squeeze on David a few years back. Fertilizer was in short supply, and the cost of shipping was through the roof."

"I heard about it," I answered coldly.

"Don't look at me like I'm shit on your shoe, Iris. I gotta eat too. My group's gotta eat. David pays for big ticket items like diesel and fertilizer in proprietary information. Stuff no one outside your city has. Generator maintenance manuals. Water filtration diagrams. Bee-keeping guides. Candle-making. You know what I'm talking about. Thing is, that's a finite resource. I know David signs all his bloody letters 'Knowledge is Power' but you can only sell information once. After it's out there to the masses, it's out there. And it's closing on twenty years since the end of the world, now. Most people have already got all the information they need to survive. What David's selling, it's not so valuable anymore. Not many customers are buying."

I swallowed loudly. "So you figured you'd just starve us out."

Maisie pinned her ears back, big nose sampling the tension in the room.

"Naw, Beetle. David was the one who held out. I told him I needed a fair trade. Information that was still worth something to offset the cost of bringing him diesel and fertilizer. You have any idea how much I pay to hire an eight-horse team for a trip from the coast to your city, Iris? I needed something bigger in return. Hydroelectric power schematics. Instructions on battery construction. And David just won't let any of those big-ticket items go. It's like squeezing water out of a stone."

"He paid when the crops died," I stated bluntly.

"Yeah, he threw us a few bones. But every supply run we dropped off after that, he threatened to eliminate the middle-man. I laughed it off, at first. Figured he was just sore, but you wanna know what he told me the last time I was there? He said, 'Nate, the best way to kill a snake is to cut off its head.' Just random and out of the blue like that."

I shuddered.

"Next thing I know, I'm lying on the road, bleeding out next to a dead horse." Nate leaned forward and lowered his voice conspiratorially. "See, it made sense to him, sending someone to shoot me. David figures he's some indispensable leader, and your whole city would fall apart without him at the head, and he thought my URL group worked the same way. He figured, if he killed me, and my people saw it was him who'd done it, they'd scatter. Then, your city could deal direct with our suppliers on the coast. Cut out the middleman. Cost-saving measures. That's what corporate is all about, yeah?"

"Zuse," I whispered, mind boggling with connections. Some small part of me had still believed that our city was good, that we were examples of civility and protectors of knowledge. But, if what Nate said was true, we were no better than marauders, gunning down people who dared to cross us. Sol, and I had wanted to be a part of it once. A Search Engine. A cog in the corporate machine.

"It didn't work though. Kahn's assassination attempt." Nate straightened, rubbing behind Maisie's ear as she leaned into his leg. "My connections are loyal to my URL group. We have a fair deal going here. Everybody does their job, sticks to their territory, and gets their piece of the pie. And it works. It's taken over a decade to build that trust. And all those rail runners, even the idiots you met, Mitch and his crew, they're still smart enough to see that David would shortchange them any chance he got. They've heard how he runs his house. They've seen how trigger happy his blue helmets are, and they want no part of it. They'd keep trading through my URLs, even if I was dead. As far as David knows, that's what they're doing right now."

"Kahn still thinks you're dead?"

Nate nodded. "And I'm not dumb enough to stick my head up again and invite him to take another shot. David doesn't like loose ends. It's best if he keeps thinking he won. And when your mom sent that note asking if you could come and stay with me, my heart just about broke." Nate swallowed and rubbed his hands against his thighs. "I knew Anne must have been backed against a wall if she was asking for my help, but I couldn't let her know I was alive when her boss figured he'd already taken care of business. I'm sorry, Beetle. You know how insecure pigeon mail is. Anyone can intercept it."

That was a shitty apology, I wanted to say, but instead I said, "We missed you."

Nate sniffed and blinked at the roof before murmuring, "I was hardly ever around anyways, Beetle."

"We still missed you."

Maisie leaned into Nate harder, whining and staring up at him until he patted her head and straightened. "Oh, hey. I almost forgot." He reached into his jacket pocket and pulled out a small, thick book with water-wrinkled pages.

My survival guide.

"We found this in your pack. Everything was soaking wet in there, and your clothes needed a wash. Christie dried it out page by page in front of the fire last night."

I assumed Christie was the woman with the nose-piercing. I wondered what she was to Nate. "Thank you." I took the book and thumbed through its pages. Ink splotched around the edges but, thank Sol, most of it was still readable. I felt like crying again, over a stupid book. Because I'd nearly ruined it. Because it belonged to Johan, and he'd given it to me.

"This is the kind of thing I'm talking about, Iris. This here is worth more than copper." Nate pointed at the book. "Information like this, printed on a large scale. Affordable for the masses. That's what people need, not selling snippets to the highest bidder and charging them through the nose for it. If my hunters had a book like this, maybe they wouldn't be losing half the traps on our lines."

"You're losing traps?" I frowned. "What are you using to anchor them? Because if we use anything shorter than a twenty-inch stake, every animal bigger than a rabbit just pulls it out. Soil is too sandy on most of our lines. You have good dirt here or no?"

Nate chuckled, blue eyes twinkling as he shook his head.

"What?" I snapped.

"Nothing, Beetle," he said. "You're amazing, that's all."

"For reading a book?"

"For knowing shit about trapping in a city full of suits. For crossing the interior alone in the most raggedy-ass boots I've ever seen. And for threatening my rail runners with a crossbow."

"I wasn't the one doing the threatening."

"Nobody messes with my Beetle." Nate grinned. "You teach me how to shoot that bow in a few days?" He waved his hand toward my feet. "After you're all healed up, of course."

I scanned the room again. "Where is my bow?"

"In the front closet downstairs. We figured you wouldn't be doing much target practice from bed, but I can bring it up if you feel more comfortable with it here."

I would, but it felt like asking for a security blanket. "No, that's okay."

"I'm serious though, Iris. I'd love your help on the trap lines, if you wouldn't mind? I have a small crew, and we just started trapping this spring. Took over some lines from an old fellow who used to supply us. He, uh, passed this winter." Nate leaned closer to me. "And I've gotta be honest with you, we've got no idea what we're doing out there, Iris. You and your book would be a Godsend."

"I'd like that." An understatement. How many times as a child had I imagined tagging along with Uncle Nate as he walked through the wilds. Sasquatch and Beetle.

"Good." Nate stood and Maisie did too. "Look at me. I've gone and talked your ear off. I just ..." He flexed his hands and blinked rapidly. "It's just so good to see you, Iris. I-I'd like to give you a hug, but I don't know if you're too old for that shit now, and I don't want to be some sort of creepy uncle."

"I'd like a hug." I held out my arms. "I'll let you know if it gets creepy. Pinky swear."

Uncle Nate folded me into his arms and crushed me in a bear hug. His beard scratched against my scarred cheek, and he smelled like all the best memories of my childhood.

"I'm proud of you, Beetle," he whispered. "And I missed you too. So much. We're going to do big things, you and I."

And my heart swelled in my chest. *Big things.*

CHAPTER
TWENTY-ONE

ain snaked down the window, fat drops smacking against the thick pane like angry bees before migrating into vertical streams. I pressed my forehead against the cool glass and tapped the volume button on the thin music player in my lap until bass thudded in my ears and angsty lyrics filled every hollow in my head.

I didn't know the band.

Christie had given me the MP3 player pre-loaded with music, and I was so thrilled to jam those ear buds in and drown out my frenetic, circling thoughts, I didn't ask questions. Honestly, at that point, two days into being stuck in a bedroom with swollen feet that wouldn't support my weight and a mind that refused to switch into low gear, I would have blissfully listened to someone reading the fine print of a generator maintenance manual on repeat rather than spend another second alone in my head. Speaking of generators, there weren't any here.

As far as I could tell, there wasn't any power at all, not in the main house or in any of the dozens of mobile homes crowding the yard. Kerosene lanterns with curved hurricane shades shone through the windows at night. I kept the MP3 player charged with a hand-crank flashlight with a USB charging port. Five minutes of winding yielded two blessed hours of music and two sore hands. That's how I'd passed the last forty-eight hours as an invalid in Nate's compound, in two-hour increments, broken by five minutes of cranking. Christie brought my meals and Nate brought Maisie.

Both evenings, before dusk, when the URLs ate their supper, Nate's farmhouse swelled with the sounds of boots clomping, silverware clattering, and later people playing card games and clinking glasses. The house was big enough to hold almost *half* of Nate's compound at a time. People shuffled in and out, laughing and prodding at each other like they hadn't spoken in years. The sound of it filtered up through the bedroom floorboards, and Nate apologized every time he came up to check on me, promising that I'd meet everyone soon enough.

I didn't want to meet anyone though. Even if I could walk, I wouldn't want to wade downstairs into that unfamiliar crowd. Their boisterous noise grated my overcharged nerves. I just wanted Nate. And his visits.

He listened more than he spoke, stretching his legs and leaning as far back as the wicker rocker would allow as I pet his dog and babbled on about Johan's humanitarian efforts and Vannevar's spite. I'd never spoken to anyone who listened like Nate did. I'd forgotten that from my childhood, the way he set everything else aside and focused on you completely, like you were the most important person in the world, how he commented and asked pertinent questions in all the right spots. Talking to Nate was effortless, because he made you feel like what you had to say mattered. No wonder people bent over backward to work with him. He was CEO Kahn's polar opposite —even more than Johan—approachable, engaging, and always wearing that self-effacing grin.

I was still blinking at the rain, zoning out on music, when a wet nose nudged my hand, and I jumped. "Maisie. Zuse, you scared me."

The German shepherd licked her lips and pressed her big wedge of a head against my thigh. Behind her, Nate leaned against the doorframe, lips moving, blue eyes bright with amusement.

I plucked my ear buds out. "Sorry. Didn't hear you."

"No wonder." He crossed the room to stand beside me and peer out the window. "You looked worlds away. What were you seeing out there?"

"The window. It looks like it's melting when water runs down it." I traced a finger down the glass, smudging it.

"I keep forgetting. Windows are a bit of a novelty in the city, aren't they? You telling me you've never watched a storm out a window before, Beetle? You worked in a glass house for Christ's sake, didn't you?"

"The greenhouses aren't glass. They're Plexiglass, and they're opaque. Glass is expensive and fragile." I shrugged. "And windows let in sunlight and ruin the faraday effect of metal Seacans. It's practical."

"It's a damn shame, is what it is. David keeps you all caged up in dark closets."

I bristled. I didn't know why. Everything Nate was saying was true, but it felt like he was insulting my home, and I missed everything about that place right now.

Johan had said I could never go back.

"You know what?" I asked. "This feels a lot like a cage too, a bigger one with a window, but a cage all the same."

Nate turned. I felt his gaze on me but couldn't meet it. Instead, I focused on his reflection in the window and how he rubbed his chin when he was uncomfortable, just like Vinton did. "Shit, Beetle," he said, "I don't want you feeling like that in my house. The door's right there. It's not like it's locked or anything. You're welcome to come on down anytime."

I jabbed a finger at my bandaged feet. "I can't walk, Nate! It's been two days and my mind is melting in here with nothing to do. I can't even bloody pace! There's nothing to read except my own survival guide, and I'm wearing out the pages on that. Every time Christie sees me sitting up, she tells me to rest. My biggest adventure is a trip to the fragging bathroom, so yeah, Nate, the window's pretty damned fascinating, okay?" I hadn't meant for it to come out in a bitter pile. Sol, I sounded like a whiny child.

Silence settled miserably between us. Mom would scold me at this point. Dad would tell me to calm down and come talk to him when I was ready. Uncle Nate did neither of those things. He nodded once, slapped the windowsill hard enough that Maisie jumped, and said, "Come on. Let's go."

"Go?" I gaped as he turned toward the door. Maisie's claws scraped on the floor as she bounded to his side. "Where? I-I just told you I can't walk."

"No biggie. Can you butt scoot down the stairs?"

"Can I *what?*"

"Scoot down. On your butt. Look, I'd offer to piggyback you, but that'd plant me firmly in Creepy Uncle territory. Besides, I'm afraid I'd bang the hell out of your feet on the way down. If I help you to the stairs, can you get down them without falling?"

"Yeah, I guess."

Nate grinned and held out his hand. "Well, let's go then, Prisoner Beetle."

Shit. What had I gotten myself into?

With my arm around his neck and Nate supporting most of my weight, I hobbled out of the bedroom on shaking legs, feet throbbing with each step.

He sat me down at the top of the stairs and shooed Maisie away from my face. "Don't tell Christie this," he said. "But I've slid down these stairs on my ass a time or two myself. She makes this mean blueberry moonshine, and she'd cut me off for sure if she ever suspected I got fall-down-the-stairs drunk on the stuff."

"Your secret's safe with me."

"Good. You need me to spot you?"

"I'm not fall-down-the-stairs drunk, Nate. And I'm not a toddler. My feet just hurt."

"Right. You wait for me at the bottom, then. I'll be right back." And before I could protest, he thudded down the stairs with Maisie trotting behind him.

There is no dignified way to butt scoot down the stairs, in case you're wondering. Once I got to the bottom, I couldn't shake the feeling that I didn't belong there, like a kid up past their bedtime, just waiting to get caught.

The front door stood ajar directly before me, painted a cheerful red with a large window overlooking a deep front porch. Moths ricocheted off the kerosene lantern outside. The main floor smelled like varnish and apple crisps. Christie baked like sugar was a limitless commodity. We'd had dessert with supper *every* night since I arrived, and my stomach ached when I thought about my family on their rations of beans. Were they still eating? Was Johan protecting them like he said he would? A clock ticked around the corner. Deeper in the house, floorboards creaked.

I swallowed the irrational fear that Christie was going to come scold me. The woman was short and soft spoken despite her hard features, but she exuded the sort of comfortable confidence of a woman you didn't cross. How in the hell would I explain to her that Nate had told me to butt scoot down the stairs and wait for him there?

My uncle bounded onto the front porch and pressed through the door, rain slicking his hair. "You ready?" he asked breathlessly.

"For what? We're going outside? It's raining." I shouldn't have complained. I should have kept my damned mouth shut.

"Here." Nate rummaged through the front closet and pulled out an umbrella. "Storm's almost spent. We'll be fine with this."

"Nate, I can't walk."

"I know." He held out his hand again, that crooked grin bunching his cheeks. "Just a few more steps, promise."

I took his hand and leaned into him. We were already shuffling through the front door when Christie rounded the corner.

"What in the hell are you two doing?"

"Prison break," Nate said. "Can't talk now."

"It's raining. Jesus, Nate."

"We've got an umbrella. And our chariot awaits."

Christie shook her head and snorted. "I'll make some tea for when you come back."

The chariot was a wheelbarrow with a plaid wool blanket and a throw cushion. I giggled at the absurdity of it as Nate set me inside and propped my feet up with the pillow. "Hold the umbrella. I'll give you the grand tour. Place always looks best right after a rain."

Nate pushed me around the yard pointing out their pigeon loft, goat pens, and beehives. He swung wide around a long row of semi-truck trailers he said they used for storage and carted me out to the gardens.

I gasped. Sol Almighty. These gardens were massive. They made Johan's operation look like child's play. How did he water and fertilize them all? I drew deep breaths of rain and lilacs as clouds churned above us and vast orderly rows of potatoes, cabbage, and beans shuddered in the soft breeze. A windmill stood like a sentinel at the center of the plot, flanked by a huge water tank. "Holy shit, Nate," I breathed.

"I saved the best for last." He set the wheelbarrow down and stood beside me, staring out at the endless rows of varying green. "I figured you'd appreciate them more if you could see them."

"This is huge. Sol, how many Gardeners do you have?"

"We don't really pin people into roles here. We have our specialties, but everyone takes shifts taking care of the essentials. If one of us learns something new, we teach everyone else. I can't let people leave a hole behind when they go. I told you about how that's biting us with the trap lines. All that information in one man's head and when he died, it was just gone. My people can't afford to lose knowledge like that." He shrugged. "In this world, we've got to be Jacks of all trades."

"And masters of none."

Nate kneeled down to inspect a cabbage head. "Look, Iris, I know your city is a big believer in specialization, but we're hand-to-mouth out here. We don't have a big ole library full of texts to study at our leisure or pass on to our kids. We've only got what we can scrounge and whatever information David figures is dispensable enough to sell off, and that's getting pretty thin."

Hand-to-mouth? Dessert every night was living hand-to-mouth? I fidgeted with the tassels on the wool blanket but kept my mouth shut.

"I've been working on something that's going to change all that, and I've been dying to show it to you." He peeled an inner leaf from the cabbage plant, stuffed it in his mouth and crunched on it. "You notice anything different about this garden?" He spoke as he chewed.

I scanned the spikes of green onions, clouds of orange marigolds, purple bobbing chive flowers and tripod bean poles. Hills of well-spaced potato plants fanned out into the distance. "It's bigger than anything I've ever seen. Your potatoes aren't flowering yet."

Nate smiled, took a stick that Maisie was jabbing against his leg and waited for her to sit before hurling it back toward the yard. "What if I told you, these were test plots?"

"Test plots? What are you testing?"

Nate leaned toward me, eyes twinkling. "I brought you some seeds from this garden."

"The snap peas," I breathed.

"They grew, didn't they?" He urged. "With nothing but dirt and water. *Without* supplemental fertilizer."

My throat went dry, and my hands started tingling. "You grew all this without fertilizer?"

Nate nodded. "We've been shipping up different strains of seeds from down south for years. It's taken us ages to fine tune it all, but this season, we finally cracked it. Nothing died. We can grow anything we want."

"Outside. Without fertilizer?" I gripped at the sharp sides of the wheelbarrow. "Oh my Sol, Nate. This is meg. This is gigabyte."

"You think David Kahn might want a piece of this?" He smiled slyly.

My stomach dropped. "You can't hold this over someone's head, Nate. This could save lives! It's not some bargaining chip."

He straightened, face sobering, and blue eyes more intense than I'd ever seen them. "Everything's a bargaining chip in this world, Beetle. Nothing comes free. You know that. And this will save lives. I can't afford to ship your city diesel if David doesn't give me some solid information to sell. He can't power his city without me shipping him fuel or feed his people without my fertilizer. There's a simple solution to all of it, and it works for everyone."

"He's not going to sell you all his proprietary information. He won't have anything left if he does."

"It's about time his little bubble burst." Nate snorted. "How long does he think he can shortchange his trade partners or shoot them dead on the road? I'm not the bad guy here, Iris. I'm willing to offer him a fair trade. My URLs and I will sell him our fertilizer-free seed stock. Hell, we'll come and plant his gardens for him, if he wants, but I want full city citizenship for all my people. None of that cred system bullshit, either. That'd have to go. I want access to his library, and I want to start printing books so that anyone who wants to buy information—for a fair price—they'll come buy it from us."

"You want to buy your way into the city?" I asked.

"I want us to work together, Iris." His voice cracked. "I don't want to die for my job or fight over scraps. I want to be one big family again. And I'm willing to feed your whole city to do it."

Nate wanted to feed people, like Johan, but on a massive scale. "What have you been waiting for?" I choked.

"A way in, Iris. Enough of your people have got to want to change how they run their business. Enough of them have got to be sick of Kahn and his cronies lapping up cream while they only get water. And they won't listen to some stranger from the outside who's supposed to be dead. They won't believe we've got gardens like this if they haven't seen it. I've been waiting for you, Beetle. I need your help."

No, you don't, Nate. This is too big, and I hurt everyone I try to help.

CHAPTER
TWENTY-TWO

You been handling these bare-handed?" I squatted on the trail and pointed at the half-concealed steel snare. "Because most animals can smell it if you have, and if I can pick it out on the trail, you haven't hidden it well enough." I pointed to a branch that had been obviously dragged across the path. "Look at that. It doesn't look natural. They'll just go around it if it doesn't look right."

Nate hunkered down beside me cradling his shotgun across his lap. "Gloves then. I'll make sure my people are wearing gloves. Anything else?"

"You can't let any of the metal ones rust. Wash them in lye, grease them, and make sure your trappers are wearing buckskin gloves or some other natural fibre. Nothing manmade. Anchor them deep and you should be set, so long as someone is checking them often enough. You don't want anything suffering, and you don't want predators stealing your catches either."

"You're a godsend, Iris." Nate stood.

I shook my head and adjusted my crossbow on my shoulder. "I didn't know any of this a year ago, either. Johan and his book taught me. It's no big deal."

"It is to us. I won't forget this."

"Teach me how to shoot your gun, and we'll call it even."

"Deal." Nate tossed his head and laughed. "Let's trade. I've been dying to get my hands on that crossbow. There's a clearing up ahead. We can fire a few shots there."

Nate thoughtfully kept the pace slow. It had been ten days since I arrived, and I could walk, but my feet were still tender. Christie had gifted me a pair of boots that actually fit. They were felt lined and supportive, utterly unlike the work boots I'd worn on my escape from home. It was good to be Outside and mobile again.

We stopped to drink at a stream where the water ran cold enough to make my teeth ache. The trail dipped, and ponderosa pines opened into a meadow backing onto the boulder-strewn base of a mountain. A wren's bright trill burbled from the top of a standing dead tree.

Nate walked me through the steps of firing his shotgun. We plugged our ears with wads of cotton. It kicked more than the crossbow did, but if I hugged the stock into my shoulder, the recoil wasn't as bad as I expected. I showed Nate how to cock the bow free-hand and with the rope puller, and afterward we wandered around the meadow together gathering up the bolts he'd fired, our feet raising swarms of mosquitoes from the fescue grass. We whooped and slapped each other's arms. It was just how I'd imagined adventures with Nate would be as a little girl.

When we arrived back at the compound, Nate returned the shotgun to his armory, a root cellar with a thick wooden door dug into the hill behind the main house. It contained a few dozen shotguns and a workbench stacked with ammunition boxes and shot shell hand-loading equipment.

"We home load all our own cartridges. It's more economical." Nate patted the thick wooden bench proudly. "You wanna store your bow in here? I keep it padlocked." He pulled a small key threaded on a chain from below the collar of his T-shirt.

"I'd rather keep it in the house with me, thanks." I don't know why, but I clutched the bow tighter, like I thought Nate was going to snatch it out of my hands or something.

"No worries." He waved me off. "Christie wanted me to ask. She's, uh, uncomfortable with it in the front closet, but I keep my .22 in there in case of midnight fox runs on the hen house. She got used to that. She'll get used to the bow too. I'll find her another spot for her umbrellas." He winked and ushered me out of the cool cellar and back into the bright, trimmed backyard.

"So, You and Christie …" I cradled the crossbow over my shoulder and side-eyed Nate. "You some sort of item, then?"

He blushed. "Some sort, yeah."

"Should I start calling her Auntie Christie?"

"Hell no." Nate made a choking noise. "She'd throat punch anyone who called her that. We're … companions."

"Kids? Gonna start firing out some little cousins for me?"

"Jesus, Mary, and Joseph. No, Beetle." Nate coughed. "Definitely no kids."

"Why not?" I focused on someone trotting across the lawn toward Nate. One of the group who'd brought me in, but I didn't know her name. "You always seemed good with us, Vinton and I, I mean. You seem like a natural." I'd never seen Nate's cheeks so red.

"I, uh, I can't have kids, Beetle. Never could. Not even before the collapse." He reached over and tugged on my braid, as he'd done so many times when I was a stubborn girl with scraped knees. Before I could apologize, he turned to face the woman approaching us. "You got news, Alice?"

The woman puffed to a stop, wiping wisps of damp gray hair from her sweating temples. "Nate. Shit. Where have you been? It came this morning. From Pigeon King." She thrust a thin, curled ribbon of paper at Nate, and he took it, scanning the tiny print.

"Thanks," he murmured.

"Yep." She saluted with a crooked grin and turned to go.

"Hey, anyone else read this yet?"

"Nope, just me in the loft today, Nate. You know how much I love the smell of pigeon shit."

"Let's keep this between us for now, yeah?"

She waved dismissively over her shoulder. "What happens in the loft stays in the loft."

"Pigeon King?" I glanced over Nate's shoulder, but he held the p-mail close to his chest.

"It's Johan's code name. I messaged him when you got here. Told him his package arrived so he'd know you were safe."

"Johan knows you're alive?" I squeaked.

"What? No, you're the only one who knows, Iris. He thinks he's messaging my group, and he's usually a prompt responder. I figured maybe something got at his pigeon, so I sent him a duplicate, just to be sure." Nate sighed, scrubbed his beard and strode toward the house. "Let's go inside, yeah?"

"Okay." My breath tangled in my chest. I sucked in several shallow inhales before stumbling after my uncle and asking the question burning up my throat. "Is he okay?"

"He is," Nate answered shortly. "For now, he is."

"What the hell is that supposed to mean?" I hurried across the lawn with my feet burning and my chest stiff.

"In the house, Iris."

I followed him into the kitchen without stopping to take off my boots. Christie straightened from a huge bowl of dough she was kneading. Her gaze flitted to the paper my uncle held, and she slapped her floured hands against her jeans. "It came."

"Yeah." Nate grumbled.

"What came?" I barked. "Zuse, you're both scaring me."

"Sit." Christie waved us toward the kitchen table. "I'll pour you both some tea." She pinned me with a hard glance. "Jesus, Iris. Could you put the crossbow away first?"

I'd forgotten I was holding it. Heat flushed my cheeks as I stomped back toward the front of the house. By the time I stowed the bow in the front closet, Nate and Christie were already both clutching steaming teacups and bending over the p-mail.

I pulled a chair out without lifting it, letting it squeal loudly across the floor before sitting.

Christie's thin face bunched into a frown as she passed me a chipped cup of tea, but Nate just pushed the ribbon of paper toward me. "Read it."

Something squeezed deep in my chest as I recognized Johan's immaculate printing.

> Ell was tracking package and found Frances
>> Burnett. He confiscated everything. A few blue
>> helmets on our side. We've taken greenhouses.
>> Ell has Bank and Cache. Abort foxtrot drop.
>> Send rations and weapons instead? Will pay in
>> black tea and surplus foxtrot.
> P.K.

"What is this?" I tugged at my braid. "Who's Frances Burnett?"

"It's code, Iris," Nate answered. "Frances Burnett was an author centuries ago. Wrote a book called *The Secret Garden*. Johan's telling us that Kahn found his gardens."

I scanned the p-mail again, stomach plunging. "And Ell?"

"Elliot. Elliot Marple. That's what David's name was before he changed it. Before the collapse. Looks like Kahn's search parties were scouting for you after you took off, and they found the gardens instead." He snorted. "Of course, the greedy bastard would want to get his fingers in that pie. He doles every crumb of food through that warehouse of yours, doesn't he? God forbid anyone eat without paying him first."

"Food Bank." I nodded, fingers trembling. "Ell has Bank and Cache. David's taken Food Bank? What's that mean?"

Nate leaned toward me, his voice low and careful, like I was a cracked glass already leaking water. "It means he's trying to starve some of your people out. I'm assuming all those ones that Johan's been feeding from the gardens. Looks like some of your security guards are on Johan's side and helped him take over the greenhouses, and, from the looks of it, the pigeon loft too. He's asking my URLs to send him food and weapons. He wants us to supply him via our fertilizer side drop. Looks like he's setting up for an uprising."

"A protest?" Christie frowned.

Nate pinched his lips together before speaking. "Don't need weapons for a protest. This is going to be something bigger, I'm afraid."

"Like some sort of civil war?" I rasped.

"Yeah, Beetle," Nate wiped a hand down his face. "Like some sort of civil war."

I didn't realize I'd stood until the chair clattered back behind me. The table jiggled and tea sloshed from our cups. I turned and left the kitchen with cotton filling my head and saliva flooding my mouth.

"Iris!" Nate called.

"Give her a minute," Christie's low voice ordered.

I stumbled up the stairs and sagged onto my bed with my boots still on. Thoughts clotted in my head, pressing against the backs of my eyes. Johan and Olivia were barricaded in the greenhouses. My family would be among those being starved out, and they couldn't run. I'd left them trapped there with Vinton and his chair.

"Oh Sol, no," I gagged.

Rioting in my city. Johan asking for rations and guns. All

because Kahn had found the gardens. And he wouldn't have been out there if he hadn't been searching for me. I'd fragged it all up, again. Everything I touched. Everything.

NATE DIDN'T COME up until the light outside my window had softened to dusk and numbness settled into my chest like clotted cobwebs.

He tapped the doorframe with one knuckle. "Mind if I come sit?"

I didn't answer, but I sat up.

He eased into the rocking chair with a deep sigh before pulling a silver flask from his pocket, uncapping it and swallowing twice. Wincing, he offered it to me. "I think this calls for something stronger than tea, Beetle."

I accepted the flask, wiped the rim, and took a careful sip. Bitterness smoldered down my throat and bloomed in my hollow chest. Even as my eyes watered, I took a second sip and this time, after the burning, I picked up the mellow aftertaste of blueberries.

"Nate," I croaked, "you have to get my family out before the fighting starts."

He sniffed and blinked at the ceiling, running his tongue over his teeth before answering. "Honey, you know I'd love to do that, but it isn't as easy as all—"

"Yes, it is!" I jammed the flask back toward him, heedless of the liquid sloshing over my hand. "You said your people are loyal to you. Those rail runners were going to hurt me, but when you showed up, they changed their programming real quick, didn't they? You can make them go pick up my family and bring them here. It'd take no time at all on the rails, Nate. You could send a bird, and you could get them out. They could stay here where it's safe until it's all over."

"Those people listen to me because they get paid, Iris. They take a percentage cut of the cargo they deliver. That's how it works. And it doesn't work with human cargo."

"I saw people, Nate! On a cargo train on my way here," I pressed. "They weren't runners. They were passengers."

"Were they tied?" Nate's blue gaze pinned me.

"What?"

"I said, were they tied? They look happy to you when you saw them, Iris?"

"What the hell is that supposed to mean?"

Nate steepled his fingers and exhaled. "Let me put it another way. Did Johan pay you to be his gardener?"

"What?" My mind reeled at the change in subject. "No. I had too much debt. I told you, I'm red-lined for life."

"Did you get a choice to work for him? Could you have quit your unpaid job any time you wanted?"

"Of course not. Kahn would have expelled me. I was an indentured worker. What are you saying Nate?"

"I'm saying there's plenty of *indentured workers* out here, Iris. I'm saying that passengers pay to ride, and they've got to pay every rail rider along the way too. It's bloody expensive to ride the rails. Those weren't people you saw. They were cargo, Iris. Someone bought them. Someone paid those runners to move them."

"Zuse, Nate!" I gaped at him in horror. Johan said Kahn would sell me. "You run slaves?"

Nate shook his head emphatically. "No, I don't. I do *not* deal in that sort of thing, Iris. But my rail runners are free to pick up side jobs from anyone they want, and you've already seen that some of them don't have the greatest moral compasses."

"Understatement," I mumbled.

"Look, the point here is, if I don't pay my runners, they don't move goods for me. Simple as that. If I'm going to spend goods shipping guns and rations to Johan, I don't have anything valuable left to trade to my runners to bring back extras, understand? And I'm gonna go ahead and assume that your family doesn't have much in the way of liquid assets right now?"

I licked my lips. "They could steal something to trade."

"Really?" Nate drawled. "Civil unrest in your city, and you don't think Kahn's locked up every valuable asset he's got. Your folks still have access to his system?"

"No," I deflated. "Kahn already locked them out of our system once. If he's starving out people, my family would be among those whose wristbands are locked. He'll punish them because I ran."

"What about yours?" Nate pointed at my arm.

I twisted the silicone band around my wrist. I hadn't taken it off since I got here. Like the crossbow and Johan's survival guide, it was a relic of my home, and I felt naked without it. "It's useless. They deactivated it."

"Not useless." Nate's eyes flashed in the gathering dark. "Not to Kahn. I bet he'd love to get a whiff of where his fugitive Beetle has run off to. He tried to assassinate me over fertilizer, Iris. One thing I know about David: He doesn't like losing. And he lost you."

Nate was right. Kahn made a public example of me just for cracking solar panels. He lost me to Johan then Vannevar set me up as a thief. If David thought I stole from him after he'd dismissed me, he wouldn't lose the chance to make an example out of me a second time. Capture me. Sell me into slavery. Probably my family too.

My jaw tightened. "A-are you suggesting turning me in?"

"Nah, Beetle." Nate took another swig from the flask. "I'm suggesting using you as bait. That bracelet of yours is valuable because the chip in it has your ID on it, yeah?"'

I nodded.

"We send it back to Kahn, he'll be chomping at the bit to find you. We'll just make sure we send it with some terms."

"Won't work." I sagged. "He'd demand payment first. He'd want me before he lets my family go, and once he has me, he won't keep his end of the bargain."

"Well then we'll make sure the terms are *extra* persuasive." My uncle's emphasis on the word made me look up from my lap. He was still clutching the flask in one hand, but now he held up a small wedge of dark plastic in the other.

"What's that?" I squinted.

"I believe it's an external flash drive, Beetle."

"I *know* what a fragging USB stick is, Nate," I snapped. "What's on it?"

He turned it end over end in his fingers. "A virus. A real pretty one, Iris. I paid through the teeth to get this. Some whiz out west designed it for me to wipe out a very specific sort of programming. Something like, oh, I don't know, David's food cred accounting software? But he's not stupid enough to plug in some random USB into his precious network now, is he?" Nate raised his eyebrows and fixed me with a stare I recognized from my youth. *Figure it out. Wind up that big brain of yours, Beetle.*

"Unless ..." I licked my lips. "Unless it was giftwrapped in something he wanted, something that would throw him enough to curb his better judgement. You don't want to use me as bait. You want to use me as a Trojan horse."

"Bingo." Nate leaned back in the rocking chair with a grin. "Sounds like a heck of a deal, doesn't it? I get your family out of Dodge, they stay here 'til the civil war simmers down, and all it costs you is the chip out of your bracelet. Soon as Kahn scans it and knows it's you, he'll be falling over himself to read the *terms* we've listed on this stick. And we wipe the slate clean for every citizen in your city. What do you think your people will do if they see a big fat zero on their cred balances?"

"They'll all turn on Kahn," I blurted. "They'll think it was him, that he's trying to starve out the whole city."

Nate took another long swallow from his flask and wiped his mouth. "That'd sure give Johan a leg up now, wouldn't it?"

Thoughts flailed through my head. "You just said you couldn't afford to bring my family back here, and now you're telling me it will only cost me my wristband? Which one is it, Nate?"

He leaned forward, alcohol on his breath, but blue eyes sober and cold. I'd never seen this side of him before. It was like a switch had flipped and rerouted the warmth that usually filled my uncle to the brim. "David tried to kill me. He'll do it again. He'll find out I'm alive, and he'll be as hungry to finish me as he is you. I want to join your city, but not with Kahn in it. If Johan's raising a fuss, now is the perfect time to take David out.

"Now, I can't afford to bring your family here, Beetle. Hell, let's be honest, I can't even afford to ship Johan guns, but I can call in some huge favors that I'll have to repay later. And I can't repay them, unless I have something to trade down the road. I need access to Kahn's library. I want tradable information and the safety of a city for me and my URLs. You want your family safe and then you want to go home. A home where someone like Johan is running things, instead of Kahn, sounds like a pretty sweet deal now, doesn't it?"

Nate back home with us. Hunting and growing food without hiding it. No more creds or Firewalls or Shareholders or David. Johan teaching everyone to provide for themselves from the wilderness. It did sound like a sweet deal. I wanted to say so, but instead, I held myself still, hands clutching my knees, afraid that even the slightest nod would tie me to a deal I hadn't seen all the angles of.

"You don't have to decide right now, Iris," Nate murmured. "It's a hell of a lot to take in, I know. How about I let it sit with you for a day or two. I'll source some weapons for Johan, and he can pay me in black tea and birds. We can send a pigeon with your chip and the USB stick any time after that. Sleep on it, yeah? That sound reasonable?"

It did. I nodded slowly. Soldamnit, it sounded perfectly reasonable, but my gut still ached with doubt long after Nate left the room. Sasquatch and Beetle against the corporate world. It seemed impossible.

CHAPTER
TWENTY-THREE

I didn't sleep well that night. By the time an ashen dawn eased over the horizon, my room reeked of stale breath and my stomach felt like it had been stewed in its own acid. I wanted to stay in bed and wrap numbness around me, but my mind was a prickling ball of raw nerve endings. I needed to eat more than I needed to avoid Nate and Christie, so I dressed, skulked down the stairs, and warily entered the kitchen.

"You look as high-strung as a racehorse." Christie smiled crookedly over her teacup. Peeled eggshells littered the blue china plate in front of her. "Come. Sit. He's already gone down the line this morning, working on procuring munitions for your Johan. I'll get you some tea. Ginger?"

"Ginger is good." I swallowed against the sourness in my throat.

"Toast and eggs?" Christie reached up into a tall cupboard for a mug, and I marvelled at how tiny she was, slight like a child. She baked and cooked decadent food all day, but only ever ate in small bites. I hadn't seen her fill her plate or her belly yet. She was nothing but cobwebby white-blonde hair and bird bones, but she'd built a firewall of no-nonsense practicality around herself so formidable, it masked her diminutive stature.

"Just toast, please." I sat at the table. My hands felt spidery and restless, so I grabbed a folded cotton napkin from the stack at the center of the table and picked at its elaborate edges. White embroidered geese with bright orange feet patrolled around the yellow fabric square. Nothing like the geese we had at the lake.

Christie lit the burner under a black cast iron pan and plopped a pat of butter in before sawing off two thick rounds of cornbread from the loaf on the cooling rack. "I've got to work in the gardens today," she said. "You should come with me. Nothing better than fresh air and murdering weeds to soothe the savage mind, yeah?"

"Sure." I smiled faintly.

"And stop being so damned agreeable. I'm not going to bloody bite you. I might slap you though, if you don't stop tearing apart my mother's good napkins."

"Sorry." I pushed the crumpled yellow fabric away from me, cheeks warming.

She laid the bread slices into the sizzling pan and glanced over her shoulder, pale eyebrows raised. "You navigated the interior as a fugitive with a crossbow over your shoulder and your feet shredded to ribbons. That takes tough. No call for ceremony or maidenly manners here. This isn't the damned city."

"Okay."

Christie snorted, shook her head, and poured me a cup of tea. Once both sides of the bread were browned, she plucked them from the pan and slathered them with butter and Saskatoon berry jam.

I was several mouthfuls into the sweet stickiness with crumbs on my cheeks when she plopped into the chair across from me and demanded, "Well?"

Well what? My mind revved as I chewed, trying to ascertain what Christie was asking.

She studied me, eyes dark and reserved, fingers toying with the simple gold stud in her nose. When I didn't answer, she leaned forward, braced her elbows on the table and said, "Well, let's be straight with each other. Tell me one damned thing that's rolling around in that mind up there without filtering it."

I chewed slowly. "The bread's a bit dry." Crumbs sprayed from my mouth. "And the tea is weak."

Laughter exploded out of her small frame, shrill and unrestrained. She slapped the table and leaned back, jabbing a finger toward my chest. "Better! We'll make a country girl out of you yet."

I helped clear and wash the dishes. Christie and I dressed in long-sleeved cotton over-shirts, wide-brimmed hats, and dark goggles; and headed to the gardens. She showed me how to use a single wheel cultivator to clear the space between the double-row carrots, and then followed me with a stirrup hoe, scraping away clumps of weed seedlings in between plants.

The cultivator with its curved wooden handles polished by countless hands felt good in my grasp. "How long have you known Nate?" I asked.

"Known him or known *of* him?" Christie straightened, pushing her goggles up her nose and leaving a ridiculous smear of dirt behind. "The man's like a living legend around these parts."

"Sasquatch." I grinned.

"He told me you called him that." She shook a clod of dirt off the hoe.

"When I was a kid, I thought he looked just like one. That great big beard, caked in mud. The way he walked. He used to tell me he had to beat women off with a stick."

"Wouldn't he like to think so!" Christie huffed. "Five years, going on six now. That's how long I've known your uncle, and—

God as my witness—there's been no swarms of girls to fend off yet. He's lucky *I* put up with him."

We worked in silence for half a row length. The morning sun on my back poured warmth into every tight muscle between my shoulders. Fat earthworms gleamed between my feet as I peeled back neat strips of fresh soil and turned under feathery weeds. The scrape of metal combed out my tangled thoughts and calmed my jittery legs.

It could be like this in the city if Johan and Nate ruled instead of Kahn. People that weren't Shareholders could have a real chance at life, their own gardens, learn skills that applied to the world as it was now. But Zuse, why did it have to take violence to get there? Was my family getting shot at right now? Were people dying?

I couldn't stand to think about it, so I blurted, "How did you two meet? You from around here?"

Christie grunted and bent down to yank out a long taproot by hand. "Ain't no one from around here except Nate. He told me this land was the only place he could afford, back in the day. Because it was close to the railway, they sold it to him cheap. Guess it's kind of worth its weight in copper now. Funny how the collapse changed things. No, I'm from the island. All of us pre-collapse folks got pushed out five years back when Victoria flooded and a shipping company armed a vigilante gang to shake up all us acreage owners on the outskirts." She shrugged. "Mainland has a bit more elbow room anyways. I met Nate on the road. I was a horse tender for a caravan, and he was trading grain for 'a nice reliable ride' as he called it." Christie's teeth flashed in a rare, sly smile. "I told him I was a nice reliable ride, *and* I came with a horse. He laughed that laugh of his—you know the one—and something about those blue eyes just called to me." She sniffed and waved a hand around the gardens and the dozens of cobbled together mobile homes surrounding them. "And here we are."

"You traded yourself for a bag of grain?" I squinted at her.

"I traded my horse. Just so happens the animal and I were a package deal."

"You still have him? The horse, I mean?" I leaned into the cultivator as it snagged on a thick snarl of root.

"No, I don't." Christie's voice cracked. "Nate told you about how he got shot, yeah?"

I nodded.

"He told you about the horse?"

I remembered Nate recounting Kahn's ambush, how the horse had collapsed, kicking and screaming, and how long it took for him to realize it'd been shot and so had he. "Shit," I said. "I'm sorry."

She pinched her lips, nodded, and jammed the stirrup hoe back and forth, uprooting a few, spindly, purple carrots along with the weeds. "His name was Theo. He had human eyes, you know? I sold my acreage to ship him over from the island with me. That damned horse was the longest relationship I ever had in my life. Twelve years Theo and I were together. You get attached." The tendons in her neck stood out as she stabbed at the soil between her feet. "So, it's not just Nate who has a bone to pick with David Kahn. There's a lot of us tired of corporate jackasses with guns trying to push us out of the picture. It's always some middle-aged white douchebag with a suit and a smile like a snake's, you know? That's going to change. You can help change it, Iris."

"Shit," I said, standing straight with Christie's words fading in my ears as I stared at the row of potatoes we'd worked our way toward.

"Are you even listening?" Christie said.

"Look at that." I pointed, my mouth drying. "You know what that is?"

Near the end of one row of potatoes, dark brown blotches, like paint stains marred several of the plants' leaves. I leaned closer with my breath held. *Potato blight.* Swallowing, I backed away, searching for signs of spread to other hills.

"What?" Christie asked.

"Late blight. A lot of it. It's a fungus, and once it infects one plant, it'll travel for miles on wind or in water. It'll kill every potato and tomato in this place for years. It overwinters in tubers that don't get dug up." I scanned the potato field before me. The sheer size of it. "Shit, Christie, this is bad. You have any plastic bags? We need all your gardeners over here. We need to dig these plants up, seal them, and burn them; or this'll spread fast." I swallowed. This late in the season; it was nearly unstoppable. "We need to scan every leaf on every plant in this field."

Christie, me, and three other people on gardener duty combed the potato fields and the tomato rows until noon. Sweating and sunburned, we carted six bags of infected plants to the garbage pit for burning. After a tense, silent lunch, Christie and I re-applied our sunscreen and went back to cultivating, even though I was tired and didn't want to work anymore. I couldn't stop moving. Every time I did, I thought of my city and rioting and people getting shot. That would happen whether I helped Nate or not. It would be worse if I helped. If that virus red-lined everyone, I'd be the catalyst that made the fighting escalate.

"Nate said you were a good kid," Christie said, reading my thoughts in my posture. "Shit, you saved our bacon today out there, Iris. And I know you'll do the right thing when Nate asks you." She was smiling, but her words raised an irrational, instant anger in me.

I didn't answer her. Instead, I gripped the cultivator handles tighter as we moved toward the onion rows. *I'm not a damned horse, Christie. Don't you dare try to lead me.* I wanted to say it, to be as brash and unapologetic as she was, but the sun was thickening my blood into sap. I didn't have the energy for fiery words. Particles of dirt crunched between my teeth as I clenched them. Sweat ran down my back and itched between my breasts. I laid into the cultivator until its metal wheel squeaked, and I pushed ahead of Christie, waiting for her to yell or press her side of the argument.

But she did neither. She kept placidly prodding at weeds while I stewed.

"Nate doesn't even own a Soldamned computer! None of you do," I finally blurted, letting go of the cultivator and swinging back to her. "He wants me to help him insert a virus into Kahn's system, and he doesn't even know what's on that flash drive, does he? What if he got shafted, huh? What if some guy in a suit with a slimy smile just sold him a snake oil USB stick, and we send it to Kahn using me as bait, and it does nothing but tell him exactly where I'm hiding?" I flapped my hands and hated myself for it. *Frag, Iris. Grow up and articulate.* "What if Kahn comes down the rails and shoots my family while they're on their way to me? Huh? Have you guys thought about any of this stuff? Like really thought about it?"

Christie nodded slowly and let out a long exhale through her nose. "I see." She smacked her lips. "When you said you called him Sasquatch, I didn't really think you literally thought of your uncle as some sort of half-witted primate."

"I didn't say that," I snapped.

"Well, your tone bloody well did." She stabbed a dirty finger at me. "Look. Just because we don't talk like your elite city snobs, just because we didn't know what goddamned potato blight was, doesn't mean we're stupid, doesn't mean we're not capable of thinking through the intricacies of a plan. Jesus, Iris!" she spat. "You want to know if Nate's *thought* this through? Come with me."

She threw down the stirrup hoe and stamped toward the house. A defiant part of me wanted to fold my arms and plant my feet out here among the onion stalks, but it was too damned hot for stubbornness, so I followed her back toward the farm-house with its invitingly shaded front porch.

Christie had already kicked off her boots and left her over-shirt, hat, and goggles strewn in a trail leading from the front foyer to the living room. I unlaced my boots, set them in the closet, and sighed at the coolness of the old hardwood floors radiating through my sweaty socks.

"In here," Christie called sharply as I padded into the living room with its overstuffed couches, generous brick fireplace, and sweeping bay windows.

I hadn't spent a lot of time in here since I arrived. This was where Nate's people gathered most nights, arriving in steady streams to sprawl on the well-worn furniture, break out board games, and drink blueberry moonshine while bending Nate's ear. They came and went in waves, and I still found them all far too loud and chaotic for my tastes. I preferred the solitude of the bedroom upstairs with music blaring in my ears and Maisie's ribs pressing against my feet as she sighed in her sleep.

"You coming?" Christie's voice barked from behind the half-closed oak pocket door to the right of the fireplace. Heat radi-ated through my gut like coals stoked by the wind. I wasn't a child. If she thought she could scold me like one, she had another thing coming.

Rolling my shoulders back and stretching my neck until it popped, I shouldered the sliding door aside and stepped into an office that looked strikingly similar to my mother's but with a more lived-in feel.

Christie scanned the shelves behind the broad, worn desk. From floor to ceiling, every ledge was crammed full of leather-bound books with thin spines and hand-stamped titles.

Nate has books! I held a tingling breath deep in my chest. My uncle had held Johan's ragged survival guide like paper was a rarity. I took in the rest of the room while Christie ran her finger over each title, mumbling sour words beneath her breath.

The delicate scent of old paper, cured leather, and citrus wood polish permeated the room. A tall, tapered beeswax candle in a brass holder stood like a sentinel on the window ledge. Blue-tinted glass panes divided by thick muntins provided a view of the shaded backyard and the root cellar armory beyond. Bright yellow goldfinches sparred for choice perches at the birdfeeder on a post nearby.

Inside, Nate's desk was flanked by two worn wingback chairs on my side and a cracked leather chair with scrolled wood arms opposite. The desk was bare, save for a kerosene lantern, an ashtray—I'd never seen Nate smoke—and a mug full of aggressively sharpened pencils.

"Here we are." Christie hooked a green book off one of the lower shelves and spun with it held to her chest. She stood there wide-stanced, jaw set, and brown eyes as sharp as the knives in her kitchen. "You doubt that your uncle thinks things through?" she asked quietly. "You have any idea what all of this is?"

"N-Nate's library?" I stammered and willed myself not to wilt in the face of Christie's compressed fierceness. This collection of books was miniscule compared to the endless rows of shelves in our Cache, but it was still impressive. Even Johan didn't have this many books.

"He color codes it." She stabbed toward the shelves. "Blue is seasonal weather patterns, temperature trends, and crop yield history per year. Red is freight documents; black is travel registers; brown is communication logs; light blue is supplier contact lists; that tan one is a diesel fuel consumption chart for your city; and the green ones are transactions." She slammed the green book onto the desk hard enough to make me jump before turning back to the shelves and snagging a brown book down.

"You think Nate is stupid enough to risk your life on a USB stick that hasn't been proven?" She cracked open the green book and flipped pages recklessly enough to risk paper cuts.

"I didn't mean it like—"

"Come here." Christie's eyes narrowed, blonde hair blooming in wisps from under her hair band.

A cold image overwhelmed me: Vannevar with slit eyes and blonde hair haloing her face as she slunk toward me with her gun trained on my head. My lungs felt stuck together, like wet paper bags. The back of my neck prickled, and my legs braced to run.

Christie looked up. "Jesus, I'm not going to murder you with a bloody book, Iris. Just come here!"

I stumbled around the side of the desk, cracking my hip on the corner hard enough to make my eyes water. *Pull yourself together.*

"Read this." She tapped a paragraph midway down the page but didn't wait for me to digest it. "September 20th year 12 Seller: Grainger Technologies. Client: Nathaniel Wray. Item Description: One flash drive containing Taps Closed Operating System. Price: Deed for one 3000W diesel generator with inverter and five-year contract for discounted diesel supply. Generator to be delivered upon satisfactory implementation of TCOS."

Nate's last name was Wray? Mom had never told me her maiden name. It didn't matter in the commune where everyone chose new names for themselves when the world ended. "I-I don't know what any of that means."

Christie shook her head and let a dry laugh press past her lips. "Course you don't. It means your uncle saved a man and his family from some marauders five years back. Not the first time he's done it, or the last. This particular man's name was Clinton Grainger. He's from down south and he used to run a tech company before the collapse, but there's not much call for that now is there?

"He owed Nate a favor, and, it just so happened, your uncle needed a man of his abilities. Tell me, Iris. When the diesel tanker comes to fill up your thirsty city, what direction does it come from?"

"Through the tunnel." I frowned. "From the west."

"Always west?"

"Yeah. I mean, I think so." I scrubbed my neck.

Christie grinned crookedly, but it wasn't a warm smile this time. "What if I told you there was a refinery to the east, in Alberta, a diesel supplier?"

"That doesn't make sense." I picked at my braid. "Something like a refinery needs a huge source of power. There aren't any of those up here. All the big hydro dams are down south."

"The big ones, yeah, but not *all* the hydro dams." Christie sniffed. "Five years back, Nate got word that this small-scale refinery was positioned to sell higher quality diesel to your city and ship it at lower rates than Nate could offer. Diesel is one of our biggest movers and we only get bulk prices from down south if we buy enough inventory to supply *your* city. If we lost you as a buyer, we'd lose our competitive edge everywhere else."

"Taps closed." I twisted my wristband. Frost prickled through my core as the meaning of it leached in.

"Nate called in Grainger's favor. Had him design a custom virus for us and paid him handsomely, of course." Christie's smile was hard. "We got one of our URLs hired on as janitorial staff, and when she plugged in the virus, it brought the refinery's PLC system to its knees. They didn't have the processors to replace what they lost." She steepled her fingers. "We shut them down, Iris."

"Zuse," I blurted, bracing myself against the desk.

Christie reached past me and opened up the brown book. It was filled with strips of p-mail, pasted onto each page and ordered by date. She flipped a quarter of the way through the entries before pausing. "There. There's your confirmation. This was from our *janitor*."

I swallowed and squinted at the yellowed strip of paper.

Taps closed successful. All systems down. Extended unplanned shutdown with no ETA for replacement processors. Freezing temperatures have turned much of the place into an ice cube. Critical damage sustained.

"And here's the confirmation of Clinton Grainger's generator delivery." Christie poked at the green book again, but my head was swimming too much to focus on it. "Your uncle isn't a stupid man, Iris. He's worked with Grainger in the past. He's used these viruses before, quite effectively, and if he can knock out a damned refinery with one, Kahn's city will be a piece of piss. He wouldn't risk you or your family if he wasn't certain this would all work. So *yeah,* I think it's safe to say we've thought it all out."

Mother of Sol. A fragging refinery. Nate just hung them out to dry. And they hadn't shot at my uncle like Kahn had. This could work. I could be the catalyst that pushed Kahn and Vannevar and every other snake out of my city. We could grow as much food as we needed. We could print books like Nate said. Help people. Really help them. What could be bigger than that? And suddenly I knew it in my bones, I would do it. I'd give Nate my wristband. I'd help him and Christie because they'd saved me, and they would save my family too.

CHAPTER
TWENTY-FOUR

When Nate got home that night, I slipped my wristband off and gave it to him.

His eyes widened as he focused on it. "Shit, Beetle. You sure?"

I nodded and a wide, boyish smile bunched my uncle's face. He scooped me into a hug that lifted me clear off my feet, and spun me around, whooping, red-faced, blue eyes crinkled and ebullient, the epitome of the Nate I idolized in childhood. I couldn't help but beam along with him.

For supper, Nate insisted on making his specialty, pan-fried chicken. Christie groaned about him spattering grease all over her kitchen, but her mouth was soft as she grumbled and her brown eyes warm and engaging. No hint of the fire I'd ignited earlier showed in her thin face. She paired Nate's chicken with baked potatoes drenched in butter and chives, and roasted asparagus with mushrooms.

At first, guilt stuck in my throat. I had an opulent table set before me and my family probably hadn't eaten at all today. Was this how Robert felt in his rich house? Was he in that house still, or was he on Johan's side? I froze behind my empty plate while Nate piled steaming food on his. My discomfort became obvious enough that my uncle slowly lowered his spoon and cleared his throat.

"Look, everyone else could have this too, if we get rid of Kahn, Beetle. You're doing the right thing. You don't have to feel guilty about eating."

I nodded because I didn't want to speak past the lump in my throat. Christie took my plate and filled it. "You worked hard today, Iris. Out here, honest work earns you a decent meal. We're going to send that pigeon tomorrow, and Kahn will be on his ass by night fall. We'll get your family out of the crossfire, and the whole thing will be over before you know it."

The spicy smell of battered chicken overcame me. It was hard not to feel safe in Christie's warm, kerosene-lit kitchen with Sasquatch smiling earnestly across from me. It was easy to forget the city for a while. Rich food and hearty laughter stuck to every hollow between my ribs, and by the time we'd polished off our elegant dishes of fresh raspberries and clotted cream, I felt a fullness that had nothing to do with the meal we'd just shared. This was the right thing to do.

The thought radiated through me like soft sunlight. Nate was right. Kahn needed to be stopped. He wasn't going to sell me or my family or anyone else. When he scanned the ID chip on my wristband, our CEO would be hungry enough to see what the accompanying ransom was. And why would he suspect a virus? Until Christie's revelation today, I hadn't heard of another instance of malware warfare in decades. Other than our city, there wasn't another settlement with functioning computer networks for hundreds of kilometers. We could shut down Kahn's skewed cred system and save my city. For the first time in my life, I could contribute to something significant, something big. Never mind Soldamned optimum battery operating temperatures, I could give Johan's humanitarian efforts the push they needed to take root and flourish. I could help

Nate, like I'd always wanted to. And our family would be whole again.

I pressed away from the table, closed my eyes, and imagined Mom, Dad, and Vinton laughing and trading barbed jokes around the table with us. I would fix this, and they would be secure and safe until the violence blew over. And maybe it would make up for every other frag-up I had piled on their plates.

NATE TOLD me he sent two pigeons the next morning. One was addressed to David Kahn containing my ID chip and the flash drive, and another addressed to my mother with the simple coded message: *Peanut butter and onion sandwiches in the tunnel.*

"What the hell is that supposed to mean?" I snorted.

He chuckled and smoothed down his beard. "It's, uh, this password Anne and I made up as kids."

"Computer password?"

"No, no. If our mom was sending someone to pick us up from school, they had to know the secret password before we'd go with them. Anne's gonna lose it when she sees it. She and I are the only ones left alive who know what peanut butter and onion sandwiches means." Nate shook his head. "Soon as she sees that p-mail, she's going to know I'm alive and that I'm coming to pick her up in the tunnel."

Tingles crept up my spine and multiplied in my chest. My family. I hadn't realized how much I'd missed them until the possibility of seeing them was only days away. "How long for the pigeon and for your rail runners to get here?"

Nate squinted and peered upward. "If the weather holds, the birds can make the trip in under a day, easy. I've instructed my runners to keep a man covertly posted at the tunnel starting tonight. If your family packs fast, and my runners relay through the night, they could be standing on the front porch three mornings from now."

Three days. I digested it slowly. Three days until Vinton slapped my back with his strong hands and greeted me with some asshole brother line he'd been saving for weeks. Three days until Dad hugged me like I was breakable and demanded to hear every detail of my escape over a cup of mint tea. Three days until Mom broke through her hard, polished corporate mold, rolled the tightness out of her shoulders and laughed without caring about the gap between her teeth. Sol, I ached to see them, hold them at arm's length, and prove to myself they were whole and well and safe.

The next day, it was too hot to work in the gardens. Nate was holed up in his office and Christie was fretting over a batch of sourdough bread in the kitchen with the screen door open and a cooling rag dripping water down her neck. My room felt hotter than the generator room back in the city, and my limbs screamed for movement.

"I'm thinking of checking the trap lines," I told Christie, and immediately she shook her head.

"Bad idea. I mean, you can check with Nate, but I'm pretty sure a crew already headed out that way this morning, and—between you and me—they're a touch trigger happy. I wouldn't want to risk getting bush shot just because I was searching for some shade." She shrugged, whisking flour and water together.

"How about south? Clear that way?" I'd seen a jagged line of cool Jack pines in that direction.

"Should be clear all the way to the river and the rails. You can take the access road, but it's a switchback path that takes twice the time and it's dustier than a desert. The game trail straight south over the ridge is rougher, so watch your feet if you take that route. No shame in turning around if they start to smart." Christie scooped some starter into a fresh mason jar and mixed in the flour and water. "Gonna be back for lunch, or you want me to pack something?"

"Don't trouble yourself. I'll make a sandwich." I started for the ice box.

"Take a thermos of water too, yeah? And cover up."

"I'll stick to the shade," I promised.

It was easier said than done. Past the southern tree line was only a thin band of wooded valley before the terrain jutted into a bare ridge stippled with yellow bursts of scotch broom. The sun hung heavy and white in the sky, harsh enough that even through my goggles it made my eyes sting. I backtracked to the trees where I'd passed a small marsh, braving swarms of small, vicious mosquitoes to smear sour-smelling, tarry mud over my arms, the back of my neck, my cheeks and nose. Cinching my wide-brimmed hat lower, I gulped several swallows of icy water from my thermos before picking my way up the brittle ridge.

I was pouring sweat, and my clothes were streaked with mud by the time I reached the generous basin with its chalky, blue white-water river. The rusted rail line curved beside it, a thin centipede of metal and oil-soaked wood. A cool wind followed the valley and swayed the stands of cedar that flanked the tracks. My legs felt like wilted plants, but my feet only itched a little as I eased down the hillside, weaving around lichen-laced boulders until I reached the quiet shade of the nearest clump of trees with a view of the glistening river, a cool boulder to press my back against, and a good line on the tracks.

It was too soon to watch for my family, but I couldn't help it. I was that little girl again, waiting for someone I loved to come up the rails, prickling with excitement for the reunion I knew was coming. Something about the breeze ruffling the water and the steady line of black railroad ties smoothed my thoughts, pulled them into line when they would otherwise have jumped the track. The high-pitched murmur of mosquitoes filled my ears, even as they failed to find purchase on my mud-crusted skin. Shadows swung over emerald clods of moss, pale plates of bracket fungus, and tender curls of fiddlehead ferns. Far above me, a raven claimed a treetop like a throne, puffed out his throat, and warbled a sundry series of calls and clicks. He stopped when the rumble of wheels down the rails drifted up from the west.

I slipped around the far edge of the boulder; it was broad enough to conceal me and short enough to peer over.

In minutes, a four-horse flat-deck clattered around the western bend. The horses moved at a brisk trot, open-mouthed and covered in lather. Their driver balanced wide-stanced behind a snarled barricade of barbed-wire and a wooden spike palisade wall. He wore a full-faced motorcycle helmet—which must have been sweltering in this heat—and an exposed flak vest. Behind him, five guards with wicked-looking rifles cradled across their laps sat on stacked crates. They wore helmets too, scuffed skull-caps with spray-painted neon symbols. One of them had glued a sprig of barred hawk feathers down the side of her headgear, and all of them looked casually comfortable despite the heat and their carapace layers of mismatched body armor.

No slaves. None that I could see.

I leaned forward as the group neared the tall trestle bridge across the river. Unlike the overpass I'd hid under to avoid my first supply train encounter, this one wasn't decked. Open gaps between the ties framed the river far below.

The driver heaved back on the reins and shouted at the horses to slow. Two of the guards peeled aside a section of the wire barricade, swung their weapons over their shoulder, and hopped down onto the tracks.

My heart seized illogically in my chest. *They can't see you, stupid.* But I couldn't draw a deep breath, even as it became obvious that I wasn't the reason the two guards had disembarked.

Wordlessly, their compatriots handed them down a thick stack of wide planking. I watched as the pair laid a path across the gaps in the bridge rails for the horses to safely traverse. As soon as the animals eased over the temporary platform, the guards shifted the already crossed planks to the front. It was a slow process, but the crew performed it with a disenchanted sort of efficiency that spoke of familiarity. In little over a minute, the supply train was over the bridge, the planks were reloaded, and the guards had vaulted easily back up to their crates.

Such odd-shaped crates. They were wooden, long, thin, and stacked four layers deep. On top of them, interlocked like bricks, was a layer of dull green metal boxes with hinged lids and big toggle latches. Each bin was no bigger than one of Christie's bread pans. I'd seen something similar before, but my mind couldn't place where. I blinked at the retreating caravan for several numb seconds before it struck me. I knew where I'd seen a metal bin like that. In Nate's armory, in the root cellar. Those were ammunition boxes.

Holy shit, I leaned into the coolness of the boulder. An entire layer of ammunition boxes. There must have been hundreds stacked on top of the crates. And those long, thin wooden boxes … My mouth dried and tension plucked at the tendons in my neck. Those were guns. A mountain of guns. This was Nate's munition delivery to Johan.

Zuse. I bent double, narrowly avoiding smacking my forehead on the boulder. Blinking down at the mushrooms between my feet, I gagged against a fear so thick it pressed air from my lungs. I'd never seen so many weapons in one place in my entire life, and they were heading toward my home, into the hands of people like Johan and Olivia, maybe even Robert. None of them were Firewalls. How many, besides the Browsers, Olivia, and her oupa had ever held a gun in their lives, let alone shot one?

Oh Sol, what had we set into motion? I'd stupidly thought that, when Johan asked for guns, Nate would send a few rifles from his armory down the line, not a whole fragging shipping car. What kind of uprising wanted firepower like this? Oupa was a pacifist. What the hell was he planning?

"WHY SO MANY GUNS?" Nate and I sat on the front porch rockers beneath a dim kerosene lantern and a cloud of moths. We passed his flask back and forth between us. It had taken me five sips to work up enough heat in my throat to spit out my question. "I saw the shipment go by today."

Nate shrugged, loose-shouldered, and blurry-eyed. "I told you how it works. There are an awful lot of rail runners who'll take their piece of the cargo as they move it. That's how they get paid. Besides, there was food on that shipment too. It wasn't all guns."

It looked like all guns to me, I wanted to say, but even drunk, Nate steered the conversation easily.

"Hey, did I tell you, I found myself a crossbow? Like yours?" he said. "It didn't make it on this shipment, but it's coming on the next train. We could hunt together, when I get some time. How about that?" He held out the flask, and I took another swallow even though my teeth already felt fuzzy.

"How about you put me on the work roster?" Nate wasn't the only one who could pull a conversation where he wanted it to go.

"What?"

"I'm not an invalid anymore. I'm going crazy waiting for them to come, Nate. Give me *something* to do," I pleaded. "Christie's going to skin me if I step into her kitchen one more time to ask her if she needs help."

"She never needs help," Nate said quietly, smiling and pushing off from the front deck rocking chair to scan the moonless sky. "All right. I'll talk to Alice first thing. She'll put you on the schedule for tomorrow."

Two days after Nate sent the pigeons, I learned how to milk goats with a boy named Isaac, harvested honey and checked for mite infestations in the beehives with Rhea, and finished the day mucking out chicken coops. On the third morning, I picked up a delivery of ice slabs from the rail runners with Orin. The older man spoke perhaps three words the entire time we pushed the handcart up the long serpentine access road from the tracks to the compound, and maybe a handful more as he expertly carved chunks from each ice slab for me to deliver to each house's ice box. Every moment, I expected a railway lookout to tear through the yard and inform me my family had arrived. I kept my gaze pinned to the access road even as I chopped wood that evening, but the ice blocks were the only thing to arrive by rail that day.

"That bird I sent should have been back by now," Nate murmured as he passed my room that night. "I'll send another pigeon in the morning, yeah?"

"Okay," I gulped, digging at a wood splinter in the palm of my hand.

Maisie crept across the room and whined quietly until I scratched behind her ears. She stayed until I fell asleep.

My family didn't come on the fourth day either. Nate didn't eat supper with Christie and I, and when I knocked on his office door, he barked "Come" in a voice as cold and commanding as my mother had ever used.

I slipped past the pocket door and closed it behind me. Nate slumped over three strips of p-mail and a communication log, reading glasses perched on his nose and a pen clutched in his hand.

I froze where I stood. I'd never seen him like this, hunched over a desk, wearing glasses, stress hollowing his face. It seemed like an utterly foreign environment for my Sasquatch.

"What do you need, Iris?" His gaze flicked to mine, and it looked tired.

"I-I was just wondering if they …" I couldn't finish. My uncle had pinned me with a stare so hard the rest of my words died on my tongue. He looked like Kahn.

He peeled the glasses off his face, folded them, and set them on the desk before rubbing the bridge of his nose. "What kind of asshole do you think I am, Iris? You'd be the first to know if I heard about your family, all right?"

I glanced at the curls of paper before him and nodded slowly. "I just … You said you were going to send another bird?"

"Another bird won't make a difference now." Nate stabbed a finger at one of the p-mails on his desk and raked his fingers through his hair. "There was a mudslide, up past Lytton last night. It's blocked the rails and my shipment to Johan, and it's gonna take days to clean up the mess. If that first bird didn't reach your folks, they aren't coming until the tracks are cleared."

My stomach sank and my cheeks prickled with heat. First to know. A mudslide last night. If I hadn't come in here, when exactly had he planned on telling me?

"Look, Christie and I are going to go and take a crew up to help clear debris."

"I want to come."

"Naw, Beetle, I don't—"

"Nate, I'm coming," I barked.

"No!" He slapped the desk hard enough to rattle the ash tray. "Jesus, Iris, the whole point was to keep you away from Kahn, not run you up the damned rails to him. Stay here where it's safe. I'm doing everything I goddamned can, all right?"

"All right," I choked and left the office, but it wasn't all right.

CHAPTER
TWENTY-FIVE

Nate's crew left before dawn the next morning. I padded through the empty house after they were gone. My uncle had locked the pocket door to his office but didn't latch the window. With most of the compound still sleeping, it was easy enough to pry a butter knife under the sill and climb in from the backyard unnoticed.

Maisie whined from the living room and nosed the crack under the door until I fumbled around the desk in the gloom, unlatched the pocket door, and let the German shepherd press against my legs.

I lit a kerosene lantern and pulled down the latest brown stamped book from Nate's shelves. Like the communication log Christie had shown me, this one was split into incoming strips of p-mail and handwritten copies of outgoing messages. I scanned the outgoing column for the past week.

June 29th to Seattle Trading Company: Request shipment
of 200 Remington Model 870 MCS and 100 cases of
12-gauge shells in exchange for 20% future shares in
acquired copper mine. I'm calling in a favor, Lars. You

> *still owe me for recovering hijacked shipment two*
> *years back.*

Nate owned a copper mine? Where? I scrubbed the scars on my cheeks and kept reading.

> *June 29th to RK ranch: Request shipment of three sides of*
> *beef smoked and wrapped and as much canned chicken*
> *as you can spare in exchange for 10 Remington Model*
> *MCS and 10 cases of 12 gauge shells. How is salt*
> *block supply?*
> *June 30th to Little City PK: Aborted foxtrot drop.*
> *Requested supplies shipping July 1st. ETA one week.*
> *June 30th to Grassland Supply: Request shipment of ten*
> *salt blocks in exchange for one barrel of blueberry*
> *moonshine.*
> *July 1st to Little City Attn David Kahn: We know posi-*
> *tion of AWOL citizen Iris Ecosia. Willing to*
> *exchange for proprietary information. See included*
> *details.*
> *July 1st to Blue Mountain Ice: Request one shipment of ice*
> *blocks in exchange for four cases of candles.*
> *July 3rd to Lytton runners: acknowledge delay. Sending*
> *clearing crew stat. Move shipment to cover. Meet at*
> *side yard #2.*

The page was blank after that. I read it through again, swallowing against the burn of acid in my throat. There was no outgoing p-mail to Anne Ecosia. Maybe he forgot to write it down. I scrambled through the previous pages, exhalations whistling out of my nose. Bullshit. Nate recorded the fragging ice delivery. He hadn't forgotten to record peanut butter and onion sandwiches in the tunnel. I breathed against the sickness shifting in my stomach. Maybe Nate didn't record personal messages. I could write one and send it today and see if a worker at the pigeon loft recorded it.

Maisie crowded my legs, and I pushed her away, closing the log and lifting it to its spot on the shelf with hot tears pooling in my eyes. A ray of morning sunlight pressed through the window and illuminated something in the gap between books. Sniffling, I squinted at a white illustrated page, stuffed behind the stack of brown communication logs. Reaching behind them, I fished out a palm-sized, sturdy-bound book and recognized it immediately.

Johan's survival guide. But it couldn't be. This one was newer. Its printed pages weren't worn ragged and water warped, and its back cover wasn't missing. I flipped through sections on mushroom foraging, emergency first aid and snare-setting, pages I knew by heart. Numbness crept up my fingers, leeched into the bones of my arms and settled deep in my chest wedged against my heart.

Nate had a copy of Johan's survival guide, and he hid it. Why? My uncle had gushed over mine like it was irreplaceable. He'd asked me for help with the trap lines when he already owned the book I learned from? It didn't make sense.

And then it did. Slowly. Painfully. Nate was a trader. He'd wanted something from me, and he knew he could get it if I felt needed, if I felt *useful*. So he'd used me. My hands shook. If Nate had read the survival guide, he had already known every-thing I did about trapping when he spun his pretty story about needing my help setting snares. He came out there with me and nodded at every idiot piece of advice I spouted because he knew we'd bond over a day in the wilderness together. Soldamn him.

I left the survival guide on the corner of the desk, and I didn't lock the office when I left.

That morning, I was on the roster for soap making with Mark, but I didn't go. Instead, I bee-lined for the pigeon loft that stood on stilts beside the goat pens. I climbed the ladder and pressed the trap door open. Dust and the sharp tang of bird droppings tickled my nostrils.

"Can I help you?" Orin, the man I'd hauled ice blocks with, stood above me.

I climbed the rest of the way into the loft and then forced an embarrassed smile onto my face and stared hard at my feet while I spoke. "Yeah, Orin. I was wondering if there's any way to get a message to my boyfriend." It had to be a purely personal message, and Robert was the most personal thing I could think of. I hadn't lobbied to pull him away from the fight and bring him here, and I didn't even know what side he was on, but I wanted him to know I hadn't forgotten him.

Orin picked up a paper cup from beside an open notebook, and spit tobacco juice into it. "I don't send birds without Nate's permission."

I straightened to my full height. "Well, I'm Nate's niece, and he left me here in his stead."

Orin chewed thoughtfully but didn't move.

"You can read the message before I send it, and if Nate is pissed off when he gets back"—I shrugged—"send him to me. Tell him I told you I had permission."

Orin shook his head. For a moment, I thought he'd denied me, but then he shuffled to the desk, tore a thin strip of paper from the back of the journal, and grabbed a pencil.

"Make it quick," he said.

I took the stubby pencil and wrote as small as I could.

> *Little City: Attention Robert Lycos. My printing hasn't*
> *improved. I miss you, Pen Pal. Tell me about your*
> *favorite romantic movie. I need a happy ending.*

I wanted to ask him what side he was on, if his Dad was still sick, if they were eating, what state the city was in, but I couldn't. Johan had controlled the pigeon house, but that was days ago. I had no idea if he still held it, and if anyone else intercepted this bird, I didn't want anything in this message identifying me and pinpointing my location. Besides, this message was supposed to be purely personal and unimportant, something that wouldn't merit writing down. Because I needed to prove that Nate didn't record personal p-mails, and that was why there was no mention of peanut butter and onion sandwiches in the tunnel on the communication log pages. I needed to know if he sent the bird to fetch my parents or if he lied.

So, I stood and watched Orin huff and shake his head as he read the ribbon of paper. Then I watched him copy the message into the notebook, pressing his pencil hard enough that the ratty page snagged and tore. Rolling my p-mail tight, he slipped it into the tube of a red-banded city-bound bird and released the pigeon out the loft window.

He wrote it down before he sent it. My stupid, pointless message, and Orin still wrote it down. Nate lied. He didn't send the bird. I swallowed carefully and another voice in my head parried. Just because it was in a raggedy notebook in this loft, didn't mean it would make it into Nate's log.

"Anything else?" Orin crossed his arms.

Yeah Orin. I'd like to look through that notebook you've got there and see if there's a message sent to my parents. Of course, he wouldn't let me do that. I'd been lucky that he sent the pigeon to Robert. I would have to sneak in later. "No, Orin. Thank you."

I climbed down the ladder and stared at the nearest water tank. My skin itched with anxiety. If Nate could be lying about sending the pigeon, what else might he be lying about? Test crops? I bet he supplemented every plant in these damned gardens, just like we did. I grabbed a stirrup hoe so it looked like I belonged and headed for the tank. Other gardeners straightened and followed my path with wary eyes but said nothing as I stomped by. *Nate's ward.* That's what most of them knew me as.

What had my uncle told them about me that they all treated me like I was made out of glass?

I climbed onto the wooden access platform of the holding tank, a white, poly nine-hundred-gallon. Unscrewing the access hatch, I peered inside. I'd mixed the powdered supplement Nate supplied us countless times in our own water tanks, both at the greenhouses and Johan's covert garden. It tinted the water blue once dissolved. But, this water was colorless. Other than the strands of algae carpeting the ribbed sidewalls of the tank, it looked like drinkable, normal water. I resealed the tank and stepped off the platform.

Nate's compound used a series of windmill wells and diesel pumps to distribute water evenly across his massive gardens. There were eight other holding tanks. Maybe they concentrated the fertilizer in one tank and diluted it into the rest as needed?

I passed between rows of plump cabbages, then a stand of radishes and beets before reaching the second storage tank. It was half full, but like the first, I found no evidence of soluble fertilizer. A hopeful twinge threaded through my chest. Maybe Nate hadn't lied. These were actual test plots, and he was willing to share all these hybrid plants with my city. Without the heavy cost of supplementation, we could expand and grow cheap, accessible food, just like my uncle.

But as I checked the remaining seven holding tanks in the vast gardens, that thread of hope frayed into fear and confusion. *None* of the tanks were supplemented. Nate wasn't growing a *few* test plots. *None* of the gardens, as far as I could see, were supplemented. How could Nate possibly justify risking his entire food supply on test crops he'd admitted were only recently proving themselves? He'd never seemed like a man to take stupid risks.

I stumbled toward two gardeners in wide straw hats pruning tomato side shoots. Their fingertips were green from pinching out the fragrant plants.

"Hey, where's the fertilizer?" I asked breathlessly and the pair answered me at the same time.

"We don't use it here," the dark-haired man with thick arms said.

"In the truck trail—" The shorter man's reply was cut off by a wallop across the chest from his compatriot.

"That's Nate's *ward*," the first man hissed.

"Ah, we don't use it here." The short man offered an awkward smile, even as he rubbed his chest. And then they both turned away from me pointedly.

I'd never been good with social cues, but this time I knew it wasn't me. As the two men rushed away from me, I knew it wasn't my lack of eye contact or my tone of voice. These people had been told to lie to me. Zuse, what the hell was Nate doing? This whole damned day felt like it was slipping out of my grip, watery and indefinable.

I charged back to the pigeon loft, hoisted myself up the ladder and slammed open the trap door. Pigeons burst into flight in their cages and feathers billowed into the air.

"Hey!" Orin bellowed.

Sweeping past him effortlessly, I snatched the ragged notebook off his desk, rolled it into my back pocket and plunged back down the ladder while he protested.

I sprinted back toward the farmhouse in a daze and locked myself in Nate's office, pulling the communication log back off the shelf. Information expanded in my head like a thunderstorm as I scanned the scrawled writing in the notebook. Nate had to use fertilizer. If it was in a truck trailer, he had to use it. When the other man said, 'We don't use it here,' he must have meant not in that plot. There had to be more gardens I didn't know about, but then why have his men lie to me?

I found the page in the rough notebook from July first, the message to Kahn, the ice delivery, it was all there, exactly the same as what had been transcribed into the formal communication log later.

There was no outgoing message to my parents. I sagged in the office chair, and then read the notebook front to back, but there was no mention anywhere of peanut butter and onion sandwiches.

Nate hadn't sent the first bird or the second one. My parents weren't coming. Nate lied about needing my help. He only wanted my wristband. *Oh Sol.*

I stumbled out of the office to my bedroom, feeling sick and shaky. For the rest of the afternoon, I lay on top of the quilt, paralyzed and confused. A normal person wouldn't be frozen by this. They'd be able to work out the snarls. A functioning mind could follow all these fraying ends to their source, but my thoughts just kept twisting like earthworms baking under the sun until they felt brittle and mummified.

Nate was the only person who had ever made me feel like I was smart because of my differences, but he was lying to me. I wasn't smart. I was gullible, and a horrible realization dawned on me.

I didn't know Sasquatch at all.

FOUR DAYS AFTER THEY LEFT, Nate and Christie returned in the middle of the night. I woke to doors slamming, the muzzled tones of restrained voices arguing, and Maisie barking until Christie snapped at her to shut up.

The old house creaked, clicked, and settled as it adjusted to full occupancy again. Heat coiled in my stomach like an aggravated snake, and I strained to decipher voices and recognize footfalls. Maybe he brought them. Fragile hope swarmed my chest, sharp and tingling like driven snow.

I listened for Mom's clipped voice, Dad clearing his throat, or the creak of Vinton's chair, but there was only Christie's feet padding quickly up the stairs, past my door to the room at the end of the hall. She slammed the door behind her. Downstairs, a glass thudded onto a table. The low rumble of the office pocket door opening then closing rattled through the walls. Maisie's claws clicked across the living room as the big German shepherd paced, and then silence swallowed the house again.

Frag it. I clenched my jaw. *It's been four damned days. I'm done waiting.* I swept my bedspread aside, dressed hastily, and took the stairs two at a time. But when I got to the living room, the sound of Orin's voice in Nate's office stopped me in my tracks.

Shit! Was he ratting me out already?

"Let's not get into this, Nate. There's plenty of other ways," the old man's voice rasped.

Nate's voice was slurred when he answered back, "I don't have a damned choice, Orin. We had guns. Now they're gone and the trading company is breathing down my neck for payment. I don't have anything else. Just that city. Just those people. I can't just let them leave once we have control. Now, do you have a source or not?"

"I think we should talk about this in the morning when you're sober."

"I think you should answer the damned question," Nate growled.

A long pause and then, "Theoretically, if I had a source …"

"Theoretically."

"Well, there's a big demand for bodies for the coal mines out east. An accident took out a bunch of Coaltana's workforce this summer, and they'd pay handsomely to replace them."

"Coaltana, we ship to them already, yeah?"

"We do. Mostly canned fish. Some diesel."

"So we've got birds trained to fly that message route, yeah?"

"You could send a message, sure, but Kahn's people are soft.

You'd probably lose half of them on the train ride over. Middle of winter. The other half wouldn't be cut out for hard labor. It's not worth it. You wouldn't get full slave price for a bunch of carpet-walkers, Nate."

It was the most I'd ever heard Orin talk, and suddenly I didn't want to hear another word out of the man's mouth ever again. *Slaves.* Bile pressed up my throat, and I clapped my hand over my mouth and held my breath. Nate said he didn't deal in slaves.

"I'd take what I could get for them," Nate said.

"You're drunk."

"Women. Kids. All of them. They're worth more out of that city than in it."

"Go to sleep, Nate. We'll talk in the morning."

My knees buckled. I hit the couch and tumbled into it, heat filling my head, hands tingling. *Sol, no.* This wasn't right. Nate said he didn't deal in slaves.

The pocket door trundled open. I jumped as Orin walked out, but he only glanced at me as he closed the door behind him, passed the couch, and kept going. The front door slammed. A slim gap in the pocket door flooded the dark living room with lamp light. I gulped against the dizziness swamping my skull and counted to ten before pushing off from the couch and barging into my uncle's office.

Nate jumped. Amber liquor sloshed in the glass he clutched, and he growled, "I said, I'll come up when I'm damned well ..." Red-rimmed eyes focused on me through clumps of greasy hair. Nate's cheeks were wet. He was crying. His face was pale, and there was blood on his jacket. Lots of blood. One large stain, brown and deep, pulled on my gaze like a black hole.

"Now is not a good time, Iris." Nate's back curled, like some feral, cornered animal.

"W-what happened?"

"*Get out!*" he roared.

I stumbled back, tripping over the dog behind my legs and falling into the living room. Breath coughed out of me as I landed hard enough to make my teeth clack. Maisie's anguished howls flooded the room as she skittered away with her long tail tucked.

Nate lunged around the desk, crossed the office in two strides, and filled the entire doorway before closing the door between us. Vases jiggled on the fireplace mantle. The lock clicked, and Maisie and I panted in the dark while the air thickened around us, a blanket of shock. Liquid poured beyond the oak pocket door, Nate refilling his drink.

The bloodstain on my uncle's jacket still burned into the back of my eyes like a reverse image. No matter how many times I blinked, I saw its outline.

He wants to sell your people, Iris. He's covered in blood, and he just said he wants to sell your people as slaves. Sol Almighty, what's happening?

CHAPTER
TWENTY-SIX

felt like I'd swallowed the sun and it was deep in my belly, a white-hot nuclear furnace churning out looping flares and tugging on all of my soft organs with an inescapable gravity. Heat radiated from my core, pressed acid up my throat, and left the taste of anger like ashes in my mouth.

I stared at my bedroom ceiling until morning, eyes itchy, marinating in a rage that seemed too big for me to contain. One thought screamed in my mind above all the others.

That was not Nate. Whoever spoke about slaves to Orin last night, whoever chased me out of his office bore no resemblance to the uncle I loved. There'd been no smile lines around his eyes or softness in the set of his mouth. All of it had been wrung out and replaced with something raw and wounded. So which had been the front? The bearish uncle with mischief radiating from his eyes or the man I'd glimpsed last night: hollow, agonized, and stretched thin over a frame of secrets?

"Only one way to find out," I whispered to myself. "Crack open some secrets." Rolling out of bed still dressed in my clothes from yesterday, I marched down the stairs, jammed my feet into my boots, and ignored Christie calling me from the kitchen. I let the screen door slam behind me and sucked in a breath of air that smelled of pine needles and leaf litter. It should have calmed me, but it didn't. The fire in my belly vaporized every inhalation I drew in. I scanned the gardens.

Dewy plants hunched below a cottony line of mist. Several workers stood clasping mugs and huddling near the closest water tank. *Nate said your city could be like this, but he meant for his people, not yours.* Women and children, he'd said. All of them. Zuse, I couldn't think about this and do nothing anymore. Veering away from the gardeners, I stopped at the wood pile to yank a splitting axe out of its chopping block. Swinging it over my shoulder, I strode purposefully across the front yard.

Eight white semi-trailers with faded decals rested in the overgrown grass bellied up against the northern flank of the gardens, just beyond the diesel slip tank.

I'd circled the trailers enough times in the past days to wear a path around them. Not once had I seen workers remove or load anything into them. Thick, rusted padlocks hung snuggly on all but one door latch. One trailer, the furthest from the house had a shiny lock and packed soil beneath its doors.

Stopping in front of it, I lined up the axe blade against the edge of the padlock, widening my stance and hoisting the axe over my head. Bending my knees on the downward arc, I drove all of my weight into the strike. The axe glanced off the lock and buried itself in the soil near my right foot.

I snorted. *Chop your toes off, Iris. That'll bleed out the anger real quick. No full slave price for you.*

Flicking my braid over my shoulder, I adjusted my feet and angled my next blow. It struck true. Vibration twanged through my wrists and buzzed up the bones in my arms. Metal clanged loudly enough to startle a covey of grouse from the scrub edging the gardens. Nate said we could teach people to hunt. He said we could sell books, and now he wanted to bloody sell people instead?

Pulling my gaze from the birds' awkward, whistling flight, I surveyed the trailer lock. It was dented, but intact. I raised the axe for another swing. It hit high and punctured the sheet metal of the door, but the next two blows struck with satisfying precision, cutting the thin morning air with deep wrenching, gong-like tones that reverberated through the ribs of the trailer and echoed down the valley.

"Hey," a wavering voice sounded behind me. "Stop!"

I reeled to face its owner, axe held high, teeth bared, and cheek twitching. *Come make me.*

It was one of the gardeners from the group at the tank. I recognized the bright band on his hat. As I took a slow, deliberate step toward him, his throat worked, and his eyes widened like a spooked horse's. He turned and trotted toward the main house.

Good. I squeezed the axe until my hands ached and swung back to the battered trailer. Bring him. Bring everyone. Let's see Nate ignore me now. I knew his secrets. I knew his lies. The axe hit the lock with a peal that sang through my teeth, and the padlock shank sheared off.

Gripping the cracked rubber of the latch, I heaved upward and twisted. Hinges groaned as I swung the wide doors open. The smell of ammonia with chemical undertones stung my nostrils. I'd smelled it every time I slit one of those brittle plastic bags open to dump its contents into the greenhouse tank. That odor had crept into every fiber of my backpack from hauling bags from the drop point to the garden cistern. It felt like years ago that I'd nearly fainted in Greenhouse Five, spilling powdered fertilizer everywhere and blubbering to Olivia about Nate dying.

"Worth its weight in copper," she'd said.

What were we worth? I wondered. How much would Nate sell us for?

I slid the splitting axe into the trailer ahead of me and

boosted myself into the mostly empty space. Wooden pallets leaned on end against the side walls. Two pallets of stacked fertilizer bags sat at the front end of the trailer, one sealed with shrink wrap, the other unwrapped with half its contents missing.

My mouth went dry. I tried to swallow, but just made a clicking noise in my throat instead. Dragging the axe behind me, I shuffled toward the bulky pallets. Sol, I'd never seen so much in one place. I ran a hand over a dusty bag, peering down at the familiar faded label: *twenty-twenty-twenty Mastergrow general-purpose water-soluble fertilizer.* This was what lost me my citizenship. A bag like this was what Vannevar used to frame me for grand theft, what Johan traded his most valuable carrier pigeons for, and what Nate held over all of our heads. Fingers of heat curled up my throat, and I resisted the urge to bury the splitting axe deep into the closest bag.

"Hey, Beetle."

I turned, hot tears filling my eyes at the sight of Nate—*my Nate*—framed by the trailer doorway.

"Don't," I snarled as his soft eyes studied me and then lowered to blink at the axe in my hand. *Don't you dare put on this face after the one you showed me last night.* I sucked in through my nose and blinked at the trailer ceiling until my eyes cleared. "Don't call me that."

"Hell of a wakeup call." He indicated the axe. Maisie trotted up beside him and nosed his hand.

"How's your head feel this morning?" I countered.

Nate smiled tiredly, blue eyes raw, but still brilliant. He groaned as he hoisted himself onto the trailer bumper.

"Don't," I barked again, raising the axe. I wanted to break something. The lock hadn't been enough and the fertilizer was too soft and my uncle had snagged every one of my emotions carelessly. He was pretending last night never happened. He was acting as if I hadn't seen the blood, as if he hadn't talked about my people as nothing more than cargo to be bought and sold.

"What? You gonna turn into an axe murderer now, Iris?" My uncle stepped into the trailer and held his open palms out at his sides. He wasn't wearing his jacket, just a faded T-shirt and jeans.

"You should talk, slave dealer," I spat.

Nate's mouth opened and closed like a fish, but he recovered quickly, eyes ashamed, head dropping sheepishly. "You heard … Look, I'd never actually do something like that. I say stupid things when I'm drunk, Beetle, but that's all it was. Just talk. I'm sorry you heard it."

"Sorry I heard it, or sorry I caught you?"

"You can go and ask Orin right now. He'll tell you it was all nonsense. He'll tell you he was just humoring me until I sobered up. It's not the first time he's pacified me while I was shit-faced."

Orin will tell me whatever you order him to. I shook my head and changed tack. "Whose blood was all over your coat last night?"

"Could we talk about this inside?" Maisie leaped up beside Nate, claws skidding on plywood.

"No. We. Can't!" I pounded the axe head against the floor, and the dog cowered but stayed put. "Do not backburner me, Nate! We are talking about this *now*. Whose. Blood?"

His beard trembled. He held my gaze with wounded eyes and opened his mouth again, but nothing came out, not for several breaths. "Alice's," he finally said, voice breaking. "You met her when we came back from the trap lines together, remember? She brought Johan's p-mail. And, uh, she came with Christie and me to help clear the mudslide."

"What happened?"

Nate's chest hitched. Maisie wriggled into him, her whine almost too high-pitched to hear. "They shot her, Iris." My uncle's eyes swam with tears. "She's dead, and I had to tell her family that last night."

"Kahn?" I choked.

He shook his head and pressed the heels of his hands against his eyes. "No. Marauders. That gun shipment was like a sitting duck. We tried to hide it in a rail siding while we cleared the tracks, but those sons of bitches sniff out anything that stands still for too long, and they ambushed us. They shot her in the head, Iris. I held her and she looked at me and ..." Nate's words thickened, and he made a strangled sound. "We lost the whole shipment and four of my rail runners, but Alice ... Alice was a grandma. She shouldn't have been out there. I shouldn't have brought her."

"So you wanted to sell us to make up for losing your guns."

Nate sighed long and low. "Beetle, I told you, I don't deal in slaves. I swear it. I was just scared and angry and drunk out of my head last night, okay?"

"Are the tracks clear?"

"What?" Nate gaped at me, face slack.

"Did you get the tracks cleared?"

Maisie left Nate's side and slunk toward me. Something about my dead tone caught those big ears of hers and let her know I needed her more than my uncle did right now. She always knew.

I buried my hand in the deep sable hair between her shoulders.

"No, Iris. Jesus! We ran for our lives. We brought Alice home. What the hell kind of question is that?"

Don't let him guilt you. I raised my chin and even though fire pounded behind my eyes, I deadened my face and spoke evenly. "So, you're saying that you didn't bring me my family like you promised."

"Come on now—"

"You didn't even send the bloody bird for them, did you?" I

held onto Maisie like I couldn't stand without her. "You left them to starve out under Kahn's thumb. You promised them food and guns, and you didn't deliver. You've conveniently armed a local band of marauders to the teeth, and my city's main supply line is *still* completely cut off. And now nobody is even clearing the slide, because you all ran home?"

"There's the line to the east." Nate spoke through his teeth.

"*Nothing* comes from the east," I hollered. "You made damned sure of that, didn't you? And now you're our only supplier, and we're under siege. You say you're not selling us as slaves. You say you're going to help. So what do you expect my starving people to do then? What?" I shrugged. "Buddy up real quick to the suppliers in the east? Are there even any left, or did you take them all out like you did with the gas plant?"

The whites of Nate's eyes flashed, and his mouth sagged, just slightly.

He didn't know Christie told me about the gas plant. Good.

"What do you want me to do, Beetle?" he rasped.

"Stop *bullshitting* me, Nate!" I screeched. "I'm not nine years old anymore. Stop lying. Stop pretending you value my fragging opinion on trapping and social economics and tell me what the hell this is all about." I waved to the pallets.

"You wanna know about the fertilizer?" Nate's lips twitched.

"Don't patronize," I hissed. "I want to know about it all. And you're going to tell me."

Nate's crooked smile hung persistently, unfazed by my sharp words, but his eyes grew cold. "See now, Iris. I don't have to tell you a damned thing, because you don't have anything left to trade with. I've already got everything I needed from you."

I resisted the urge to rub the strip of pale skin at my wrist where my ID band used to be. Instead, I shifted my grip to Maisie's collar and raised the splitting axe in my hand. "I have your dog," I said quietly.

Nate's face twisted. "You wouldn't."

Of course, I wouldn't. I felt sick for even thinking it, but I couldn't let him see that. So I held the blade over Maisie's beautiful wedge-shaped head, looked my uncle dead in the eye, and said, "Oh, I don't know, Nate. You do stupid things when you're drunk. I do stupid things when I'm desperate. I'm a hunter, remember? I've knocked plenty of animals over the head when that was the only option left."

"Don't." He held out his hand.

"Sit down." I motioned toward the trailer wall, and my uncle sidled over and slid down it.

Gripping Masie's collar firmly, I stepped backward and sat on the half-empty pallet of fertilizer with the axe across my lap. There were ten steps between us if Nate tried anything stupid.

I waited.

"It's a long story, Beetle," Nate sighed.

"Oh, I've got all day, *Sasquatch*."

CHAPTER
TWENTY-SEVEN

Before the collapse, I drove trucks. Mostly dry-van haulers like this." Nate flicked a hand toward the trailer ceiling. "I didn't own my own rig, didn't want to be tied to a truck payment—hell, I'd just bought this place—so I was a company driver.

"All their tractors were fitted with GPS monitoring and kill-switches. If you sped, you got automatically ticketed. If you took the truck too far from its assigned route, you couldn't get it to start again once it shut down. You'd have to call the hotline to disable the kill-switch and get you going again. I guess it prevented people from stealing their rigs."

Nate rolled his head back, letting it thud against the wall. His Adam's apple bobbed. "You know, I feel old as shit saying this, but I remember exactly where I was when the collapse started. Hauling a load, just outside of Brassey Creek, a thousand klicks from home. It wasn't anything momentous. My GPS glitched. Then it said no satellite signal. That happened, sometimes. I didn't think anything of it, but when I stopped to take a piss, and I came back out, the truck wouldn't start. I tried to phone the hotline, but my phone wouldn't work. No big deal. Cell coverage sucked in Northern BC at the best of times.

"I walked back into the gas station to use their phone, and the two attendants were crowded around a TV. They couldn't get a single channel. Landline worked though, so I called the hotline, and they walked me through how to disable the kill switch. I didn't turn the truck off again until I got home.

"I read later that week in the paper that a solar flare had taken out most of the satellites, weather, imaging, commercial … everything. My company disabled the GPS kill switches on all the trucks so we could keep working. A week later, I'm at a loading dock in the Surrey terminal, eating my supper in the truck and scanning radio channels—they were all static—when there's this explosion on the far side of the lot. Like lightning, white enough to burn my eyes, but the sky was clear that night. Other drivers had been reporting Northern Lights as far down as Seattle. It was wild." Nate stared at the ceiling like he could see through to the sky.

"A transformer exploded," he said, "on the pole across the street. The whole parking lot smelled like ozone. Everyone froze watching it, but I got this feeling in my gut, like this was something big. Power wasn't just out in the freight terminal. I couldn't see lights anywhere on the horizon. The warehouse wasn't even finished loading my truck, but I just pulled out of the loading dock, sealed the doors, and started driving.

"From Surrey, all the way past Abbotsford, there were transformers puking out smoke. The blackout had swept across the whole city, far as I could see. I drove home, parked the trailer behind the house, and ate canned chili by candlelight. When the power didn't come on the next morning, I unhooked the trailer and drove the tractor back into the city.

"People were already looting. That's when I knew it was bad. Glass everywhere. Honest to God, one guy walking down the sidewalk hauling a king-sized mattress." Nate's face sobered. "I got scared. I hooked up to the first unlocked van hauler I found, drove it home, and parked it beside the first one. No one stopped me. The cops didn't show up at my front door. The truck kept starting every morning, so I kept going. I mean, I got a bit more savvy, started busting open doors, checking loads, and only hauling home what I thought people would pay for.

"First, it was freeze-dried food. Folks hoarded bleach at the start for some reason, so *that* was a hot commodity for a bit. After that, it was propane and space heaters, then sugar, flour, and powdered milk. Alcohol. You get the picture."

"You spent the apocalypse looting on an industrial scale?" I snapped.

Nate snorted. "I didn't just loot. I drove up to check on your mom. Before the collapse, Anne was a secretary for that crazy old rich guy who had your *city* built to his specs. You know the rest. He died during the collapse, and your mom stayed, along with all the others who built the place. She was happy clicking keyboards in her little commune. I asked her if she needed anything and drove her up goods from time to time, but when the roads started clogging up with abandoned vehicles, and sink holes big enough to swallow cars, I couldn't make the drive as often as I wanted.

"Then the marauders started laying out spike belts and road-blocks to catch people like me. I kept hauling, taking back roads instead of mains, but none of those were built for loaded semis. It only took a few winters of no maintenance for all the roads to crumble, highways and secondaries. One day, the truck over-heated up past Kamloops, other end of the lake from you. I just got out and left it there in the middle of a desert of cracked pavement. I walked the rails home. They were still clear. And on that long walk I realized, if I wanted to keep moving product, I'd have to do it by rail, and I'd need help. That's how this all start-ed." Nate smiled vaguely. "That's my comic book origin story."

"I don't know what that is," I said.

"Sorry. Before your time."

He was still deflecting, I realized. Steering the conversation where he wanted it to go. Soldamnit, the man was slippery. "Explain this." I smacked the broad side of the axe against the fertilizer bags.

Maisie licked her lips and laid her head on my thigh, blissfully unaware of her abducted status.

Nate frowned at her, cleared his throat, and scrubbed at his beard. "This is the first trailer I took. The one from Surrey. I didn't even read the manifest that night. When I got it home, I found out I was the proud new owner of twenty pallets of bulk fertilizer and two skids of industrial weed killer." Nate's forehead puckered. "Neither of those are at the top of people's post-apocalyptic shopping lists, in case you're wondering." He waited for me to smile along with him and when I didn't, he blew a long sigh. "You gotta understand, Iris. Things were pretty desperate at the start."

"Define *desperate*, Nate. Was it selling-a-whole-city-including-women-and-children-to-a-coal-slaver desperate?" I gripped Maisie's collar so tight, the leather edges bit into my fingers.

"It wasn't like that. I'm not like that. I'm just a guy trying to *live* out here." He sighed. "The other trailers were sellable, but this stuff," he pointed to the fertilizer, "I couldn't offload, and I had to eat. I had to fuel up the truck and bring product home." He shrugged. "So I got creative."

"Zuse, I don't know if I want to hear what creative means to you, Nate." An ache swelled in the back of my throat.

My uncle stood, so I did too, dragging Maisie up with me. His fingers flexed as he paced. "I didn't hurt anybody, Iris. It was just a con."

"Meaning what?" I snapped.

"Meaning your city was a backward little cult!" Nate shouted back, his words dripping with a sudden vitriol that startled me. "They were an easy mark then, and they still are, now. Look at them. Exactly the same as the day they took over that place. Clacking around in shiny shoes and suits. Talking like they're in some computer program and pretending the world never ended. Looking down their *noses* at the rest of us while we bring them *everything* they need to live. Walled off. Isolated, vulnerable, and stupid. That's what Kahn's turned you all into."

"You. Be. Careful," I hissed, holding the axe over Maisie as her ears pinned back against her head.

"Or what, Iris? You've got it all under control here? Holding all the cards?" Nate shook his head. Then he whistled short and sharp.

Maisie lunged toward him, wrenching my arm hard enough to send me sprawling. My knees hammered against the trailer deck. One of them tore open on the tie down rails. Fingers twisting, I lost my grip on the collar. The splitting axe clattered and skidded toward my uncle. I dove for it, but Nate was closer.

He scooped it up and backed away. Maisie pranced at his side like we were playing a game. "Now you sit!" Nate barked, eyes hard and voice cold.

My rear end hit the floor at the same time Maisie's did, both of us obedient dogs.

"Goddamnit, Iris, open your eyes. I conned your city, because they're easy to con. They believe *anything*."

I shook my head, still panting, knees throbbing. Blood seeped through the tear in my pants. "We're educated citizens. We hold the single largest cache of information since the Collapse."

"Bullshit!" Nate bellowed. "You've got no bloody common sense! Half of the shit in your cache isn't even true. It's from the goddamned *Internet*, Iris." Nate shook his head. "But Kahn just eats that garbage up, doesn't he?" He started ticking off fingers. "The sun poisons plants. You can't grow anything outside. Solar flares fry anything with a computer chip." Crouching over me, Nate lowered his voice. "I'll bet he still has you unplugging and bagging up every scrap of electronics you own, every time he sees a sunspot, doesn't he?"

A horrible heat pressed up my throat as city procedures ran through my head. "The flares create induction currents—"

"And they're slow enough that they only affect large grids, not small gadgets. Just because some opportunistic, asshole country set off a few EMP weapons over Midwestern USA at the start of the collapse, David Kahn thinks the sun is out for his laptop. Wasn't too much of a stretch to make him believe that it was out for his crops too."

The air thickened between us. Maisie panted and nipped at Nate's fingers.

I pressed my palm over my shredded knee. "What did you do?" My words left me in a hoarse whisper.

My uncle straightened to his full, terrible height. "I just fed him some information. I made him believe if he didn't buy my supplemental fertilizer from overseas—that I paid through the teeth for—his crops would all die. The sun would kill them."

I gagged. Thoughts streamed through my head faster than I could process them. "But Olivia said. Sh-she said they *did* all die when you stopped sending fertilizer. Every plant ...""

Nate shrugged and spoke gently. "There were two pallets of weed killer, Beetle, and your greenhouse water tank has a rainwater collection line. Any time David started doubting me, I snuck into your city, and dumped a few jugs down the downspout diverters."

Oh Sol. Oh Sol, no. Air pumped out of me, thick and hot. "No. Johan's gardens. They died too."

"I followed him from the fertilizer drop point. I knew where they were the whole time."

"Y-you could have starved us all." I swayed, saliva flooding my mouth and dizziness clotting in my head. "I *helped* you."

"Yeah, you did, Iris. Thank you for that. I got the pigeon last night from Johan. He says all of your computers are down. You know what that means?"

"Kahn plugged in the virus."

"The sun can't take out small electronics." Nate tapped the axe head between his feet. "But *I* just wiped out every computer in your city."

My stomach compressed, cold and leaden. "You said the virus would only target the cred system programming."

"It's easier to build a virus to destroy a whole network. When in doubt, keep it simple, Beetle."

"Simple, Nate?" I wailed. "Wiping out the last existing computer network for a hundred kilometres is simple? Selling my people to the highest bidder is *simple*?"

"Jesus, I'm not selling anybody, Iris! I promise. But your city is *over*. Don't you see that? Every big operation has an end date. Economies. Civilizations. Cities. And yours has reached it. Kahn is running out of things to trade, and I just made it a nice clean cut instead of a slow death. He doesn't even know what he's sitting on."

"What he's sitting on?" I repeated dumbly.

"Kahn's not the only one with proprietary information." Nate preened. "I did some research on your mom's old boss, and do you know why he picked the spot he did for your little commune? Wind that big brain up, Iris. Didn't you ever wonder why it was in the middle of the bald-ass badlands?"

I shook my head. The trailer started tilting at a sickening angle. Shock pooled in my limbs and hummed in my ears, but Nate didn't seem to notice or care.

"Your so-called city is right on top of the largest remaining deposit of natural copper in the western hemisphere." Nate paused to let me absorb that.

The communication log p-mails I'd read in his office scrolled through my head. *Request shipment of 200 Remington guns and 100 cases of 12-gauge shells in exchange for future shares in acquired copper mine.* I bent over, clutched my stomach, and squeezed my eyes shut.

"You know what people need right now, Iris?" Nate continued, unsympathetic. "What they need sixteen years into an apocalypse? It's not goddamned books. It's batteries. They're all reaching their end of life now, and copper is skyrocketing. I bet I'd be sitting real pretty if I had some of Kahn's proprietary information on say ... battery construction, *and* I was the sole supplier of copper for the west coast. Wouldn't that be something?"

"You never planned on joining the city." I choked on the realization.

"No, Iris." Nate turned his back on me and vaulted down from the trailer, his dog following him. "I plan on taking it. One way or another, I plan on taking it."

Hinges groaned and the trailer's doors swung inward.

"No." I gulped, scrambling to my feet. "Nate, no!" but as I slammed into the doors, the locks clicked home, and the trailer plunged into darkness.

Maisie barked frantically outside.

I hammered on the door until my fist ached. When I stopped, my uncle spoke, his voice muffled by the barrier between us.

"I'm gonna give you a little time to cool down and decide whose side you're on, Iris. And if you behave, I might even go get your family."

I closed my eyes, took a slow, steadying breath, and bellowed, "Eat shit, Nate."

CHAPTER
TWENTY-EIGHT

Mom used to tell me my anger was like a wildfire and, if I didn't control it when it was small and smoldering, it would break free and burn everything it touched. I'd witnessed what fires did to the terrain around the lake. Once, when I was five or six, a summer burn scoured right to the edge of the city. In the aftermath, I'd stood out there on the border, gawking at the black skeleton plains, certain it was my fault. The burnt grass looked like wads of dead spiders and steel wool. My anger had escaped somehow. How many times had I swallowed hot rage since then?

When Nate locked the semi-trailer and walked away, I didn't swallow. I went berserk. Heat rolled over me, crackling through my limbs and snuffing out every other emotion. Pressure burst out of me in hot screams. I vaguely recall hammering the trailer walls with my fists, kicking like a trapped animal, and savoring the pain it caused. Pain was the only thing strong enough to sweep out the thoughts cutting through my brain, and I couldn't weather those thoughts right now. Pain was pure and simple. I could regulate it. So, I threw myself against the walls until my knuckles peeled and bled, and my toes bruised and swelled. I stamped and paced in the dark even though my torn knee throbbed, and I screamed until my throat felt like I'd swallowed sandpaper.

When I couldn't kick or scream anymore, I tore into the fertilizer bags, heaving them onto my shoulder and hurling them against the trailer doors where they burst and rained powder across the floor until the air was thick with dust that choked me, and I tripped and fell over half-empty bags in the dark. Dust caked on my sweaty skin, stung in my wounds, and clogged my throat. As I hacked and spit, I remembered that Olivia and I wore masks when we poured the stuff because it was dangerous to inhale, but I didn't care. It was probably bull-shit anyways. It was all bullshit the whole time. Nate had been selling us snake oil. Now he was selling us.

I couldn't judge how many minutes or hours ticked by as I sagged against a battered wall and eventually sunk down in the dark, but the sun swung high enough overhead to turn the trailer into a sweltering oven. My clothes clung to me, twisted and stifling. I couldn't breathe. Sweat oozed from every pore as I sat and focused on deep inhalations and slow releases. Fertilizer powder crunched underfoot every time I shifted. Garden tools clacked outside, but I wasn't strong enough to call out for help. Blanketed in blackness, burned out from anger, I could only whimper as all my circling thoughts returned to roost and started stabbing at all my soft bits.

Nate was a fraud. Sasquatch was all an act. I'd never known him. I'd loved a version of him that didn't even exist, and I'd thought he loved me back.

"No," I countered out loud, fresh tears stinging my gritty eyes. I wouldn't accept it. Nate—my Nate—loved me. He was real. He had to be. I had not imagined the man who had shown me how to catch salamander larvae in the shallows at the lake and taught me how to suck nectar from purple clovers. The uncle who'd re-braided my hair when it got in my eyes without pulling like Mom did and howled at coyotes with me when no other adult would, that man was the real Nate.

Then who was the dead-eyed asshole who drunkenly suggested selling my people into slavery? Who was the prick who casually admitted to planning to take my city, and thanked me for being his accomplice before locking me in a trailer with no air?

I cringed at the memory of Nate's blue eyes gone cold. Had I imagined it? We'd both been angry. Sol, I'd threatened to club his dog with an axe, and that sure as hell wasn't me. Nate had admitted to saying things he hadn't meant, in the heat of the moment. When he let me out of here, I would apologize for yelling, and then coax Sasquatch back into existence, because that was the Nate my city needed, the one who wanted to share knowledge and print affordable books and re-unite with my family. He'd been a foundation of my childhood, and I'd crumble if those playful blue eyes and unapologetic laugh weren't the genuine deal. The Nate I knew couldn't be a lie, and I could prove it. If I could keep my damned temper under control and stop barging into the man's office uninvited, I could bring the real Nate back.

Despite the heavy heat and the dizziness hanging like cobwebs in my brain, I stood and paced. The scab on my knee cracked open and bled freely and my knuckles throbbed, but I didn't mind. It was better than the boredom burning me up from the inside. I felt like if I didn't find something to focus on soon, I'd claw my way out of my own skin. I needed stimulation, noise, something to latch onto but there was nothing in here save the fertilizer and me. So I paced. I pulled long swathes of plastic wrap from around the pallets, twisted them into ropes and tied them into knots. I shook out my hair and re-braided it, even though it felt gritty and greasy. And I stacked words in my head like blocks, one by one, building the perfect convincing conversation in my head. My uncle was a good man, and I could make him reconsider what he'd said. If I used the right words, I could make him see Johan and the rest of my city as valuable allies.

I was weaving plastic rope in the dark when the trailer latch clattered and squealed, and the rear doors swung open. White, blazing light knifed into the stale space, blinding me. Fresh air washed my cheeks, and I sucked in deep breaths that smelled like honeysuckles and barbecue smoke.

"Jesus Christ. You're a mess," Nate grumbled.

I clutched the woven plastic between my fingers and peeled my eyes open to blink at my uncle's silhouette.

He was holding a small rifle—probably the .22 from the front porch closet—lazily propped over his shoulder. "If I let you out of here to clean yourself up, and you try anything stupid, we're coming right on back, understand?"

I nodded, licked my lips and immediately regretted it as the chemical taste of fertilizer burned my tongue. "Could I have some water?" I croaked.

"After you shower and change. Come on." He stepped back to give me room to exit and didn't offer a hand to help me down when I balanced on the trailer's edge, limbs slack with heat.

We crossed the lawn in silence. Nate didn't put the gun away once we got inside. Instead, he followed me up the stairs, cradling the rifle in the crook of his arm and waiting wide-stanced in the hallway when I crossed the threshold into my bedroom.

A flash of silver caught my attention, and I glanced at a newly installed hook and eye latch screwed into the outer door-frame. It was oddly dark inside the room. My gaze rose to the window beside the bed. Slats of wood had been nailed across it from the outside and only cracks of light seeped through. *Oh Sol,* my throat spasmed, *he's just moving you from one cell to another.*

"Get your clothes and get into the bathroom," Nate said coldly. "You're tracking dust all over."

I opened the dresser top drawer with shaking hands and pulled out a clean pair of pants, underwear and a T-shirt big enough to fit two of me. Then I sidled past my uncle with my head down, padded into the bathroom, and shut the door behind me. I stood under a cold shower until my skin was numb, tingling and red, and my torn knee bled freely.

Nate didn't say a word when we crossed the hallway back to the bedroom. He just shut the door behind me and flicked the latch outside closed. I knew because I checked if the door would open after he left. I sat on the edge of the bed, mouth dry and heart pounding as I scrubbed at the old scars on my cheeks. Dust motes bobbed and swirled in the slats of light cutting through the dimness. My knee and raw knuckles throbbed. As my eyes adjusted, I noticed a glass on the nightstand and a jug of water, sweating with condensation. I drank the whole thing, and then I curled onto the bed and slept.

A knock on the door woke me, Christie with my supper. "Bit of a day, huh?" She swept into the room, pushed the jug on the nightstand to one side, and set down a steaming plate of barbe-cued chicken, pasta with peas in cream sauce, and a tray bun with a pat of butter on the side.

"I'm, uh, not supposed to be in here, but easier to ask forgiveness than get permission, right?" She tucked a set of cutlery rolled into a napkin beside the plate and then stood there, lingering while my mouth filled with saliva. "He says stupid things when he's drunk, but he'd never act on them. He's a good man."

"I know." That's what I was counting on.

"He's just got a lot on his plate, and Alice … Well, that hit all of us hard. Just give him a bit of time, and he'll come round, all right?"

Anger licked at my belly. *How dare she offer advice like we're old friends instead of prisoner and jailor? Or a master and a slave.* Breathing against the bitterness in my throat, I motioned toward the boarded-up window and spoke tightly. "Looks like I have all the time in the world, don't I?" *Now leave so I can eat my damned chicken.*

She did. And when she came back later for the empty plate, she didn't notice the missing butter knife.

I expected Nate to come to my room late smelling of blueberry moonshine, but he was quietly sober when he tapped on my door hours after sunset. I sat up and studied his blank face as he closed the door behind him and crossed the room to settle into the wicker rocking chair.

"A bird came for you today." Nate pulled a strip of paper from his pocket and held it out to me.

All of the towering phrases I'd painstakingly built all afternoon toppled in my mind. Maisie whined and scratched at the door from the hallway outside, but Nate didn't seem to notice. His face had resigned itself to a tired frown, and his knuckles were white as he clasped the paper. I took it and read it.

> *To: URLs of Nate. Attn: Iris. Re: happy endings. Don't have one for you yet, but I'm working on it. Pigeon King still holds greenhouses. More people joined us when Kahn crashed computers. We took generators, garages, and Cache. All Browsers are with us now. Motorcycles headed out to pick up shipment blocked by rail. Meet you at Lytton?*
> *Love R.*

"Robert," I whispered. He was on our side. We were winning, and he and Vinton and the Browsers were coming.

"*Love* Robert." Nate flicked a finger toward the paper. "That your boyfriend, Iris? He riding out, a knight on a motorcycle coming to get you?"

He's still mad. Make the first move. Bring the old Nate back. I straightened, forced my gaze not to skirt away from my uncle's face, and said, "I'm sorry about Maisie. I was mad. I'd never hurt her."

My uncle blew a long, soft sigh. "I know you wouldn't. You don't need to say sorry about that. I'm sorry I suggested something as stupid as slavery when I was drunk. Now what are we going to do about these Browsers, Beetle?"

My chest tingled and my next breaths came shallow. *Beetle. My Nate. Hold onto this.* "This is good, Nate. There's ten motorcycles all together. We can go back. Even with the rails blocked, we can move families out. Vinton says the marauders mostly ignore them, because Browsers are always armed with handguns and their usual cargo is just old computer parts. We can go back with them. We can ship food and reinforcements using the bikes before the marauders ever found out we were moving something they wanted."

"Your people will want the gun shipment I promised them. The gun shipment the marauders took that I still have to pay for."

I scooted to the edge of the bed, willing him to look up. "They want help, Nate. They'll take any kind they can get. And I still want to help too. You said we could do big things together. We can still get rid of Kahn. We can be a family again."

My uncle looked up. Relief flooded his face like rainwater soaking into parched soil. A broad, boyish smile bunched his cheeks and crinkled his eyes. "I'd like that. Very much." Blinking up at the ceiling, he unclasped his hands, reached into his pocket and withdrew something else.

I recognized the thin cord dangling between his fingers and the slim black device tucked in his palm. *The MP3 player.* Unexpected tears stung my eyes. I'd raked the room for it after supper and had only been able to find the hand-crank flashlight, but not the player or earbuds. I had told Nate how much I hated silence. He'd brought the music player back as a peace offering.

"I can't tell you how much I missed you and Vinton. Hell,

even Anne and John. I've wanted this, a secure place for my people, my family, for so long. Sometimes, I just go crazy wishing for it."

Suddenly, I didn't want to push. I didn't want to talk my uncle into anything. I just wanted him to stay. *Do it now, while he's still smiling. You can convince him.* "And our city would be lucky to have you, Nate, but you've got to understand that I've got a lot of family, not just Vinton and Mom and Dad. Not just Robert and the Browsers."

Robert's face rose in my mind, and suddenly I wished he was here beside me already. He'd know what to say, how to frame his words wisely. "There's so many good people caught in the middle of this, and they deserve a chance too." I gulped.

"A chance?" Nate's smile froze on his face. He leaned away from me and scrubbed a hand down his face. "A chance! Iris, you haven't been around this as long as I have. All those people in your city *have* had a chance to adapt, to change, to join the real world for *sixteen* damned years, and none of them did. They all just keep playing pretend, staring at their screens and shining their shoes." He shook his head. "They're stuck, Iris. And that city nest isn't big enough for all of us. Look, I won't sell anyone, but they need to leave. Sometimes, you've got to push the runts out, so the ones more likely to survive can eat."

I shuddered. "No. That sounds like something Kahn would say. Not you, Nate."

"I've *tried*, Iris. I've tried to talk to Anne, and she cut me out of your family."

"She's watched me starve since then, Nate. She's seen how Kahn treats people. She sent the pigeon to you, didn't she?"

Nate sniffed. "Yeah, she did."

"And Johan. You've always been allies. People will side with him. With you. He has Cache now. We could make books, like you said. You were right, what you said about an end date coming. I've lived in the city for sixteen years, Nate. I've been on the inside. And people can feel it coming. They're hungry for change, and you can bring it for them. You don't need to take it by force, you don't need to drive us out. Join us and push Kahn out, and you'll be their hero."

"I killed their computers, Iris. That's like killing their god. I'm no hero."

"You are to me," I whispered.

Nate's throat worked. His fingers shook as he turned the MP3 player in his hands.

Push. Do it now.

I licked my lips. "You could save us. *All* of us, Nate. And people would never forget that. You could give them a fresh start instead of pushing them out. You could share the wealth."

Nate's eyes flared. He bolted out of the chair so fast that I cringed. "Share the wealth?" he spat, standing over me. "'Cause that's what they've been doing this whole time, isn't it, Iris? *Sharing the wealth.* They got their fresh start taking over a cushy commune that wasn't even theirs! Did they share then? I've had to *beg* for scraps of information. Your people looked at me like I was dirty every time I walked their streets. And Johan has been dragging his heels for years. He could have pushed Kahn out years ago. I begged him to. But, no!" Nate's hand knifed through the space between us. "No, he waited until Kahn *shot* me, and he didn't even start his damned revolution then.

"I'm *done* sharing, Iris!" he shouted. "They want a fresh start? Johan can give them one out in the bush. They can crawl out of their air-conditioned, wood-paneled offices and learn to live off the land like the rest of us have. It's my turn now, under- stand?" His cold blue gaze pinned me, like a predator deciding if he was hungry enough to consume his cornered prey.

As I held my breath and shrank away from him, my uncle stuffed the MP3 player and ear buds back into his pocket.

"You know what, Iris? Maybe it's best if you sat this one out. Stay here where it's safe. Me and my team will take the guns from the armory tomorrow, and we'll meet your Browsers. I don't need them, just their motorcycles and their weapons. We'll do our best not to hurt anyone, but I need to take that city, now, before the marauders do. I don't have time to change minds anymore, and I can't afford extra mouths to feed. Everyone who wants to be on my side already is. It ends here."

He left, and he took the music player with him. The rattle of the latch locking made my throat close. My chest turned to stone as the realization struck me.

He was done with me. My own personal end date.

Nate loved me, but he'd always intended to use me. He wanted to be family, but he was leaving tomorrow to hijack the Browser's motorcycles, ransack my home, and scatter my people to the wind. He knew silence felt like death to me, but he took the MP3 player regardless, because he was done with me.

Nate wasn't the carefree, jovial wanderer of my childhood, but he wasn't just a cold, calculating, dictator either.

He was both.

I blinked down at the p-mail in my hands, studying every letter of it as my eyes blurred with tears. Robert was coming to Lytton, and I wouldn't get to see him or Vinton. My uncle would intercept them, hold them at gunpoint, and then what? Dump them in the wilderness? Abandon Vinton in the middle of nowhere and take over my city? I couldn't believe it. *Nate's just tired and angry and desperate.* My thumb ran over the soft swirls of Robert's tidy printing. The penciled letters smudged, highlighting the angled indentations of a separate message. I wiped the wetness from my eyes and held the paper close to my face.

Someone had opened this p-mail, laid another piece of paper on top of it and wrote hard enough to leave imprints of their words on this strip. The first letters were '*Attn*'.

A coded message? From Robert? I rubbed my thumb further down the strip highlighting four faint words before the phantom message ran off the side of my paper. But those four words were legible, and they stopped my heart when I read them.

Attn: Coaltana re: Workers

This wasn't a secret message from Robert. Coaltana was the coal company that Orin had said would pay for slaves. *Son of a bitch, Nate. No!* He had said he wouldn't sell people. He'd promised. Breath leaked out of me leaving me aching and hollow, pulling every last scrap of my hope with it. I took several gulping inhales and each one burned my throat more than the last.

He's left you no choice, Iris. He had lied to my face just now. He had promised not to sell people into slavery on the same day he sent a message to a slave company inquiring about workers. I had to end this. I had to break the Nate I loved to stop the Nate I hated from rising up. I had to destroy Sasquatch and Beetle forever.

I sobbed. I mourned the loss of us. I allowed myself to wallow in it for one whole hour while Maisie paced and snuffled outside my door.

And then, when the house went utterly silent, I took the butter knife out from under the mattress.

CHAPTER
TWENTY-NINE

Somebody should have told Nate how stupid it was to lock someone in a room with a mind that wouldn't shut off and then leave them with only one viable option to focus on. When something challenged me—really motivated me—my frantic brain was capable of shifting into this sweet spot where everything calmed like the lake first thing in the morning. My mind reeled in all its frayed wires and plugged them all into the problem until every minuscule facet of it was covered. I could rapidly absorb information that would overwhelm a typical person and run hundreds of scenarios at once with ease, as long as there was a reward firmly in sight. And escaping was the ultimate reward. I could save my family, rescue my city from Nate's end date, and make up for everything I'd ever fragged up.

When I was certain the rest of the house slept, I eased the absconded butter knife out from under the mattress, along with a sock I'd stuffed with the chicken breast from supper. Then I peeled my pillowcase off and filled it with the remainder of my spare clothes from the dresser and the hand-crank flashlight.

Crouching behind the bedroom door, I pressed the butter

knife's blade under the cap above the top hinge and levered the hinge pin up. It was well-oiled, but it still took several minutes to pry it free. I was able to pull the remaining hinge pins in under five minutes. Tucking my toes under the crack in the door, I lifted the panel free of its hinges, pulled it to the side, and reached around to pop up the hook latch. Once I moved my pillowcase into the hallway, I re-hung the door and latched it. Now, if Nate or Christie woke to use the bathroom, they'd see my door locked as it should be. I needed every second of head start I could wring out of this plan.

Claws clicked on the hardwood as Maisie trotted up the stairs. I held my breath, reached into the pillowcase, and wordlessly offered her the barbeque-stained sock stuffed with chicken. Her big ears perked, and she accepted the gift daintily. I kissed her lovely broad head, and she wriggled down the stairs beside me before retreating with her delicacy to her rug in the living room.

Next step was the kitchen.

Padding past the oven, I snagged a lighter from the junk drawer and a jar of pears from the pantry. Then I returned to the front entry. I could hear Maisie licking her sock as I edged open the front closet and pressed my feet into my fertilizer caked boots. Nate's .22 was propped up with the umbrellas, and behind it, my crossbow and Johan's hiking backpack. I liberated all of them, along with a box of shells from the top shelf, before slipping through the front door and creeping off the porch into the cool night. With each step, I expected lanterns to flare and Nate's angry voice booming through the farmhouse, but the moonless night greeted me with only the whine of crickets and the lulling vibrato of tree frogs. Stuffing everything except the weapons and the flashlight into the hiking pack, I adjusted the shoulder straps and crept into the gardens, choosing a path that avoided the lighted windows of the pigeon loft on stilts. It was manned twenty-four seven, and

I had work to do before I planned to draw the attention of the posted worker inside.

The closest water storage tank to the house would shield me from sight of the pigeon loft, and it had a two-inch drain at its bottom. I fumbled in the dark until I found it. Unscrewing the cover cap, I cranked open the drain valve and stepped over the rush of water spewing into the dirt. Then I headed toward the potato crops.

My eyes adjusted to the dark. As I moved between rows of billowing plants, they looked like ribbons of gray, stacked clouds. I couldn't make out the next water tank for a reference point, but the creak of the central windmill whined through the darkness. When I judged I was in the right spot, I set down my weapons and crouched, hissing as the scab on my knee cracked open. Clicking on the hand-crank flashlight, I shielded its bright beam with one hand. The faint light seeping between my fingers was enough to see by without risking being spotted out here in the fields. Muted light swept over several clods of dirt before I found what I was looking for.

Dark patches on foliage. A blighted plant.

Setting the flashlight between my feet, I gripped the plant at its base. When I pulled it, the wet smell of decay oozed from the crumbling dirt. Holding back a gag, I dug until my fingers encountered the slimy, spongy ruin of a potato. I pulled it up, and then dug up three more tubers before flicking off my flashlight.

Two water tanks supplied the potato field and one larger one irrigated the tomatoes. I climbed all three in turn, opened their top access hatches and listened to the plop of a blighted potato settling to the bottom of the tank. My additions were small enough that no one would notice them until it was too late. Blight would spread through the irrigation water to rot the compound's entire potato and tomato crops. Nate had attacked my home with a virus. I'd retaliate with a fungus.

Wiping the rancid smell off my hands, I froze, scrambling for my next move. *Come on, Iris. You've played this out in your head a hundred times in the last few hours.* And then I had it. Diesel! Diesel was next. I headed for the slip tank. Three yellow jerry cans sat in the gravel below the tank. Two felt empty as I hoisted them, but one jug was half-full. I topped it off, and when I was finished, I bent the butter knife from the house into a crooked *L*, jammed it against the trigger on the tank's fill nozzle and left the slip tank puking diesel onto the ground in my wake. I headed back toward the farmhouse, veering into the backyard.

The armory lock was thicker than the one I'd broken on the semi-trailer. Even if I hadn't cared about the noise it would make, I was fairly certain I couldn't break this padlock, nor did I need to. I didn't have to get inside Nate's armory. I just had to make sure nothing got out. My uncle planned to arm his team in a few scant hours to raid my city, and I was going to make sure they didn't have the resources to do it.

This place had been a root cellar before it was an arsenal. That meant it had to have a stack on it somewhere for ventilation. I clambered over the mounded soil roof, sweeping through vegetation until my foot struck something solid with a hollow *thunk*. A PVC vent line with a chimney cap, a little thicker than my arm, sprouted through the thick grass like a black mushroom. If I remembered correctly, below this, Nate's hand-loading work bench was pushed against the back wall, stacked with boxes of fresh ammunition. *Perfect.*

The pillowcase was thin and tore easily into strips. I shredded my spare T-shirts too, and, when I had a respectable pile of rags, I doused them all with diesel, snapped off the plastic vent cap, and started shoving the fuel-soaked rags down the hole. My crossbow bolts were too short, but I found a stout stick that was long enough to shove all the way down the vent line. I wrapped my last rag around it, poured the remainder of fuel from the jerry can down the pipe, and chased it with the lit torch.

A low whomp rumbled the ground beneath my feet. Flames mushroomed up the vent and singed my hair. Staggering, I fell back, blinking, blinded, and fully expecting every person in Nate's compound to fly awake and seize me where I stood. But, as I froze, crouched amongst the waving seedheads with the smell of burned hair filling my nostrils, the only sound I could pick up was the crackle of eager flames echoing up the cellar vent.

Go, before the ammunition starts going off. The blotchy after-image of the flash fire still swam across my vision as my fingers scrambled through the grass for my crossbow and Nate's rifle. I found both, tucked them against me, and sprinted around the house, taking a wide route toward the pigeon loft.

A silhouette pressed against one of the small windows, peering toward the backyard where I'd set off my explosion. They hadn't seen me yet.

Only after dumping my weapons and pack on the far side of the goat shed, did I backtrack to climb the ladder to the loft. As the trapdoor opened above me, I bit the inside of my cheek hard enough to make tears well in my eyes.

"The armory's on fire!" I sobbed as I pulled myself up the last few rungs. "Did you hear it?"

A face swam into view past my tears. Orin. Goddamned Orin who wrote hard enough to tear paper. It was probably his message I had read. *Attn: Coaltana re: Workers.* I baulked and then caught myself. *You need to do this, Iris. No stopping now.* He offered a hand, and I took it and climbed fully into the loft with the man who'd sent an inquiry about enslaving my whole city. "I think someone's attacking us," I babbled. "It's right behind the house. Get Nate!"

"He's in the house, isn't—"

"Get Nate!" I howled hysterically, clawing Orin's arm and hauling him toward the trap door.

He descended the ladder in a daze. When he started trotting toward the farmhouse, I turned from the window, grabbed a multi-tier travel cage and started stuffing disgruntled pigeons inside. The birds growled and puffed up, but they were easy to catch when they were sleepy. It took two cages, and the birds were definitely overcrowded, but I managed to scoop all twenty-three birds from their lofts. There'd be other pigeons, still en route with messages somewhere, but this was the bulk of Nate's high speed communication system.

The cages were fitted with thick leather straps. Ignoring the outraged squeaks and flying feathers, I shrugged one cage over my shoulder and hauled it down the ladder. By the time I returned for the second, the snap of gunfire ricocheted across the compound, and the scent of spilled diesel wafted in the breeze. Startled murmurs, pounding feet, and flaring lanterns followed. I glanced toward the farmhouse and the pale orange glow beyond.

Time to go.

Lugging the cages behind the goat shed, I lashed them both to my hiking pack and allowed myself three breaths to consider my weapons. I knew the crossbow, but it was slow to reload and Nate's rifle had a seven shot magazine. Reluctantly, I secured my bow to the hiking pack, eased the entire awkward load up onto my back, and cinched the straps even as they cut into my shoulders. With the .22 cradled in my arms and pigeons crooning at my back, I eased out into the vast gardens and away from the waking chaos of the compound.

People would congregate around the water tank closest to the house. That's where they'd set up the diesel pump and hoses to try to douse the flames, and that's when they'd discover both tanks, the water and the diesel, were rapidly emptying.

The crack of ammunition exploding echoed through the valley. I peered back at the farmhouse one last time, knowing I'd never see it again, breathless with the repercussions of what I'd set into motion in a little under half an hour. I'd crippled my uncle's major crops, destroyed his weapon cache, drained his fuel, and wiped out his communication system. And no one was even chasing me yet.

"Maybe you'd better sit this one out, Sasquatch," I murmured before swinging south toward the train tracks and home.

This wasn't my end date. This was just the beginning.

And Sol help anyone who underestimated me.

CHAPTER
THIRTY

scanned the area around the sleeping man for weapons before standing over him wide-stanced and tapping his head with the barrel of Nate's .22.

He woke with a start, arms windmilling, eyes bugged out, and rotten teeth bared.

"Darrin, I presume," I said.

The rail runner swore and scrambled off his sleeping mat, tangling in his blankets.

I stepped over the mess to keep my gun pressed against his temple. *Look tough, Iris. Or he'll see right through you and kill you.*

"Everything worth stealing is locked in the safe." The muscles in the man's neck corded as he held up his hands. "It's a combination lock. You kill me, and you can't get in. It weighs more than you do so good luck moving it."

"I don't want anything in the safe. Let's go for a ride, Darrin." It was him. Even in the darkness of this siding shed, I recognized the hollowed-out features of the man with the electric hand car. Nate had stopped him from abducting me back on that first day, appearing out of nowhere like a ghost from the dead to admonish the man. That seemed like years ago, now.

"Nate's ward." Darrin gaped as recognition dawned on him too.

"Not anymore." I pulled my mouth into a sneer and tried to imagine I was intimidating, like Kahn or Vannevar. It was difficult with cages full of pigeons flapping and cooing on my back.

"I-I can't run the car without Gren and Mitch. They're my crew."

My heart pounded between my ears. *He's testing you. Soldamnit, don't give him an inch.* "That's bullshit, Darrin!" I jabbed the rifle against his temple hard enough that he winced. "If you need them so bad, they'd be sleeping here too, and they're not. I checked. Your car is electric. I could take the damned thing myself." I couldn't. There was a chain and padlock around the wheel and axle of Darrin's vehicle. I'd checked that too, before waking him. Nodding at the key hanging around his dirty neck, I said, "What was it you said to me? 'I could shoot you. Then I wouldn't have to make room for a passenger.'"

Darrin winced again. "I'm sorry I said that. I wouldn't have shot you. I was just trying to scare you."

Ditto, Darrin. Ditto. I clicked off the safety on the rifle.

"Shit. What do you want?"

"I want a ride."

"How far?"

"Lytton."

Darrin tried to shake his head, but he couldn't move much with the barrel of the .22 pinning him. "I can't." His voice cracked. "That's way outside my territory. If another runner catches me on their tracks without paying a toll, they'll shoot me."

Leaning into him, close enough to smell his sour breath, I enunciated my words slowly. "Well, that makes it easy. I'll shoot you right now, Darrin. That's a guarantee. Or you can run me to Lytton and pay whatever tolls you have to, and then you can keep this gun and a full box of ammunition as payment. That sounds fair, doesn't it? That sounds better than your brains painting the wall behind us, yeah?"

"Yeah," he gulped. "It does."

"Well, what are we waiting for?" I smiled even though my stomach felt like cold porridge.

"Just let me get some toll fares from the safe."

"It's a three and a half hour run to Lytton. You gonna stand with the gun aimed at my head the whole way?" Darrin sniffed, his hand resting on the throttle lever, and his nervous eyes big behind the goggles he'd donned as soon as he eased the scabbed together hand car out of its siding shed. "Your arms'll get sore."

I snorted and remained standing stiffly on the cargo deck behind him. Suddenly, I had to pee, but I wasn't going to tell him that. *Note to future self: before overthrowing an evil dictator's plans and blowing up armories and hijacking rail runner cars, pee first.* The big hand-car motor whined up to speed, and trees flashed by on either side of us in shades of moonlit gray, whisking me farther and farther away from Nate's compound.

In the silence that followed, something other than my full bladder pressed on me from the inside. The enormity of what I was trying to do—and what I'd already done—gripped me by the throat. Who did I think I was? Nate had destroyed a gas refinery; he'd killed my city's crops just to sell Kahn his snake-oil fertilizer. He intended to sack my home and sell its citizens as slaves. What would he do since I'd turned on him? And what would Kahn do, just let me walk back in as a criminal? An outcast? The catalyst that started a civil war?

I bit my lip until fresh pain washed out the flood of defeating thoughts. I couldn't think like this. I couldn't afford distractions like having to piss, and I didn't have the luxury of doubt. *Just one step at a time, Iris. Focus on the next step. Just get to Robert and Vinton.*

I set the bird cages, my crossbow, and the mostly empty hiking pack down on the cargo deck, but I stayed standing with the rifle aimed at Darrin.

"Listen." He shook his head. "Even if we're playing nice and paying tolls, there's still the odd marauder out this way, and if you're sitting, you make a smaller target for snipers, yeah? I'd rather not spend my next few days scrubbing blood off my cargo deck and explaining to Nate where his ward disappeared to, if it's all the same to you."

So I sat. I ignored my filling bladder and the oozing scab on my knee. When the full moon rose over us, I cradled Nate's .22 across my thighs and pulled the jar of pears from my pack. I ate the whole thing and then, with my fingers still sticky, I pulled the rolled-up notebook I'd stolen from the pigeon loft out of my back pocket, and smoothed the pages against a brisk wind. I could make out the lettering just enough to read it if I squinted. Flipping pages until I found Orin's copy of Robert's message to me, I scanned the rest of the day's entries, and there it was.

Attn: Coaltana. re: Workers.

I clapped my hand over the rest of the words and closed my eyes. There was a chance this message wasn't about selling slaves. If I didn't read this, there was a chance that I was wrong and Nate wasn't a lying, cold-hearted asshole, and all of this had been some sort of huge misunderstanding. It was a small, stupid hope, but I clung to it for a few seconds, regardless, before pulling in a deep inhale, opening my eyes and moving my hand to reveal the rest of the entry.

We are in the process of procuring a sizable workforce.
Would trade for coal shares. Approximately 100-200

*workers available depending on shipping conditions
and whether you have open positions for women and
children as well as men. Please send rate sheets for
review.*

URLs of Nate

The pears turned in my stomach as I read the message over again. *Women and children.* "Shit," I whispered, blinking away tears as a hot, horrible pain ballooned in my chest. *Shit. Shit. Shit.* Nate had said he'd take them all, women and children. I wanted to hit something. I wanted to tear the page out of the notebook and burn it, but I'd need it as proof of what Nate's group was planning when I met Vinton and Robert in Lytton. How would they ever believe me otherwise? I didn't believe it myself. Not fully. Not until just now.

I crammed the notebook into my pack and swallowed the feelings swelling up my throat until they burned and receded into a strange numbness.

You were right, Iris. No doubts now. Nate was ready to be ruthless. If I wanted to hold him back and push Kahn out, I couldn't afford to be soft. Not now.

We faced the rest of the run in silence with the hand car's lights dimmed. Darrin only stopped at the border toll posts. Each time, I resisted the urge to hop off and relieve myself in the bushes. I couldn't think of a way to do so that didn't end with me getting abandoned or shot with my pants around my ankles. So I counted down the minutes and hours. Darrin paid our way with small rolls of copper wire and a few shells from the ammunition box I'd given him as pre-payment. Nate's gun was still loaded with a full clip of seven rounds, more than enough to keep my driver on his best behavior until I reached my family.

I wouldn't tell them that Nate was still alive, I decided. Tears blurred my eyes again, and a hole opened up in my heart that I knew would never close. He was better off as a nostalgic memory, anyways.

Goodbye, Sasquatch.

LYTTON SAT CRADLED in the curve of the river, flanked by two train trestle bridges and one collapsed highway overpass. Parked on the road, just beyond the crumbled bridge, were two motorcycles with bright headlights and alert riders. Browsers. Had to be. My chest tingled. "Stop up there, beside the bikes," I ordered Darrin.

As we crossed the trestle bridge parallel to the overpass, the riders stiffened and drew their handguns. Darrin eased the throttle and swore under his breath while I squinted past the glare of the headlights and spotted a bulky load strapped to the rear rack behind one of the riders. A thin spoked wheel. *Wheelchair. It's him.*

"Vinton!" I shouted.

"Iris?" he called back, gun arm lowering uncertainly.

"It's me." I braced myself as the rail car squealed to a halt. Scooping up my pack, crossbow, and bird cages, I kept Nate's .22 trained on Darrin as I eased toward the edge of the cargo deck. "Keep your weapons on this guy, yeah? Don't let him try anything funny."

Darrin exhaled loudly and raised his hands over his head. "Are we all forgetting I'm the only one without a gun, right now?"

"Stay right there, and you'll have a gun in a minute," I spoke softly enough that only he could hear me. "It's Nate's gun, by the way. Probably best that he doesn't know about this little trip."

Darrin winced. "I brought you fair and square like we agreed. I spent *my* toll fare to get us here."

"Thank you for that." I nodded and hopped off the car. Pigeons jostled and flapped, and my full bladder almost let go at the jolt as I landed on the gravel right of way. Turning back to the rail runner, I spoke through my teeth. "I'm gonna leave the rifle halfway between us." Pointing toward Vinton, I added, "Don't come and get it until we're gone. You set foot off that car before then, and they'll shoot you, understand?"

"Understand." Darin rolled his eyes.

"Pleasure doing business." I grinned.

"Wish I could say the same," he grumbled.

I laid the rifle at the halfway point in a dry ditch between the railway and the road. Then I armed my crossbow and kept it pointed at Darrin until I'd backed all the way to the idling diesel motorcycles.

"He hurt you?" Vinton asked, his eyes dark and interrogative below his helmet.

"No." I disarmed the crossbow. "He's just my ride. Hey, Mark."

"Hey, Iris." Vinton's partner answered me casually with his weapon still trained on Darrin.

"Get over here," my brother ordered, and I did. I stepped past his handgun, and he pulled me in a strangling one-armed hug until I squirmed. "You okay?" he asked.

I wasn't. Tears blurred my eyes, and my knees felt loose and unreliable. But I couldn't lose strength now, not out here in front of Vinton and Mark. "Stop squeezing me," I wheezed. "I have to piss."

"Missed you too," Vinton snorted.

"Are Mom and Dad all right?"

He nodded into my hair. "They're good. They're with Johan. Who else is coming?" He let me go and stared past my shoulder, down the rails.

"No one," I gulped. "Just me. I'll explain everything after I find some bushes."

"Let's put some distance between us and him before you do, yeah? Can you ride? What the hell are you doing with all those pigeons?"

"Long story." I lashed my crossbow and the pigeon cages over Vinton's wheelchair and Mark scooted ahead on his seat to leave room for me behind him. Neither of them put away their guns until they'd turned their bikes around. Vinton took lead position, and I watched him over Mark's shoulder as we picked up speed and left the rail runner and the tracks behind us. Vinton flicked a switch on his handlebars and the landing gear on his modified motorcycle eased upward.

I breathed in diesel fumes and dust, my hair slapping against the pack behind me, unraveling from its braid. I'd never trapped Vinton in an uncomfortable chair, I realized, watching my brother navigate his machine effortlessly around potholes and heaves in the road. He was in his element out here.

We stopped a few blocks away at a wide strip of green space overgrown with brush and trees. Vinton and Mark stayed on their motorcycles, guarding at a distance on either side of me while I minced toward the bushes, fumbling with the button on my pants.

"Hey, does this count as an assisted piss?" Vinton hollered, his back to me.

"What?" I frowned as I squatted.

"I owed you one assisted piss, right? This totally counts. We're even."

"Zuse, Vinton, you've been waiting all this time just to drop that line?"

"Hell, yes," he said.

WE MET with two other Browsers just outside of town. One of them was carrying a passenger who leaped off the bike as soon as we stopped.

"Iris?" he called.

"Robert?" He came. I slid off my own seat and strode toward him.

"You got my message, thank Sol."

I fell into him and lost myself in the smell of aftershave. Tears pricked my eyes. *Oh Sol*, I hadn't realized how much I missed him. I wanted to settle into the hollow between his neck and shoulder and cry. I wanted to stay there until the world was right again, but I couldn't because I had to make it right first. Robert kissed the top of my head.

"Thank Sol, you're all right," he said.

"Break it up, Lover Boy," Vinton growled, not entirely joking.

"Where are all the others?" I asked.

"We didn't want to risk all the bikes until we confirmed with the URLs where their shipment was," Robert said. "It's not in the siding near the landslide. We checked."

All of them looked to me for an explanation. "The shipment is gone. Marauders took it days ago. Shot up a bunch of the URLs people"

"Zuse," Robert exhaled.

"They kill anyone?" Vinton asked.

I nodded. "That's not all. The URLs aren't with us. They got your p-mail and were planning on meeting you here under the guise of lending you some of their own weapons, but they just wanted to take your motorcycles and guns. They planned to sack the city before the marauders beat them to it."

"That doesn't make sense." Vinton frowned.

"They're coming here with guns?" Mark straightened, alarmed.

"Not yet." I shook my head. "I slowed them down. I might have, um, blown up their armory."

"You did *what*?" Vinton raised his eyebrows.

"Badass." Robert grinned.

"I took their pigeons too." I pointed toward the cages.

"Look, this isn't the place to talk about any of this," Mark urged. "Not if there are marauders around here better armed than we are. Let's get your sister home, Vinton. If there's no shipment, we can hash this all out somewhere civilized. Back on the bikes, yeah?"

Robert squeezed my hand. "Come on, Iris. He's right." But I shook my head and pulled away.

"Kahn's not going to just let me walk back into his city after all this. You know, he won't. He tried to hunt me down when I left."

"It's not Kahn's city anymore," Vinton sneered. "And he's not going to do shit, because he's holed himself up in a bunker."

A bunker? My thoughts buzzed through my head, clumsy and bumping into each other like smoked-out bees. We had a Soldamned bunker? Robert led me to Mark's bike. I swung my leg over the seat, wincing as the scab at my knee split again.

"Are you all right?" Robert leaned close to whisper in my ear.

He must have been able to see it, fear and anxiety settling over my face. My mind was slipping out of its sweet spot. Thoughts were fraying and tangling into chaos. The motorcycles idling sounded like jackhammers in my ears, and I couldn't hold it all together anymore. I couldn't carry a thread of thought without it falling and shattering.

"I'm tired." I gulped.

He kissed my temple and stroked my hand. "Hang in there. We're almost home."

Almost home. I could hold onto that, even with the mess in my head churning like the lake during a storm. I could hold onto home.

CHAPTER
THIRTY-ONE

My heart jumped as I caught a glimpse of the lake between the green banded sediment hills before us. Flat and dark in the moonlight, it looked more like a black absence in the terrain than a body of water. *Home.* As our group of six maneuvered the bikes up the back trail toward the city, the cold, familiar scent of water, marsh plants, and clay filled my nostrils—and something else, something sour and sharp clung to the back of my throat. Ash.

"Something's burning," I mumbled to Mark.

He shook his helmeted head and hollered back, "Everything's burning."

And then the narrow valley opened to reveal the city with its streetlights darkened and its generators silent, and I saw what Mark meant. The light of the full moon was still enough to illuminate the damage. Some of the smaller office Seacans had been pushed until they tumbled all the way down the gully to the railway. Broken furniture and scattered papers trailed down the ravine. The Shareholders houses in the downtown core had burned to blackened husks. Blistered, warped panels and metal doors twisted like the tops of tuna cans. Robert's house and

Kahn's house were both among the wreckage still oozing smoke. Light posts with smashed cameras tilted over main street like broken matchsticks. Greenhouses One and Two were nothing more than ribbed frames. Their plexiglass shells looked like rows of massive smashed out teeth. As we drove closer, I saw trampled plants, shattered trays, and broken clay pots peppering the bare rows of potting benches inside. Spent ammunition shells and smashed jars of food littered the boardwalk. In a few spots, large dark stains puddled on the gravel.

Blood. Oh Sol, I gagged, jerking my feet higher. It was blood.

The whole city looked like Nate's story of the collapse, the end of the world reborn again, nothing but shattered glass and skeleton buildings. A metal overhead door squealed open before us, and we were all swallowed into the garage between the generator building and Cache. The motorcycle's diesel motor thrummed between my legs for a few more moments before Mark sighed, shut off the key, and kicked down his stand.

But I couldn't move. The wreckage of my home still burned the back of my eyes. My mouth tasted like burned plastic. *Zuse, Iris. You were so damned sheltered. What the hell were you expecting?* Nate had said civil war. Johan the pacifist was asking for weapons, and I had just hoped everyone was holed up in some civilized political siege. How had I been arrogant enough to think I could save my city? Me. A sixteen-year-old girl with a brain full of anomalies who was crashing hard after a long night.

"Iris."

I struggled to focus on the voice calling me through the choking black smoke of my own thoughts.

"Iris, come on. I've got you." I blinked and focused on Robert's face, his startling blue eyes and his kind mouth, but my gaze refused to linger on him for long. I took in my surroundings like a trapped animal. Mark wasn't on the motorcycle in front of me anymore. I was just sitting there, perched on the broad padded seat frozen with shock. Candles guttered atop metal toolboxes, dripping wax onto scattered wrenches and pliers. Mark lifted Vinton off his motorcycle and into his wheelchair. His hands moved with steady gentleness that spoke of familiarity.

Vinton never let us help him like that. The odd jealous thought drifted through my beached mind like stringy seaweed, but then I saw how my brother tucked his head against Mark's shoulder and, once he was in his chair, Vinton held his partner's arm longer than was necessary to steady himself. I imagined the minutes and hours and days he spent with Mark on broken roads in dangerous, unfamiliar territory, sifting for houses with untouched computers. There were no ramps or lifts out there. The whole world was broken, cracked, and uneven. How vulnerable Vinton must feel in a world where one loose patch of gravel could send his motorcycle skidding on its side guards, stealing his mobility.

Yet, he went on every survey run regardless, vulnerable in his paralysis, but never alone. I'd never thanked Mark before for that, for what he was to my brother. I wanted to do it then, but my tongue felt heavy in my mouth, and Robert's voice was so loud in my ears that I cringed.

"I've got you," he said.

And then I was the one being lifted from a motorcycle with gentle hands, but the closeness of it was too much. Robert's coat against my arm felt like steel wool rubbing my skin. The candlelight around us stabbed at my eyes, and the smell of diesel exhaust filled my nose. That was the problem with a mind that could process a million thoughts at once. When it frayed again, it unravelled completely.

"I can stand," I snapped, desperate to buy myself some space to breathe.

Robert set me on my unsteady feet but held my arm until I swatted him away. Through the over-sensation flooding in my head, I barely recognized the look on his face as one of hurt.

"I'm sorry. I'm just …" I couldn't find the words to finish.

"Long night. You're shutting down?" Robert whispered. "Tell me what you need, and I'll get it for you."

He understands. My throat swelled. "A bed," I croaked. "Somewhere quiet and dark."

Robert nodded and started to steer me out of the garage, but then my family was on me: Mom clutching my shoulders, her sobs shrill in my ears and her styled hair stiff against my cheek, Dad with his deep voice thrumming through my chest and his scratchy sweater and rough, ink-stained hands. I couldn't sort it all, what they were saying, whether the tears in their eyes meant happiness or sadness.

This wasn't how it was supposed to go. This isn't how I'd wanted to meet them, broken-down and weak. I wanted to tell them I saved them. I cried, inundated by it all, drowning in my family reunion, until I couldn't stop scratching at my arms or covering my ears, until Robert took me away, led me to a narrow cot, and tucked the blankets up to my chin before leaving.

CHAPTER
THIRTY-TWO

trudged through the early morning mist to Greenhouse Three. I needed to breathe in something green and unbroken. I needed to be alone and keep my hands busy before I dove back into the dirtiness of humanity. Olivia came and brought me black tea. We cradled steaming cups in our cold hands. She settled into splitting and re-potting aloe plants, and I joined her. We didn't speak until we were up to our wrists in potting soil.

"Citizen Iris, Mighty Warrior." Olivia smiled slyly.

"Shut up."

"What'd you find out, out there?" She flapped her hand overhead, indicating Outside and sprinkling dirt into her halo of red hair.

Nate's alive. I wanted to scream it. *He's alive and he loved me and he's better and worse than I ever imagined he could be.* Instead, I swallowed and spoke softly. "Nate's fertilizer was all a con."

Olivia's hands froze, still gripping an uprooted, leggy aloe plant. Her brown gaze pinned mine. "What?"

I nodded. "We don't need fertilizer to garden outside. We never did."

"That's bullshit," she sputtered and shook her head. Particles of dirt settled on her white work shirt. "Oupa's gardens, our crops in here. They all died without—"

"Nate—the URLs had a pallet of weed killer. I saw it. When we didn't pay what they liked for the fertilizer, they snuck in at night and dumped concentrated jugs into the greenhouse rain cisterns. They did the same to Johan's gardens. They knew where they were."

"Shit." Olivia pulled the plant apart roughly, her eyes shifting.

"It was just regular, water-soluble fertilizer. They'd stolen a truckload of it and couldn't find a buyer. But they grow *everything* outside, Olivia. I've seen it. Their gardens are massive. And they're thriving. They eat like Shareholders, every one of them."

"And you came back anyways?" Olivia's words were flippant, but her smirk softened them.

"I'm part of Johan's underground potato resistance. What kind of agent would I be if I didn't see Pigeon King's vision to fruition?"

We laughed, easily and without reserve, like we had as girls. We drank tea and puttered in the greenhouse until Robert found us. "Johan's called the meeting. Greenhouse Five."

I held Robert's hand as we crossed the short stretch to Greenhouse Five. Even though there was dirt under my nails and his were clean, even though everyone else filing down the boardwalk could see us, it didn't feel out of place. It felt like my hand belonged wrapped in his.

Claude's dad, dressed in his Firewall fatigues, held the door open for us. I froze at the sight of his blue helmet. My mind spun to his hard hand gripping my elbow during my public expulsion and then Vannevar's blonde curls feathering around her blue helmet as she jammed her gun against my head. I jerked back on Robert's hand.

"It's okay. They're with us now," he whispered.

"All of them?" I swallowed.

"Ever since Kahn crashed the computers, yeah."

So they didn't know we did it, Nate and I. I ducked past Claude's dad despite the prickling at the back of my neck, and he smiled as we passed, but it was dry and unconvincing. "Even Vannevar?" I pressed. "Vannevar is with us?"

Robert snorted. "Vannevar doesn't do anything except pout in her bunk, but she's with us. Kahn turned on his own people. He stole the food they stockpiled, and he locked himself in his bunker alone. I don't know what his handle was, destroying his own network. After the computers went down, he practically won the war for us."

We pressed around a makeshift table filled with heads from every department. Search Engine, Browser, Cache, Power Supply Unit, Firewall, Food Bank, Med, they were all there. Even Robert's dad, Paul, was sitting in as a representative of the Shareholders. He looked tired and pale, but his eyes were clear. His whole face hardened when he saw me. *Does Robert know his own father tried to ruin me?* I looked away from him. Now wasn't the time to reboot old grudges. Gardening was here too.

Johan. I slipped my hand from Robert's and pressed toward Olivia's oupa. He looked older and smaller than I remembered, but there was a fierceness in his warm eyes now that looked strong enough to hold up every broken building in our city.

"Iris." He wrapped his arms around me in a firm embrace that lasted long enough to convey everything he couldn't say in words. Then he took me by the arms and held me away from him, studying my face. "You look stronger than ever," he said. "Come. Sit. We've so much to talk about."

So I sat at a table amongst the kale and beans as an equal among the heads of my city's departments, and I showed them Nate's p-mail notebook. I told them what I knew. The fertilizer, the trade route monopoly, the slave runs, all of it—except Nate back from the dead and the virus I'd helped him infect our city with. I was ashamed of my involvement in that. I always would be and, besides, Nate didn't deserve to be a part of my story anymore. I was done with him.

When I'd finished, and all the questions had been asked and answered, Johan told me how the city fell.

"David had the support of most of the Shareholders, the lion's share of the food supply, and a fair amount of leverage once he held Food Bank and Cache, but the network crash changed all that. He went too far wiping out the computers. It was unlike him, a man whose religion says 'Knowledge is Power' destroying his own electronic archives."

My scarred cheeks reddened, but Johan continued, "The Shareholders feared Cache would be next. They were afraid he'd burn it rather than lose it to us, and they were furious that their amassed cred wealth was just erased. So they divided, and then yesterday, Kahn held his remaining supporters at gun point, took their food, and retreated into his house. When it burned, we found the entrance to a bunker hidden beneath it. We presume he's locked inside. The door has held up to every one of our attempts to force it open."

"You didn't know about the bunker?" I asked Johan carefully. I didn't know how many at this table knew of Johan's and Kahn's partnership.

"I didn't. I was finishing another project when David started building the city, and I didn't arrive on site until construction was well underway."

"What are the chances he has weapons down there with him?" Claude's dad asked.

Johan shook his head slowly. "David is usually well prepared, but if he had extra guns, I imagine he would have used them already, don't you?"

"Are there blueprints?" I asked. "Of the original city design? Something that would show us the ventilation system for that bunker?"

"Khan moved out all the critical information when he still held Cache," the department head answered me. "No trace of it on the drawings he left behind. Look, I don't understand why we even want Kahn out of there anyways." The man slapped his hands on the table. "Let him rot down there. The city is ours now."

Robert's dad spoke up. "We don't need Kahn *out*. We need us *in*. He isn't the threat right now."

"The URLs will have their hands tied for a while," I replied. "We should have enough time to rebuild and buy weapons, before they're strong enough to attack again."

"Buy weapons?" Claude's dad huffed. "With what? We have no valuable information left to sell. Kahn has it all down there with him."

"One of the generators." Everyone in the room stared at me like my head was on backward so I licked my lips and carried on. "The URLs didn't even have power at their compound, and they improvised. We could do the same. There's three generators. With no computer network, no air-conditioned board rooms, and no big Shareholder houses, we should be able to run on one generator with the second reserved for peak hours, right?"

The Power Supply head nodded slowly. "It's doable."

"And a big-ticket item like a high capacity generator would buy us all the guns we need and more."

"We'd have to find a trader first. We'd have to wait for the guns to ship. We don't have time for that," Johan spoke slowly.

"What do you mean?" I asked. "I slowed down the URLs. They're weaponless, and they can hardly communicate. They'll be scrambling to replace crops—"

"It's not the URLs I'm worried about, Iris," Johan interrupted me gently. "Robert, why don't you go show her. There are binoculars in the loft."

"Show me what?" I gulped.

"Come on," Robert said.

CHAPTER
THIRTY-THREE

We left the meeting, pressing past the humid atmosphere of the greenhouse back out into the dry heat of a summer morning with a cold breeze that spoke of fall. "What is he talking about, Robert?" I puffed as he guided me by the elbow up the stairs of Johan's loft, through his living quarters, and out into the pigeon loft.

The birds I'd brought in last night crowded in a quarantine cage in the corner. Other cages lined the loft from floor to ceiling. Suddenly, I thought about the pigeon I'd trained as a child. His name was Teal. I searched for his brilliant turquoise neck amongst the shuffling birds. *Don't be stupid, Iris. He's dead.* Carrier pigeons only lived three to five years, and most of them got picked off by hawks or falcons. *Get your mind back on track.*

Robert picked up the binoculars, focused on something out the window on the crest of the hill to the west, and then swore softly before handing the binoculars to me. "Right there." He pointed.

I scanned the hill where he indicated for several seconds before seeing it. Silhouetted against the sun, small, but recognizable, stood a man with a gun. Through the binoculars, frightening details sprang into focus. The gun was a semi-automatic with a large magazine. The man looked thin as a rail. A greasy strip of eye black cut across his face beneath his wide-brimmed hat. Over his shoulder, hung a torn provincial flag, like a sash. And he wasn't alone.

I counted ten other people, leaning against outcroppings farther down the hill. Eight more patrolled the hillside opposite. All of them wore torn flags and black charcoal smudged around their eyes, and all of them carried big guns. Something dropped in my stomach, cold and heavy as lead.

"Marauders," I whispered hoarsely. "The ones who stole the shipment."

"They've been standing on the hill like that for the last week. There's more of them every day." Robert sighed and scratched the back of his neck. "They're like bloody vultures waiting to close in."

"They just stand there all day watching?" I asked.

"In shifts, yeah," Robert said. "Johan doesn't think they'll be watching for long. They're cautious. I don't think marauders train to fight like the Firewalls do. They're more the hit and run type, and they're just trying to intimidate now, but they know we're weak. They saw the buildings burn. They're going to attack, sooner rather than later, and we don't have the firepower to match them. Hell, you saw the shells in the street. We hardly have any ammunition left at all. We were counting on that shipment."

"What are we going to do?" My voice came out too high, like a little child's.

"Johan thinks the bunker would be big enough to house the city's population. He said that's how David designed his other facilities that had them. We could hole up and wait until the marauders strip the place and move on. They never stay in one spot for long. They'll take what they want and leave."

"The generators. Th-the solar panels," I stuttered. "Zuse,

Robert. We can't let them take all of that from us. It's irreplaceable. We'd have nothing left."

Robert grinned, but it was a broken sort of smile, all nerves and bundled fear. "What do you suggest, Iris? We don't have any other options."

We went back to the meeting, which as far as I could tell, was the department heads arguing sullenly about abandoning their posts. *Just as productive as every other business meeting they ever had,* I thought bitterly.

After sitting through five minutes of their droning, I straightened in my seat. "Can we get back to talking about the bunker? We need to find the air intake."

Johan shook his head. "We can't get in that way, even if we knew where it was. The vent pipes are far too small to climb through."

But my mind was already shifting back to the night before, standing over the vent stack for Nate's root cellar. "We don't need to get in. We just need him to open the door and come out."

IT TOOK us three hours to find the air intake for the bunker. One-hundred feet to the north of David Kahn's ruined house, Vinton spotted it, a false boulder with an inch of clearance between the bottom of the rock and the ground it laid on. When we tipped it back, the hollow within contained a five-inch u-pipe with a grill. After that, it was only a matter of setting up the Firewalls in front of the bunker door while Robert, Johan, and I gathered enough broken furniture and crushed plants from Greenhouse One and Two to make a nice smoky fire. One of the Power Supply Unit operators modified an exhaust fan with a battery to fit over the intake and pull air in. We'd smoke out David Kahn like a bee out of a hive.

I was just bending over the kindling pile with a lighter when Vinton barked my name, and something jabbed hard against the back of my head.

"Step off. All of you," A cold shrill voice spoke, and a hand gripped me by the hair.

"Soldamnit, Vannevar, what the hell are you doing?" Robert barked.

Her gun pressed behind my ear and her arm wrapped around my throat, as she yanked me toward the overturned false boulder, using it as cover.

"What I should have done a long time ago." Vannever spoke through her teeth, and I couldn't help it, I remembered her kicking me in the street, her promise to blow my brains out in the side lot of Robert's house. The air around me thickened into syrup. The safety clicking off Vannevar's gun reverberated through my skull, and a sickening warmth spread at my crotch.

You pissed yourself, Iris.

"Get away from her!" Vinton howled.

"What do you want, Vannevar?" Johan asked quietly.

"I want her fragging head off her shoulders, that's what I want," she snarled at my ear. Then to me, "Drop the lighter, Basic Bitch."

I did. It bounced off my boot and skittered away in the dirt. I wanted to talk to her, to plead, or reason, or even scream, but I could only breathe in short, sharp gulps as Vannevar's forearm pressed harder and harder against my throat. Sol, she was strong, and she was going to kill me this time. White splotches bloomed across my vision like lazy, swirling bees.

"Let go of her!" Robert roared.

"I don't think so. She's my ticket." Vannevar purred, her arm pressing hard enough against my throat that my breath whistled. "Robert, why don't you run and go get me one of the motorcycles from the garage? Vinton's maybe—can't have him following me, after all. Basic Bitch and I are going to go on a little ride, unless you'd like me to spray little pieces of her skull all over the front of your nice shirt."

"I'll kill you first," Vinton said quietly.

"Really?" Vannevar drawled. "From your chair? I'd like to see that." Then she lifted her arm from my throat and shook me by the hair hard enough that my head snapped, and I wailed. "*Go, Robert,*" she barked.

My vision swam as I watched Robert stumble toward the garages. Vannevar only let me pull in a few breaths before tightening her grip again with slow maliciousness. "I hear marauders accept new members into their ranks if they come bearing a *ticket,* a worthy gift. I think a motorcycle and a nice little bitch to bend over should do it," she whispered to me.

Oh Sol, No.

"And when you're all used up, then I can shoot—" Vannevar flinched behind me, her words cut off.

"Let her go, Vannevar." I recognized Claude's voice.

"Stop!" Johan barked. "How are more guns to more heads solving any of this, Claude?"

"Hers isn't real," he hissed.

"Shut up, Claude!" Vannevar barked.

"What?" Johan gaped.

"I said her gun isn't real. It's a replica. Kahn never had enough guns for all of us. Half of them are just for show. There's only one partner per shift who gets a real gun and ammo, and it's me today. Hers isn't real, I'm sure of it."

Vinton leaned toward Johan. "Sol, it's the same with the Browsers handguns, Johan. I didn't know he was doing it with the Firewalls too. We signed non-disclosure agreements, all of us."

Vannevar's weight shifted. The pressure of the gun against my head lifted, and I dropped as I saw the shadow of her arm raise overhead to strike me, but her fingers still clutched my hair, and I caught the butt of her gun against my head as a glancing blow. Pain seared through my skull. I crashed to my knees amidst a confusion of feet shuffling and muffled grunts. Vannevar cried out and something substantial clattered to the ground beside me. Her gun. I reached for it and rolled away, aiming back toward my captor, but Claude already had her pinned to the ground.

Johan knelt and pressed his hand against my back. "Iris, are you okay? You're bleeding."

I was. I hadn't realized it until blood started running down my cheek. My head felt hot and raw where Vannevar had hit me. Scrambling further away from her, still gripping the gun, I nodded. "I'm good."

"There." Vinton wheeled next to me, pointing to the midpoint on the barrel of the gun I held. "It says 'Replica'. Claude was right."

Fantastic. I thought, breath sawing in and out of me as I sagged. I'd pissed my pants and the gun wasn't even real.

THE BLUE HELMETS escorted Vannevar to one of the Seacan cells behind the generators and locked her in. Johan said it took less than two hours after that to smoke out David Kahn. They imprisoned him with Vannevar and cleared the bunker within an hour. Other than a modest food supply and all of the critical documents from Cache, the subterranean space was empty and large enough to house the hundred of us who remained in an emergency. We'd be cramped, but we'd be alive.

"I don't like guns, but Sol help me, I was really hoping against reason that I'd find more of them in that bunker. And, instead, I find out half of the ones we have aren't functional."

Johan sighed and slumped in a small chair across from my new bunk. The generators were humming above us, and the bunker lights shone brightly. Elaine was stitching the wound on my head. Several beds were filled with transferred patients with gunshot wounds from the hectic weeks I'd missed. I didn't want to look at them.

Instead, I rolled my words in my mouth several times before speaking. "We could make them." I shrugged.

"Hold still, will you, honey?" Elaine admonished.

"What do you mean *make them*, Iris? We don't have any of the equipment needed to make firearms."

I winced as Elaine pulled thread through my scalp. "Not guns. We could make replicas."

"Replicas?"

"Kahn did it when he didn't have enough guns, and it worked for years. We don't need guns, right now. We just need the marauders to think we have guns and lots of them."

"They won't attack us if we seem armed to the teeth." Johan smiled slowly.

"Even if we're just armed with water pipes with wooden stocks. They only have to look like guns through binoculars."

"Strip the houses," Johan mumbled. "Carve the stocks from the wooden desks. Paint everything black—there's paint in the garage for the motorcycles. This could work, Iris."

"Until we trade a generator off for a real shipment of guns."

"I don't like guns." Johan sighed, scrubbing his face.

"I don't like being homeless," Elaine quipped. "I'll like guns well enough if they keep my roof over my head, and not a damned claustrophobic bunker roof. I feel like a hunted rabbit down here."

"Do we really need to keep this though, the city, I mean?" Johan asked carefully. "We have nothing of value left to sell. Once Kahn's critical documents are gone, we have no economy, nothing to stay here for. Wouldn't it be wiser to leave now, while we're still well provisioned?"

"Wilderness provides," I murmured.

"Frag that." Elaine snipped her last stitch and set her needle down, stripping off her gloves. "I'm not leaving my home, and you know half of the city won't either, Johan. We've been here since the world ended. Marauders aren't going to push us out now. We'll find a way."

I swung my legs off the bed and stood unsteadily, thanking Elaine and taking Johan's arm. "I need a breath of fresh air. Are we safe to go out?" I felt trapped too. It still reeked of smoke down here.

"Five minutes, and we stay within sight of Kahn's house," Johan said and led me out of the makeshift med room, up the narrow metal stairs and out into a night cradled in the familiar hum of generators and the pulsing chirp of crickets. A loon called from the lake, its cry hollow and echoing. Overhead, green and white whips of aurora borealis crackled through the sky.

Johan stopped on the boardwalk, and we blinked up at them.

"I will miss it," he said. "My books and the pigeon loft. The Greenhouses. I'll miss it all if we have to go. I love wilderness, but Kahn was right about some things. Progress. We made progress here. We built something that I don't want to lose." He paused. "But I have no idea how to keep it. Fending off marauders and URLs is one thing. Rebuilding a broken economy is quite another. These people will need to work, and not all of them are suited to hunting like we are, Iris."

I looped my arm through his and pulled him toward Cache with a slow smile bunching the scars on my cheeks.

"What?" Johan asked. "Why are you smiling?"

"No reason." I shook my head. "What do you know about copper mining, Johan? I hear it's the next big thing."

FREE PREQUEL STORY

Sign up for Shelly and Megan's newsletter to stay up to date on releases and appearances and opportunities for free content. For your first taste, enjoy this free short story "On Broken Days." You'll see first hand what happened to Vinton and why Iris is so focused on her career at the beginning of *Knowledge Itself.*

They say Outside will kill you. Yet, a pseudo life in a contained, controlled environment is worse than death for one.

ACKNOWLEDGMENTS

Big thanks, as always to Colin who supports and encourages me in everything I do and patiently lets me play in imaginary worlds. A tip of the hat to Ella, for naming Iris. It made her instantly real and relatable to me. Thanks to Cory Whitesell for graciously answering a long vague email about solar flares, EMP weapons, data centers, and SATA interface adapters. Although our story changed and evolved from its original idea, your expertise and the time you took to patiently explain IT tech to a total newbie really helped inject some realism into our pages. As always, kudos are due to my Writer Alliance crew. I'd be nowhere without you. Special thanks to Jennifer Lane, Al Hess, Essa Hansen, and Cassie Greutman who read *Knowledge Itself* in its baby stages and helped mold it into something worth reading. Patrick White, thank you so much for sensitivity reading scenes involving Vinton after he'd lost the use of his legs. We really appreciate you taking the time. Last but not least, thank you to Kelly Lynn Colby who saw the potential in *Knowledge Itself* despite its awkward original opening chapters. We are so thrilled that you warmed up to Iris and gave her the chance to shine.

-Shelly Campbell

Shelly, without you this story may have just remained a dream. Scott Walker, for always being my biggest supporter, and for always listening to my weird dreams; I love you more than I can say. Ken and Terry, Amanda, Vanessa, and Will, Avery, Spencer,

Norah, and Macy, Papa Don Murray, Colette Beresford for always being our photographer, Rob, Nate, Beckett, and Ari, Matt Betton, the son I might have had if I'd made different choices, thank you all.

-Megan King

ABOUT SHELLY CAMPBELL

At a young age, Shelly Campbell wanted to be an air show pilot or a pirate, possibly a dragon and definitely a writer and artist. She's piloted a Cessna 172 through spins and stalls and sailed up the east coast on a tall ship barque—mostly without projectile vomiting. In the end, Shelly found writing fantasy and drawing dragons to be so much easier on the stomach. Shelly's grimdark fantasy novels *Under the Lesser Moon* and *Voice of the Banished* were published by Mythos and Ink. She also has a quiet horror novel, *Gulf*, with Silver Shamrock publishing, and has co-authored *Making Myths and Magic* with Allison Alexander. It's a field guide to writing sci-fi and fantasy published by Mythos and Ink.

ABOUT MEGAN KING

Megan King has been a singer, dancer, artist, and most recently, an author, where she fills her time turning weird dreams into story ideas. She supports her arts habit by working as an optician. In her spare time, she listens to Canadian alt rock music pretty constantly and spends time with her family, which includes two dogs and a very large cat.

YOU MIGHT ALSO LIKE

When magic is rediscovered in a land devoid of it, the royal twins must compete to earn the right to be called True Heir, a title that means more than either imagined.